GUILT

Also by Keigo Higashino

Under the Midnight Sun

THE DETECTIVE GALILEO MYSTERIES
The Devotion of Suspect X
Salvation of a Saint
A Midsummer's Equation
Silent Parade
Invisible Helix

THE KYOICHIRO KAGA MYSTERIES
Malice
Newcomer
A Death in Tokyo
The Final Curtain

GUILT

KEIGO HIGASHINO

abacus
books

ABACUS

Originally published in Japan as *Hakucho to Komori* by Gentosha
First published in the United States by Minotaur Books in 2026
First published in Great Britain in 2026 by Abacus

1 3 5 7 9 10 8 6 4 2

Copyright © 2021 by Keigo Higashino
Translation copyright © 2026 by Giles Murray

The moral right of the author has been asserted.

*All characters and events in this publication, other than those
clearly in the public domain, are fictitious and any resemblance
to real persons, living or dead, is purely coincidental.*

All rights reserved.
No part of this publication may be reproduced, stored in a
retrieval system, or transmitted, in any form, or by any means, without
the prior permission in writing of the publisher, nor be otherwise circulated
in any form of binding or cover other than that in which it is published
and without a similar condition including this condition being
imposed on the subsequent purchaser.

A CIP catalogue record for this book
is available from the British Library.

ISBN 978-0-349-14861-8

Printed and bound in Great Britain by Clays Ltd, Elcograf S.p.A.

Papers used by Abacus are from well-managed forests
and other responsible sources.

Abacus
An imprint of
Little, Brown Book Group
Carmelite House
50 Victoria Embankment
London EC4Y 0DZ

The authorised representative
in the EEA is
Hachette Ireland
8 Castlecourt Centre,
Dublin 15, D15 XTP3, Ireland
(email: info@hbgi.ie)

An Hachette UK Company
www.hachette.co.uk

www.littlebrown.co.uk

Cast of Characters

Tsutomu Godai: Detective, Homicide Bureau, Tokyo Metropolitan Police

Nakamachi: Detective sergeant, Homicide Bureau, Tokyo Metropolitan Police

Tsutsui: Assistant inspector, Tokyo Metropolitan Police

Sakuragawa: Unit chief, Robbery-Homicide, Tokyo Metropolitan Police

Kensuke Shiraishi: A lawyer; murder victim

Mirei Shiraishi: Kensuke's daughter

Ayako Shiraishi: Kensuke's wife

Tatsuro Kuraki: A person of interest in the Shiraishi murder investigation

Kazuma Kuraki: Tatsuro's son

Yoko Asaba: Restaurant manager; person of interest in the Shiraishi murder investigation

Orie Asaba: Yoko's daughter; person of interest in the Shiraishi murder investigation

Hiroki Anzai: Orie Asaba's ex-husband

Tomoki Anzai: Orie and Hiroki's son

Shozo Haitani: A murder victim from 1984

Takahiro Horibe: A lawyer

Azusa Sakuma: A lawyer

1

AUTUMN 2017

Outside the window, the lower half of the sky was red and the upper half was gray. Dense clouds were beginning to blanket the sunset. There had been no rain forecast when he checked the weather earlier.

"Got an umbrella, Nakamachi?" Tsutomu Godai asked the young detective beside him.

"No. Do you think it's going to rain?"

"It's not looking good."

"Did we pass a convenience store? If it starts raining, I'll just go buy one."

"No need for that."

Godai looked at his watch. It was almost 5:00 PM. Since the start of November, there had been endless chilly weather. *Please don't rain*, he thought. The last thing he wanted was to use the detective from the local precinct as his errand boy.

The two of them were in the office area of a backstreet workshop in Tokyo's Adachi Ward. It wasn't a proper meeting room, just a small space for receiving visitors. Product samples were arranged on shelves against one wall: pipes, valves, joints, and the like. The firm obviously dealt in plumbing supplies.

Godai heard something and turned around. A young man came in and bowed politely.

"I'm Yuta Yamada," the young man said.

Godai rose to his feet. He held out his Tokyo Metropolitan Police badge, explained that he was a Homicide Bureau investigator, then introduced Nakamachi.

The two detectives sat down across the table from Yamada.

"Shall we get straight to it? We'd like to ask you a few questions about Mr. Kensuke Shiraishi. I believe you know him?" Godai asked.

"Yes," said Yamada. He was a thin fellow with a pointed chin. But why was he reluctant to make eye contact? Did he have something to hide?

"What's the nature of your relationship?"

"My relationship?"

"Your relationship with Mr. Shiraishi. Can you tell us?"

After a moment or two, Yamada lifted his head and looked at Godai, puzzled. "What's the point? You already know the answer. That's the reason you're here."

Godai smiled. "Yes, but we want to hear it from you. Please, indulge us."

An expression that was equal parts annoyance, anxiety, and confusion flashed across Yamada's face. He lowered his eyes again and spoke.

"He was my lawyer when I was in trouble."

"For what offense? And when?"

A wrinkle appeared between Yamada's eyebrows. He was getting angry. Why were they asking him these questions when they already knew the answers?

Always get people to tell you their story in their own words. That's an ironclad rule of investigation. But Godai had another reason. It was always easier to get people to show their true colors if you got under their skin. Angry people generally make bad liars.

"It was an assault. Happened about a year ago. I was working at this karaoke joint. I beat up my boss. At the same time, someone ran off with the proceeds from the till, and I got prosecuted for theft as well as assault. I told the police it wasn't me, that I hadn't taken the money, but they wouldn't listen to a word I said.... Anyway, Mr. Shiraishi was my lawyer."

"Prior to the trial, had you ever met Mr. Shiraishi?"

Yamada shook his head. "No."

Godai nodded. Kensuke Shiraishi had been Yamada's court-appointed lawyer. He had already confirmed that.

"How did the trial go?"

"I got a three-year suspended sentence. All thanks to Mr. Shiraishi. He showed them that the boss was lying when he accused me of stealing the money. On top of that, Mr. Shiraishi proved that my boss was harassing me daily. Without Mr. Shiraishi, I'd have ended up in jail."

Everything Yamada said tallied with the two detectives' research.

"Have you met with Mr. Shiraishi lately?" Godai asked.

"He dropped by a couple of weeks back. During my lunch break."

"Why?"

Yamada cocked his head to one side. "No particular reason. He was like, 'Just swung by to see how you're getting on.'"

"And what did you two talk about?"

"Nothing special. He asked me how it was going. It was Mr. Shiraishi who got me this job."

"What was your impression of Mr. Shiraishi? Was there anything different about him? Did he say anything that struck you as odd?"

Yamada tilted his head to one side and thought for a moment. "I can't be one hundred percent sure, but I did feel that he wasn't quite his normal self, like he had something else on his mind." Yamada waved a dismissive hand. "But that was just my impression. I may be imagining things. I don't want you attaching too much weight to that."

Yamada was clearly anxious about them taking anything he said as fact. Having been through the court system, he knew that irresponsible remarks could land you in trouble.

"You know what happened to Mr. Shiraishi, right?" Godai asked.

"Yes, I know." Yamada nodded, and his face seemed to stiffen.

"How did it make you feel?"

"How did it . . . ? I was shocked."

"How so?"

"It just seemed so impossible. For Mr. Shiraishi to be murdered like that. Makes no sense. Why would anyone do such a thing?"

"Any idea who might have done it?"

"None." Yamada's voice was emphatic.

"Were there people who had it in for Mr. Shiraishi?"

"Dunno. Seems unlikely. I can't believe Mr. Shiraishi had any enemies."

There was genuine emotion in Yamada's voice. Initially, he had been reluctant to make eye contact; now he looked him straight in the face.

2

IT ALL STARTED with a phone call.

Someone reported a suspicious vehicle parked on the street. According to dispatch center records, the call came in at 7:32 AM on November 1. The caller was a security guard at a company near Takeshiba Pier.

There was a navy-blue sedan parked illegally opposite the elevated Yurikamome driverless train line.

A couple of traffic cops were sent to the scene. The case was elevated to the Criminal Investigation Department after they'd found a corpse in the back seat of the car. The dead man was dressed in a dark gray suit and had been stabbed in the stomach. He hadn't bled profusely, perhaps because the murder weapon was still in the wound.

His wallet hadn't been taken. It contained around seventy thousand yen and a driver's license.

His name was Kensuke Shiraishi. He was fifty-five years old and lived in Minami-Aoyama. According to his business cards, he was a lawyer with an office near Aoyama Boulevard. No cell phone was found.

When an investigator called the family, they were about to file a missing person's report. He had a wife, who was a year younger than he was, and a daughter, who was twenty-seven. Shiraishi hadn't come home after leaving the previous morning and was unreachable. The two women came to the police station. When they were confronted with Shiraishi's body in the morgue, they wept as they confirmed his identity.

According to his wife and daughter, Shiraishi had both a smartphone and an old-fashioned flip phone. He used the flip phone for work and the smartphone for staying in touch with his family. The murderer seemed to have made off with both devices. While the flip phone was completely offline, the smartphone was still on the network.

They quickly pinpointed the location of the smartphone using GPS data. It was found near the Sumida River Terrace, a walkway parallel to the river just beneath the embankment. There was blood on the phone and spatter on the ground nearby. His flip phone was not found.

A task force was set up that day, and Godai and his team from the Homicide Bureau of the Tokyo Metropolitan Police Department were called in. The meeting was held at 1:00 PM. The local head of CID provided them with a rundown of the case.

Using location data from the smartphone, he explained, they'd managed to trace the victim's movements. The victim left his home at 8:20 AM on the morning of October 31 and reached his office at 8:30 AM. He'd spent the day in his office until a little after 6:00 PM, when he'd gotten into his car. After roughly thirty minutes, he arrived at Tomioka in Koto Ward. He'd parked in the lot attached to Tomioka Hachimangu Shrine. After spending around ten minutes there, he left and went to the Sumida River Terrace, a little before 7:00 PM.

Given the blood on the smartphone, it looked highly likely that the Sumida River Terrace was the site of the murder. That early in the evening, there would normally be plenty of joggers and walkers along the river. But due to ongoing repair work nearby, the terrace was blocked off, making it the ideal place to commit a crime. The murderer had known the area well, if he lured the victim there.

The dead body was transferred to the back of the car. The victim was thin and only weighed about 130 pounds, so a strong man could have carried him easily enough. The car was found in Minato Ward. It wasn't known if it had been driven directly there or if the driver stopped off somewhere en route, but they assumed the murderer had driven the car. At present, they had no idea why the body was moved.

Once the head of CID completed his briefing, they discussed next steps and decided what the different investigators would do. Godai was paired with Nakamachi, a detective sergeant from the precinct. Nakamachi was a tall, sharp-featured fellow of twenty-eight, exactly ten years Godai's junior, and Godai thought after a few minutes' chat that Nakamachi had his head screwed on right. The two of them were tasked with looking into all the people associated with the victim. Their first job was to interview the family.

Kensuke Shiraishi's house was a modestly sized detached house in the Western style. Godai was a little surprised. Given the address, he'd expected something grander.

He found himself sitting opposite Shiraishi's wife, Ayako, and Mirei, his daughter. The two women seemed levelheaded, despite the circumstances. They had divided up the jobs of arranging the wake and the funeral and of contacting people, they explained. Ayako was petite with a classic Japanese face, while Mirei's features were stronger and more striking. *She looks like her father*, Godai thought.

After offering his condolences, Godai asked about Shiraishi's behavior when he left the house that morning.

"I don't recall there being anything different about him yesterday, no," Ayako said, a grief-stricken look on her face. "He didn't say anything about meeting anyone after work or expecting to come back late." She paused. "But recently, he wasn't his normal, cheerful self. He often seemed distracted, preoccupied. I just thought he was working on a difficult case."

Neither of them knew what Shiraishi was working on. He never discussed his work at home, they explained.

Godai pushed on with the questioning. Did they have any thoughts about the incident? Had anything out of the ordinary happened recently?

"Can't think of anything," Ayako said with conviction. "My husband wasn't the sort of person to have enemies, though. He was always very straight in his dealings with people. I can't begin to tell you how many thank-you letters he got from his clients."

Surely, though, as the counsel for the defense, he ended up angering the victim? When the wife was stumped by that question, the daughter spoke up.

"Look, I admit that my father could be perceived negatively by the victim. Dad never went into specifics, but he often talked to me about what being a lawyer meant to him. His approach wasn't just about getting a lenient sentence for his clients; he also did his best to make them aware of the gravity of their crimes. As my dad saw it, being a lawyer meant examining every crime carefully enough to understand its gravity. Given that, I just can't see anyone hating him enough to take his life." As she spoke, Mirei grew increasingly upset. Her voice grew ragged, and her eyes reddened.

Finishing up, Godai asked the two women about Shiraishi's movements just prior to his murder. Were they familiar with Tomioka Hachimangu Shrine, the Sumida River Terrace, or Kaigan District in Minato Ward?

Mother and daughter both looked equally nonplussed. Shiraishi had not mentioned any of these places, they said.

Ultimately, Godai didn't learn anything from them. "Call me if you think of something," he said, handing over one of his cards. Then he and Nakamachi took their leave.

Their next destination was Shiraishi's office. It was on the fourth floor of a shiny silver-clad building with a café on the street floor.

They were met by a Ms. Setsuko Nagai. The job title on her card was personal assistant. A bespectacled woman of around forty, she'd worked for Shiraishi for fifteen years.

According to Nagai, Shiraishi dealt mainly with criminal cases, traffic accidents, and juvenile crime. Did he have any clients who held a grudge against him?

"Oh, we see all sorts here," said Nagai. "Some clients say the craziest things. They're busy insisting they've done nothing wrong and are innocent, when Mr. Shiraishi can see they're clearly guilty. Mr. Shiraishi was very patient with clients like that and would take the time to explain the situation. You know, 'At the end of the day, it's always better for you to be up-front and honest with me.' If the client refused to change their story despite his best efforts, that limited Mr. Shiraishi's options for defending them. All he could do was regurgitate the same lying nonsense in the courtroom. You can't expect a light sentence with a baseless defense that generates. Of course not. So yes, we sometimes have clients who blame Mr. Shiraishi even though they're the ones who dug their own graves."

Godai could sympathize. He had arrested his fair share of suspects like that himself.

"Even after sentencing, Mr. Shiraishi always followed up and did his best for his clients. Ultimately, most accepted their situation. Plenty of clients who'd bad-mouthed him after the verdict would then thank him after they'd done their time."

Listening to Setsuko Nagai talk about her boss, Godai found words like *warm* and *empathetic* came to mind.

Godai then asked Ms. Nagai the same question he had put to Shiraishi's wife and daughter earlier. What about the victims? Might they be angry with him?

"People often threatened him when he was negotiating out-of-court settlements. Victims are justifiably angry, so what else can you expect? While Shiraishi was doing his best to keep things amicable, they sometimes thought he was trying to pull a fast one."

Even so, Nagai added, she couldn't think of a specific case where the victim loathed him enough to kill him.

"I don't actually know that many lawyers other than Mr. Shiraishi. Personally, I think he was a very moral person. When he pled a case in court, he was just as mindful of the victim as he was of the client he was defending. The idea that a man like that would be murdered because of a grudge or some sort of festering old hatred—it's unthinkable. Though God knows, there's no shortage of crazy people out there, so I suppose I can't rule it out completely."

Did she have any idea of what might have motivated his murder? Godai asked. Nagai groaned.

"Mr. Shiraishi is involved in a few difficult ongoing cases. There's no reason why killing him would be to the other side's advantage, though. Maybe he was murdered because of something in his private life. But as far as I know, Mr. Shiraishi had no money troubles, and I never heard any strange rumors or gossip about him. All I can suggest is that some crazy person killed him with no motive."

At this point, Godai again brought up Tomioka Hachimangu Shrine, the Sumida River Terrace, and Kaigan District of Minato Ward. None of these places meant anything to her.

After securing all the documentation related to Shiraishi's recent cases and a list of recent incoming calls, Godai and Nakamachi left the office.

The two detectives then proceeded to interview several of Shiraishi's recent and former clients. Without exception, they were shocked by his murder. Nearly all of them made the same comment.

"I simply can't believe that anyone would hate Attorney Shiraishi that much."

3

THE TWO DETECTIVES decided to grab an early dinner on their way back to the precinct. Nakamachi suggested they stop at the Monzen-Nakacho District.

After changing trains, they arrived at Monzen-Nakacho Station a little after 6:00 PM.

There, they stopped at a robata-yaki barbecue joint, which specialized in steamed rice with clams, a local delicacy. Just the thought of the dish was enough to make Godai's mouth water.

Inside, a man in a white smock was busy grilling vegetables and shellfish. Godai chose a table at the back of the room; a counter was never the best place for a confidential discussion.

Over a couple of beers, edamame, and cubed tofu, Nakamachi sighed as he flipped his little notebook open. "Everyone we interviewed said the exact same thing."

"No one could believe anyone would hate Mr. Shiraishi enough to murder him? For all I know, they're right. He probably did handle every case that came his way with seriousness and sincerity, just as his assistant said. When you're a lawyer, enmity comes with the territory. There are cases that end in murder, but it's rare. No, we're probably better off dismissing the whole deep-seated grudge theory."

The waitress brought the draft beers and the edamame to their table. "Cheers," said Godai, picking up his glass and taking a big swig. The slightly bitter liquid seemed to penetrate deep into every cell of his tired body.

"Okay then, what are we left with if we throw out the whole grudge angle? Ms. Nagai suggested the motive could be something personal, unconnected to his work."

"It's anybody's guess." Godai cocked his head as he grabbed a handful of edamame. "There's no sign of financial distress and no extramarital relationships. What does that leave us with? Envy, maybe?"

"Who would be jealous of him?"

Godai took his notebook out of his jacket pocket. "Kensuke Shiraishi. Born in Nerima Ward, Tokyo. Earns himself a law degree from a respectable national university and passes the bar exam thereafter. Starts his career working for a law firm in western Tokyo. At twenty-eight, he marries the girl he's been seeing since college. Strikes out on his own at the age of thirty-eight to start his own firm. Lay out the facts like that and you can see that his whole life has been smooth sailing, one unbroken line of success. There's reason enough there for people to feel jealous of him."

"Yes, but would they actually kill him for it? I mean, his career seems normal enough."

"That normality could be exactly what someone would envy—like a rival student from the same university, say. You know how it is. There's no shortage of aspiring lawyers who have to jettison their ambitions after failing the bar exam."

"True."

"Let's say that such a person did have murderous intent. Wouldn't it be more of an impulsive thing? I can't see envy of that kind translating into acquiring a knife and then stabbing him with it. Honestly, I'd feel silly proposing a theory like that." Godai shrugged at himself and slipped the notebook back into his jacket pocket.

Godai had described Shiraishi's life as smooth sailing, but life had not always been easy for him, according to his wife, Ayako. His family wasn't well off; all the schools he'd attended were public ones; and his father died in an accident when Shiraishi was still in junior high. Shiraishi had contributed to the family finances by working different part-time jobs during high school. And until she passed the year before last, he had also helped look after his mother when she got dementia. His life had its fair share of problems and hardships. Godai wondered if that was why he'd opted to work as a court-appointed defense attorney, a famously ill-paid branch of the legal profession.

They polished off their edamame and cubed tofu appetizers, then ordered the house specialty: Fukagawa-meshi, or steamed rice with clams.

"Putting motive aside for now, what do you think he was doing in this part of town?" Godai asked. He was staring vacantly at a piece of paper that was tacked to the wall.

"Yeah, doesn't seem like the sort of place our victim would go."

Godai crossed his arms over his chest and sank into thoughtful silence.

The first place Kensuke Shiraishi had driven to after leaving his office was the parking lot beside Tomioka Hachimangu Shrine. His car was plainly visible on the security camera footage. They had spotted him getting out of the car after ten minutes or so. During that time, no one had approached his vehicle.

The murderer must have told Kensuke Shiraishi to park in the parking lot, then contacted him while he was parked there, with instructions to move to the Sumida River Terrace, the site of his murder.

The murderer could have chosen anywhere in Tokyo for the crime. The investigation team attached a lot of importance to Shiraishi stopping off at Tomioka Hachimangu Shrine. And there was a reason for that. Location data from his phone showed that he'd visited the area twice in the last four weeks.

His first visit was October 7, and the data showed that he'd walked around a lot. The second visit was October 20. That time, he'd gone more or less directly to a café on Eitai Boulevard. He'd parked his car in the same shrine parking lot both times.

The detective in charge of canvassing spoke to the staff at the café. He'd found security camera footage of Shiraishi, who was carrying a small briefcase, entering and exiting the café. Unfortunately, none of the staff could recall his visit. That suggested he hadn't drawn any attention to himself.

So why had Kensuke Shiraishi come to this part of town? The investigation hadn't found anyone connected with any of Shiraishi's cases who lived, worked, or studied in this district.

The steamed rice with clams was brought to their table. Godai couldn't help smiling as the aroma wafted from the steam basket.

"How about we forget about the case for a while?"

"All for it," Nakamachi replied, his gaze fixed on his own steam basket.

Once they had finished their dinner, they went to have a look at the café that Shiraishi visited. It was in a two-story building. The first floor only had the serving counter, so they went upstairs after buying their coffee. One of the tables was free, but it was so close to the tables on either side that the detectives instead opted to sit next to each other at the counter by the window.

"The location data tells us that he spent almost two hours in this place. What do you think he was doing for two whole hours in a coffee shop in a part of town that he didn't normally visit?"

"He was meeting someone. That's the logical explanation."

"Sounds reasonable. But you were at the team meeting, so you know that Shiraishi was on his own, both when he arrived and when he left. Arriving is one thing, but normally when people leave a place, they leave together."

Nakamachi grunted his assent.

"So if he wasn't meeting anyone, what would he be doing for two hours in a place like this? Reading, maybe. Or maybe doing the same thing they're all doing?" As he said this, Nakamachi jerked his thumb over his shoulder.

Godai cast a discreet glance over the rest of the café. Most of the patrons seated at the tables were busy fiddling with their smartphones.

"Hardly think so." Godai grinned. "Can't see him trekking all the way to a strange part of town just to do that. Besides, wasn't there a café on the first floor of Shiraishi's own office building?"

"Was the victim a coffee aficionado who tracked down this place because its brew was a cut above the ordinary? . . . No, I don't think."

"Cute theory. Trouble is, this place is a chain."

"I know, I know." Nakamachi raised the paper cup to his lips, a disappointed look on his face.

Godai took a swig of coffee. He turned to face the window that overlooked Eitai Boulevard. Something must have occurred to him, as he gave a little snort of laughter.

"What is it?" Nakamachi asked.

"Okay, so the man spends two hours in a single coffee shop without reading a book or using his phone. That's not normal behavior. But when you think about it, there are people who do precisely that—and have zero choice in the matter, aren't there?"

Nakamachi looked mystified. Godai jabbed a finger at his face.

"I'm talking about *us*. I'm talking about *detectives*. On a stakeout, we have to stay in the same place for hours on end."

"Yes, I suppose we do." Nakamachi's mouth dropped open in surprise.

Godai swiveled his finger and pointed at the cars driving up and down the boulevard outside.

"Just look at that. Isn't this a great place for a stakeout? Most of the major shops and restaurants in Monzen-Nakacho are located on this street. From here, you get a bird's-eye view of anyone who's entering the establishments on the opposite side of the street."

Nakamachi looked down at the busy boulevard. "You're definitely right there," he muttered. "So you think he was monitoring someone's movements?"

"Not sure that *monitoring* is quite the right word. After all, Shiraishi was no detective. Let's say that he was waiting for someone to show up."

"Someone on foot?"

"Maybe. It could have been someone who came by car and parked at the side of the road, or else someone in one of the restaurants. There's any number of potential scenarios. All we can say for sure is that this is a fantastic place for keeping an eye on things. Plus there's coffee thrown in."

Nakamachi's eyes were shining with excitement. "Should we report this to the higher-ups?"

Godai smiled wanly. He gave a curt, dismissive wave of the hand. "No, not yet. For now, it's not even a theory; it's pure speculation. If the squad leader and the unit chief had to listen to every silly hunch, nothing would ever get done."

"I guess not." Nakamachi looked slightly deflated. "I was just hoping we'd have something to tell our colleagues in the incident room."

"I get it. Still, you don't need to feel embarrassed about coming up empty. It's not the hunting dog's fault if he finds no prey. It's the hunters who release the dogs in a place where there's no prey to be caught. No, we can go back to the incident room with our heads held high." As he said this, Godai gave the younger detective a pat on the shoulder.

Four days had now passed since the discovery of the body. What Nakamachi worried about was that none of the other teams had turned up anything significant.

The detectives were using the call logs of the victim's phones to track down anyone who had recently been in touch with Shiraishi. Although the flip phone remained lost, the phone company had provided them with his outgoing call records. Yuta Yamada's number was on the list.

Between them, Godai and Nakamachi spoke to more than thirty people. As well as Shiraishi's clients, both past and present, they had visited other lawyers he worked with and the accountant who handled his firm's finances. They had even dropped in on his barber. Everyone told them the exact same thing: His murder was inexplicable. A colleague went so far as to say that if the person responsible asked him to handle his defense, he would rather jump off a bridge than take the case. Godai and Nakamachi got back to the incident room late in the evening. Assistant Inspector Tsutsui, their supervisor for the case, was still there, so they summarized their findings for the day.

Tsutsui was a squared-jawed man with a striking head of prematurely gray hair. He barely reacted when his two subordinates reported that they had uncovered nothing of interest.

"You've done well. Go back home and take it easy. I'm sending you on a road trip tomorrow." Tsutsui slid a single sheet of paper across the desk toward Godai.

"Where to?" Godai picked up the sheet of paper. It was a photocopy of a driver's license. The portrait photo showed a scrawny-looking man, around sixty years old.

The address was in Anjo, a town in Aichi Prefecture.

4

THE BULLET TRAIN from Tokyo was busier than Godai had been expecting. He was pleased to find a seat in one of the unreserved cars. Getting to Mikawa-Anjo Station would take about two and a half hours. Sitting in a window seat, Godai took another look at the paper Tsutsui had given him.

Tatsuro Kuraki, sixty-three years old. That was the man he was going to meet. There wasn't much more information than that.

Shiraishi's law firm kept a record of all incoming calls. These records showed that a "Kuraki" had called from a cell phone number on October 2. Setsuko Nagai, Shiraishi's assistant, remembered the call, which she had patched through to her boss, but she knew nothing about Kuraki other than that he was a man, and had no idea what the call was about.

Kuraki wasn't on the firm's client list. He'd only called once, and there was no record of him ever visiting the office.

In the end, they decided to call the number and speak to the man himself. A female officer made the call in the hope that Kuraki would be more forthcoming with someone of the opposite sex.

Without going into any of the specifics of the case, she asked him for his full name and his contact details. He was cooperative and provided his full name—Tatsuro Kuraki—his address, and other details. The officer didn't detect any hint of alarm in his voice.

Tsutsui then reached out to Kuraki to say that they would appreciate if he could make the time to see them. Kuraki said that since he was not working, he was available anytime.

According to Tsutsui, Kuraki had been pretty persistent in asking why the police wanted to interview him. That was to be expected. Kuraki probably thought that a detective wouldn't go to all the trouble of coming to see him unless it was important. One didn't need to have skeletons in one's closet to feel nervous about something like that.

"The officer will give you more information when he sees you," was all Tsutsui said. They had no idea if Kuraki was involved in Shiraishi's murder, but another ironclad police rule was to give out minimal information prior to an in-person meeting.

That was how Godai had ended up on the train to Mikawa-Anjo today.

Godai reached Mikawa-Anjo Station a little before 11:00 AM. When he emerged from the station, he found himself in a parking lot with a handful of cars in it. With few large buildings and no billboards, the place had a slightly pastoral feel.

There was a single taxi waiting at the taxi stand. Godai showed the driver the map he'd printed in advance.

Looking out of the taxi window, Godai noticed that the road and the sidewalks were generously wide. There were no high-rises to be seen, but such buildings as there were sat on spacious lots. Anyone used to a place like this would struggle to live in the densely packed residential districts of Tokyo.

Less than ten minutes later, the taxi came to a stop. "It'll be somewhere around here," the driver said.

"Here is fine."

Godai paid the fare, got out, and set off, checking his whereabouts on the map. The houses lining the street were a motley bunch, some old and some new, each one with enough space to park a car. Several houses had multiple cars parked outside.

The house with Kuraki's nameplate on the front gate also had a carport out front, containing a small gray car with a lucky charm dangling from the rearview mirror.

There was an intercom just below the nameplate. Godai pressed the button and waited.

"Hello?" came a man's voice.

"I'm here from Tokyo."

"I've been expecting you."

A few moments later, there was the sound of a lock turning, and the front door opened. The man who appeared had the same rather thin face as on his driver's license. He was physically sturdier than Godai had been expecting.

"My name's Tsutomu Godai. Thanks for seeing me." He pulled out his Tokyo Metropolitan Police badge, took a step forward, and held it up for the older man to see, before quickly stuffing it back in his pocket and pulling out a business card.

Kuraki squinted as he scrutinized the card. "Come on in," he said, gesturing Godai inside.

Godai thanked him, ducked his head, and stepped into the house.

Kuraki led him into a Japanese-style room just off the entrance hall. There were rattan-style chairs and a table on the tatami-mat floor. Up against one wall stood a small Buddhist altar, above which hung a photograph of a woman: It looked like a funeral portrait.

"That's my wife," said Kuraki. "She passed sixteen years ago. She was a little older than me. Fifty-one at the time."

"Too young. That's tragic. Was it an accident?"

"No, it was something called *acute myeloid leukemia*. With a bone marrow transplant, she might've made it, but we didn't manage to find a donor."

"Ah, right . . ." Godai mumbled.

"So here I am, an old man living all on my lonesome. I haven't brewed up a proper cup of green tea in a teapot for years now. Will you be okay with the bottled stuff?"

"Fine by me. But don't go to any trouble on my account."

"No? Well, as you wish. Please, sit down."

"As I believe my colleagues informed you over the phone, Mr. Kuraki, your name came up in the course of an ongoing investigation. We found your telephone number among the incoming calls of the Shiraishi Law Office in Tokyo. We are currently investigating Mr. Shiraishi's murder."

Pausing, Godai looked at Kuraki to gauge his reaction. There was little change to the expression on the old man's gaunt face. He only gave the slight hint of a nod.

"Were you aware that Mr. Shiraishi had been murdered?"

"After your colleagues called me yesterday, I went online and saw what happened. It was quite a shock. I can certainly see why the police might want to come and see me." Kuraki's tone was calm and unruffled.

"That should speed things up a bit. I'm here today to ask you why you telephoned Mr. Shiraishi. What was the nature of your relationship?"

Kuraki ran a hand over his closely cropped head. "We had no 'relationship.' I never actually met the man. That was the first and the last time I spoke to him."

"So why did you call him?"

"I was calling him for advice."

"Advice?"

"Yes, legal advice. I'm dealing with a financial issue. I'm involved in a dispute. That's why I called."

"Why did you call Mr. Shiraishi's firm in particular?"

"Anywhere would have been fine. When I looked up lawyers online, Shiraishi's website said they offered simple legal consultations by phone—and that the service was free. I never intended to become a full-fledged client, so it made no difference where they were based—Tokyo, Osaka, wherever."

Kuraki delivered this speech briskly and confidently. It struck Godai as convincing enough, as simple as it was persuasive.

"What were you consulting him about?"

Kuraki frowned at Godai's request. "Do I have to tell you?"

"There's no obligation. Still, I'd be grateful if you could."

Kuraki grimaced and shook his head. "I'm sorry. I can't tell you. It's a privacy issue. Not just my privacy—it's about other people's too."

"I see. Well, I suppose I'll have to let that one go."

Godai scratched his head with his pen, unable to come up with a follow-up question.

There was the sound of a ringtone. It was Kuraki's cell.

"Where'd I put the thing? Oh, it's over there. Would you excuse me a minute?" Kuraki said.

"Of course. Go right ahead. Would it be okay if I used your bathroom?"

"Feel free. It's just across the hall."

Godai watched Kuraki hurry to grab his cell, before heading to the toilet. As he made his way back to the tatami living room, a votive slip stuck on one of the wooden pillars caught his eye. Godai's whole body stiffened at the sight of the characters on it.

It read *Tomioka Hachimangu Shrine*; beneath that in smaller script were the phrases *For the safety and well-being of my family* and *For prosperity in business*.

Godai took his phone out of his inside pocket and was preparing to take a photograph when he heard footsteps. Kuraki reappeared at the far end of the corridor.

"Is everything all right?" Kuraki asked.

"Yes, fine." Godai slipped his phone back into his pocket.

He sat back down across the rattan table from Kuraki, his frame of mind quite different from a couple of minutes ago.

"Do you go up to Tokyo from time to time?" Godai asked. He could hear the edge in his voice.

"I do, yes. Because of my son."

"Your son? Where in Tokyo does he live?"

"Koenji. He went to university in Tokyo, got a job there, and ended up staying."

"Right. And do you visit him regularly?"

Kuraki thought for a moment. "Several times a year, I guess."

"When were you last in Tokyo?"

"When was it? I reckon it would be . . . oh, about three months ago."

"A precise date would be extremely helpful."

Kuraki gave him a searching look. "Why?"

"I'm sorry. Procedure." Godai ducked his head apologetically. "Please understand, we ask these sorts of questions of everyone with any sort of connection to the case."

"But all I did was make one phone call. I'm hardly 'connected to the case.'"

"I can only apologize," Godai repeated.

Kuraki sighed. "Give me a minute," he said as he picked his cell phone up off the table. Godai noticed that it was not a smartphone. With a look of intense concentration, Kuraki pressed its buttons. Godai got the feeling this was merely playacting designed to confuse him, the detective from Tokyo.

"It was August 16," said Kuraki, his eyes fixed on the phone's little screen. "I've got the text messages I sent to my son here. I stayed for a couple of days. My son doesn't usually come back here for the summertime Obon holiday, so I go see him instead. I do it every year."

"Do you stay at your son's place when you go to Tokyo?"

"Yes. He's single. It's no trouble for him."

"Could I get your son's name and contact details?"

Kuraki looked at the floor and blinked a few times. Clearly, he was reluctant to oblige.

"My son's name is Kazuma. He works for—"

Kuraki went on to give the name of one of Japan's largest advertising agencies and provided Godai with his son's phone number. Godai briskly noted it down.

"What do you like to do during your visits to Tokyo? Any favorite places you like to visit?"

"Depends. A few years ago, I went to the top of the Tokyo Skytree. It's certainly very high. Honestly, though, that's about all that can be said for the place."

"What about shrines and temples? Everyone likes a nice temple visit."

"Shrines and temples? Don't know, really. I don't dislike them, but I'm not wild about them either."

"I noticed a votive slip from Tomioka Hachimangu Shrine stuck onto one of the pillars in the corridor outside the toilet. It looks quite new. I suppose you're the person who put it there?"

"Oh, that thing? No, someone gave it to me. I'm not a very religious person, but it was a gift, so I thought I'd better put it up."

"Someone gave it to you? Meaning you've not yourself been to Tomioka Hachimangu Shrine?"

"No, I've not. It was a gift."

"Who from? Who gave it to you?"

Kuraki was looking at Godai with open suspicion. There was a wary look in his eyes.

"Why would you even ask a question like that? How can it matter who I got the stupid thing from?"

"That's up to me. Just tell me who gave it to you."

Kuraki inhaled deeply and briefly shut his eyes. Perhaps he was scanning his memory, but Godai suspected that he was playing for time—again.

"I'm awfully sorry." Kuraki had reopened his eyes. "I can't remember."

"You can't remember? Come on. Only someone close to you would ever give you a votive slip from a shrine as a present."

"You're welcome to think that if you want. I simply can't remember, and there's nothing I can do about it. I'm sorry. I must be losing it. It's an age thing."

I can't remember. That had to be one of the worst answers a detective could ever get in an interview. When people went for *I don't know*, you could always throw a piece of material evidence at them and argue that there was no way they didn't know. With *I can't remember*: There was nothing you could do.

But Godai knew he was onto something. His trip to Aichi had not been wasted.

"You told me earlier that you called Mr. Shiraishi's firm to ask them for some rudimentary legal advice. Did you consult any other law firms about the same issue?"

Kuraki shook his head. "No, I did not."

"By talking to Mr. Shiraishi, were you able to solve the matter to your satisfaction?"

"No. Quite the opposite. Shiraishi's response couldn't have been more unhelpful. All he said was that I could figure the whole thing out for myself if I did a little research online. The service was free, so perhaps I was a fool to expect anything better. I realized the whole thing was a waste of time, and I didn't bother consulting anybody else." Kuraki was holding Godai's gaze and speaking with complete composure. He appeared to be laying out the facts honestly—but he could be putting on a show of extreme self-assurance to fool Godai.

Either way, Godai felt that now was not the right time or place to push the matter. There remained one last point he needed to check.

The detective glanced at his watch.

"I've already taken up too much of your time. This is my last question. Were you in Tokyo on October 31?"

"October 31 . . . Sounds like you're asking me for an alibi."

"I know it's an odd question, but we ask everyone we interview the same thing. I hope you can understand that."

There was a pained expression on Kuraki's face as he turned and looked up at the calendar hanging on the wall.

"The thirty-first of last month? Unfortunately, I didn't do anything special on that day. It was just a normal, ordinary day, like every other."

"Meaning what exactly?"

Kuraki turned back toward Godai. "Meaning that I didn't go out anywhere and that no one came here to see me. I was right here at home. All day."

"I need you to prove that—"

"Not possible." Kuraki shot back. "I have no alibi for that particular day. Regrettably."

There was no note of apology or deference in his answer. *I'm going to have to find out why this man's so confident*, Godai thought.

He looked at his watch again. It was just past noon. "Okay. That's fine. Thanks for your time."

"I'm sorry. I doubt I was much help."

Godai looked Kuraki right in the eye. "That remains to be seen."

"It does, does it?" Kuraki held the other man's gaze.

"Thank you." Godai began making his way to the entrance hall.

"Oh, Detective," Kuraki called out to him. "One thing . . ."

"What?"

"About when I was last in Tokyo. I told you I'd been to see my son over the Obon holiday. I forgot that I'd made another visit since."

Godai pulled out his notebook. "When was this?"

"It was October 5. I had no particular reason for going. I just wanted to see my son, so I went there. I stayed overnight and came back here the next day. There was nothing special about the trip. That must be why the whole thing slipped my mind."

October 5—Godai dug into his memory. Kensuke Shiraishi's first visit to Monzen-Nakacho had been on October 7.

Why had Kuraki opted to tell him this just as he was on his way out? Had he really forgotten about it? It could just be one of those things. On the other hand . . .

Perhaps Kuraki was expecting the police to pay his son a visit—in which case, concealing his October 5 visit wasn't a smart move. It would come out as soon as they pulled some threads. Why, then, Godai wondered, had Kuraki tried to keep it secret in the first place?

"Thank you for all your help," Godai said, leaving these questions for later. "Appreciate it."

Kuraki walked him out. Godai stopped briefly beside the pillar with the votive slip on it.

"Would you like me to get in touch if I manage to remember who gave me that thing?" Kuraki asked.

"That would be great."

"I'll put my thinking cap on. Can't guarantee it will come back to me."

"Either way, I'd be grateful."

Godai slipped his shoes back onto his feet, then turned and looked up at Kuraki. "If something comes up, I'll come back."

Kuraki's shoulders tightened. He gave a small nod. "Sure. You're always welcome."

"Goodbye."

Godai left. He heard the door being locked as soon as it shut behind him.

He was heading for the sidewalk when a thought struck him. He went over to the car in the drive. He craned forward slightly, squinted, and looked through the windshield. There was a lucky charm made of red silk dangling from the rearview mirror.

His hunch was right. It was embroidered with the words *Tomioka Hachimangu Shrine: Safe driving amulet*.

Would Kuraki claim that the amulet was another something he'd been given by a forgotten someone?

Godai went out onto the street. He wondered why Kuraki had refused to admit to buying the votive slip himself. Had he done so, he wouldn't have had to tie himself in knots with a phony excuse about having forgotten.

Of course, there was always the possibility that Kuraki was telling the truth. It could have been a gift. Perhaps he'd pretended not to remember to avoid revealing that person's name.

Godai quickened his pace, looking around for a cab to take him back to the train station. *I've got a lot to do when I get back to Tokyo*, he thought.

5

Tatsuro Kuraki's son, Kazuma, worked in a building on Yasukuni Boulevard in Kudanshita. Rather than go to Kazuma's office, Godai called him from the street. The son sounded taken aback when Godai told him he was from the Tokyo Metropolitan Police. "What's this in relation to?" Kazuma asked. His father must not have told him anything.

Luckily, Kazuma was in the office and had the time to step outside for a few minutes. They arranged to meet in one of the old coffee shops in the neighborhood. Nakamachi was accompanying him today, and the two detectives found a table at the back of the coffee shop.

"What game do you think Kuraki's playing?" Nakamachi said. "Why didn't he warn his son that detectives from the TMPD might come and speak to him? Or did he think we weren't going to follow through?"

"He's a slippery customer, that one," Godai said, speaking with conviction. "He knows that I'm suspicious, and he has a pretty good idea why I want to speak to his son. My guess is that he thought there was nothing to be gained from warning him. He knows that it would look bad if their stories were too neatly coordinated. That's why he told me about his visit to Tokyo on October 5. My gut feeling is that even if Tatsuro Kuraki is somehow involved, the son probably isn't."

Godai was being deliberately cautious. In fact, he didn't just think Kuraki was involved—he was pretty sure that Kuraki was the murderer. Kuraki calling Shiraishi on the phone. Shiraishi's subsequent visit to Monzen-Nakacho. The votive slip on the pillar. The amulet in the car. Everything about the man was suspicious. Godai's superiors shared his opinion, and they had another investigator looking into Kuraki's connections. Meanwhile, a large team of investigators was on the ground at Monzen-Nakacho, canvassing the local residents with Kuraki's photograph.

The door of the coffee shop opened, and a man stepped inside. Godai put his age at around thirty. He had a handsome face and a strong, straight nose. *A chip off the old block*, thought Godai, noticing how similar his eyes were to his father's.

The other customers were all solo women or couples. Visibly anxious, Kazuma Kuraki quickly spotted the two detectives and made his way over to them.

"Are you the ones who called me?"

"That's right. Sorry to bother you when you're at work." Godai handed him his card.

When he saw that Godai was from the Homicide Bureau, Kazuma Kuraki frowned dubiously. The silver-haired proprietor brought water over to their table, and Kazuma ordered himself a coffee.

"So what exactly do you want to talk to me about? This is quite nerve-racking."

Kazuma was at least honest about his feelings, Godai thought. "I'm sorry if I got you worried. Our inquiry is simple enough. We just have a few questions about your father."

"My father?" Kazuma looked surprised. It was obviously the last thing he'd been expecting. "By my father, you mean Tatsuro Kuraki?"

"That's right."

Kazuma blinked and scowled. "What's my father supposed to have done? I suppose you know that he lives in Anjo?"

"We know that. We also know that he comes up to Tokyo from time to time."

"Yes, he does, but . . ."

"When was the last time he came to Tokyo?"

"Wait a minute." Kazuma held up his hands and looked first at Godai, then Nakamachi. "What sort of investigation is this? How is my father involved? I really don't want to answer any questions until you fill me in."

"Be reasonable," Nakamachi said with a grin. "You don't need to know what we're investigating to tell us when your father last came up to Tokyo."

"No." Kazuma glared back at them defiantly. "But if I'm going to share private and personal information with you, I think it's the least you can do."

Tension hung in the air. Kazuma's coffee arrived. He made no move to pick it up.

"You should try it," Godai said with a conciliatory smile. "This place is famous for its coffee. It would be a shame for it to get cold. Please."

Kazuma grudgingly added milk to his coffee.

"There was a murder," Godai said just as Kazuma picked up his cup. "Someone was killed here in Tokyo. Our job is to speak to everyone who had contact with the victim, or we believe to have had contact with the victim. Contact is not limited to meeting in person; it includes any sort of communication—like phone, emails, letters, whatever."

"And my father is one of the names on your list?" Kazuma was still holding his cup in midair.

"Precisely. He called the victim."

Kazuma took a small sip of coffee and put the cup back on the table.

"I don't suppose you can tell me the identity of the victim?"

"I am afraid we can't. If you want to know, I suggest you ask your father."

"Have you been to see my dad?"

"I saw him just yesterday. He was the one who gave me your contact details and told me where you work."

"He never said a word to me."

"He must have his reasons. Anyway, that's all I can tell you at this stage of the investigation. Now I need you to answer my question. When was the last time your father came to Tokyo?"

"Give me a minute," Kazuma said. He pulled out his phone and made a few taps and swipes. He was obviously checking his calendar. "It was October 5." That was the answer the detectives had been expecting. "Strictly, though, it was more like October 6."

The detectives' ears pricked up.

"What?" Godai blurted out. "What do you mean?"

"I don't know when exactly he arrived in Tokyo on the fifth. But he didn't get to my place until around one in the morning on the sixth."

"What had he been doing till then?"

"I don't know. When I asked, he just said he'd been wandering around, exploring. That's what he always does when he comes to town."

"He always does that? Don't you two ever have dinner together?"

"Quite often when he first started coming here, but not for several years now. With my schedule, it's difficult to make time, and we find that having breakfast together the morning after works better for us. There's no point in us hanging out. We don't really have that much to talk about."

"Does your father always leave for home early the next day?"

"I think so, but honestly, I don't know. There's a diner near my apartment that opens early. We eat there, and then we go our separate ways."

"How often does he come up to Tokyo?"

"About once every two, maybe three months."

That fit with what Kuraki had said.

"How long ago did you move to Tokyo?"

"I came here for university, then stayed, so four years of university plus eleven years since I graduated. Fifteen years all told."

"And when did your father start coming to visit?"

"It started when he retired. 'Now I've finally got the time,' he said and started coming up."

"And the frequency of his visits has always been the same?"

"Pretty much."

"Has anything out of the ordinary happened to him while he was visiting? It could be something good or bad; it doesn't matter. Was he ever like, 'Can you believe what happened to me today?'"

"Let me think." Kazuma leaned forward and propped his forehead in his palm. "I suppose there was the occasional small thing he told me about. Nothing I can remember, though. Sorry."

"When your father comes up to Tokyo, does he usually go around on his own? Did you get the impression he was meeting other people?"

"If he was, he never said anything about it to me. He doesn't know anyone in Tokyo, and he never said anything about making any new friends either. I think he was always on his own."

"I see. If you don't mind, I just have a couple more questions. Does Monzen-Nakacho bring anything to mind? Or Tomioka Hachimangu Shrine?"

"Monzen-Nakacho?" His bewilderment seemed genuine enough. "What do those places have to do with anything?"

"I'm sorry, but we're not at liberty to share that information. Just one more question. Has your father discussed any legal issues with you?"

"Legal issues? What sort of legal issues?"

"Anything, really. Maybe something related to financial matters or ownership rights."

"No, he's never brought anything like that up."

"Thank you. That's all the questions I had. We appreciate your cooperation." Godai snapped his notebook shut.

"I'd like to ask a question of my own," piped up Nakamachi. "How do you feel about your father's visits?"

"How do I *feel* about them? What's that even supposed to mean?"

"Like you, I'm not a Tokyoite, so I know what it's like. Having your parents come to see you too often can be annoying. Once every couple of months strikes me as fairly frequent. Haven't you asked yourself why he comes here so often? There's only so many sights to see. Have you ever suspected there might be another reason for his visits?"

Kazuma had a deep frown line between his brows and a hard curl to his lips as he picked up his coffee cup. After swallowing a mouthful of coffee—which was probably lukewarm by now—he thumped the cup back down on the table.

"Look, I don't know anything about your family or your relationship with your parents. In our family, our policy is live and let live. My dad likes to come up to Tokyo. Whatever. It's none of my business. That's why I'm not *suspecting* anything." Kazuma directed his gaze at Godai. "Listen, I've got work to do. Can I go?"

"Of course. Thank you for your help."

Godai ducked his head in a bow. By the time he looked up again, Kazuma was already striding toward the door.

"That last line of attack of yours worked like a charm." Godai grinned at Nakamachi. "Looks to me like Kazuma Kuraki already had suspicions of his own. When you had the indelicacy to point it out, he went to pieces."

"Suspicions of his own? Do you think . . . ?"

Godai gave a snort of laughter. "The father comes up to Tokyo regular as clockwork, but never tells his son where he's going. He only shows up at the son's place in the middle of the night, and he leaves the next morning without bothering to have a proper conversation with him. There's only one possible explanation for behavior like that."

"A woman?"

Godai nodded forcefully. "I'm willing to bet that it's his girlfriend who gave him the votive slip and the amulet from Tomioka Hachimangu Shrine. If we can find her, we can start making progress on this case."

"Sounds to me like we've finally got something good for our colleagues in the incident room." Nakamachi's eyes crinkled shut as he smiled with unadulterated glee.

6

THE POLICE TRACKED a possible girlfriend later. The investigators doing the door-to-door interviews with Tatsuro Kuraki's photo found the lead. A clerk at a liquor store claimed to have seen Kuraki on several occasions when making deliveries at a local restaurant. Kuraki, he said, had been one of the customers seated at the counter.

The restaurant, Asunaro, had been operating for over twenty years. While the owner was nearly seventy, it was actually her daughter who ran the place and was possibly Kuraki's girlfriend.

"You're the ones who interviewed Kuraki. You should be the ones to speak to her." Assistant Inspector Tsutsui handed Godai a map on which Asunaro's location was marked.

Godai immediately left, taking Nakamachi with him. He told Nakamachi there was somewhere he wanted to visit on the way.

The place was the café that Kensuke Shiraishi had visited twice. Just like on the previous occasion, they went to the second floor and sat next to one another at the counter that overlooked Eitai Boulevard.

"Hey, Godai," Nakamachi said excitedly. "We're definitely on the right track here."

He was holding up the map that Assistant Inspector Tsutsui had given them.

Godai glanced at it. Before leaving the police station, he'd checked the map and seen that Asunaro was right opposite the café. It didn't take a wild leap to guess that Kensuke Shiraishi had been watching the comings and goings at the restaurant.

"We don't want to jump to conclusions, but I don't think there's much chance we're wrong." Godai picked up his paper cup as he said this. Somehow the completely ordinary chain-store coffee it contained seemed to taste special today.

Asunaro opened at half past five. At half past four, the two detectives got up and crossed the street. Asunaro was on the second floor of an old and rather small building. There was a staircase, and at the top, a little Sorry, We're Closed sign hung on the door to the restaurant.

They entered. The first thing to strike Godai was the smell of dashi broth. Only after that did he take in the appearance of the place. A youngish woman was standing behind a plain wood counter.

She wore an apron over a tracksuit. Despite her casual outfit, her face was carefully made-up; her neatly plucked eyebrows were especially striking.

"Sorry, we're not open till half past five," the woman said.

"We're not customers." Godai held out his badge so the woman could see it.

She froze, a ladle in her hand and a mystified look on her face. She took a deep breath. "I see," she said. "Why are you here?"

Although she looked young at first glance, on closer inspection, Godai could make out the crow's-feet at the corners of her eyes. Even so, she certainly didn't look like she was in her forties. Her face was small with delicately sculpted features.

"Are you the manager here?"

"No. Mother is the manager. She's just stepped out to do some shopping."

"She is Mrs. Yoko Asaba?"

"That's right."

"Clearly, you also work here. Do you mind telling us your name?"

"My name's Orie Asaba. Listen, what are you doing here?"

Her eyes darted anxiously.

Godai presented her with a photograph. "Do you know this man?"

Orie looked at the photograph, and her eyes widened slightly. "Uh-huh," she said with a nod.

"Do you know his name?"

"He's called Kuraki. He comes here from time to time."

"And do you know his first name?"

"Pretty sure it's Tatsuro, but don't quote me on that." She didn't sound all that confident.

"When was he last here?"

Orie thought for a moment. "Early last month, I think."

"How often does he come?"

"Several times a year. Sometimes he's regular as clockwork; sometimes there's more of a gap between his visits."

"When did he first start coming?"

"I can't be too sure. Five, maybe six years ago."

That tallied with what Kazuma had told them about his father. It sounded like Tatsuro Kuraki stopped by every time he came to Tokyo.

"Do you know why he comes here? Did a friend of his recommend it to him?"

Orie tipped her head quizzically to one side. "He never said. I think he just dropped in at random and took a fancy to the place."

"Does he come here alone or with someone else?"

"No, he's always alone."

"And what does he do with himself when he's all alone like that?"

"What does he do? Given that we're a restaurant, he has something to eat and he enjoys a drink or two."

"What time does he get here, and when does he leave, roughly?"

"He usually gets here at about seven. And I'd say he normally leaves just before we shut up shop."

"What's closing time here?"

"Last orders is at eleven, and we close at eleven thirty."

"Where's he like to sit?"

"Wha—?" There was a look of confusion on Orie's face.

"Regular customers at a bar or restaurant usually like to sit in the same place. I thought maybe he had a favorite spot."

"Right." Orie nodded. "It's there." She pointed at a seat at the end of the counter up against the wall.

Godai looked where she was pointing and tried to picture Kuraki there. Sitting in a spot slightly removed from the other patrons and spending four and a half hours drinking all by yourself until closing time—that wasn't something you would do unless a place mattered to you.

No, that isn't it. Perhaps it's about a person rather than a place.

"Listen." There was a hint of firmness in Orie's voice. "What sort of investigation are you working on? Has something happened to Mr. Kuraki?"

When Godai said nothing, Nakamachi stepped in. "You just need to answer our questions. The less you know, the better," he said gently.

"That's not fair. How can you subject me to the third degree and not expect me to be curious? What am I supposed to say to Mr. Kuraki the next time he comes? He may not come often, but he's a nice guy. He's really sweet to me and my mom. Can I tell him about your coming here today?"

"You're more than welcome," Godai shot back. "Seeing as we've already interviewed him."

"Really?"

She seemed a little shocked, and she looked away. Godai scrutinized her face. If Orie was in a relationship with Kuraki, he would definitely have told her about the detective who had traipsed all the way from Tokyo to Aichi Prefecture to interview him. But the expression on her face counted for next to nothing. *Women are all actors*, he told himself.

"We're not subjecting you to the third degree, but we haven't even asked you any difficult questions." Godai was looking directly into Orie's perfectly made-up face. "Now we will. First, I want you to tell me everything you know about this Tatsuro Kuraki. Doesn't matter how trivial. Nakamachi, are you ready to take notes?"

"Ready when you are, sir." Nakamachi had his notebook open in front of him and a pen in his hand.

"Go on, then," Godai said to Orie.

"It's easy enough for you to ask the question, but I actually don't know much about him. Mr. Kuraki isn't a big one for talking about himself.... He told me that he lives out in Aichi Prefecture, while his son lives here in Tokyo. He drops by every time he comes to town, and he usually brings us some sort of a present from Aichi. What else . . . ?" Orie tipped her head to one side and appeared to rack her brain. "Oh yes, he's a fan of the local baseball team, the Chunichi Dragons. And he's got too much time on his hands now that he's retired. What else . . . ?" She sighed and slowly shook her head. "I'm sorry. He must have told me more about himself. It's just not coming to me right now."

"Take your time and see what comes back to you. We'll be dropping in on you again. More than once, I suspect."

Orie frowned unhappily. *The woman's an open book. She doesn't want us coming back, and she's not acting this time,* thought Godai, seeing her response to his remark.

There was the sound of a door opening behind them. Turning around, Godai saw a little old woman in a beige cardigan, with a white plastic shopping bag in each hand. She stood there, rooted to the spot. Her small, bespectacled face was a mass of fine wrinkles, but Godai recognized her as Orie's mother. The family resemblance was obvious.

"You must be Mrs. Yoko Asaba?"

Ignoring Godai, she looked over at the counter where her daughter was.

"They're from the police," Orie said. "They're here to ask us about Mr. Kuraki."

"We appreciate your cooperation," said Godai, showing her his badge at the same time.

Yoko didn't even bother to look at it. She walked up to the counter and handed the two bags she was carrying to her daughter. Only then did she turn to face the detectives. "What? Are you trying to tell me Mr. Kuraki's done something wrong?" she asked.

"I can't yet speak to that. Which is the reason we're going around interviewing people. Yourselves included."

"Oh, I get it. Look, I've no idea what you're investigating, but if you suspect Mr. Kuraki, then you're way off the mark. The man doesn't have a bad bone in his body," Yoko said briskly.

"I'll bear that in mind." Godai felt a twinge even while the words were coming out of his mouth. There was something not quite right about what the older woman had said, though he couldn't quite put his finger on it.

"Was it Mr. Kuraki who told you about this place?" Yoko asked.

Godai grimaced and waved a hand. "I can't tell you that."

"Apparently, we're supposed to answer their questions and not ask any of our own," said Orie from behind the counter, her voice heavy with sarcasm.

"Oh yeah? Well, in that case, let's get this over as fast as possible. It's nearly opening time. I know it's not the politest thing to say, but personally, I've always loathed the police." Yoko looked straight up at Godai as she said this. There was a frighteningly cold gleam in her eyes.

"Okay then. This question is for both of you. Have you heard of a certain Kensuke Shiraishi? He's a lawyer."

"Not someone I know. How about you?" Yoko asked Orie. When the younger woman wordlessly shook her head, the mother said to Godai, "And nor does she, apparently."

"Okay. Moving on, Tomioka Hachimangu Shrine is not far from here. Is that somewhere you like to visit?"

"Yeah, we go there. I mean, it's just around the corner."

"Do you buy votive slips and amulets there?"

"Yes." Yoko nodded. "Look up there." A votive slip of the kind Godai had seen at Kuraki's house was stuck just below the ceiling of the kitchen area.

"Do you ever give the votive slips and amulets as presents to other people?"

"To our best customers. All the time."

"Does that include Mr. Kuraki?"

"Mr. Kuraki?" Yoko clapped her hands together. "Come to think of it, I did give him one. It was quite a few years back. Maybe three. It was to thank him for the presents he's always bringing us from Nagoya."

Yoko's answer set Godai's mind whirring. Given what she had said, Kuraki's claim that he couldn't remember who'd given him the votive slip didn't ring true. Now what Godai had to figure out was why Kuraki would want to stop him finding out about this restaurant.

"From what you've both said to me, I get the impression that you're close to Mr. Kuraki. What about your other regulars? Is Mr. Kuraki friendly with any of them?"

"I don't really know. You can see how small this place is. You run into the same people again and again. I think he's made a few friends, yes."

"What sort of customers do you have here? Can you give me an idea?"

"That's an impossible question to answer," Yoko said with a smile. "If you want to find out, visit us during opening hours and use your own eyes and ears. You'll need to come as a regular customer, though. Flash your badge around the way you did just now and I'll sue you for interfering with the business."

Godai broke into a crooked smile. "I'll be careful," he said with a nod.

"Detective, listen. If you've got any more questions, can't you wait for another day? We've got a thousand and one things to do," Yoko said, looking pointedly at the clock on the wall.

As she spoke, Godai realized what was behind that uneasy feeling he'd had when she first came in.

It was her intonation. There was the faintest regional accent in her voice. Godai was sure that he had heard something like it recently.

That's it. The taxi driver at Mikawa-Anjo Station had spoken in the same way. That intonation—it was a Mikawa accent.

"Is something wrong?" Yoko was looking at him warily.

"No, nothing wrong. I just have one last question for you. On October 31, were you open for business as normal?"

"The thirty-first of last month? I don't think we took any extra days off then, no."

"Were you both working here that day?"

"Yes, we were. Luckily for us, we're very busy. There's no way one of us can handle everything. What's so special about that day?"

"I'm sorry, I . . ."

"Oh yes, I forgot. We're not supposed to ask you questions." As Yoko said this, she gave a shrug.

Ignoring this, Godai said, "Thank you very much for your help. If you don't mind, I'd like to get an address and phone number for each of you."

Yoko scowled. "Planning to chase us down at home too?"

"Right now, I've no such intention. It's just to be safe."

With a sigh, Yoko grabbed a piece of notepaper and jotted down an address and two cell phone numbers. Apparently, the two women shared an apartment in Toyocho.

"Where were you ladies born?" Godai lifted his gaze from the notepaper and looked fixedly at Yoko. "I can tell that you were definitely not born here in Tokyo."

Yoko's face was now blank and expressionless.

She exhaled slowly, exchanged a look with her daughter behind the counter, and then turned back to Godai.

"You're very perceptive. I was born in Seto in Aichi Prefecture. When I got married, I moved to a place called Toyokawa and lived there till my mid-thirties. I came to Tokyo sometime after the death of my husband."

"That explains it. I imagine you and Mr. Kuraki must enjoy talking about your hometown."

"No, that's not something we've ever discussed. I haven't told him I was born in Aichi. He could probably tell, but he's never asked me about it. I never mentioned it myself, so maybe he was being tactful and staying away from the subject."

"Why should he do that?"

Her face still as blank as a Noh mask, Yoko took a deep breath. "I don't like the idea of you poking around and checking up on me, so I'll just come right out and make a full confession. I just told you that I loathe the police. Well, I have a very good reason for feeling that way."

"What is it?"

"My husband..." Yoko's eyes reddened, her wrinkled face tautened, and her lips twisted. The emotion on display was deep sadness. "My husband was murdered by the police." The sound that came out of Yoko's mouth was closer to a groan than anything else. "He was the suspect in a murder case. They arrested him, and he never came back home. He hanged himself in a police cell."

7

THE INCIDENT TOOK place on Tuesday, May 15, 1984, at a multi-tenant building near a train station. A financial adviser was murdered. The victim was Shozo Haitani. He was fifty-one years old and unmarried. One of his employees found him and called it in around seven thirty that evening. The victim was stabbed in the chest. The murder weapon was a kitchen knife."

Although Assistant Inspector Tsutsui was speaking softly, his voice reverberated around the small meeting room. Seated around the table with Tsutsui and Godai were all the top brass.

"Junji Fukuma was arrested on May 18, three days after the crime," Tsutsui went on, looking down at the file in front of him. "Based on what happened next, it seems very likely that he'd been arrested for a different offense, though what exactly that was isn't clear. We know little about Fukuma other than that he was forty-four years of age. Four days later, he took his own life in one of the police station cells. He used his own clothing to hang himself. With the suspect deceased, the case was referred to the prosecutor. The prosecutor dismissed the case. Most of the documentation related to the investigation was destroyed in May 1999 when the statute of limitations expired."

Godai had compiled the document from which Tsutsui was reading based on research and what Yoko Asaba had told him. Although Asaba remembered the precise time and date of her husband's arrest, she seemed not to know the broader details of the case.

"One day, out of the blue, this pack of cops and detectives piled into our house and took my husband, Junji, away. He said he'd be back in no time. He told me not to worry. Next thing I know, he's hanged himself in his cell and is dead."

Godai could not forget the look on Yoko's face as she calmly gave her account of events. Even more than thirty years later, it was obvious that the emotional scars hadn't healed.

By contrast, any official record of the case had all but vanished. After contacting the Aichi Prefectural Police, Godai managed to get an outline of the incident, ascertaining what had led to the suspect's arrest. Portions of the text that Tsutsui had read out were taken from newspaper articles.

"And you said the person of interest spoke to you about the incident?" asked Sakuragawa, the unit chief in Robbery-Homicide.

"Yoko did, yes," Godai replied.

"When a couple of detectives showed up at her restaurant, she must have realized that we would run a background check. Since Toyokawa's only a small place, she knew it wouldn't take much sniffing around for us to learn about the case, so she and her daughter decided to be up-front and tell us all about it."

"Right, then. How do you think we should go forward?" asked Sakuragawa, eager to hear his colleagues' opinions. "We've been struggling to explain why Shiraishi went to Monzen-Nakacho three times in a single month, including on the day of his murder. We have absolutely no idea of the motivation for those visits. The one possible link we have is this man, Tatsuro Kuraki. I'll get Godai and Nakamachi to keep looking for connections between Kuraki, the Asunaro restaurant, and the victim. The problem we have is how deeply we should dig into this thirtysomething-year-old case."

The horse-faced precinct commander groaned loudly. "It's such a nasty, sordid story."

"Couldn't agree more."

"The last thing the Aichi Prefectural Police want is for us to start digging into this case. The death in custody of a suspect is about as bad a screwup as there is. They don't just want to forget about it; they want to pretend it never happened."

"I'm sure that's right," Sakuragawa said. "That's why I'm asking for your advice."

"Is there any chance that either of the women who run the restaurant killed Shiraishi?"

"Godai says no. They were busy working at the time of the murder."

"In that case, even if the restaurant itself may have some connection to the crime, there's not much point investigating the two women who run the place."

The precinct commander was clearly dragging his feet. He was anxious not to antagonize the police of another prefecture.

"Hey, Godai," called out the chief of detectives. "What's your gut feeling? Do you think the two women are involved?"

Godai gave a small shake of his head. "To be honest, I don't know. Originally, we thought the daughter might be seeing Kuraki. But now, I don't think so. What bugs me is Tatsuro Kuraki failing to mention their restaurant to me. I also find his claim of not remembering who gave him the votive slip implausible. My sense is that Kuraki was more anxious to conceal the existence of the mother and daughter than the restaurant itself. So—"

"Okay. Enough." The chief of detectives thrust out a hand to cut Godai off and turned to the precinct commander. "I don't expect the Aichi Prefectural Police will want us to look into the matter, but the person who was in charge at the time will be long retired now. They'll probably be willing to talk."

The precinct commander nodded grudgingly at Sakuragawa. "Fine. So I can leave this to you?"

"I'll talk to my superiors. They'll arrange for cooperation from the Aichi Prefectural Police." As Sakuragawa said this, he shot a meaningful look at Tsutsui and Godai. They were no longer needed.

"If you'll excuse us." Godai and Tsutsui bowed and left the meeting.

"This could turn into a real can of worms," said Tsutsui as he walked down the corridor.

"It happened in 1984." Godai sighed. "That's when I started school."

"It's no surprise that all the investigation records are gone. All it means is that we'll need to speak to the people who handled the case."

"Won't most of them be dead by now?"

"If they were the same age then as we are now, they should be—what—well into their seventies by now? If they're still alive, we'll be the ones who look crazy." Tsutsui tapped a finger to the side of his head.

Godai managed a sardonic grin, but he felt slightly down. Even if they succeeded in finding someone with a clear memory of the 1984 case, they certainly wouldn't be keen to revisit it. There was little chance they'd be greeted with open arms.

8

"I'VE NEVER HAD miso katsu. What about you, Godai?" Nakamachi asked. He was sitting beside Godai, scrolling on his phone.

"No, I haven't either. Meant to have it last time I was in Nagoya but never got around to it. To be frank, I'm not excited about it."

"What? You should be more open-minded."

"My mom's always saying that's the reason I'm not married. If you get one, then I'll have one too. Let's find a good place once we're done with our work."

"There are loads of places. We're in Nagoya after all." Nakamachi still had his eyes glued to his smartphone.

The loudspeaker announced that the train would soon be arriving in Nagoya. Godai checked for his ticket.

It was now four days since he'd sat in with the top brass. Godai had been ordered to pay a second visit to Nagoya, this time to Tempaku Ward in the eastern part of the city. Nakamachi, happy to be out of the office, was in high spirits.

Given the sheer length of time that had passed, not to mention the statute of limitations, barely any documentation of the 1984 case still existed; that was only to be expected. The Aichi police had actually been very cooperative and patiently tracked down the whereabouts of the investigators who'd worked the case. Reduced to relying on the memories of people of an advanced age and with no records to consult, it must have been a headache.

The person they'd found was the man Godai and Nakamachi were on their way to see. He'd been the lead investigator but was now a seventy-two-year-old retiree.

Unfortunately, no one could plausibly argue that the investigation into Kensuke Shiraishi's murder was progressing well. The knife that had served as the murder weapon was a model sold through large retailers, and the murderer had left nothing else at the crime scene. No useful footage had been found on any of the security cameras in the area. And since locating Asunaro, the restaurant where Kuraki was a frequent visitor, the team going door-to-door had come up with nothing new.

Now, they were checking up on all his recent movements. Whenever he spent any length of time in a café or restaurant, they reviewed any relevant security camera footage. If there was no security camera in the establishment itself, they turned to cameras in the neighborhood. Although it was a job that demanded dogged perseverance, so far, everyone on the footage had been colleagues and clients of Shiraishi.

A friendly-looking fellow in glasses, around thirty, walked up and greeted the two detectives in Nagoya Station.

They flashed each other their IDs. He was a Sergeant Katase from the Aichi Prefectural Police, who had been assigned as their guide.

"We appreciate your going to all this trouble," Godai said.

"No big deal. You'd do the same for us," Katase said with a grin.

K ATASE PULLED HIS car around. Nakamachi was halfway into the front seat when Godai stopped him and climbed into the front himself. It would be easier to talk to Katase that way.

"I'm guessing our request must have been a royal pain in the ass. I mean, the case is more than thirty years old," Godai said once they were on the move.

"Personally, I thought it was fun. Looking into an incident from before I was even born was a whole new experience for me." Katase's tone was relaxed and easygoing.

"Did you track down the investigators yourself?"

"Yeah. The guys you're looking for are now just ordinary old geezers."

Katase explained that the man they were going to meet was a certain Shigenori Muramatsu. At the time of the 1984 murder, he'd been a police sergeant at the local precinct, leading the investigation.

"He's still of sound mind and has hung on to his old investigation records."

"What? How come?"

"They're only his personal records. He never chucked out the old notebooks and files he used throughout his career. Apparently, they include some information on the case you're interested in."

"I see."

Godai too had all his own investigation records safely stowed away in his apartment. Despite knowing that they were of no possible use to anybody, he couldn't bring himself to throw the things away. They were a testament to what he'd gone through to dig up all that information.

After half an hour of driving, Katase brought the car to a stop. They were parked beside a kindergarten in a middle-class neighborhood.

Katase led them to an old, detached house of a hybrid Japanese-Western design. It had a driveway large enough for two cars, though just a single kei car was parked there.

Katase spoke into the intercom. The front door opened, and a gray-haired man appeared. He was smaller and friendlier-looking than Godai had been expecting. No one's idea of a former detective, really.

Muramatsu waved them genially into the house. He directed them to a small Western-style living room overlooking a modest garden, where they sat down around a marble coffee table. Formal greetings were exchanged before Muramatsu's wife brought in some Japanese tea. A placid woman with short hair dyed a light brown color, she was very elegantly made-up.

"Thank you for making the time to see us."

Muramatsu responded to Godai's grateful bow with a relaxed and dismissive wave of his hand.

"Oh, I've nothing but time. I was working as a parking violation inspector until recently, when they finally managed to get rid of me! All day, every day, I've nothing but time on my hands. I'm happy to help you any way I can." The man's tone was almost too glib.

"As I'm sure you've been told, we recently learned that a person of interest in our investigation was born in Aichi Prefecture and was the wife of the suspect in a murder here."

Muramatsu nodded gravely at Godai's words. "So I gather. The woman now lives in Tokyo, does she? I must have met her a couple of times. Still, I can't picture her face."

"We have no idea if there's any link to our case, but it might be worth our while to learn more about the 1984 case."

Muramatsu grunted and nodded rather smugly. "Well, if that's what you want, then you've come to the right man, if I do say so myself. I was closely involved in that case from beginning to end. I was one of the first people on the scene. The person who called it in was still in the room where it happened, standing beside the body."

"Really?" Godai's eyes widened in surprise.

Muramatsu extracted an old university notebook out of a paper bag beside his chair, picked up a pair of spectacles from the table, and put them on. "I can still recall that day vividly. I'd just finished eating dinner at home when the call came, and I rushed out to the crime scene. It was on the second floor of a building near Higashi-Okazaki train station. It was an office with a rather dodgy-looking plaque saying *Green Enterprises* on the door and a fellow in a suit stabbed to death inside. There was a bloodstained knife on the floor next to him. The knife turned out to be something they'd had in the office, suggesting that the stabbing was not premeditated but had been done on impulse, probably in connection with an argument of some kind. A task force was quickly set up. As soon as we started looking into things, we discovered that Haitani, the victim, was up to his neck in mischief. One isn't supposed to say things like this, I know, but the fellow got what was coming to him."

"What sort of things was he doing?"

"You gentlemen are probably too young to remember it. Have you heard of the East-West Trading Company incident?"

"The East-West Trading Company incident... I vaguely remember studying it at the police academy. Large-scale fraud, wasn't it?"

"They got their customers to buy gold. Told them it was an asset that could only go up in value. Nothing wrong with that—the only problem was they wouldn't actually hand over the physical gold to their customers, and instead, they issued them pieces of paper, which they had the balls to refer to as 'securities.' They insisted they would keep the physical gold safe on the company premises. That wasn't the case. The company never purchased the bullion in the first place; they just helped themselves to the money they got from their customers. Plenty of people—many of them on the elderly side—were taken in. Of course, it's not the sort of scam you can sustain indefinitely. As more and more people started making official complaints, the company's dirty tricks were eventually laid bare. The company collapsed, and whatever assets remained were returned to the victims. The sums were pitifully small, though." After having delivered this speech, Muramatsu took a sip of tea.

"Was there a link between the two cases?"

"An indirect one. Like I said, East-West Trading itself collapsed, but plenty of people from the firm, both the executives and ordinary employees, launched new scams of their own. Scams involving golf club memberships, palladium futures trading, getting people to buy worthless precious stones at inflated prices—they would do anything to trick their customers out of their money. It would always end with the scammer doing a runner or the company going into planned bankruptcy. They liked to target old people who lived alone. They would call people indiscriminately until they found someone old who lived alone, then they'd deploy every trick in the book to scam them. They would tell them lies, like, you know, your pension will be automatically cut if you have too much money sitting in your bank account, so you're better off investing your savings with us. They were all scumbags, but Shozo Haitani, the victim, was a real hyena."

Godai leaned forward slightly. They seemed to have finally come to the link with the Higashi-Okazaki case.

"These fraudsters were always on the lookout for marks. Haitani got to know them and started introducing them to people he thought they'd be able to scam. He had previously worked at a life insurance company, and he got the names from customer lists he'd stolen when he quit. He had information on people's ages, incomes, savings, sometimes even the makeup of their families. For anyone who was planning on committing any kind of fraud, he was a great guy to know. Haitani would take the salesmen of these dodgy outfits with him to the house of whichever old person they had decided to target. He would introduce them, pretending it was part of the follow-up service for life insurance products the old folks had already purchased from his former employer. Believing that there was a connection to insurance they already held made them that much easier to trick. And apparently, this Haitani fellow had the gift of gab. Sometimes he would even bring along small presents. The lonely old folks were completely disarmed and treated him like a member of the family."

"I can see why someone would want to stab him."

"Quite. The main thrust of our investigation was to speak to Haitani's victims. When we started looking into it, we discovered that at the time of his murder, the proportion of people who realized they had been tricked by him was surprisingly low. I heard there was even one old woman who, when she heard he was dead, burst into tears and was like, 'How could such a terrible thing happen to such a nice young man?'"

"Impressive," murmured Nakamachi.

"One name that came up in the course of our investigation was that of a man called Junji Fukuma. Fukuma was the owner of an electrical appliance store who'd started speculating in palladium futures after an introduction from Haitani. At just forty-four, he was one of Haitani's younger victims. It was his knowledge about electronics that was his downfall. After doing a bit of research, he decided that palladium was a very promising metal. When it came to futures trading, however, he was a rank amateur. They repeatedly got him to buy when the market was high and sell when it was low, with the result that he squandered whatever money he had in no time at all. Meanwhile, what do you think the representative of the futures company was doing? Selling whenever Fukuma bought and buying when Fukuma sold, making himself a mint in the process. Every penny Fukuma had went straight into the company rep's pockets."

"That's so blatant," Godai said with a grimace. "Why did Fukuma keep on trading?"

"Because the sales rep had promised to guarantee his principal. Fukuma was convinced that he'd get back all the money he had originally put in, even if he didn't make a profit. Trouble was, the sales rep then went AWOL. That was the point at which Fukuma realized he'd been scammed and complained to Haitani. He was like, 'I know you were in on it, so give me back the money I lost.' There was no way that Haitani was ever going to agree to that. He just stuck to his guns and said that while yes, he had made the original introduction, he knew nothing beyond that. Haitani had his nephew manning the office phone. According to him, Fukuma had visited the office on multiple occasions." Muramatsu adjusted his glasses and squinted at his notebook. "A witness saw Fukuma on the day of the murder. A delivery boy who passed him on the building's staircase thirty minutes before the emergency call came through. Naturally enough, Fukuma was asked to present himself at the station."

"Did Fukuma admit to the crime?"

Muramatsu's mouth turned down at the corners. He shook his head. "He admitted to having gone to the office and met Haitani there. And he admitted to punching Haitani—but denied having stabbed him."

"What?" Godai asked. "Fukuma punched him?"

"Yes, apparently, he did. And he was willing to admit that. There were signs of internal bleeding on the victim's face, so we arrested him for assault right away."

So that's what happened. Godai could now make sense of things. Still, it would be difficult to describe that as an arrest for an entirely different offense.

"That's how he ended up in police custody?"

"Yes. He was indicted for assault, and then he was questioned."

"And was it you who questioned him, Mr. Muramatsu?"

"The prefectural HQ sent over an assistant inspector and a sergeant to handle Fukuma's interrogation. What were they called now . . . ?" Muramatsu consulted his notebook. Their names, apparently, were Assistant Inspector Yamashita and Sergeant Yoshioka. "Those two were notorious for the harshness of their interview technique. They were the go-to combo for browbeating a confession from a suspect who said anything slightly nuanced—like, 'I punched the guy, but I never stabbed him.' When we heard those two had been put in charge of questioning Fukuma, we expected them to clear things up in no time. Some people thought they were too brutal, but that's just the way investigations were handled back then."

As soon as the subject of Fukuma's questioning came up, Muramatsu had become defensive.

"Did you sit in on any of the interviews, Mr. Muramatsu?"

"No, I didn't. It was the stenographer who told me what was going on in the interview room. Yoshioka was the one who asked most of the questions. He was very aggressive and would just push and push and push. Fukuma was terrified of him. Then Yamashita would step in, rebuke Yoshioka, say something nice to Fukuma, and get the message across that things would only get more unpleasant if he didn't hurry up and confess. The stenographer was sure that he would quickly crack and confess under that much pressure." Muramatsu sighed wearily. "But no one imagined it would end the way it did."

"I heard that he hanged himself."

"That's right. He took off his clothes, rolled them into a long rope, slipped them around the window bars, and hanged himself." Muramatsu picked up his teacup. He had already drunk it all. He looked in the cup and put it back down on the table. "Anyway, that's everything I can tell you about the case. There's no doubt that there were failings in the supervision of the cells. I don't think there was anything wrong with the investigation itself, though."

Godai nodded. Based on what he had heard, he was inclined to agree with Muramatsu.

Muramatsu called to his wife, who was sitting in one corner of the room, and asked her to make a fresh pot of tea. He then turned to Godai. "Is there anything else you want to ask me?"

Godai drew himself upright in his chair. "Was there a man by the name of Kuraki who had any sort of connection to the case? The full name is Tatsuro Kuraki."

"Kuraki?" Muramatsu repeated. He thought for a moment. "I can't be sure. I mean, this incident happened over thirty years ago. All I can say for certain is this: There was no Kuraki among the key figures in this case."

Muramatsu fished another file out of his paper bag. Something that was lodged inside it fell onto the floor. It was a small black leather notebook. Muramatsu put the notebook back in the bag, then handed the file to Godai.

"This is a full list of the people that Haitani introduced to his fraudster pals. Some of them were tricked into buying fake antique vases, and others were lured into pyramid schemes. It's like a department store of fraud."

Godai took the file and passed it across to Nakamachi. "Take a look. See if you can find Kuraki's name in there."

"Yes, sir."

Godai watched as Nakamachi flipped open the file, then returned his gaze to the paper bag. "The notebook that fell out just now—was that the one you used at the crime scene?"

"You mean this one?" Muramatsu pulled the notebook out again. "Yes, it's the one I had at the scene."

"Mind if I have a look?"

"Be my guest. In those days, I bought notebooks like this in bulk. Used a new one for each new case."

"Sounds very practical."

Godai opened the old notebook. "May 15. Arrive on crime scene at 7:55. Green Enterprises on 2nd floor of Yahagi Bldg. Vic. is a Shozo Haitani," it said on the first page. The writing was just about legible. Looking at it, you could sense the nervous excitement of a young detective who'd had been dragged away from his dinner.

The next page started with a note about "Masahiko Sakano, vic.'s nephew, answers the phone." From there on, the writing got even messier and harder to read.

"What's this page about?"

"Where? Sorry for the god-awful handwriting. Where? Show me."

As Godai passed the notebook over to Muramatsu, Nakamachi handed the file back to him. "There's no Kuraki on this list."

"No?"

Hardly a surprise, Godai thought. Kuraki had been around thirty at the time. That made him an unlikely target.

"This is from my interview with Haitani's nephew," Muramatsu said. "I mentioned him a couple of minutes ago. Haitani had hired his sister's son to man the office phone. This is the guy—Masahiko Sakano. He was there when we got to the crime scene. We got much of what we needed to know from him right then and there. Look, see? He was standing in the street outside after calling the emergency services from a pay phone."

"What?" Godai looked hard at Muramatsu. "Didn't you just tell us that the person who called it in was standing beside the body and hadn't left the room?"

"Yes, I did say that. That's certainly how I remember it. Weird." Muramatsu began leafing through the old notebook. "Oh, okay. I've got it now," he eventually announced in a loud voice. "I remember now. Sorry. I muddled things up. There were two people."

"Two people?"

"Two people found the body. One was the nephew, who called it in; the other was the guy who was in the office. Let's have a look. Here we go. The nephew described him as a driver."

"A driver? What, a taxi driver?"

"No, not a taxi driver. Yes, here it is in black and white." Muramatsu drew the book away from his face. Even with his reading glasses on, he was finding his writing difficult to decipher. "'Man who caused road accident driving him to and from the office.' Oh yeah, it's starting to come back to me."

"Go on."

"My memory's pretty vague on this. It wasn't anything important. Haitani had suffered some minor injuries in a traffic accident, and the other party in the accident, the person responsible for it, was acting as Haitani's driver until he recovered. Haitani's nephew went up to the office together with that second man, and they both discovered the body. We didn't turn up anything problematic on that second man, so we eliminated him from our list of suspects very early on." Muramatsu noisily flicked through his notebook as he said this. Suddenly, he gasped, and his hand stopped moving.

"What's wrong?"

His eyes bulging behind his glasses, Muramatsu held the notebook out to Godai with one hand, while pointing at the page with the other.

Godai half rose to his feet and peered at the page.

It was a barely legible welter of scrawled words and phrases. One word, in larger letters than everything else, stood out.

It was the name *Kuraki*.

9

AFTER THEY LEFT Muramatsu's house, Katase drove them back to the station. This time, Godai sat in the back and called the incident room.

"Oh, I was just about to call you," said Sakuragawa as he picked up. "Let's hear what you found first. Did you get something good?"

Godai told Sakuragawa what he had learned from Muramatsu.

"That's a bit of a bombshell. Turns out, Kuraki does have a connection to that old case after all."

"It wasn't just that his name was there in Muramatsu's notes. Afterward, when we combed through all the files Muramatsu had on the case, we found a copy of the signed consent-to-fingerprint form. The name Tatsuro Kuraki's there, written in his own hand."

"So now we have a link connecting him and the Asunaro restaurant. This is how puzzles get solved. It's about patiently putting the pieces together one by one."

"Did you turn up something at your end as well?"

"More than a mere something. The team that was reviewing the security footage hit the jackpot. We have Mr. Shiraishi going into a café near Tokyo Station on October 6. Then, two minutes after Mr. Shiraishi goes in, there's footage from the same camera near the café door showing someone else going in. I probably don't need to tell you who it is."

"Kuraki?"

"Who else? I need you two to get over to Kuraki's place and interview the guy. I'll send Assistant Inspector Tsutsui and his team as backup. I'm also going to call the local precinct. We'll see how things go. Maybe we can get Kuraki to come to the local police station."

"Wouldn't it make sense to check on Kuraki's whereabouts before we descend on his house?"

"No need. If he finds out that detectives from Tokyo are trekking out to see him for a second time, he'll realize that things are getting serious. And if he is involved in Shiraishi's murder, then he's a real flight risk. So you should head there now. Better safe than sorry."

"You're right, sir. We'll head there directly without giving him a heads-up."

Godai ended the call and relayed what Sakuragawa had said to Nakamachi.

"Seems like things are finally getting moving." Nakamachi's eyes were glimmering.

"He must be sending the backup team to surveil Kuraki's house in case he runs. Sounds like Sakuragawa thinks he's the perp."

"I'm jealous," said Katase from the driver's seat. "This is exciting. I wish you the best of luck."

"Appreciate it," said Godai.

"THERE'S ONE THING I can't figure out. What's the connection between this murder from thirty-plus years ago and the one we're currently investigating?" Nakamachi asked.

Godai was sitting in an unreserved seat, his arms crossed on his chest as the bullet train raced toward Tokyo.

"And I'll tell you something else that bothers me. Yes, Kuraki was involved in the old case, but as far as the investigating team was concerned, he was not a person of interest. Put in movie terms, he was nothing more than an extra. But if that was the level of his involvement, then why is he still dwelling on it?"

"Search me. I've no idea." Godai shrugged.

When they reached Mikawa-Anjo Station, they headed straight for the taxi line. Godai instructed their driver to take them to Sasame.

In front of Kuraki's house, Godai took a deep breath, walked up to the front gate, and pressed the intercom button. He waited a moment or two. There was no response. He exchanged a look with Nakamachi.

"Has something come up?" came a voice from behind them.

They swung around. It was Kuraki. He held a paper bag.

"There's something rather urgent we need to speak with you about," Godai said.

"Really? Well, in that case, come on in. I'm afraid I can't offer you anything." Taking the key out of his pocket, Kuraki walked past them.

They went into the house. Kuraki ushered them into the same room as on Godai's previous visit. "Just give me a moment, please," he said. He pulled a bunch of flowers out of the paper bag, arranged them in front of the household altar, and pressed his palms together in prayer. Seen from behind, he appeared shrunken.

"Sorry about that," Kuraki said, sitting down across from the two detectives.

"Do you replace flowers on the altar regularly?" Godai asked.

"Only when the mood takes me. Today, for some reason, I felt like doing it." Kuraki smiled wanly. He seemed physically feebler than at their last meeting. "So, what is it that you want to ask me about?"

"It's about the last time you visited Tokyo. You traveled up to Tokyo on October 5 and returned home the following day. What was the purpose of your visit?"

"I told you last time you were here. I wanted to see my son."

"Your son and no one else?"

"What are you getting at?"

"We know you went into a café near Tokyo Station in the afternoon of October 6."

The skin of Kuraki's face tautened visibly. He was struggling for words.

"You look a bit shocked. You must be wondering how on earth we found that out." Godai went on, scanning the other man's face. "Here's the short version: Tokyo is awash in security cameras. In fact, though, there are surveillance cameras installed pretty much everywhere. Once upon a time, pay phones were a handy tool for con men. Now, if we discover that a person has made use of a pay phone, we can sift through all the footage from the vicinity of all the pay phones in Tokyo. Because in almost one hundred percent of cases, there's a security camera installed nearby that enables us to capture an image of anyone making a call. You were caught in the meshes of the surveillance state. And I should mention that we also have clear footage of the person you met in that café. You know who I mean: Kensuke Shiraishi, the lawyer."

Kuraki said nothing. He was staring at some vague point in the middle distance. When Godai looked more closely at Kuraki, he could see that he was not in a state of shock. If anything, his eyes suggested that some sort of internal struggle was underway.

"Last time I was here, you told me that you had spoken to Kensuke Shiraishi on the phone but that you had never met him in person. You told me that you called him because his office provided free legal consultations. The truth is that a few days subsequent to that call, you traveled up to Tokyo and met Mr. Shiraishi face-to-face. What's going on? I'd appreciate an explanation."

Kuraki said nothing. He just sat there, motionless and frozen.

Godai shifted so that he could make eye contact with Kuraki. "We also went to speak to Yoko and Orie Asaba."

Kuraki's eyelids twitched slightly.

"Yoko Asaba told us that she gave you that votive slip from Tomioka Hachimangu Shrine. Why did you pretend to have forgotten? It's not the sort of thing anyone forgets."

Kuraki shut his eyes. Godai could not catch his eye even if he wanted to.

"Why do you go to Asunaro? Why did you keep your visits there secret from even your son? And you weren't up-front with the Asabas either. You never told the two women that you were one of the men who discovered the body of the man who scammed their loved one. Why not?"

Kuraki reopened his eyes and slowly got to his feet. He walked over to the family altar and once again put his hands together in prayer.

"Mr. Kuraki . . ."

"I've had enough."

"Sorry?"

Kuraki turned around and faced the detectives. His expression was serene and quite different from before.

"I did it all. I'm guilty on all counts."

"All counts . . . ? Are you telling us that—?"

"That's right." Kuraki nodded. "I killed Shiraishi. And I also stabbed Shozo Haitani to death."

10

THIRTY YEARS AGO

I WAS WORKING FOR a components manufacturer in Aichi Prefecture. Before I bought my house, I used to commute by car from an apartment near the train station.

One day, on my way to work, I had a collision with a bicycle. The person on the bicycle was injured. Shozo Haitani.

I say he "was injured," but it was just a few bumps and bruises. Haitani was cunning, a nasty piece of work. I was very contrite and apologetic, and he tried to take advantage of that and made all sorts of extortionate demands. My covering his medical costs was fair enough in principle, but the sums he demanded were completely outrageous. To make things worse, he insisted that I drive him to and from his office. This went on for a few weeks.

Then Haitani wanted me to pay for the repairs to his damaged bicycle. Once again, the sum he was demanding was completely unrealistic. He claimed that instead of repairing the old one, it made more sense for him to buy a new bike. That's when I lost it. "There's no way I can pay for that," I came out and said. At that point, Haitani threatened to inform my company about the accident.

You see, I hadn't told my employer about the collision. The firm I worked for was a subsidiary of one of Japan's giant automakers. They were acutely sensitive about traffic accidents. Even a minor accident would have a negative impact on your job assessments throughout your career, all the way up to retirement.

I couldn't bear the thought of having this man on my back for the rest of my life. I grabbed this knife from the kitchen area of his office. I wasn't intending to kill; I just meant to threaten him. Haitani couldn't have cared less. He taunted me. "Go ahead. Stab me if you've got the balls for it." I went berserk. Next thing I knew, Haitani was on the ground. The knife in my hand was all covered in blood. Haitani was dead.

I knew I had done a terrible thing. The best thing I could do was get out of there as fast as possible, so I wiped down the knife and left. I had just gotten into my car when I saw Haitani's nephew on his way back into the office. I acted like I had just arrived, got out of the car, and, together with the nephew, went back up to the office. That's how the two of us discovered the body.

Naturally enough, the police interviewed me. They didn't have enough evidence to treat me as a suspect. I was never detained, and they never interviewed me a second time.

And something I had not been expecting happened: Someone else was arrested for the crime. It was a man by the name of Junji Fukuma. Fukuma and Haitani were at loggerheads over a money issue.

If I'm completely honest with you, I was like, "Thank God. I'm safe." I was praying that the whole thing could be neatly tied up. As you would expect, Fukuma denied having committed the crime. The police didn't want to listen to him.

I suppose my prayers were answered. As you know, Fukuma took his own life, and the police promptly stopped asking questions.

From that day forward, I have borne a heavy cross. In some corner of my mind, I've always blamed myself for costing a man his life—well, not a corner; it's front and center. I have an overpowering sense of guilt. But I never got up the courage to turn myself in. Not only was I frightened of going to jail, but my wife and I had a newborn son. Whenever I thought about him, I knew I couldn't turn myself in. I couldn't let my wife and son be known as the family of a criminal.

Several years later, I realized how wrong I'd been. Japan was in the throes of an economic boom. Everyone was making money hand over fist in real estate or the stock market.

I went to Toyokawa City for work. I had gone into some random local hole-in-the-wall restaurant with a colleague. We were busy discussing our investments when the woman who ran the place piped up. She mentioned one of the electrical appliance stores in the neighborhood. Several years earlier, the store owner had fallen victim to an investment scam and lost everything he had. He'd gone to complain to the financial adviser who had him invest and ended up stabbing him to death in a fit of rage. Then the store owner had gone and hanged himself while in detention.

I asked the restaurant owner what the name of the store was. I was filled with this . . . dread. I shuddered when she said it was called Fukuma Electronics. It was *that* Fukuma.

According to the restaurant owner, his widow had left town, taking her young daughter with her. Running the store alone was hard enough, but what really did it was being ostracized from the community. They'd been subjected to every kind of vile harassment that the family of a murderer might receive.

My head was spinning. I had protected my family. The price for that was plunging another family into misery. What I did was unforgivable.

Nonetheless, I still couldn't confess. Protecting my family and myself still came first. I managed to convince myself that coming out and telling the truth would make no difference at this stage.

In May 1999, the statute of limitations on the case ran out. That didn't make me the slightest bit happy. If anything, the guilt deepened. That was when my wife got sick. Leukemia. I saw her death a few years later as a divine punishment. Rather than punishing me, God had taken my wife's life.

I decided to hire a private investigator. The first thing I wanted to find out was what Fukuma's surviving family members were doing. I found a detective agency in the phone book. Some honest, hardworking outfit.

Despite getting me an answer within a week of my initial request, they didn't overcharge.

According to the report, Fukuma's wife and daughter had started using the wife's maiden name, Asaba. The wife had opened a little restaurant in Tokyo, where the daughter, who'd graduated from high school, was helping out. Photographs the detective took showed the two of them leaving their home. Although their ages were wide apart, the similarities in their appearance and manner made them look more like sisters than anything else.

I felt relieved. It *was* a relief. I'd been afraid that they were living on the streets somewhere. Of course, they must have gone through a lot to build the kind of life they now had.

Should I go and check up on them myself? No, what would be the point this late in the game? If I went and confessed or made an apology, they'd probably think I was only doing so because the statute of limitations had safely expired. It would be traumatic for them, and they would probably tear into me for being smug and self-serving—

After a great deal of agonizing, I once again decided to do nothing.

Another ten or so years passed. I retired. I had this idea of taking advantage of my retirement by doing something new and different. The first thing that came to mind was the Fukuma family—I mean, the Asaba family. I wanted to see with my own eyes how they were getting on.

By now, our son was working in Tokyo. Using him as a pretext, I went to visit and did what I called some "sightseeing" by myself.

My biggest worry was that the restaurant had shut down. However, Asunaro was still up and running. After reminding myself not to get flustered or say anything stupid, I went on in.

The two women were in the restaurant. Although they were that much older, they were the same mother and daughter from the detective agency's photos. No doubt about that. I struggled to control my emotions. There was joy at finally being able to meet these people I thought about for such a long time; there was crushing, intense guilt; and finally, there was gratitude that the two of them had managed to survive what I put them through.

Naturally enough, neither Yoko nor Orie had any idea who I was. They were very welcoming to me. Everything they put in front of me was delicious; I could see why they had been in business for over ten years. In fact, the first day I was there, they were very busy.

On my way out, Orie came to the door to see me off. When she said she hoped I'd be back, I promised to return soon. I know it was reckless, but I had just felt so happy there.

Less than two months later, I went back to Asunaro. The ladies remembered me and gave me a warm reception. The pangs of conscience didn't disappear entirely, but the truth is I felt relieved, even content.

I ended up going over and over again until I became one of the restaurant's regulars. That description may come across as a little arrogant given that I only went once every two or three months, but I think the Asabas singled me out for special treatment because I came from so far away.

If only I had left things there.

The two women seemed to have achieved a level of contentment. I told myself I should just keep an eye on them. But the better I got to know them, the more I started wondering if there was something I could do to make amends.

That was when I bumped into Mr. Kensuke Shiraishi.

It must have been the end of March this year. I was at the Tokyo Dome. My son got me a ticket for a Giants-Dragons game. It was a fabulous seat, in the infield stand.

The game was still in its early stages when a silly accident took place. The man next to me dropped the thousand-yen note with which he was trying to pay one of the roving beer vendors. By a stroke of bad luck, the thing fell into the cup of beer I'd just bought for myself. The man was very apologetic and bought me a replacement.

That was how we got talking. He was alone too.

There's nothing better than talking about baseball while watching baseball. And what do you know, I discovered that he too was a Dragons fan. I just assumed he must be an Aichi man, but no, he turned out to be a Tokyoite, born and bred. He was one of those so-called anti-Giants—you know, people who became Dragons fans when the Dragons stopped the Giants winning the league championship for a tenth time in a row back in 1974.

The game ended just before 9:00 PM. That was good for me. My last train left at 10:00 PM.

But I had a problem. I had just left my seat when I realized my wallet had disappeared. It had been in my trouser pocket! I couldn't believe it! Then I remembered that I had been to the bathroom once.

I rushed to check the bathroom. Mr. Shiraishi came with me. We didn't find my wallet there. Next, we went to the service center. No one had handed it in there either. I was desperate. The departure time of my train was getting closer all the time, and I couldn't buy a ticket. To make matters worse, my son was out of town on a business trip.

It was then that Mr. Shiraishi took twenty thousand yen out of his wallet. He was like, "Here, take this." That took me by surprise. We had only just met, and we hadn't introduced ourselves properly. All we'd done was chat about baseball.

Mr. Shiraishi handed me one of his business cards and told me to simply mail the money. I first discovered that he was a lawyer when I read it on his card.

There was no way I was going to say no. I hastily took the money, thanked him, and left. In the taxi for Tokyo Station, I remember thinking that the world is a place full of kind and good people.

I forgot all about Mr. Shiraishi until September. I was watching a program about Respect for the Aged Day on TV. It was a special feature on inheritance and wills. I had an idea while I was watching the show. Here was the perfect way for me to make amends to the Asabas: On my death, I could pass all my assets on to them.

I didn't know if this was legally feasible, and I had absolutely no idea how to go about it.

That was when Mr. Shiraishi popped back into my head. I decided to get his advice. I called him, told him I had something I wanted to discuss with him, and requested a meeting. He agreed instantly.

As you already know from your investigation, I met with Mr. Shiraishi on the sixth of October. It was he who chose the café near Tokyo Station as the venue. I thanked him again for helping me with my wallet, said it was lovely to see him again, then broached the subject.

Could I bequeath my assets to strangers, not blood relations? The answer, according to Mr. Shiraishi, was yes. It was perfectly doable provided you left a legally valid will. Whether I could leave them all my assets was dependent on the posture of my legal heir or heirs. My sole legal heir is my son, Kazuma. Even if I made a will in which I bequeathed *all* my assets to people outside the family, he still had the right to inherit a maximum of half. In other words, I could leave all, or almost all, my assets to the Asabas as long as I was able to get my son to agree.

With that issue out of the way, Mr. Shiraishi asked me if the person or persons I planned to leave my property to were aware of my intentions and had given their consent. When I told him they knew nothing about it, he suggested that I should add a clause to the will explaining my motivation. The more convincing my reasons, the more likely my son would relinquish his rights to his share.

Despite our having only met once before, Mr. Shiraishi was very kind to me. He couldn't help but be curious about why I wanted to leave my money to complete strangers, but he didn't press the issue. Perversely, this only made me want to tell him everything. I also thought that being frank might make it easier for him to draw up the will. More than anything, though, I just wanted someone to confide in. I felt sure that Mr. Shiraishi was a man I could trust.

"There's something I need to get off my chest," was my lead-in. Then I filled him in on the whole story right up to the present day. Mr. Shiraishi was shocked. As I spoke, his expression became graver and graver.

Once my explanation was over and done with, Mr. Shiraishi said that he understood the situation and my desire to bequeath my assets to the two women and that he would be happy to help me.

One thing Mr. Shiraishi did not condone was my basic approach. If I was serious about wanting to apologize and make amends, then surely I should do so while I was still alive rather than after my death?

That wasn't something I'd been expecting him to say. While I knew in my bones that Mr. Shiraishi's suggestion was just and right, the reason

I was planning to hand over my property to the two women was precisely because I felt unable to tell them directly. Mr. Shiraishi, however, was unwilling to accept that. "That's not an apology or amends; that's just you running away from your responsibilities," he said. He'd been getting more and more agitated over the course of our conversation. He became harsh.

I realized that seeking Mr. Shiraishi's advice and sharing my secret had been a huge mistake. I asked him to forget about the whole thing and pretend the meeting had never happened. Then I left.

When I got back home to Anjo, my nerves were still on edge. I couldn't shake the feeling that Mr. Shiraishi might take matters into his own hands. I had even told him about Asunaro.

Soon after, I got a long letter from Mr. Shiraishi. He made the case that I needed to find some way of apologizing to the Asabas directly. He added that he would help me and was happy to sit in on any meetings I had with them.

It was a passionate piece of writing, brimming with a mission and sense of justice. But Shiraishi's passion only inspired terror in me. I started worrying that, left to his own devices, he might divulge everything to the Asabas. The fear only grew with every passing day.

When I didn't reply to Mr. Shiraishi's first letter, a second one arrived a few days later. It said all the same things as the first one, but more of it was devoted to attacking me. The statute of limitations may have run out, he wrote, but that didn't wipe away my sin. A lawyer is meant to protect the rights of suspects, but he would never assist in the active concealment of a crime. If anything, he felt compelled to bring the crime to light. What choice did he have?

I panicked. I saw the second letter as an ultimatum. If I wasn't going to tell the truth to the Asabas, then Mr. Shiraishi would.

I had to stop him no matter what. The time I spent with the Asabas, mother and daughter, gave meaning to my life. I was ready to acknowledge that only telling them the truth after my death was equivalent to "running away," as Mr. Shiraishi said. At the same time, I couldn't bear to lose the relationship that had become important in my life.

On October 31, I finally decided. I caught the train for Tokyo. While on the train, I went over what I was going to do from every possible angle to make sure my plan was flawless. Yes, that's right. At that point, I had already made up my mind that Shiraishi had to die. I had a knife concealed inside my jacket.

I reached Tokyo Station around 5:00 PM. I called Mr. Shiraishi's cell and asked if it would be possible for us to meet. He said he could meet any time after 6:30. We agreed to meet at 6:40 at the parking lot next to Tomioka Hachimangu Shrine. I told him to wait for me there.

In the time remaining, I went and walked around the area. I needed to find somewhere with no people. Since it was around six, the whole area was quite lively. I walked to the Sumida River. The minute I passed beneath the elevated expressway that runs parallel to the river, the number of people dropped off dramatically.

That was how I came across the construction site on the riverbank. The area where the construction workers parked their vehicles was empty. And even better, the section of the Sumida River Terrace promenade below the Kiyosu Bridge was closed. There was absolutely nobody there.

This is the perfect place, I decided.

I called Mr. Shiraishi just after 6:40. He was already in the parking lot. I told him I had been walking around and ended up getting a bit lost. I was near the Kiyosu Bridge. Could he come and meet me?

Mr. Shiraishi showed up in his car a few minutes later. He must have noticed me standing near the construction site, as he parked the car nearby and got out.

I told him that I had something I wanted to discuss and headed down the stairs to the Sumida River Terrace. Although Mr. Shiraishi followed, he was clearly getting uncomfortable. "What are we doing in a place like this? Weren't we supposed to be going to the Asabas' restaurant?" he complained. His nasty, aggressive tone was what prompted me to act.

I looked around. There was no one else about. Seeing my opportunity, I stabbed Mr. Shiraishi in the stomach with the knife I'd brought with me.

Although Mr. Shiraishi fought some, he soon stopped. I wasn't sure what to do with his body and ended up taking it to his car. I guessed it would be better for me if he was discovered somewhere else.

After placing the body in the back seat of the car, I climbed into the driver's seat and drove away. However, I was unfamiliar with the area and had no idea where to abandon the vehicle. I'd only been on the move for a couple of minutes before I parked on the side of the road, took the lawyer's phone off him, and fled.

Everything had worked out well. Now I would be able to keep seeing the Asabas, the same as before. Along with this thought, a crushing sense of gloom overcame me.

I've killed another man. And worse, this time, he was completely blameless.

My life is one long story of regret and remorse. I am still the same person I was thirty-three years ago. I disgust myself.

What I did to Mr. Shiraishi and to the Asabas is truly unforgivable. Now, I must make my apologies to Mr. Haitani and Mr. Fukuma in the next life.

I deserve the death penalty.

11

FOAM SPILLED ONTO the table when they clinked glasses. They gulped down their beer, which tasted extraordinarily good.

"There's nothing like a pint after clearing up a case," Nakamachi said cheerfully.

"Especially a difficult one."

"Come on, Godai. You did a great job. You've definitely earned some big brownie points for your performance review."

"Please. I couldn't care less. Besides, I can't take all the credit. The guys from the other teams all did a great job too."

Godai cupped his chin in his hands and gazed over the countertop. A man in an old-fashioned white smock was busy grilling vegetables, chicken, and seafood. They were back in the robata-yaki restaurant. Last time, they'd sat at a table; this time, they were sitting side by side at the counter.

Two days had elapsed since Tatsuro Kuraki gave a full confession. They were now gathering corroborating evidence for everything he'd told them. So far, everything matched.

Godai had found Kuraki's confession almost too much.

The facts of the case were a complete surprise. Junji Fukuma, the man who had taken his own life, was innocent. His wife, Yoko Asaba, and his daughter, Orie, had been discriminated against, had their names dragged through the mud, and their lives permanently knocked off course.

At the same time, Godai could understand Kuraki's psychology. When he heard Muramatsu's account, Godai had felt nothing but loathing for that Haitani fellow. Kuraki must have felt profoundly humiliated. Impulsively stabbing Haitani seemed understandable enough. His subsequent behavior was the problem. Even the most moral person would debate before turning themselves in to the police. That's just normal. With the benefit of more time, Kuraki might well have changed his mind. But the fact that someone else was arrested in his place had a huge impact. Humans are basically weak creatures. His thinking, *If I can get away with it, then why not give it a go*, was only human.

And after that, unable to forget the mistake he'd made, he'd gotten to know the Asabas, mother and daughter, and his desire to atone had only grown stronger. All that spoke to the man's sincerity.

His interactions with Kensuke Shiraishi had been a terrible case of two people acting at cross-purposes. As Kuraki himself admitted, he'd behaved in a selfish and irresponsible way, but the case could be made that Kensuke Shiraishi's response had also been problematic.

"Wonder what those two will make of this?" Nakamachi said somberly. "The Asaba mother and daughter. You've not yet told them the truth, have you?"

"The brass told me to keep my mouth shut for the time being."

"But we're going to have to tell them at some point."

"Yeah, at some point." Godai felt a lump in his throat. Likely as not, that unpleasant task would land in his lap.

"How will they feel when they discover that one of their regulars, someone they'd been especially nice to, is the actual killer who let their husband and father take the fall for his crime?"

Godai did not answer Nakamachi. He just finished his beer.

"Either way, things worked out fine." Nakamachi sounded more cheerful now. "At one point, we had zero leads and we all thought the investigation had run aground. The head of Homicide even said that the Sumida

River Terrace case looked like it would never get solved. Instead, we managed to find the real culprit in a decades-old case on top of everything else. It's an impressive feat."

Godai was about to pop a roasted gingko nut into his mouth. His hand stopped in midair.

Kuraki's statement had cleared up plenty of questions about the old case. But there was one big question which remained unanswered.

Why hadn't Kuraki been arrested three decades ago? Why had he been eliminated from the list of suspects? Normally, the person who discovers the body is the prime suspect. All Kuraki had been able to tell them was that he had no idea why it had happened that way.

Had they really cleared everything up nice and neatly? Or was there another labyrinth to navigate in this case? Godai did his best to bat the thought away.

12

Looking down from his sixth-floor apartment, he thought of how Tokyo was quite different from his hometown. A mass of buildings of all shapes and sizes crisscrossed by a convoluted pattern of narrow streets. The town where Kazuma had been born and raised had only sprawling, low-rise buildings with plenty of space between them. He hadn't been back recently, but things probably hadn't changed much. The place had its own reality, so it didn't need to change.

He took a few deep breaths. Despite the urban setting, the wintry air was cool and refreshing. He slid the glass door shut behind him, pulled the lace curtain across, and turned around. The stocky, middle-aged man in the dining chair was still sitting in the same position as a few minutes earlier.

"Sorry about that," Kazuma said as he sat down on the opposite side of the table.

"Feeling a bit more composed?" the man asked.

"I dunno," Kazuma said. "How can I put it? My mind's not functioning quite right."

The man nodded several times. "That's understandable enough."

Kazuma lowered his gaze and studied the man's business card. *Takahiro Horibe, Lawyer*, it said.

Kazuma had been in the office a little before lunch when he had gotten a call. He was surprised enough that the caller was a lawyer but stunned by what came next: His father, Tatsuro, had been arrested. For murder.

He remembered something. That detective from the Homicide Bureau who had come to see him a couple of weeks ago. Godai. He'd barraged him with a boatload of questions about when exactly his father had come up to Tokyo and what he did with himself on his visits. The detective had said it was related to a murder investigation but hadn't gone into any detail.

Kazuma had called his father that night to find out what was going on. Tatsuro's response was short and to the point.

"It's nothing to do with me. No need to worry."

His father's expressionless tone gave Kazuma a bad feeling. Nonetheless, he didn't press. The detective had simply said that they were looking into Tatsuro because they had found a record of an incoming call from him on the victim's phone. Kazuma did his best to convince himself that the police were just being overzealous. His father would never be involved in a murder!

The lawyer—Horibe—had said he needed to have an in-depth talk with Kazuma. Could they meet somewhere away from prying eyes? Keen to find out what was going on, Kazuma suggested they meet at his condo, then canceled all his afternoon appointments and left the office, citing "family issues."

On his way back to his condo, Kazuma started trawling through online news sites. Inputting the name *Tatsuro Kuraki* quickly yielded results. According to an article he found, his father had been arrested three days earlier. He was suspected of murdering a lawyer named Shiraishi. The authorities would soon be revealing further details about his motives.

The whole world seemed to go dark, and he almost dropped his cell phone. *This has to be a nightmare. A lawyer called Shiraishi? Who the hell is that?* Kazuma had never even heard of the man.

For the last couple of days, Kazuma had been so busy that he hadn't bothered to read the news. He did have a TV, but most days, he never got around to switching the thing on. Regardless, weren't the police supposed to inform the family of people they arrested?

Horibe had arrived at Kazuma's condominium and explained that he was a court-appointed lawyer. In murder cases, a court-appointed lawyer was automatically assigned to any suspect who wanted one.

Horibe had with met Tatsuro for the first time that morning. Tatsuro—who struck him as almost preternaturally calm and appeared to be in good health—had promptly started talking about his crime in a matter-of-fact way. His account had been so coherent and free from contradictions that Horibe had been able to get it transcribed and was planning to use it as Tatsuro's official written statement.

Horibe talked Kazuma through his father's statement. Kazuma was startled enough to find that it went back more than thirty years, but surprise turned to shock when he learned what had happened all those years ago. *Tatsuro had knifed someone!*

Statute of limitations up. Yoko and Orie. His father wanting to make amends. His father confessing to Shiraishi, his father murdering again...

Horibe was only halfway through his account, and Kazuma was already quite bewildered. He simply couldn't believe that the lawyer was talking about his father. He repeatedly interrupted with, "Did my father really say that?" Horibe's response was the same every time: "I am simply repeating the statement that Tatsuro Kuraki gave to me."

The statement read in its entirety, Kazuma was dumbfounded. Dazed and incapable of coherent thought, he felt feverish. Next thing he knew, he had sprung to his feet, slid open the glass door, and was feeling the wind on his skin.

Kazuma raised his eyes from Horibe's card and looked at the man himself.

"So what is the situation with my father right now?"

Horibe nodded and adjusted his gilt-framed spectacles. "The case has already been referred to the public prosecutor, and the prosecutor has started looking into it. They are still reviewing and verifying the facts, and there are a great many things they need to confirm with Tatsuro himself, so he will be kept in custody at the police station for the foreseeable future.

Since your father has admitted to the crime and made a full voluntary statement, I don't think his detention will be extended. As soon as he is charged, he will be transferred to the Tokyo Detention Center."

The lawyer's words seemed to flow individually through Kazuma's mind unconnected from each other or reality.

He sighed heavily. "All right, so what do I need to do?"

"As a lawyer, I always urge the family members to cooperate fully to help reduce the penalty. I intend to plead extenuating circumstances."

"Okay, but what should I do specifically?"

"There's something else." Horibe extracted an envelope from his briefcase and placed it on the table. "Tatsuro gave me this."

The words *To Kazuma* were written on the envelope.

"May I read it?"

"Of course," Horibe said.

Kazuma picked up the envelope. It was unsealed. Of course. The police must have read it.

Kazuma unfolded the paper and pressed the sheets flat. There were neat rows of tidy script.

I can picture the look of annoyance on your face as you get ready to read this. Maybe you're so furious with me that you just want to rip the thing up and throw it away. Honestly, I don't mind if you do. I know I have no right to object. I just hope you will read the letter through to the end before you destroy it.

What I did to Mr. Shiraishi was inexcusable. I am acutely aware that an apology won't make things any better; even so, all I can do is apologize to you from the bottom of my heart. The thought of all the trouble I've already caused you and am going to cause you in the future fills me with sorrow.

I imagine that my lawyer has filled you in. Everything has its roots in a mistake I made a long, long time ago. Regrets are futile at this stage, but I still regret what I did. I was a fool.

I will be atoning for my crimes for the rest of my life. I may not have that long to live, but I want to be properly repentant in the time I have left.

There are three things I want to say to you, Kazuma. The first is this: I understand if you choose to disavow me as your father. No, let me rephrase that. I want you to do so. I want you to embark on a new life, one where you forget that Tatsuro Kuraki was ever your father. For my part, I have no intention of trying to keep in touch with you, so you don't need to write to me either. Nor do you need to come and visit me. If you do, I will just refuse to see you. Of course, you don't need to attend my trial. They may ask you to provide some sort of testimony. I want you to refuse.

The second thing I wanted to tell you was about your mother. Chisato had no idea that I had murdered Haitani. And she went to her grave in ignorance. Her integrity and honesty—including the love she felt for you, her only child—are unclouded and unsullied. Although I encourage you to expunge the fact of my being your father from your mind, please never forget that Chisato was your mother.

Last, I want you to deal with the Sasame house. Do whatever you want with it. The title deeds are in a drawer in the big chest. Sell the place off at a fire-sale price. Hire a company to dispose of the house's contents. There is nothing in there that I want to leave to you.

I am so sorry for what I did. My greatest concern is that a dark future awaits you, all because of your father's foolishness.

Please, take good care of your health, and I hope you somehow manage to salvage a good life for yourself.

After refolding the four sheets of paper, replacing them in the envelope, and putting the envelope back on the table, Kazuma sighed. His mind was a blank. A feeling of intense hopelessness was spreading through his chest.

"What do you make of that?" Horibe asked.

"I don't know what to say." Kazuma frowned and scratched his head. "My father wrote this letter himself. That means there's no question of any sort of mistake or wrongful charge. My strongest feeling is, why? For my father to do things like that, it just doesn't . . ."

"I know exactly what you mean. Tatsuro struck me as a very genuine and serious individual. He certainly doesn't look like a murderer. Both the police and the prosecutor's office tell me that he is responding to their inquiries in a sincere manner. One can only imagine that he committed this latest crime because he was at the end of his tether."

"Maybe, but . . ."

Kazuma's voice trailed off. He couldn't get a handle on his feelings. There was anger: Why did his father do anything so damn stupid? And there was doubt: Had there really been no other way to solve the problem? Ultimately, though, what he felt most strongly was incredulity.

"Mr. Horibe, um . . . My father, my dad . . ." He had to moisten his lips with his tongue before he could go on. "Will he get the death penalty? I remember hearing somewhere that people who've killed one person don't get the death penalty but that anyone who's killed two people or more does."

Horibe adjusted his glasses again. The lenses glinted as they caught the light.

"I plan to do my utmost to prevent that. While your father undeniably took two people's lives, the statute of limitations has run out on the first case. On top of that, his desire to make amends to the family of the man who died by suicide after being arrested shows that he has gone through considerable emotional pain and has demonstrated remorse. Whether I can get the jury to believe that he atoned—that will be the decisive factor."

"If that was the case, then surely the other side will argue that he should have manned up, come out, and apologized under his own name, just as the lawyer Mr. Shiraishi told him to."

Horibe grimaced and nodded. "You're right about that. At the same time, don't you think they will see something very human in his psychology? The way it became harder for him to reveal the truth because he got to know the family? Shiraishi's point of view was valid, but what I plan to stress is that he really drove Tatsuro into a corner. At the trial, it's not the facts of the case we'll be arguing. No, it's his state of mind."

"Will that determine whether he gets the death penalty or not?"

"A prison sentence is also a possibility," said Horibe soberly. "So my basic strategy will be to show that Tatsuro is deeply remorseful and is at heart not the kind of person who kills people. To do that, I will need the testimony of people close to him, that means his family."

"Yes, but . . ." Kazuma gestured at the envelope on the table. "It says in there that he wants me to disavow him and not to appear at his trial."

"Don't you think that that's proof positive of just how remorseful he is? He doesn't want to try for a reduced sentence. You remember what he said about not having that long left? I think that means that he is resigned to getting the death penalty. I plan to put this letter forward as evidence. Plus, I want you, his son, to plead extenuating circumstances. I need you to take really good care of that letter."

Kazuma heard what the lawyer was saying, but the words didn't quite register. It took him several seconds to realize that the "son" in question was himself.

"There are a few points I need to check with you." Horibe had his notebook and pen at the ready. "You had no knowledge whatsoever of the 1984 incident, did you?"

Kazuma shook his head. "I knew nothing about it. I mean, I wasn't even one year old at the time."

"It was in the autumn six years ago, after his retirement, that Tatsuro started visiting Tokyo on a regular basis. Is that right?"

"I believe so."

"Did he always stay here with you?"

"Yes, he did. He usually turned up around midnight."

"Did Tatsuro offer any explanation for why he was out so late?"

"He told me he'd found a bar that he really liked and that he'd been drinking there. He always smelled slightly of alcohol."

"Did he tell you anything more about the place?"

"Just that it was in Shinjuku. And even that was a lie," he murmured. "I didn't tell the detective that."

"What detective?"

"A detective came here a couple of weeks ago to ask me about my father. He also asked why Tatsuro always got back so late. I wasn't completely honest with him. I told him I didn't know."

"Why did you lie?"

"Why? Well, um . . ." Kazuma faltered briefly, sighed, and then went on. "It was kind of awkward. I thought I was not the only reason my father had for coming up to Tokyo."

"You suspected"—Horibe glanced up at him—"he had a woman."

"That's right," Kazuma said with a nod. "But I didn't blame him for it. It's been years since my mother died, and my dad's still in his sixties. Why shouldn't he have some fun?"

"But was he really having fun? Did he look happy when you saw him?"

"I'm not sure." Kazuma cocked his head quizzically. "He wasn't in a bad mood, nor was he dancing on the ceiling. My father's not a young man, and he's never been the frivolous type."

Given the crimes he had committed, perhaps he wasn't the most sensible of men either, Kazuma thought.

"You never spoke to Tatsuro about the bar or this woman, right?"

"No, I did not," Kazuma stated with conviction.

Horibe look down at his notebook. "Tatsuro committed his first murder on May 15, 1984. That date, the fifteenth of May, does it bring anything particular to mind?"

"Sorry?" Kazuma didn't understand the point of Horibe's question.

"Let me explain." Horibe leaned forward slightly. "Did Tatsuro pray at the household altar or go somewhere special on May 15 every year? The ideal scenario for us would be his going to visit someone's grave."

"Oh, I get it," Kazuma said. "You're asking if my father was somehow honoring the person he killed?"

"Precisely, precisely," Horibe said. "Refraining from alcohol, copying out a sutra—those would be good too. Does anything like that come to mind?"

"May 15," Kazuma said. He shook his head. "No, it's no use. Nothing comes to mind. I can't recall that being a special day for the family or for my dad."

"Keep thinking." Horibe frowned disapprovingly. "Even the most brutal people don't forget the dates they've killed someone. That's going to be all the more true for Tatsuro, because he is a fundamentally decent man. I doubt he forgave himself for what he'd done."

Kazuma's brow furrowed as he reached back into his memory. Everything Horibe said made sense, but still nothing came to mind. It was hopeless.

"Have you tried asking my father directly?"

"No, not yet. Evidence like this would be more persuasive coming from a third party. His claiming that he used to say a prayer for his victim and beg his forgiveness every year would just come across as hypocritical."

Sounds all too plausible when it's put like that, Kazuma thought. "I'm sorry, I really can't think of anything."

Horibe nodded, looking resigned. He glanced at his watch and shut his notebook. "There's nothing we can do, then. Still, I'd like you to think about what I said. Will you contact me if you think of anything?"

"I'll try. Don't get your hopes up, though."

"Just do your best. I'm sure something will come back to you. This will impact your future too. If you tell people that your father's serving time in prison, no one will know what he's done. If people find out he's an inmate on death row, there's only one crime he can be guilty of. It's a big difference. A devastating difference, in fact."

Kazuma started at the words *inmate on death row* and the fervor with which they were uttered. It was not a phrase he'd ever imagined would be part of his life. "What should I do now?"

"You should go about life normally. You don't want to do anything that will draw attention to you. It's the media you really need to look out for."

"The media?" Kazuma echoed. The thought had not occurred to him.

"A murderer who evaded justice once goes on to commit a second murder. It's the kind of story the media will jump all over. If they get wind of it, chances are someone will be banging on your door. Journalists are an obstinate and heartless breed. They'll provoke you: They'll stop at nothing to get a statement or some sort of rise out of you."

"Can't I just blow them off?"

"Being too offhanded is probably not a good idea. I can imagine them writing a headline like KILLER'S SON INSISTS THAT FATHER'S CRIME IS NOT HIS PROBLEM."

The lawyer's words made Kazuma dizzy. He dropped his head in his hands.

"It's fine for you to be honest with the media if they ask you how you're feeling right now. Just say you can't believe it, that it's been an awful shock. That's not a problem. What you absolutely must not talk about is the motivation behind the crime or any of the details. If they keep the pressure on you, just tell them that your lawyer gave you strict instructions not to discuss anything likely to come up at the trial. If they mention the victim and his family, bow your head and say that you would like to apologize sincerely on your father's behalf. That's how you can come safely out the other side."

Kazuma glanced up at the television on the wall. Picturing one of those tawdry, gossipy news shows on the screen, he saw himself bowing deeply, surrounded by a pack of journalists and commentators.

"Give me a call if you think anyone's violating your privacy. I'll file an official complaint."

While Horibe was being supportive, Kazuma also felt the lawyer was preparing him for the worst. There was no way of knowing what was going to happen next.

"Any further questions?"

Kazuma racked his brain. Nothing came to mind. The whole situation was changing so rapidly he could barely keep up. Catching sight of the letter on the table, something occurred to him.

"Is . . . uh . . . visiting allowed? I know my father says that he doesn't want me to come and see him."

"There aren't any restrictions on visiting. I thought you'd want to go and see him."

"I really want to hear what he has to say for himself."

"Of course. I'll let Tatsuro know. Is there anything else you'd like me to say to him?"

"No," Kazuma said, shaking his head. "Not right now, at least."

"How about I tell him to take good care of himself? When it comes from a family member, a simple message like that can do wonders for morale."

"Oh. . . . Uh, okay. Tell him that from me."

"Will do. I'll be in touch again soon." Horibe rose to his feet.

W HEN KAZUMA GOT back to his apartment after walking the lawyer out, he flung himself onto the sofa. He had no idea what to do with himself in the days ahead.

He reached for his phone, which was nearby. He might as well check his schedule for tomorrow. Just then, he remembered that he had given "family issues" as his excuse for leaving work early and had told his boss that he would fill him in tomorrow.

What in God's name am I supposed to tell him? He felt as though a high wall had suddenly materialized in front of his eyes.

At that moment, his phone started to ring. The screen showed an unregistered number.

He picked up. "Is that Kazuma Kuraki?" a man's voice asked.

"Yes, that's me."

"I'm calling from the Tokyo Metropolitan Police," said the voice at the other end.

13

GODAI AND NAKAMACHI arrived at an apartment building that was one in a line of identical buildings.

The elevator had seen better days. On the way to the fifth floor, Godai checked his watch: it was 2:50.

"We're a bit early. Let's wait here," Godai said to Nakamachi as they exited the elevator. Waiting in the hallway would arouse less suspicion among the neighbors than hanging around outside the apartment door.

As Godai gazed down at the residential streets from the hallway window, he tried to sort through his thoughts. If he was honest with himself, his view of the case was still murky. He had no idea how people were going to respond to his questions. Today's interview was the kind of job that depressed him most.

Although Kuraki's arrest had already made the news, the Tokyo Metropolitan Police had yet to make an official statement. Out of consideration for the local police, the policy of the upper ranks was to keep Kuraki's motive under wraps.

"I wonder how they're feeling," said Nakamachi. "They must be pretty antsy, wondering what we're going to ask."

"Listen, no one's going to be relaxed after hearing that a homicide detective wants to interview them. Even if they have nothing to hide, they might be aware that Kuraki's been arrested."

"You didn't mention it, right?"

"I didn't. But they could have seen it on the news. Or found out on the internet after my call."

Godai had contacted Orie, rather than her mother, who was contemptuous of the police.

Orie had sounded calm and collected on the phone. She didn't ask why he was calling, so Godai suspected she knew it was about Kuraki.

Nakamachi consulted his watch. "It's about time."

"Shall we?"

They set off down the long corridor. They came to a stop in front of apartment 506, double-checked the number, and pressed the button on the intercom. "Hello," came a woman's voice almost instantaneously. It sounded like Orie.

"This is Detective Godai. We spoke earlier."

The door clicked open. Orie Asaba stuck her face out. Her hair was pulled back with a hair band. She was lightly made-up and was wearing a gray sweater and jeans.

"Thanks for seeing us. We appreciate it," Godai said.

Orie nodded and gestured for the two men to come in. "This way."

"Thank you," Godai said and entered. The detectives removed their shoes and donned the slippers that were waiting for them just above the concrete step.

Orie took them to the end of a zigzagging corridor. They found themselves in a modest living room with a couch, a few chairs, and a table squeezed in. Yoko, who was sitting on one of the chairs, got to her feet when the detectives came in. She was wearing a purple cardigan and was nicely made-up.

"First off, I want to thank you for assisting us with our inquiries the other day," Godai said.

"No big deal," Yoko said, dropping back into her chair. Her face was blank, but her tone made it clear enough that she wasn't pleased to see them.

"Please, sit down," Orie said, indicating a two-person couch perpendicular to her mother's armchair.

The two detectives murmured their thanks and sat down. Godai casually ran his eye around the room. A framed photograph on a shelf caught his eye. Orie Asaba and a boy, probably twelve or thirteen years old, standing next to one another.

"Who's that in the picture?" Godai pointed at the photograph. "The son of a relative of yours?"

"It's my son," said Orie. She sounded defensive.

"Oh? I didn't realize."

"My ex-husband has custody."

Godai debated probing further, when Orie excused herself to the kitchen and began taking down cups and saucers, obviously planning to offer them tea.

"You really don't need to," Godai protested.

"I think we can offer a cup of green tea," said Yoko. "In return, I hope you'll keep this nice and short."

"I'll do my best. Today, we want to ask you about Mr. Kuraki."

Yoko took a deep breath. "We heard that Mr. Kuraki's been arrested."

"So you knew?"

"One of our regulars at the restaurant told us last night. Said he'd seen it on the news. The police bundling this guy who looked a lot like Mr. Kuraki into a police car and driving him away. *That can't be him*, he thought, when the news anchor said, 'The suspect in the case, a certain Tatsuro Kuraki.'"

"He's suspected of murder. Detective Nakamachi and I are handling the investigation."

"I know. I checked the news as soon as the customer told us. He's suspected of killing a lawyer, right?"

"That's right."

Yoko's lips curled with distaste. She gave a small shake of the head. "Nonsense."

"What is?"

"Mr. Kuraki killing somebody. It's got to be a mistake. I mean, why in

God's name would he do a thing like that?" Her lips were thrust out, and she spoke with vehemence.

"We are currently looking in detail at the facts of the case and his motive."

Godai wondered how Yoko would feel if she knew what had motivated Kuraki to commit the crime.

Orie came back carrying a tray with teacups on it. After wordlessly placing a cup in front of each of the detectives, she arranged a cushion for herself on the floor and sat down with her feet neatly tucked underneath her.

"You need to reinvestigate this whole thing properly," Yoko declared. "Mr. Kuraki would never do anything like that. It's a mistake. It has to be."

"I'm not so sure."

"I know it is. Stupid police are always happy to arrest people without a shred of evidence," Yoko muttered venomously. "Never stop to think that those people might hang themselves in their cells."

"Kuraki made a full voluntary confession," broke in Nakamachi, no longer able to restrain himself.

"Nakamachi!" Godai rebuked him.

"Sorry."

"Detective Godai." It was Orie's turn to speak. "What did Mr. Kuraki say in his confession?"

"I'm afraid I can't share that information with you," Godai replied. "We're currently gathering the necessary corroborating evidence."

Orie didn't seem particularly disappointed. "I see," she said in a muffled voice.

"I simply can't believe it," said Yoko, her eyes fixed on the floor.

"You told us that Mr. Kuraki, the suspect, used to come to your restaurant several times a year," Godai continued. "He would turn up about seven in the evening and stay till closing time. Is that correct?"

Godai looked at the two women in turn. They exchanged a look and then nodded in unison.

"Correct," Orie said.

"Have you ever met Mr. Kuraki outside the restaurant?"

"Outside the restaurant?" Orie once again glanced at her mother. "Have we?"

"Give me a moment." Yoko cocked her head to one side. "No, I don't think so."

"Did he ever invite you out?" Godai asked. Now he was looking at Orie.

Orie looked back at him, astonishment writ large on her face. "Invite me where?"

"You told us that Mr. Kuraki often stayed in your restaurant until closing time. He never invited you out for a drink somewhere else afterward? Or suggested going for a meal on the restaurant's day off?"

"Do you mean me?" Orie had her palms pressed to her chest and a puzzled look on her face.

"Either of you." Godai transferred his gaze from Orie to Yoko, then back again to Orie.

"No. Never."

"Why should he do anything like that?" Yoko broke in, speaking over her daughter. "Mr. Kuraki came to our place because he liked the food. Why should he want to go anywhere else?"

Godai scratched at his temple. It wasn't easy: How could he say what he wanted to say more tactfully?

"Last time, you told me you gave Mr. Kuraki a present from Tomioka Hachimangu Shrine. What about the other way around? What kind of presents did he bring?" Godai was trying a slightly different tack. "This is a question for both of you."

Yoko replied, sounding very relaxed. "He would always bring a little something with him when he came to visit. Sweet rice jelly, custard pudding, prawn crackers, things like that. Aichi Prefecture's famous for tasty sweets and snacks."

"Anything more than little gifts like sweets or snacks from Aichi? I'm talking about—how should I put this?—proper, serious presents. Accessories, things you can wear."

Yoko frowned uncomprehendingly.

It was Orie who replied.

"Detective, are you asking if Mr. Kuraki liked me or my mother?"

Godai winced reflexively. "Well . . . uh . . . I suppose I am," he managed to stammer.

"*Ridiculous*," said Yoko, spitting out the word. "Me, at my age? If Mr. Kuraki had any feelings, it would have to be for my daughter. Well, Orie?" she asked. "Did he ever come across like that to you?"

Orie thought for a moment. "He was always very sweet to me, so I certainly knew he didn't dislike me. Honestly, though, I never thought about it. He never said anything to me."

"And he never gave you any presents?" Godai insisted, fully aware that he was being annoying.

"No, never." Orie's response couldn't have been clearer.

"What does any of this have to do with his arrest?" Yoko asked tetchily.

"We are trying to find out why Mr. Kuraki came up to Tokyo on such a regular basis," said Godai, rolling out a line he'd prepared in advance. "It struck us as unlikely that he would come all the way here just because he fancied having a drink in his favorite restaurant."

"The reason's got to be that his son lives in Tokyo. At least, that's what I've heard. Don't you think so?" Yoko looked at her daughter for support.

"We don't think that the presence of his son in Tokyo is enough to explain the frequency of his visits."

The women lapsed into silence. Godai wondered if his comment had unsettled them.

"Let me just double-check this point with you. You never felt that the suspect, Mr. Kuraki, had any special feelings for you?" Godai scrutinized Orie's oval face.

She shot a quick glance at her mother, then said, "Like I just said, the thought never even crossed my mind."

"Can you consider it? Looking back, is there any incident that might suggest he had feelings for you?"

Orie cocked her head to the side, a bemused expression on her face.

"Look, if that's the approach you're going to take, we can keep doing this forever. Mr. Kuraki was always nice to me and, like I told you a minute ago, often brought us little gifts from Aichi. So I suppose that yes, he must have had some feelings for me. But please don't ask me to tell you what kind of feelings they were, because I don't know. All I can say is this: Nothing he ever said or did suggested that he was in love with me."

"I see. Allow me to ask you another, somewhat intrusive question. Are you currently seeing someone? You don't have to answer if you don't want to."

"No, I'm not seeing anyone," Orie snapped back.

Godai nodded and turned to Yoko. "Mrs. Asaba, you told me that you got the news of Mr. Kuraki's arrest from one of your customers. Could you give me the customer's name? And their contact details too, ideally?"

"I really don't want you to drag our customers into—"

"I promise not to cause any trouble," Godai said, interrupting Yoko mid-sentence. "I'd also appreciate it if you could give me the names of any other customers who were friends with Mr. Kuraki. We're investigating Kuraki as the prime suspect in a murder. We can't just let it go." Godai leaned forward and stared intently at Yoko.

The corners of Yoko's mouth turned up in something like a smile. "I don't have contact details for all our customers, you know."

"Whatever you have."

Yoko nodded, took a small breath, and turned to her daughter. "Have you got the customer register?"

Orie rose reluctantly to her feet.

AFTER LEAVING THE Asabas' apartment, Godai was not in the mood to go straight back to the incident room, so he invited Nakamachi to a café. Although he was planning to have a coffee, he changed his mind and ordered a beer instead. Despite raising his eyebrows, Nakamachi asked, "Mind if I join you?"

"Be my guest. It's my treat."

They found a couple of seats away from the street and slaked their thirst with beer.

"Well, I managed to ask everything I wanted," Godai said.

"You struggled with how to phrase that last question, didn't you?"

Godai smiled and nodded. "They must have thought I was asking the dumbest things. 'Do you think Kuraki was in love with you?' They were like, 'So what?'"

"When the trial gets underway, 'so what' won't be good enough."

"All I know is that the prosecutor will want to have a clear answer, one way or the other." Godai downed his remaining beer in one gulp. "It's a pain in the ass."

Kuraki had admitted to the murder. There would be no arguing about the facts of the case in court. The focus would be on whether he could plead extenuating circumstances.

Kuraki claimed that the time he spent with Yoko and Orie Asaba gave meaning to his life. The defense lawyer was likely to argue that wanting to protect the one thing that gives meaning to your life is a natural and understandable instinct. The prosecutor apparently intended to counter this by making the case that finding meaning in the time spent with the family members of a man who had been falsely charged in your place was perverse and narcissistic, proof that Kuraki was unrepentant. The prosecutor suspected lust was behind Kuraki's feelings toward the Asaba women.

So Godai's superiors had ordered him to secure either proof or testimony that would corroborate Kuraki being infatuated with one of them, ideally Orie.

From his encounters with Kuraki, Godai came away with the impression that he was a thoroughly decent man. Even if he had desired Orie, which Godai found hard to believe, he would have suppressed those urges, knowing that a relationship was morally wrong. Today's interview was a depressing experience.

When they got back to the incident room, Godai relayed the substance of his interview with Yoko and Orie Asaba to Assistant Inspector Tsutsui.

"About what I expected," Tsutsui snorted, sounding unimpressed.

"How so?"

"I got to interview Kuraki's son. He suspected that the reason his father came up to Tokyo so often was because he had a woman. But the father never told him in so many words, he said. He was only guessing as to the reason."

When Godai met with Kazuma Kuraki, he'd been adamant that he and his father kept out of one another's lives.

"Mr. Kuraki told us that he has no special feelings for either of the Asaba women. I see no reason to doubt him," Godai ventured.

"I agree. I suppose the prosecutor who's handling the case is eager to dig up anything that will help turn the jury against the defendant. He really doesn't want them to think that Kuraki's a fundamentally decent man." Tsutsui again snorted as he said this. "Let's leave it there for now. Write everything up in a report."

"Yes, sir," said Godai. As he headed back to his desk, he overheard Sakuragawa speaking on the phone.

"Don't just show the photograph to the conductor; show it to the staff in the station too. . . . Listen, we don't know for sure that he used the automatic gates. Goddammit, I shouldn't have to tell you this sort of thing." His anger was evident from his voice.

Godai leaned down so his face was close to Tsutsui's. "Still haven't managed to pinpoint which train Kuraki took?"

Tsutsui scowled and nodded.

"The security camera footage was no good, so we're gambling on finding a witness. I don't think we can expect much."

"Was the return train to Nagoya a no-go too?"

"Yes. Which is why the chief's so cranky," Tsutsui said, lowering his voice and glancing across at Sakuragawa.

Several investigators were hard at work gathering evidence to corroborate Kuraki's confession. His claim that he took a bullet train to Tokyo on October 31 was part of that. Although Kuraki said that he caught the train at Nagoya Station, he claimed not to recall the precise time it departed. Working backward from Kuraki's purported arrival around 5:00 PM, the investigators had examined footage from all the security cameras in and around Nagoya Station. Nonetheless, they were unable to identify Kuraki with any certainty. Some of the investigators had then gone to Nagoya Station to show Kuraki's mug shot to the train conductors and other station staff. They hadn't managed to pinpoint his return train either.

"What about that place? Monzen-Nakacho, I mean?" Godai asked quietly.

The expression on Tsutsui's face grew sourer. Wordlessly, he shook his head.

"No luck there either, huh?"

"There aren't many security cameras in the backstreets, and no one remembered Kuraki. It all looks pretty hopeless."

"Doesn't it strike you as odd, Assistant Inspector Tsutsui?"

"What?"

"The way we're completely failing to find any corroborating evidence. Like from the car. Even though Kuraki claims to have driven the thing, we got no evidence off it. Do we have a case?"

"Hey, not so loud." Tsutsui clucked his tongue and snuck a glance at Sakuragawa.

"This isn't good, is it?" Godai repeated, speaking more quietly this time.

Kuraki claimed to have loaded Shiraishi's body in his car and then driven to another part of town. The trouble was that no fingerprints, hair, or DNA from Kuraki had been lifted from inside the vehicle.

"Forensics says that this sort of thing happens," Tsutsui said unhappily. "Just because Kuraki was in the car doesn't guarantee that he left any hair or DNA behind. As for fingerprints, Forensics said that the handle of the knife had been wiped down."

"But Kuraki didn't say anything about wiping off his prints in his statement. When he was asked what had happened to the prints, didn't he initially say that he couldn't remember? It was only *after* it was suggested that he'd wiped them off that he said that yes, perhaps so."

"If he says he can't remember, there's nothing we can do."

Godai shook his head and scratched his scalp, mussing up his hair. "The whole thing is fishy."

"So what do you suggest?"

"Don't you think we need to do some more digging? There's no guarantee that Kuraki's telling us the truth."

"What do you think he's lying about?"

"I don't know. That's why I want to investigate. It's just weird that we can't substantiate *anything* that he told us. It's starting to feel like a wild-goose chase."

"Don't say anything like that in front of Sakuragawa." Tsutsui scowled at him. "I'll admit that we don't know if everything Kuraki told us is true or not. He could come out and suddenly say something quite different at his trial. Regardless, the fact of his guilt isn't going to change. That's good enough for us. We've done what we're supposed to do."

"You mean him knowing confidential info about the case?"

"Yes. You agree, don't you?"

In his confession, Kuraki had stated that he had killed Shiraishi at the Sumida River Terrace close to the Kiyosu Bridge. Since the police had not revealed the crime scene location to the general public, this was a piece of information that only the perpetrator would know. That was practically equivalent to physical proof in court.

"Do you think that's enough to take him to trial?"

"From what I've seen of Kuraki, I wouldn't expect him to pull a one-eighty and deny everything. Stop overthinking things. Just go and write up your report. Come on." Tsutsui clapped Godai on the back.

"Yes, sir," said Godai rather half-heartedly. Probably, he suspected nothing was more important than the answer to whether Kuraki was in love with Orie Asaba.

"That reminds me. I was able to confirm the Tokyo Dome business with Kazuma, the son," Tsutsui said. "Around March, he did give Kuraki a ticket for a Yomiuri Giants–Chunichi Dragons game."

"What about the father losing his wallet?"

"He knew nothing about that. Perhaps Kuraki kept it to himself because it's a bit embarrassing." Tsutsui turned to his computer screen. As far as he was concerned, the conversation was over.

Godai walked off, unsatisfied.

There was still one more thing for which they had not found any proof.

The night before, Godai visited the Shiraishi home, following a hunch. Again, he found himself sitting opposite Shiraishi's wife, Ayako, and daughter, Mirei.

He couldn't rest until he verified that first fateful encounter between Kuraki and Shiraishi.

Had Shiraishi told them about a Dragons game where he met a man named Kuraki, who'd lost his wallet? Godai asked the two women.

They both claimed to have heard nothing about it. And, naturally enough, not to have heard the name *Kuraki* either.

In fact, both women seemed very surprised that Shiraishi had gone to the Tokyo Dome solo for a game.

"My husband was a Chunichi Dragons fan. That much is true. He got invited to plenty of games. But he was never committed enough to go and watch a game on his own," said Ayako, her face creased into a puzzled frown.

Ultimately, Godai left the Shiraishi residence without anything supportive of Kuraki's statement. As he was on his way out, Mirei, the daughter, asked him how the case was progressing.

"We heard that a man by the name of Kuraki's been arrested, but no information about his motive or anything else. Please tell us. Did he kill my father? Who is he? What was his relationship with my dad?"

Mirei was a beautiful woman with well-sculpted features. When she put that face to work—raising her eyebrows—she was hard to resist, almost overpowering.

Even when Godai gave her the boilerplate response about not being able to discuss an ongoing investigation, she refused to give up.

"On the news, it said that he admitted to the crime. So, did he admit to the murder but not tell you why?"

He had to admire her tenacity.

When Godai reiterated that he was unable to reveal details of an ongoing investigation, Mirei said, "But I'm family, for God's sake! You must be able to tell me something. If you've arrested the perpetrator, surely you're duty-bound to share the truth with us? We loved him. How can you treat us this way? It's not normal."

Godai understood her anger. He wanted to tell Mirei what was in Kuraki's confession. However, there was no guarantee that she would keep what he told her to herself, and he couldn't afford any leaks. Even if he swore her to secrecy, she might not keep her word. The wisest course of action was to tell her nothing, and all Godai could do was bow his head and apologize, hurrying away.

What was he to make of the fact that Shiraishi's family knew nothing about the episode at the Tokyo Dome? Perhaps the lawyer had thought it too trivial to mention. That was hard to dispute—but it was a funny anecdote someone would share with family. What the wife and daughter had said about Shiraishi being unlikely to go to a game on his own also bothered him.

Either way, I owe it to these two women to dig deeper into this case, Godai thought, recalling Mirei's pleading eyes.

14

THE DAY AFTER Horibe's visit, Kazuma took a sick day. In his current mental state, there was no way he could do his job properly. His boss had been perturbed the day before when Kazuma said a family member was in trouble. But Yamagami never would have imagined that one of his subordinates' fathers had been arrested! Kazuma promised to explain later, but his spirits sank when he thought about it.

Kazuma hadn't eaten and barely slept. He had no idea how to deal with what awaited him. Horibe had talked about the media probably showing up at his door.

Kazuma stared at his phone. Any minute now, he felt, it might light up with a call from some journalist asking questions. Or maybe they would just show up on his doorstep instead?

With a heavy heart, he forced himself to read through all the articles he could find online about the case and switched the TV channel to one of those gossipy talk shows. The best way for him to get some idea of what was in store for him and his father was to keep on top of the situation.

To Kazuma's surprise, there was nothing new on his father's case. With new stories breaking every day, no one would bother with a detailed follow-up unless someone famous was involved.

Kazuma spent the whole morning lounging around in bed. Nobody contacted him. The day before, after Horibe had left, a couple of detectives came to see him. They had asked a number of very specific questions, like whether he had given Tatsuro a ticket for a baseball game or if he had spotted any sign that Tatsuro was in a relationship with a woman. While he had his own suspicions, he told the detectives that he had no reason to think so. Anyway, how could that be relevant to the investigation?

Kazuma checked his phone again, ignoring his text messages. If he read the messages, he'd have to respond. It was too much trouble. *They're probably not important*, he told himself.

By the afternoon, he was starting to feel hungry. He wasn't in the mood to make anything for himself, so he went out. At his favorite local café, he ordered a coffee and a sandwich, then searched on his phone using the terms *family*, *perpetrator*, and *trial*.

He quickly found several relevant articles. Most of them were on law firms' websites. According to them, the only contribution that the family members of the accused could make in court were to observe proceedings "in a sincere frame of mind" and provide testimony as character witnesses. If the family members wanted to plead extenuating circumstances, they'd have to explain in detail how they could assist the accused's rehabilitation.

The day before, Kazuma had not been ready to accept what was happening to him; now, as he read the legal articles, the reality started to sink in. One question loomed large: Why would Tatsuro have done something so awful? Although Horibe had talked him through the background, he still struggled to make sense of it. Kazuma needed to hear the truth from his father.

Kazuma choked down what remained of his sandwich, went to a quiet corner of the café, and called Horibe. The lawyer picked up almost immediately and asked him what was wrong.

"I just want to know when I'll be able to see my father," Kazuma said.

"Right now, he's shuttling between the police station and the prosecutor's office. That makes it difficult. You'll stand a better chance of getting to talk to him after he's transferred to the detention center."

The lawyer paused.

"I should add that I've just come back from seeing your father. He insisted again that he does not want to see you. He probably feels too ashamed. Your visit may only put him under greater psychological strain."

Horibe recommended giving it a bit more time.

Kazuma was irritated. Horibe had no idea how this was affecting him. Still, taking it out on the lawyer wouldn't be fair. "Okay," he said and ended the call.

He left the café and went home. Although the thought of his work was weighing on him, there was not much he could do. He wrote an email apologizing to the person he'd canceled on the previous day. It shouldn't have been hard, but he struggled to find the right words. In the end, writing a single email took him the better part of an hour.

Just past 5:00 PM, a call came from Yamagami. Kazuma felt a burst of panic when he saw his boss's name on the screen. He picked up. "Hello, Kuraki here," he said.

"It's me, Yamagami. You okay to talk right now?"

Kazuma detected a note of gloom in his voice. Or was he imagining things? "Yes, what is it?"

"I heard you weren't feeling well. How are you doing now? Think you can drag yourself into work tomorrow?"

"Ah . . . yeah, I think I'll make it."

"Good. Could you come in an hour early?"

"An hour early? Yes, I can do that."

"Sorry for asking. Right, then. See you tomorrow."

Yamagami was about to end the call.

"Listen, boss," Kazuma blurted out. "Is there something urgent you need to discuss with me?"

Initially, his question was met only with silence. *I knew it. I was right*, he thought. *The writing is on the wall.*

"Kuraki," said Yamagami. His tone was suddenly stiff and formal. "Are you free right now?"

After discussing possible meeting places without being able to settle on one, they finally agreed that Yamagami should go to Kuraki's apartment. Yamagami wasn't keen on meeting anywhere near the office in case one of their coworkers spotted them.

Kazuma had a terrible feeling he knew what Yamagami wanted to talk about and wasn't surprised when Yamagami began. "I think you've guessed why I'm here. It's your father."

"Did the police contact you?"

"No, we've heard nothing from the police. It was our human resources department. Was I aware that Mr. Kazuma Kuraki's father had been arrested?"

"Human resources?" *Why on earth should they have contacted Yamagami?* Kazuma wondered.

"From the look on your face, I'm guessing you don't know."

"Don't know what?"

"Um . . . I don't quite know how to put this." Yamagami interlocked his fingers on the table and ran his tongue over his lips. He was clearly struggling to find the right words. "We got a strange call at the office switchboard around lunchtime today. The caller asked if we had a Kazuma Kuraki on the staff. Naturally, the operator's response was to say that she wasn't at liberty to give out that information. When the caller asked why not, she explained that it was a privacy issue. At that point, the caller asked, 'Not because he's the son of a killer?' and hung up. The operator reported the call to her manager. He then called human resources, who started looking into the matter. They quickly found that a man who appeared to be your father had been arrested for murder. They also discovered that your name was attached to his on the internet."

"My name?" Kazuma was confused. "How did that happen?"

"Social media. Not long after your father was taken into custody, somebody posted a comment saying, 'The dude they arrested lives just around the corner from me.' Somebody else then posted your father's address and mentioned that he had a son. One thing led to another, and then someone put your name online along with a high school photo."

Kazuma gasped in shock. "Are you serious?"

"I'm afraid so."

"Do you mind if I take a quick look?"

"Go ahead," Yamagami said.

Kazuma did an image search for his own name. There was his own face, from high school. He felt faint.

"You've got to be kidding!"

"Sign of the times," Yamagami said sympathetically. "Information wants to be free. Once it's out there, there's no stopping it. I suppose someone who saw the photo of you decided to check you out. Or perhaps someone who just happened to know where you worked. And this person who saw those posts decided to call the company directly and ask about you. . . . I'm guessing that's how it went."

Kazuma sighed. "What a screwup."

"When did you hear that your father had been arrested? Yesterday?"

"Yeah, his lawyer got in touch. I'm sorry. At the time, I didn't know how to tell you."

"You were upset. Of course you were. The problem is what we should do now."

"According to my father's lawyer, the best thing we can do is to try pleading extenuating circumstances."

"That's not what I mean." Yamagami waved his left hand lightly. "I'm talking about the company. About your job."

"Oh . . . Of course. I'm sorry."

The conduct of the trial had nothing to do with Yamagami or the firm.

Kazuma pulled himself upright and looked his superior in the eye. "That's something I should be asking you about. What do you want me to do? Can you keep me on at the firm?"

Yamagami sat up a little straighter in his chair and gave a brisk little nod. "You're not the one who's been arrested, so you don't need to worry about being fired or anything. But it may be difficult for things to continue along normal lines. . . ."

"Meaning?"

"After HR reached out, the board of directors met to discuss how to handle the situation. The information about you is out there; there's no putting that particular genie back into the bottle. We are likely to get inquiries from outside, and there may be criticism directed at you. The upshot is that the directors decided it would be best to transfer you to a job where you don't have to interact with anyone outside the firm, at least for a while."

"You're . . . reassigning me?"

"On a purely temporary basis. We have no way of knowing what the impact will be. Give it a little time and, who knows, maybe it will all fade away. At which point, you can come back."

"What department am I being transferred to?"

"I need to liaise with the different departments. Could you take a leave of absence until I've sorted it all out? A couple of weeks, let's say."

"That's a long time."

"You see, the truth is," Yamagami began, sounding rather embarrassed, "we're not sure how word got out, but rumors are running rampant inside the company. The CEO wants to calm things down fast."

"You mean that if I showed up at work, work would be the last thing on anybody's mind!"

"Well"—Yamagami nodded—"I suppose that's about it."

"What about tomorrow? You told me to come in an hour earlier than usual."

"Forget about that. I'll handle your application for leave myself."

Kazuma swallowed and nodded. "Yes, sir."

The look on Yamagami's face suggested he had something more he wanted to say, but he just got to his feet and said, "Okay, I think that takes care of everything."

Kazuma also stood up and bowed. "I am very sorry to cause the firm so much trouble."

He heard Yamagami drawing in a deep breath. "I don't get it," his superior said. "Why did your father do what he did? Was he in financial trouble?"

"Oh . . ." Kazuma stammered.

Yamagami, looking panicked, flapped his hand from side to side. "No, no. You don't need to answer that. I shouldn't have asked." Then he patted Kazuma a couple of times on the shoulder. "I'll be in touch" were his parting words.

As he left the apartment, he almost seemed to be running away.

After saying goodbye to his boss, Kazuma picked up his phone. He itched to see what people were saying about him online, though he knew there was nothing to be gained from looking. It was obvious enough that no one would have anything nice to say and it would only make him more upset. Doomscrolling would be a mistake.

He was about to put down his phone when he noticed that he had a new email. He looked more closely. The subject was "Hey, it's Amemiya." Masaya Amemiya was a colleague who had joined the advertising firm the same time as Kazuma. He was Kazuma's closest friend at work, and they occasionally went out for drinks together. Kazuma had gotten a text from Amemiya the day before but hadn't bothered to look at it. Amemiya must have decided to send a follow-up email.

Kazuma opened the email.

> All sorts of rumors are flying around. Let me know if there's anything I can do for you. Don't feel pressured to reply to this. Take good care of yourself. Amemiya.

Kazuma wondered what to do. After a few minutes, he just typed the word *Thanks* and pressed Send.

15

AT THE BICYCLE shop on Eitai Boulevard, a boy clambered onto the saddle of a new blue bicycle as his father looked on. The proprietor of the store, Fujioka, a short, thickset man of around fifty years old dressed in gray overalls, was explaining the ins and outs of the bicycle to the pair.

Godai inspected the rows of colorful bicycles inside the store as he waited for their exchange to end. Now and then, Fujioka glanced in his direction.

As soon as the father and son left, Fujioka went over to him, forcing his lips into a smile. "Apologies for keeping you waiting. Are you interested in a bicycle?"

With a wry smile, Godai thrust a hand into his jacket pocket.

"I am afraid that's not why I'm here." He flashed his police badge. "You are Mr. Fujioka, right?"

Fujioka, his mouth hanging open, looked at Godai and mumbled something.

"Could you answer a few questions? It's about Asunaro in Monzen-Nakacho."

Fujioka blinked and nodded. "Oh... yeah, no problem. Come this way."

There were a couple of stools at the back of the shop. Once they were both seated, Godai showed Fujioka a photograph.

"Do you know this man?"

Fujioka took a deep breath as if to calm his nerves. "That's Mr. Kuraki . . . isn't it?"

"That's right," Godai said, returning the photograph to his jacket pocket. "Did you know he's been arrested?"

"Yes, I heard the news. Quite a shock." Fujioka paused. "But is it true?"

"Is what true?"

"You know, that stuff about Mr. Kuraki killing someone. It must be a mistake, surely?"

Godai smiled wanly. "Why do you say that?"

"Well, he seems like such a nice guy, a gentle soul. He doesn't get nasty when he drinks. I've never even heard him raise his voice."

Godai pulled out a notebook and a pen. "So you became very good friends with Mr. Kuraki at Asunaro?"

"I don't know about 'very good friends'; 'drinking buddies' is more like it. I go there a lot on my own too, you see, so we'd often end up at the counter, drinking together."

"What did you talk about?"

"All sorts of stuff. General chitchat, politics. Lately, we've been talking a lot about health issues, different diseases. Old-geezer stuff."

Being asked about Kuraki or seen to be a known associate of a murderer did not seem to bother Fujioka unduly. He mostly seemed to be earnestly saying that Kuraki was a good and honest man.

"Did you talk baseball?"

"Baseball? Yeah, baseball we talked a lot about. Kuraki's a Dragons fan, and I'm a Giants guy. We follow the games on our phones. Depending on who's winning or losing, it's an emotional roller coaster."

"Mr. Kuraki sometimes went to watch live games in the stadium. Did he ever talk about that?"

"Him going to games? Come to think of it, he did mention it. Just once. Told me he was going to the Tokyo Dome for the first time in his life."

"When was that?"

"Start of the current season, I think."

Finally, a corroboration of Kuraki's statement.

"Did he say anything about having a funny experience at the ballpark?"

"A funny experience?"

"Like meeting someone or losing something."

Fujioka grunted in response to Godai's question. "I talked to Mr. Kuraki the day before he went to the Tokyo Dome, then he went straight back to Nagoya the next day. We didn't meet till several months later, so we didn't discuss the game."

Godai was disappointed. He wasn't going to be able to verify that Kuraki and Shiraishi had met from Fujioka's testimony.

"Pardon me." It was a female voice. A middle-aged woman stood at the open storefront on the street.

"Yes, madam." Fujioka got to his feet and hurried to help her. He handed her a bicycle that was in the store. It must have been in for repairs.

Fujioka rang her up, saw her off, then returned to Godai.

"Have you any more questions for me?"

"Yes, I would appreciate you telling me what Mr. Kuraki was like at Asunaro."

"Completely normal, I'd say. He never got into it with anyone. He'd just sit there, quietly enjoying his drink."

"A female proprietor runs the restaurant with her daughter. Was there a vibe between Mr. Kuraki and the two women?"

"Sorry, a 'vibe' . . . ?"

"Do you think Mr. Kuraki had feelings for Orie Asaba? That's what I'm asking."

The question did not appear to surprise Fujioka, despite the groan he emitted. "Orie is a good-looking woman. Still, I'm not sure about Mr. Kuraki. Maybe it's his being so much older than she is, but I don't think he saw her as an object of attraction as a woman. Or rather, he deliberately stopped himself from seeing her like that."

The phrasing struck him as funny. Godai was curious. "What do you mean by he didn't see her 'as a woman'?"

"No, well..." Fujioka rubbed his forehead. "I'm not really sure if I should say this."

"This will be off the record, if that helps."

Fujioka wiped the back of his hand across his mouth and shot an anxious glance around the store. "It looked to me more as if Orie had a serious thing for Kuraki."

"Orie?"

"I don't think I'm the only person who got that impression," Fujioka continued, lowering his voice. "Some of the other customers gossiped about it. I know that for a fact."

"Did you ever ask Orie herself?"

"Oh, please. I'd never do that. Detective, don't mention what I told you just now to anyone. I'm begging you."

Godai pictured the faces of the two Asaba women. *No way could Yoko be ignorant of her daughter's feelings, especially if the restaurant's customers are gossiping about them.* But neither had mentioned anything about it. Maybe they just didn't want to share their most intimate feelings with a detective.

16

SIX DAYS AFTER his previous visit, Horibe returned to let Kazuma know that his father had been formally indicted and moved to the Tokyo Detention House. Apparently, Tatsuro was quite calm and ready to give Horibe free rein in how he handled the trial.

"I have a copy of the written indictment. It all tallies with what Tatsuro told me himself. I gather that he's looked over it and confirmed that he has no objection," Horibe said, choosing his words with care.

"Last time, you said you weren't going to contest the basic facts of the case," Kazuma said rather dully. He felt resigned, fatalistic.

"That's the plan, yes."

"So the trial will be just a formality. . . ."

Horibe frowned slightly and shook his head. "Not quite. That would mean the prosecutor gets the verdict he wants. What I plan to do is plead guilty while also aiming for the lightest possible sentence."

"It's all well and good to say, but my father admitted everything. What can you contest?"

Horibe flipped open his notebook.

"The most crucial aspect is premeditation. The degree to which a crime is premeditated has a major impact on the severity of the sentence."

"Yes, but—" Kazuma dug into his memory. "From what you told me last time, my father traveled to Tokyo with the specific intention of killing someone. He scoped out a place to commit the crime, and he lured his victim there. That seems pretty damn premeditated."

"You're right. That is, in fact, exactly what the indictment says."

"Meaning that we haven't got a leg to stand on."

Horibe removed his glasses. "True. However, if you look carefully at Tatsuro's account, you start finding discrepancies. Take the exchange between Tatsuro and Shiraishi at the Sumida River Terrace, for instance. Tatsuro says that what triggered his final resolve to kill was Shiraishi's aggressive tone when he asked, 'What are we doing in a place like this? Weren't we supposed to be going to the Asabas' restaurant?' Now, what do you think of the phrase *triggered his resolve to kill*? Doesn't that suggest that he hadn't actually decided to kill Shiraishi until just before he actually did so? Tatsuro may have felt that he had no choice, but if he was conflicted about doing so, that puts things in a different light."

"Uh-huh," Kazuma grunted. "That makes sense. But there's still the matter of him having brought along a weapon."

"I think there's hope there." Horibe turned over the page of his notebook. "The knife that was used in the murder was a folding outdoorsman's knife. It's sold in various retail chains, and you can also buy it online. Tatsuro claims to have bought it so long ago that he can no longer remember where. And the police haven't been able to refute that either. Therefore, *he did not buy it for the specific purpose of committing murder.* I think it's reasonable to argue that the idea of committing the crime came to him impulsively and he just grabbed it on his way out of the house, all without really knowing what he was doing. What do you think? We can't say there was *no* premeditation, but it doesn't seem terribly well planned either, does it?"

"When you put it like that, no. . . ."

"Shiraishi was giving Tatsuro a hard time. Tatsuro felt cornered and came up to Tokyo. He brought a knife with him, thinking he *might* kill him if it came to that. But he wanted to solve the problem through discussion.

However, Shiraishi's demeanor pushed him off the deep end, and he resorted to murder—that's the case I plan to make in court."

As Horibe expounded with so much confidence and fluency, Kazuma had the sense that he was looking at someone quite extraordinary. When he first heard the details, he wondered why on earth his father would do something so stupid. But when the case was presented in these terms, he could understand, at least to some extent.

This man is a true lawyer, Kazuma thought.

"It's also important to show remorse," Horibe continued. "I told you that Tatsuro responded in a frank and honest way to the questions of the police and of the prosecutor. Even before that, though, Tatsuro made his confession at a very early stage in the investigation, only the second time the detectives talked to him. He's not trying to wriggle his way out of trouble by lying. This will be regarded as proof of him acknowledging his guilt and being remorseful. That certainly won't go down badly with the jury."

"But the prosecutor will try to prove otherwise, won't he?"

"That is his job! I expect the prosecutor to focus on the selfish motives for the crime. When it comes to Tatsuro's attitude to the old murder—the one on which the statute of limitations has expired—I expect the prosecutor to argue that had Tatsuro felt any genuine remorse, then he would have come forward like Shiraishi urged. When the prosecutor deposed Tatsuro, he ripped into him on that subject. I suspect that the way Tatsuro responded will be a point of contention in the trial. It's not something I can be sure about until I have thoroughly reviewed the prosecutor's records. I have just asked for access to those."

Listening to Horibe's explanation, Kazuma saw the trial would be a tangle of different strategies. The best contribution he could make was to step aside and let the lawyer do his job.

"Ultimately, the biggest problem we have is Tatsuro himself." Horibe had lowered his voice as if he were saying something especially meaningful.

"How so?"

"He told me that he'll let me handle the trial as I see fit. My sense is that's not because he trusts me, more that he simply couldn't care less. He's apathetic—indifferent, not at all engaged. For instance, when I ask him about character witnesses, he always says the same thing: that he doesn't want to bother anyone and he won't give me the names of any of his friends. He's even said that he doesn't want me to plead extenuating circumstances."

Horibe sighed. A strange feeling came over Kazuma. Since first getting the news of Tatsuro's arrest, everything he'd been told was unbelievable. This behavior, however, sounded much more like the father he knew. It was easy to imagine Tatsuro obstinately sticking to his guns: He had committed a crime, so he deserved to be punished, and whatever the punishment was, he should just take it lying down.

"Oh, that reminds me: What about that thing we discussed last time?" Horibe asked as he put his notebook back into his briefcase. "Did you manage to think of anything?"

For the life of him, Kazuma didn't know what the lawyer was referring to.

"May 15," Horibe said. "Did you remember if Tatsuro would do anything special on that day every year?"

"Sorry. I thought about it hard, but couldn't come up with anything."

"Oh, okay." Horibe's face fell. "I tried putting a similar question to Tatsuro in an offhand way. 'Do you ever think about the old murder?' He told me that he had never forgotten it or stopped regretting it. Even so, I didn't get the impression that he was doing anything concrete, like some sort of penance."

"I don't think so, no."

"Well, that's that, I suppose. How are you getting along? I know you're on leave from work. Has anything else happened?"

"Not really. The media haven't started hounding me yet."

"I imagine that's because the police haven't released any information. The TMPD are probably not sure how to announce the motive. Upsetting the Aichi Prefectural Police is the last thing they want to do. If they wrongfully charged the original suspect who died by suicide in his cell, then the

Aichi police will be criticized for the suicide and a wrongful accusation. Now that your father's been officially indicted, depending on what TMPD say, media may kick up a stink. Given the complete lack of consideration the media show even for victims' families, you're probably in for a rough ride."

Victims' families.

"Do you think I should go and make a formal apology? To the Shiraishi family, I mean."

Horibe cocked his head.

"I think you'd be better off not doing that, for now at least. The victim's family haven't yet been given the full details of the case. They might barrage you with questions—'Why did your father kill him? What was going on between them?' You know, stuff like that. Giving poorly thought-out answers to questions like that is the last thing you want to do. And if you go purely to apologize and can't answer any questions, they will only get annoyed. My advice is: Let's wait for the release of the official police announcement. I'd like you to stay away not just from the victim's family but from anyone with any connection to the case. Do you understand?"

"Yes. I'll be careful, I promise."

"I think that's everything for today," Horibe said as he stood up.

"Uh, Mr. Horibe . . ." Kazuma half rose from his chair. "Can I see my father yet?"

The expression on Horibe's face was inscrutable. "As I said, your father is very insistent about not wanting to cause anyone else any trouble. For now, at least, I get the impression he doesn't want to see you. His feelings may well change over time. All you can do is wait. That's the best advice I can give you."

"Seriously? There's actually something I want to ask my father. Could you ask him for me?"

"Of course. What do you want to ask him?"

"It's about the murder. . . . Not the most recent one; the one he committed in 1984. Could you ask him if he ever planned to tell me? Or was he intending to keep it secret even from his own family forever?"

Horibe, who was taking a pen and notebook out of his briefcase, froze briefly.

"That's . . . that's a pretty specific question."

"It's one I really need to have answered."

"I can see that," Horibe said, jotting something down in his notebook.

After Horibe left, Kazuma took a file down from the bookshelf. It contained printouts of old newspaper articles Kazuma found online.

He sank onto the sofa and riffled through them. They were articles about the 1984 case. Now, he knew them almost by heart.

The articles all referred to the "case of the financial adviser murdered near Higashi-Okazaki Station." The victim, a certain Shozo Haitani, had run a small business called Green Enterprises. An article published in the immediate aftermath of the murder stated that "Haitani appears to have been involved in a number of financial disputes. His murder is thought to be connected to these problems."

The next article, from three days later, reported that a suspect had been found, but the suspect's name had not yet been made public. It took another four days for the name *Junji Fukuma* to appear with the headline SUSPECT IN THE HIGASHI-OKAZAKI FINANCE ADVISER MURDER CASE KILLS SELF IN POLICE CUSTODY.

When it came to Fukuma's suicide, although the newspapers were united in attacking the police department for malpractice, they barely mentioned the original crime. Most of the articles stressed that the opportunity to get to the truth of the case had been lost with the suspect's death, but no one thought to wonder whether Junji Fukuma was actually guilty.

Kazuma crossed his arms, closed his eyes, and tried to go back in time as far as his memory could take him. The first image that appeared in his mind's eye was of Tatsuro unloading a truck. It was the day the family moved into their new detached house in Sasame in Anjo, a few years before Kazuma started elementary school. Later, his parents explained to him that they'd decided to move before Kazuma started school so he wouldn't have to change schools later on.

Until the move, they had apparently lived near Higashi-Okazaki Station. Kazuma had no clear memory of the place, only that it was an old two-story apartment building made of wood.

Near the apartment, there had been a parking lot where you could rent spaces by the month. Hadn't his father said how nice it was to not do that in their actual house? They kept the family car there. It was anyone's guess about the make, but he knew the car had been white—Tatsuro claimed he bought white cars because the government's mandatory vehicle inspection cost less for them. Kazuma had no idea if that was true.

Either way, Tatsuro had a white car. It was always rather grubby, as he seldom washed it and the parking lot was unroofed. When he hit Haitani, it was probably just as dirty as usual. He could see it: the car, the bicycle, Haitani, and his demands . . .

His father threatening Haitani with a knife, Haitani gloating, "If you've got the balls, then do it, stab me." And his father lost it, sunk the blade into Haitani's chest before he even knew what he was doing—

Kazuma opened his eyes. He went over to the kitchen, poured himself a full glass of water from the faucet, and downed it in one gulp.

However hard he tried, he couldn't see his father acting that way. Sure, Tatsuro was pigheaded, but he would never lose his self-control so completely, regardless of how furious he was. Kazuma had never seen his father be violent to his mother or to him. He didn't have a volatile temper, at least now. But had remorse for his actions prompted a change in his character?

Kazuma remembered what his mother, Chisato, had told him once. "Your father is kind and gentle toward everybody. Some people say that sometimes he's too kind for his own good, but that's what I like about him. That's the reason I married him." Surely it would never occur to a person like that to pick up a knife and threaten someone with it?

The same was true of the more recent crime too. Given Tatsuro's character, so much of what played out was impossible. Shiraishi was supposed to be pressuring Tatsuro to tell the truth to the Asabas before he died. But Tatsuro would have been well aware of that fact—his father wasn't a fool—and wouldn't need anyone else to tell him. Nor would he have been upset at having it pointed out to him. If Shiraishi was planning to reveal all to the Asabas, the Tatsuro that Kazuma knew would have simply bowed to the inevitable and accepted his fate.

Something's not right here, Kazuma thought. *Is he lying?*

Some parts were true—Tatsuro's behavior toward the Asaba women. It was completely in his character to track down Junji Fukuma's family and quietly help them.

I'd like to meet those two women, Kazuma thought. If he met them, he would have the opportunity to learn more about their relationship with Tatsuro.

The sound of his phone ringing interrupted his train of thought.

It was Horibe.

"The police have just released information on the recent case to the media. You should probably take a look at the news," said the lawyer immediately after they had greeted each other.

Kazuma ended the call quickly and switched on the TV and pulled up the news on his phone. He quickly found an article with the headline MAN COMMITS BRUTAL MURDER TO COVER UP PREVIOUS CRIME. It was accompanied by a clip from the news.

The presenter on the screen of his phone began speaking. She had a grave expression.

"The body of Kensuke Shiraishi, a lawyer, was found in a car abandoned on a street in Minato Ward early last month. From sources within the investigation, we have learned that Tatsuro Kuraki, the man indicted for Shiraishi's murder, stabbed the lawyer to death to prevent information escaping about a previous murder, on which the statute of limitations had run out, from coming out. According to our sources, Kuraki had confided his guilt to Shiraishi and asked for help atoning. Shiraishi urged him to be completely open and honest and admit to everything he had done. Terrified at the thought of the people he knew and loved finding out about his past crime, Kuraki resorted to murder—"

17

GODAI AND NAKAMACHI went for dinner at the counter of the same robata-yaki charcoal-grill restaurant. Nakamachi was on a different assignment, but Godai wanted to pick his brain.

Godai sighed and put his phone back in the pocket of his jacket, which hung on the back of his chair. Although it was December, the restaurant was hot and muggy, plus he was sitting too close to the charcoal grill.

"Guess what? The higher-ups have released information on the case—in a half-assed fashion, of course." Godai filled his and Nakamachi's beer glasses. "What's the point of an announcement if you're going to mess it up?"

"Why do you say 'half-assed'? The lack of details about ties to the old case?" Nakamachi asked, cramming edamame into his mouth. "Apparently, they're saying that even people accused of a crime have a right to privacy."

"That explanation is just for the public. Not embarrassing the Aichi Prefectural Police is the real reason. I can understand why they want to keep the details secret, but releasing incomplete information is sure to backfire on them. It seems never to cross their minds that a mysterious past case would arouse people's curiosity."

"They can't very well come out and announce the suspect who killed himself had been falsely charged. I mean, come on."

Godai glanced around the restaurant, then kicked Nakamachi under the table. "Careful. Walls have ears."

"Sorry."

"It doesn't matter how desperate the top brass are to keep it quiet; it's all going to come out once Kuraki's trial starts. The old case is central to the new one."

"Do you think the Asabas will be called as witnesses?"

"I don't know. The prosecutor can't ask either woman to provide a statement unless he can establish that Kuraki had feelings for them. No, if anyone was going to get them to testify . . . I'd guess it would be the defense."

"Seriously?" Nakamachi gasped in surprise. "Why?"

"To add to his plea, obviously. Defending counsel will use the two women to show what a decent, upstanding fellow Kuraki is." Godai piled soy sauce and grated ginger onto his shiitake mushroom before biting into it.

"Do you think they'll take the stand for him after what he did?"

"There's the rub. Was it really Kuraki's fault that Junji Fukuma committed suicide? I don't think it was. It's the investigation team who jumped to the wrong conclusion and arrested him. Yoko Asaba makes no secret of her contempt for the police."

"But if Kuraki had handed himself in to the police, Fukuma wouldn't have been wrongfully charged. . . ."

"True enough. But I doubt that Orie feels that way."

Godai had lowered his voice. Nakamachi leaned in closer.

"Did you dig up something new on Orie Asaba?"

Godai had told Nakamachi about the feelings Orie might have for Kuraki.

"One of the regulars at Asunaro is this old guy, a real estate agent. Says he's known the two Asaba women for twenty years. Anyway, this old guy told me something interesting. About a year ago, Kuraki started asking about the cost of apartments in Tokyo. Not just the rent; he wanted information about the cost of living, local taxes, all sorts of things. When the old real estate agent asked him if he was planning to move from Nagoya up to Tokyo, Kuraki said that he wasn't thinking seriously about moving yet, but there was no harm in informing himself in advance."

"I wonder how serious he really was."

"Living in Tokyo would make it easier for him to keep making it up to the Asabas until his death, if that was what he planned to do. My guess would be that he was looking into the matter pretty seriously. But that's not the most interesting bit. One night when Kuraki wasn't in the restaurant, the real estate agent told Orie about his plan to move. She couldn't have been more interested. She was all pleased and excited. You know, 'Do you think he really means to move to Tokyo?' and 'If he does make the move, when do you think it will be?' When the old guy saw how giddy she was, he couldn't help but suspect Orie was head over heels for Kuraki."

"Well, QED. So it is Orie, and not the mother, who has a romantic interest in Kuraki. In that case, I wonder if Orie'd be willing to testify for the defense."

"It's unlikely—but it's possible."

The bottle of beer they had ordered was empty, so Godai called the waitress over and ordered sweet potato shochu on the rocks.

"Since the old real estate guy has known the Asabas for years, he knows quite a lot about them. Although he had no idea that Yoko's husband had killed himself in a police cell, he remembered when Orie got married. In fact, he knew Orie's husband; he bumped into him in the restaurant."

"When are we talking about here?"

"Fifteen, sixteen years ago, he said."

The sweet potato shochu arrived. Godai picked up the heavy glass and swirled it gently. As he listened to the tinkling of the oversize ice cube, he recalled what the real estate agent had said.

"Orie's husband worked in the Ministry of Finance, and he was annoyingly good-looking," the plump old man had said, a hint of malice in his voice. "Orie's still a looker now. Back then, though, she was still in her late twenties. You ask me, half the customers at the restaurant were there just for her. When I heard she was getting married, I was heartbroken—and

I'm a married man! Couldn't be helped, though. Orie was pregnant; it was a shotgun marriage."

For the first two years after Orie's marriage, Yoko had run Asunaro with the help of part-timers. When the baby was big enough for day care, Orie returned to the restaurant, though not every day. According to the old real estate agent, she had been very happy.

"She just adored that little boy of hers. She was always telling us proudly how he had managed to run or throw a ball or say a new word."

At that point, the real estate agent's face had clouded over.

"Life's a bit of mystery. A few years later, Orie started showing up to the restaurant on a daily basis. 'Things okay at home?' I asked her, and she and her husband had split up! You could have knocked me over with a feather. I was so sure they had a happy homelife. She was probably only married for about five years in all."

After that, he never asked Orie the reasons for the divorce and had no idea why the marriage had failed.

Godai recalled the photograph of a young boy at the Asabas' apartment and wondered when it had been taken.

Godai found himself thinking about Kazuma Kuraki. He must have heard that his father had been indicted by now.

Kazuma had moved from Nagoya to Tokyo and found himself a job with a blue-chip company. By rights, he should have a bright future in front of him, but after his father's arrest, that future would be much more complicated. Just imagining the struggles that lay ahead of him made Godai heavyhearted. He reached for his glass and threw back the shochu.

18

THE CHIME OF the intercom woke him. He looked at his watch. It was after 9:00 AM. He had only managed to drop off to sleep sometime after 3:00 in the morning and felt slightly dazed.

He clambered out of bed with a sense of foreboding. No one he knew would drop in at this hour of the morning. Nor did he have a delivery scheduled.

The intercom monitor showed a man with a mustache, probably around forty, wearing a jacket but no tie.

Kazuma warily picked up the receiver. "Yes?"

"I'm sorry to bother you first thing in the morning. I very urgently need to talk with you. I was wondering if you had the time?" The man spoke politely, if slightly ponderously.

It's started. The media had found him.

"Sorry, who exactly are you?" He could hear the quaver in his voice as he asked the question.

"My name is Nanbara. I will introduce myself properly when we're face-to-face with one another. What I want to talk to you about"—the man paused for a moment before going on—"is your father."

He was from TV or the papers. A media guy of some sort. Kazuma felt conflicted. Talking to the man via the intercom for any length of time was the worst thing he could do. If he stayed outside the building's front door for too long, the superintendent and the building's other residents would notice. Kazuma didn't want them overhearing even this short conversation.

With no other ideas, he pressed the release button for the lobby door. He wouldn't let the man into his apartment; they could stand in the hall and talk.

What sort of questions would Nanbara ask? Kazuma recalled Horibe's advice. *I have to be careful not to say anything that he can use against me*, he thought.

The bell rang. Kazuma took a deep breath and made his way to the front door. He unlocked the door, but kept the chain in place, leaving a small gap. Kazuma expected Nanbara to look through it.

But that wasn't what his visitor did. Kazuma could not see him. He must have been standing at a slight distance.

"I know how you must be feeling. If you want me to interview you here like this, I will respect that," the man said flatly. "Obviously, I can't guarantee that other residents won't pass by, so it's likely they will hear at least some of what we're saying. Although that doesn't bother me, I suspect it's a concern of yours. We don't need to sit down, but we can both speak more freely if we just stand inside your entryway."

His cool tone had a far greater impact on Kazuma than clumsy threats or a bribe to talk would have. Reluctant though Kazuma was to admit it, the fellow was persuasive. Kazuma let him in.

The man bowed and gave Kazuma his card: Nanbara. A journalist, as he'd suspected. "I must apologize for barging in on you like this. I'm a freelancer. I'd like to ask you some questions about Mr. Tatsuro Kuraki. He is your father?"

"That's right. How did you find me?"

"It's not difficult to find out the address of someone whose name is trending on social media these days; you just need to pull a few strings. Looks like I'm the first to find you."

Kazuma sighed. "All right, so what do you want to know?"

Nanbara took a notebook and a ballpoint pen out of his shoulder bag. "When did you learn that your father had been arrested?"

"Last week."

"Who told you?"

"My father's lawyer contacted me."

"Did you meet this lawyer in person?"

"He called me, and then we had a face-to-face meeting, yes."

Nanbara flipped open his notebook and held his pen poised above the page.

"What did you think when you heard what led to your father committing murder?"

"Surprise. Shock. I couldn't believe it."

"Did you know Mr. Shiraishi, the victim?"

"No, I didn't. Obviously, I feel terrible about what happened. I would like to apologize to the bereaved family on my father's behalf."

Nanbara grunted and gave a little nod. He scribbled across the pages of his notebook while never lowering his eyes from Kazuma's face. *He's a pretty deft notetaker*, thought Kazuma.

"You said you couldn't believe what the lawyer said. Can you tell me precisely what part of what the lawyer said you struggled with?"

"What part of it? All of it. My father killing someone—"

"The motive as well?" Nanbara interrupted.

"Sorry?" Kazuma replied.

"What did the lawyer say about his motive?"

Kazuma opened his mouth to launch into an explanation, when he realized where this was heading. Horibe had been adamant that he should not say anything more than strictly necessary to the media.

"I'm sorry. I can't discuss any details related to the case. Because of the upcoming trial."

"No, of course not."

Nanbara transitioned smoothly to his next line of questioning. "According to the police department's statement, your father murdered Attorney Shiraishi to cover up a past crime on which the statute of limitations had expired. Is there any part of that statement that conflicts with what you were told?"

"Uh . . . I suppose not."

"Did you know about the past crime?"

"I'm sorry, but I can't answer that question. Please, try to understand my position."

"Just now, you said that you wanted to apologize to the victim's bereaved family. What about the bereaved family from the previous case? I'm assuming you would like to apologize to them too?"

"Yes, of course," Kazuma answered reflexively.

Was that the hint of a smile on Nanbara's lips? Kazuma realized his mistake. The police statement had only said "a past case on which the statute of limitations had run out"; it had not been specifically described as a murder. He'd just practically admitted it was. Nanbara had played him like a violin.

"Since you can't answer questions directly related to the case, let me try a slightly different line of inquiry. How do you personally feel about the statute of limitations?"

"How do I feel?"

"Now, the statute of limitations on murder cases has no term limit. Before, there was a term limit. Do you know how long it was?"

"Was it . . . fifteen years?"

"At one point, it was up to twenty-five years. Could you tell me how you feel about the statute of limitations being abolished entirely for murder cases? Are you in favor? Or do you, as I suspect, wish it had been left in place?"

What is he really getting at? Kazuma scrutinized the aloof expression on Nanbara's face.

"I'm very much in favor. Abolishing the statute was the right thing to do."

Kazuma thought he had given a safe and innocuous answer.

The journalist stared at him intently. "And why is that?"

"Why? Because anyone who commits a crime should pay the price."

"I see. So you don't think anyone should be exempted from punishment because of the statute of limitations?"

"Um..."

"Can I take that to mean that you think your father has *not* paid the price for his past crime?"

"Well—"

"If that is your point of view, that would make your father truly guilty of two crimes. Is that something you're prepared to say in court?"

Kazuma, confused by the endless barrage of questions, took refuge in silence.

"Kazuma," Nanbara said. "I get it. That's a lot of questions. Let's go back to square one and start again. I want you to answer this question very carefully, thinking forward. Do you think your father has properly atoned for his past crime, the one on which the statute of limitations has run out? Is that now a clean slate, as far as you're concerned?"

Kazuma remembered what Attorney Horibe had said. There was a crossroads where people were willing to accept that the past had been reset.

Kazuma cleared his throat before he started to speak. "Yes, well, I think that he's paid the price, made amends, and it's over now."

"Why do you feel like that? Because the statute of limitations has run out?"

"Yes... I, uh, suppose so."

"Thank you," Nanbara said, sounding rather pleased with himself. "Since you've already said this much, could you tell me a little more about the past case? About what age were you when it took place?"

"No, I... Look, please, you're going to have to stop. My lawyer has instructed me to not to say anything."

"One way or another, the truth will come out, despite your efforts to hide it. Instead of waiting, you should get out in front of the story. That way, the public will know you are actually sincerely sorry for what happened."

Nanbara had a way with words. Kazuma could feel himself starting almost to believe him.

"I'm sorry. I think we should probably wind this up."

"One final question, then. What sort of father was Mr. Kuraki?"

"What sort of a father was he?" Kazuma murmured, then said: "At times, he could be stern, but, all in all, he was a kind, serious, and conscientious father."

"He sounds like a wonderful human being."

"I always saw him as someone I could respect."

"He's also human. People are never perfect. Surely there were times when he was a bit prickly? Maybe times when he seemed down and depressed?"

"He could be."

"When?" There was a gleam in Nanbara's eyes.

"Just before he retired. He seemed rather down in the dumps."

Nanbara's face went icy. He did not write anything down. He thanked Kazuma and started stuffing his pen and notebook back in his shoulder bag. Kazuma realized that Nanbara had only asked the question to deduce when the first crime had occurred.

After Nanbara left, Kazuma called Horibe.

"Anything wrong?" the lawyer asked.

Kazuma told him about the journalist's visit.

"I hope you didn't say any more than the absolute minimum?"

"I didn't mean to, but I fell for his leading questions."

Kazuma gave Horibe a detailed account of the interview. The longer he spoke, the graver Horibe's responses became.

"I fell for it hook, line, and sinker. I'm sorry."

"You made a huge blunder. You went along with the journalist when he talked about murder."

"Sorry, I don't follow?"

"The presence of a bereaved family isn't limited to murder cases. You get bereaved families in manslaughter and accidental homicide cases too. With a hit-and-run, for instance, the statute of limitations is only seven years. Had Tatsuro committed that less serious category of crime, you would have reacted differently."

Kazuma frowned. He was furious at himself for his own stupidity.

"The police did not say what Tatsuro's past crime was, so that journalist used all his cunning to find out. There'll only be more like him in the future. You've got to be more careful. If anyone rings the doorbell, just pretend to be out."

"Okay. I'll do that."

I should have done that with Nanbara too, he thought.

"There's one more thing," Horibe continued. "It's not a good idea for you to answer questions about the statute of limitations. From now on, simply sidestep any questions about legal issues. Just say you're not a legal expert."

That had never occurred to him. The journalist had set the agenda. He realized that he had been pitifully gullible.

Kazuma ended the call. He was about to put his phone down on the table when he noticed an incoming message.

It was once again from Amemiya.

> Holding up okay? If you need anything, just let me know.
>
> You should probably get off all social media.
>
> Don't read anything. No one on the internet supports you. NOBODY.
>
> Probably best to delete all your accounts.

Kazuma sighed. It was brought home to him just how much friends mattered in this sensationalist, sordid era.

19

About two minutes past ten in the morning, the automatic doors slid open, and a thin man with gray hair strolled into the reception area. He wore an expensive-looking zip-up jacket.

Mirei Shiraishi got to her feet, conjured up a smile, and ducked her head. "Good morning, sir."

"The name's Tanaka," the man said.

"We were expecting you. Please, take a seat." Mirei indicated a chair opposite her desk.

With a few rapid strokes on her keyboard, she called up the relevant information on her monitor. He was a businessman, sixty-six years of age.

"Have you brought your patient registration card and consultation slip, Mr. Tanaka?"

The man opened his shoulder bag and extracted a few pieces of paper. "I've also got this," he said and placed an envelope on the desk, bulging slightly because of the cylindrical container inside. It was his urine sample.

"Thank you, sir."

After checking the name on the registration card, she pulled the envelope over to her side of the desk. She then handed him a checkup card.

"Could you write your name and address on this?"

"Sure, sure."

As the man filled in the form, Mirei got a paper wristband from the drawer and held the printed barcode up to the barcode reader on her desk.

"This okay?" the man asked, showing Mirei his completed checkup card.

"That's perfect. All right, Mr. Tanaka, I'd like you to pop this ID wristband onto your wrist. Which do you prefer, left or right?"

"Let's see. This one." The man held out his right arm.

"If you don't mind"—Mirei put his bracelet on—"I will remove this band when you've completed all your tests. You must not take it off yourself."

"Yeah, okay."

"You're all set. Could you grab a seat and wait over there? Someone will be with you in no time."

She gestured toward a cluster of leather armchairs in the waiting area. A small bookshelf contained a selection of newspapers and golf and business magazines.

The man ambled over to one of the armchairs. Mirei sat down and rubbed her forehead with her fingertips. Having to smile all the time was exhausting.

Medinix Japan was a members-only healthcare service; its links with multiple hospitals gave members access to the most cutting-edge diagnostic technologies and medical support. Mirei worked at one of the primary care facilities. It offered the latest form of PET scanning in addition to MRI, CT, and ultrasound.

Mirei heard a faint vibrating from the bag beside her. She pulled out her phone and checked the screen under the desk. It was a text from her mother.

> Attorney Sakuma is coming to the house tonight. About 7pm.

Okay, she quickly typed and pressed Send. She returned the cell phone to her bag and sat upright in her seat.

The automatic doors slid open, and a new guest came in, a woman in a fur coat. Mirei summoned a smile back onto her face and rose to her feet.

Mirei had started working at Medinix as a receptionist in April last year. Her father got her the job. A lawyer friend of his was general counsel for the company.

At the time, Mirei was working as a flight attendant. She always dreamed of travel and actively chose to pursue the job, so initially, she was motivated and enjoyed a sense of achievement. However, that excitement had faded, and she simply felt fed up. Dealing with passengers' interpersonal problems was starting to wear her down. She wanted a new challenge.

When she took the job, her father was pleased.

"They were at their wit's end because they don't want to just hire anybody. I'm sure you'll do a great job."

It felt nice, hearing her father say that. Even though she hadn't started the job yet, she felt useful.

They couldn't hire just anybody, because the job involved handling a lot of personal information. Finding someone they could trust was crucial.

And her father had vouched for her.

But he's gone. On the other side.

Mirei last saw him for breakfast on October 31. Her mother had prepared her father's favorite, a Japanese-style breakfast of grilled salmon with boiled spinach, miso, and rice.

As he plied away with his chopsticks, Kensuke had talked about how much snow there would be that winter. He loved to ski and had taken Mirei to the mountains every winter in her childhood. In the past few years, he had stopped going at all, even by himself. No amount of snowfall would change that.

Mirei replied that she didn't expect much, what with global warming.

She couldn't remember what he'd said back. He probably wasn't paying that much attention either. At breakfast, he always had his phone out to check his email.

Those were the last moments they had spent together as father and daughter. It was so ordinary.

When she got home from work, her mother was looking perplexed. She had called him, and even though his phone was ringing, he wasn't picking up.

"Perhaps Dad forgot his phone somewhere. Why don't you try calling his other phone, the flip phone?"

Kensuke had two mobile phones. For work calls, he still used a simple, old-fashioned handset.

"That one doesn't even ring. I wonder what's going on." Ayako shrugged.

At that point, neither of them was seriously worried. Kensuke was an extremely busy lawyer. His schedule frequently changed last minute, and he often got called in the middle of the night. They assumed he simply didn't have the time to answer his phone.

When the next day dawned and they still couldn't get through, they began to get worried. Mirei hastily called her workplace and told them she would need the day off.

After talking the matter over, Mirei and Ayako decided to file a missing person's report. Mirei was just about to head for the nearest police station when a call came in on the landline.

Ayako picked up. The blood drained from her face as she listened to the person on the other end, and her voice was shrill as she said, "You're one hundred percent sure that it's my husband, are you?" in a tearful voice.

The police told her they believed so but would need them to confirm his identity. The two women made their way to the police station. Ayako kept a handkerchief pressed to her eyes throughout the taxi ride. Mirei gritted her teeth and swallowed her tears. There was a whirl of questions inside her head: What exactly had happened? Why?

The hope that it was all a misunderstanding crumbled as soon as they entered the police station morgue. The man who lay there, his eyes closed, looking almost serene, was the father who had been fretting about snowfall at ski resorts the previous morning. Mirei broke into an uncontrollable flood of tears.

The police explained that Kensuke had been found in a car left parked on the side of the road. They showed them a photograph of the vehicle. It was their family car. His body had been in the back seat. That meant that someone other than Kensuke had driven the car.

Mirei and Ayako returned home while Kensuke's body was autopsied. Although they were both exhausted from grief, there were arrangements to make: the wake, funeral, informing friends and family.

As they mustered all their energy and pushed ahead with their tasks, the intercom buzzed. Godai and Nakamachi dropped by, asking about her father—a murder investigation was underway.

The detectives asked what he'd been like recently and if they'd noticed anything unusual. Mirei said she hadn't. Ayako added, *"But recently, he wasn't his normal, cheerful self. He often seemed distracted, preoccupied. I just thought he was working on a difficult case."*

Mirei wondered why she hadn't picked up on the same thing. How could she be so callous?

Kensuke never mentioned his work at home, so when Godai asked them what case he was currently working on, neither of them knew.

The last question Godai asked struck Mirei as very strange. He reeled off several place names: Tomioka Hachimangu Shrine, the Sumida River Terrace, and Kaigan District in Minato Ward. Did those places mean anything? Not to them.

Several weeks went by, and then there was the arrest of the culprit.

Tatsuro Kuraki from Aichi Prefecture. Mirei first heard about it from the news. A few days after that, Godai visited again to give them official notice. Not even to console them—no, he just wanted to confirm part of Kuraki's statement. A baseball game where her father met his murderer.

When they couldn't confirm it, Godai left empty-handed—without the courtesy to give them any more information on the case.

Days went by, and still no explanation from the police. Almost a week after the arrest of the alleged culprit, they finally got further information.

Their source, however, was not the police but an online article. Kuraki had consulted Kensuke about how best to atone for a crime he had committed in the past. Kensuke had advised him to do the right thing; instead, Kuraki had killed him.

Mirei was flabbergasted by the article. What a melodramatic motive! It was absurd to think that was why her father was killed.

However—

Somehow it did not feel quite right. It wasn't just because the motive seemed so implausible. What really nagged at her was the bit about Kensuke insisting that Kuraki disclose everything.

Would her father really have said anything like that?

Kensuke often said that defendants telling the truth always worked to their advantage in the end. But this case was different: The statute of limitations had expired. Who was supposed to benefit from Kuraki telling the truth?

When she mentioned her doubts, her mother admitted to feeling the same.

"It doesn't fit your father either. Would he really pressure someone to the point they felt cornered and desperate?" Ayako said. "But it's difficult to know what to think until we know what really happened between the two men."

Her mother was right. They simply didn't have enough information. They had no idea what Kensuke's old crime really was.

"I've got an idea," she said. "Remember Mochizuki?"

"Sure. What about him?"

Mochizuki was also a lawyer, who graduated some years after Kensuke. He now worked at a big law firm in Tokyo and made a point of offering them his condolences at the funeral.

"He suggested that we use the victim participation system."

"Ah..."

The law had recently been modified so that victims and bereaved families could take part in criminal trials. Mirei didn't know the details of the system. She'd been so sure that she wouldn't need to know—until now.

Mochizuki had told Ayako that if she and Mirei were interested in the victim participation system, he would be happy to introduce them to someone who could help. Participating in the trial sounded simple enough, but, unless you were familiar with it, the system could be confusing. If they went to the Tokyo District Public Prosecutors Office, someone there could introduce them to a lawyer; alternatively, Mochizuki had someone in mind he thought would be just right for the job.

"Let's ask for Mochizuki's help," Mirei said. "That way, we can learn more. I want to find out why Dad was murdered and see with my own eyes what sort of man killed him."

Ayako also seemed to be in favor. There was a look of resolve on her face.

They had been getting interview requests from reporters on a daily basis since the police statement. A journalist by the name of Nanbara had come by the house and been very persistent, begging to be allowed to ask just one or two questions.

"I gather that Attorney Shiraishi was of the opinion that the expiration of the statute of limitations did not expunge the guilt of a crime. Can you recall him ever mentioning this?" Nanbara had asked her while they stood on the doorstep.

It's precisely because we can't recall him mentioning it that we're having trouble accepting the motive we're being given, Mirei thought.

20

The intercom bell rang at 7:00 PM. "She's here," Ayako called to her daughter as she made her way to the front door.

Mirei checked that the dining table was clean and arranged the chairs neatly around it.

A moment later, she heard the front door open and close; a small woman followed Ayako into the living room. Her hair was cut short, and she had on a pair of large spectacles with black frames. She was wearing a dark gray suit and carrying a backpack. She appeared to be in her mid-thirties, though she could have been a little older. Mirei knew that Azusa Sakuma, attorney-at-law, was coming, but she had not imagined she would be so chic.

Mirei gestured toward the dining room table. Sakuma thanked her and took a seat. Mirei did the same.

"If you're planning to offer me a drink, I'm fine as I am. I'd prefer to focus on the matter at hand," Sakuma said, noticing that Ayako was making for the kitchen.

"Oh . . . okay." Looking a little nonplussed, Ayako came back and pulled out the chair next to Mirei.

"Shall we get down to business? For starters, how much do you know about the victim participation system?" Sakuma asked.

"We looked into it a little after Mr. Mochizuki mentioned it. With a lawyer in the family, we're a little embarrassed to be playing catch-up," Ayako said apologetically.

"The system itself is relatively new; there are a quite a few people in the legal community who aren't familiar with it either," Sakuma said. She spoke crisply and clearly. "To put it succinctly, the system allows the victim and the bereaved family into the inner circle of the trial."

"Into the inner circle," Ayako murmured.

"Yes, the way criminal trials were conducted in the old days, you had the accused, the defense counsel, and the public prosecutor. Victims only attended to provide evidence of the harm inflicted, very much in line with other witnesses and deponents. Unless they got lucky in the seat lottery, sometimes they could not even observe the trial from the gallery. That eventually came to be seen as an unacceptable situation. Multiple modifications were made to the law so victims could participate. They can both state their opinions and put questions to the defendant. That, in a nutshell, is the victim participation system." Sakuma smiled after delivering this little speech. "You said you had looked into the system. I apologize if I'm repeating what you already know."

"The thing is, we haven't the faintest idea about the specifics of what we are supposed to do."

The lawyer nodded emphatically at Ayako's words.

"It's my job to help you with that. I should stress that to help you and support you is all that I can do. I am nothing more than a *representative* of the victims, and I cannot take any action that does not conform to your wishes. In that sense, my position is very different from defense counsel, who is free to act in a way that does not necessarily conform to the defendant's wishes. Your wishes, Mrs. Shiraishi, and you, Ms. Shiraishi, are what really matter in the victim participation system. What I'd now like you to think about very carefully is what you want to do and what your demands are."

"What do you mean?" Mirei asked.

"Sentencing is the first thing. For his part, the prosecutor will recommend a certain sentence. As victim participants, you are also able to demand a different sentence independently.

"In the case of murder"—here Sakuma looked slightly uncomfortable before continuing—"the bereaved family often petition for capital punishment, regardless of the prosecutor's recommendation."

Mirei glanced sideways. She caught Ayako's eye. *What should we do?* her mother's eyes seemed to be saying.

We've got to ask for the death penalty, said Mirei's eyes, although she did not utter a word.

"What else is there we need to know?" she asked Sakuma.

"It depends on the nature of the crime. Some people want to ask the defendant about their state of mind when they committed the crime; others might ask them about their current state of mind. Whatever you do, it's important to think about the impression you want to make on the jury. Parading your personal feelings is never a good idea. Most members of the jury try their best to be objective and avoid being swayed by emotion. The greater the passion with which a victim speaks, the more the jury cools to them. Ultimately, emotional fireworks can backfire on you."

Remaining unemotional about murder, Mirei thought. *Nothing challenging about that.*

"That's all good to know, Attorney Sakuma," Ayako began, "but we know next to nothing about the crime itself. How are we supposed to ask the right questions?"

"Well, to get the ball rolling, I will call the prosecutor tomorrow and inform him that you want to participate as victims. I will then initiate the application procedure. I'll take care of everything myself, but I will need a letter of authorization from you. Could you come by my office tomorrow?"

"I'm happy to go," Ayako said.

"The court's response will be very quick. With this case, there's zero chance that permission to participate will be denied. Then we can really get started. Um . . . Are you familiar with pretrial conference procedure?"

"Yes, I read something about it," Ayako said. "It's a kind of preparation for the trial."

"That's right. It's to decide what the trial will seek to prove, who will be called to the witness stand, and what issues are up for debate. The judge, the clerk of the court, the prosecutor, and the defense attorney all take part. I'm afraid that the victim participants cannot be present for it. So what I plan to do is go see the prosecutor and get all the information I can from him. I'll put in a request for all the relevant transcripts and try to piece together what happened. Once you have read through all the documentation, you should have some idea of the questions you want to put to the defendant and the sort of penalty you think he should pay for his crime. What do you think?" Sakuma asked Mirei and Ayako.

The mother and daughter exchanged a nod, then turned back to the lawyer. "Sounds good. Let's do that."

"Great. Well, I look forward to seeing you in my office tomorrow." Sakuma stood up and picked up her backpack from the seat next to her.

"Excuse me, Attorney Sakuma," said Mirei as she got to her feet. "How long have you been doing this kind of work?"

"You mean helping victims?"

"Yes. My dad mentioned the victim participation system to me, but I don't think he did any work of this kind himself."

"I doubt he did. We're a rather unique species in the legal community. I mean, during the trial proceedings, we actually sit beside the prosecutor. Though to tell you the truth, that's the position I'm used to anyway."

Puzzled, Mirei tipped her head to one side.

Sakuma smiled. "I worked at the Public Prosecutors Office for five years. I'm a former prosecutor.

"As a prosecutor, you have to listen to what the victims say before the trial starts. Emotionally, they're all suffering, all in pain. Once the trial got underway, my job was to prove that the defendant was guilty. But no matter how hard I tried, I was never able to fully express what the victims were feeling. I could not speak for them. I thought it would be far better to get the victims or their bereaved families to make their case directly—that's why I switched to my current job." Sakuma reached up and adjusted her black-framed spectacles on her nose while looking intently at Mirei from behind their lenses. "Does that answer your question?"

"Very much so. Thank you."

"Good. We can do this," Sakuma said, hoisting her backpack onto her shoulders. For a moment, she looked to Mirei like a mountaineer getting ready to tackle some lofty peak.

21

THE TEENAGERS WOULD not stop glancing at him. They were looking at their phones and whispering to one another.

It started the second he took off his mask after sitting down. Still, it would be weird to put the thing back on just because of them. Besides, how could he drink his latte with his mask on?

Just as that thought went through his head, one of the girls got up and walked toward him. His body tensed instinctively.

The girl stopped. She was directly in front of the table where Kazuma was sitting. Raising her phone, she directed the camera lens at the wall a little to Kazuma's right and snapped a photo. After checking the image on the screen, she gave a smile of satisfaction and went back to the table where her friend was sitting.

Kazuma twisted around in his seat and looked behind him. There was a poster on the wall of a J-pop idol grinning and holding a hot dog. *So that's what they've been looking at.* He felt deflated and relieved all at once.

Lately, he had been feeling anxious whenever he stepped outside his condo. He couldn't shake the feeling that people were looking at him. He'd started always wearing a mask to hide his face.

No one, however, had accosted him. No one had come up and said, "You must be the murderer's son."

Regardless, he felt certain that it was going to happen at some point.

It all came down to social media. He didn't know who was responsible, but pictures of him were circulating online. First it had been a close-up of his face from a group photo in his high school graduation album; more recently, he had come across a photo that he had uploaded to a social media site years ago. It was him at a friend's wedding; everyone else in the shot had a black censor bar covering their eyes.

There couldn't be all that many people out there who were interested in photos like that. Photographs of the actual killer, sure, but these were only pictures of the killer's son. Despite that, when he saw the wedding picture for the first time, he felt as if he were trapped in a maze with no way out.

He took a swig of his latte. If he was being honest with himself, he didn't really want to go out at all. If he had just stayed put in his condo, he wouldn't have had to worry about being seen. At the same time, he couldn't stay cooped up. The lack of information was weighing on him. His complete ignorance about his father's crime frustrated him. Even the details he had felt inconceivable. If the trial got underway and Tatsuro was found guilty and forced to do time in jail—Kazuma doubted that he would be able to accept the reality of it.

The door opened, and a man came in. He was wearing a beige coat over a suit. Kazuma gingerly raised his hand.

It was Kazuma's friend and colleague Masaya Amemiya.

After buying himself a drink, Amemiya made his way over to where Kazuma was sitting. He made a point of not looking at him. Only after putting his large coffee on the table and removing his coat did he say, "Hey."

"Sorry to drag you all the way out here," Kazuma said.

"No worries. Like I said in my email, I like this area. I like this place. Full of life." As he said this, Amemiya brought his cup to his lips. His hair was long, and he had a wispy mustache.

"It's my first time here too. If this thing hadn't happened, I'd probably never venture this far from my neighborhood. Seriously, though, you'd probably be better off giving me a wide berth." Kazuma looked down at his coffee cup.

"You said that your father came to this part of town whenever he came to Tokyo," Amemiya said.

Kazuma looked up and nodded. "Yes, he used to go to a little restaurant called Asunaro. The place is run by a mother-and-daughter team. Apparently, my dad went to the place to see them."

Amemiya eyed him. "You're sure you want to be telling me this?"

"I trust you, man. Besides, if I don't tell you anything, how could you understand what I'm going through?"

"I won't tell anyone. But only tell me what you think it's safe to tell me. I promise not to ask any questions." Amemiya looked at Kazuma earnestly.

"Okay." Kazuma returned his friend's gaze. "Look, I'd like you to come with me to that Asunaro place. Now."

"No problem. What do you want me to do?"

"Just be yourself. The same as when we go out drinking together. From the reviews I've seen online, the food is good. We can order a few small dishes and have a drink. Just—don't mention the murder or use my name when we're in the restaurant. If you absolutely have to address me by name, then call me Shibano."

"Shibano. Okay, got it." Amemiya spelled out the name's characters on the table with his finger.

"It's actually my mother's maiden name."

"Right. I'd better not drink too much. Might forget, if I get tipsy."

"I'm sorry. I know this is a pain in the ass for you."

Amemiya snorted and waved a hand dismissively. "Don't worry. Going out for some nice food and a couple of drinks is never a pain. It's what we always do, eh? No big deal."

"I'm really sorry."

"Like I said, there's no need to apologize." Amemiya frowned. "How are you feeling? That's way more important."

"I'm doing okay, I guess."

"Really? Are you eating properly?"

"No need to worry on that score. I may not be in the mood for eating, but instinct takes over."

"Glad to hear it. Give me a call if you get bored with eating on your own. I'm always happy to join you."

Kazuma gave a pained smile. "It's nice of you to offer, but I know you're busy. Today is special. Oh, by the way," Kazuma went on, "how are things at work? Is everyone making a big song and dance about me?"

Amemiya shrugged. "No, they're not. Mentioning the incident is taboo in the firm. There was a gaggle of reporters hanging around the main entrance of the office, but I've not seen them around recently. I think they gave up."

Kazuma sighed. "I've caused the company a lot of grief. I doubt I'll be getting my old job back when I finally return to work. Still, better than being fired outright."

Not knowing how to respond, Amemiya frowned as he sipped his coffee.

"To be honest, I still can't believe it. It just doesn't feel quite real to me," Kazuma said. "Knowing my father, I just find it incredible that he did what he did. He's a stubborn man, and he loathes injustice of any kind. His lawyer told me that he's admitted his own guilt and is prepared to take whatever punishment is meted out to him. But would someone that brave and upright really kill another person to cover up an old crime? I don't think so."

Amemiya was silent, in thought. "Have you managed to see your father yet?"

Kazuma shook his head. "He says he doesn't want to see me. But I've a ton of things I want to ask him. The lawyer gave me a letter he'd written me; it was just an apology and didn't mention the murder at all. How can he possibly expect me to make heads or tails of anything based on that?"

"Which is why you're trying to investigate the case as best you can."

"I don't know about investigating—I just want to see for myself what my father was getting up to here. You probably think I'm flailing because I can't bear to accept that someone from my family could commit murder."

"There's nothing wrong with a bit of flailing. I'm more than happy to come along."

Kazuma was tempted to apologize to Amemiya yet again, but he swallowed the words and just thanked him instead.

They left the coffee shop at 7:00 PM for the restaurant on the opposite side of the street. There was a small signboard with the word *Asunaro* at the top of a narrow staircase. When they got to the landing at the top, a sign on the latticework door said Open.

Kazuma took a deep breath. He removed his mask and put on a knit cap, which he pulled down low, and a pair of nonprescription glasses with thick black frames. It was a rough-and-ready disguise in case the mother and daughter who ran the place had seen one of the photographs of Kazuma online.

Amemiya opened the door and went in. Kazuma followed him inside. Looking over Amemiya's shoulder, he could see the backs of a man and a woman who were sitting next to one another at the plain wooden counter.

"Good evening, gentlemen." An old woman dressed in a smock came bustling over. She looked around seventy, was on the short side, and wore spectacles over a heavily wrinkled face. This had to be the mother. If Kazuma remembered right, her name was Yoko Asaba.

"Just the two of you?" Yoko held out two fingers as she looked up at Amemiya.

"Yes, two," Amemiya said.

"So what would you prefer—counter or a table?" Yoko looked first at Kazuma and then at Amemiya. Kazuma hastily looked away.

"What do you prefer?" Amemiya asked.

"Uh . . . a table," Kazuma said, keeping his eyes fixed on the floor.

"Very good. How about this one?" Yoko led the two of them over to a table up against the wall. As far as Kazuma could tell, she did not suspect anything.

After they sat down, Yoko quickly brought over a couple of hot towels. Could she get their drink order to start with? Kazuma ordered a whiskey and soda, Amemiya a beer.

As he wiped his hands with the hot towel, Kazuma glanced at the counter. Another woman, wearing a short smock, like Yoko, was standing behind it. She was tall and slim with chestnut-colored hair tied in a bun at the back of her head. She had large eyes and a well-sculpted nose. Kazuma knew she was around forty, but she looked younger. It was Orie Asaba.

Tatsuro came here to see these two women. Two women who had lost a husband and a father because of a crime Tatsuro had committed thirty years ago.

It was just the sort of thing his father would do: get to know them, leave his estate to them, all to make amends. Assuming, of course, that he really had dipped his hands in blood all those years ago.

"Hey, Shibano," he heard a voice say. When he turned back around, he saw Amemiya holding the menu.

"What do you fancy? If you want me to handle it, I'll order a few things for the both of us."

"Go right ahead," Kazuma said.

Yoko Asaba brought their drinks over. She put a coaster on the table in front of Kazuma on which she placed a slender tumbler.

She gave Amemiya his beer, and he took the opportunity to order some food from her. He went for a couple of traditional Aichi dishes: deep-fried chicken wings and oden stewed in miso broth.

As Yoko walked off, Kazuma picked up his tumbler.

"Cheers," said Amemiya as he picked up his beer glass.

"Cheers," replied Kazuma and took a swig of his whiskey and soda.

He shot another glance at the counter and gave a start.

His eyes met those of Orie Asaba.

After a moment, she looked away. Now she was smiling at another customer and saying something to him.

Was it by chance that their eyes had met? Or had she been inspecting him?

As Kazuma raised his tumbler to his lips for a second time, he directed his gaze back at the counter. This time, Orie was busy preparing some food and she did not look up.

22

AZUSA SAKUMA'S OFFICE was on the third floor. Small and neat, the office was the perfect match for her. Mirei and Ayako found themselves sitting across from her in a simple meeting space fitted with a few armchairs and a glass table.

"Yesterday, I met with the prosecutor in charge of this case," Sakuma said. "He assures me the pretrial proceedings are progressing. Defense counsel is hoping that the victim participation will provide you with an opportunity to see how remorseful the defendant is."

"Really?" Ayako said coolly. Perhaps her mother did not care either way, Mirei thought. She knew she did not.

"So." Sakuma crossed her arms. "Did you read all the documentation?"

"I did," Ayako said as she pulled a large file out of a paper bag and placed it on the table. Post-it notes were sticking out of it here and there.

Sakuma had given her the file three days ago. It was a photocopy of all the statements and reports the prosecutor had in his possession, covering everything: the motives leading up to the murder and all the details of the murder itself. Sakuma had told the two women to read the file thoroughly before their next meeting: no photocopying, no posting on the internet, and so forth.

By reading the file, Ayako and Mirei finally had a clear picture of the case.

"What did you think?" Sakuma asked.

Mirei looked at Ayako.

The file had made the same stark impression on both of them.

"Well?" Sakuma prompted.

"It just doesn't seem like something my husband would do," Ayako said.

Azusa Sakuma's eyes widened. "Which part of it?"

"This part." Ayako opened the file and pointed to the relevant page. "This bit about Kensuke disapproving of Tatsuro's plan for making amends and insisting he should be open and up-front about what he'd done. How can I put it? It's just not Kensuke."

"How so?"

"How so . . . It's difficult for me to describe."

"My father," Mirei broke in, "he just wouldn't think like that."

Sakuma turned to face Mirei. "Not think like that?"

"I mean wielding justice blindly like a blunt instrument. That's not how my father thinks. Sure, atoning by leaving your estate strikes me as easy and self-serving enough. The idea that anyone who's serious about making an apology should confess up front seems like a sound argument to me too. But my father is precisely the kind of person who'd know that actually *doing* something like that isn't easy. I can't believe that he tried to pressure Kuraki."

From the corner of her eye, Sakuma noticed that Ayako was nodding along with her daughter.

There was barely any detectable change of expression on Sakuma's face as she looked down at the file in her hands, then looked up again.

"Are you saying that you don't believe the defendant's statement?"

"I wouldn't go quite that far. . . ." Ayako's voice trailed off.

"I for one don't believe it," Mirei declared. "That's simply not the kind of man my father was."

Sakuma's mouth tightened into a taut straight line, and she took a series of breaths through her nose before she spoke.

"The prosecutor has informed me that defense counsel will not be contesting any facts. My guess is that premeditation will be the main point of contention, the issue the defense is most likely to highlight. Since Kuraki brought a weapon along with him, the argument that he committed murder in the moment simply won't fly. Why didn't Kuraki stop himself? I suspect this will be the crucial issue. Rather, if there's any one issue the defense attorney is really going to lean into, I'd say that's it. He will argue that Kuraki did not want to kill Attorney Shiraishi, but Shiraishi's attitude was so overbearing and uncompromising that it left him with no choice. In other words, Kensuke Shiraishi's attitude on the day of the murder will be of the utmost importance.

"However," Sakuma went on, looking directly at Mirei, "from what you told me just now, you think that Mr. Shiraishi's supposed response when Kuraki requested his advice *before* the day of the murder was out of character. Have I got that right?"

"Yes, that's right," Mirei said with a nod.

A thoughtful look came over Sakuma's face. "The trouble is that we have to believe Kuraki's statement. There's no other witness who heard what Mr. Shiraishi said to Kuraki."

"But what Kuraki says about the letters my father sent him doesn't make any sense," Mirei said. "There was something in his statement about feeling 'pressured' from the letters he'd received."

"Yes, the defendant claims to have received two letters, both of which he has thrown away. In them, Mr. Shiraishi said that he did not want to be party to concealing a crime and would rather disclose it."

"I don't find that credible." Mirei shook her head. "There's just no way that Dad would have ever said anything like that."

"The prosecutor thought it was far-fetched too, something Kuraki had cooked up to suggest that he felt painted into a corner. Since the letters won't be appearing as evidence in the trial, he wasn't intending to bring them up."

"Leaving the letters aside, does the prosecutor believe the rest of what Kuraki said?"

"Since the defendant has no reason to lie, the prosecutor regards his stated motive as credible."

Mirei ran her fingers through her hair. "Well, I'm not convinced."

"All right, let's communicate that point to the prosecutor," Sakuma said. "Do you want to explain it to him yourself?"

"Me? Am I allowed to do that?"

"That's how the system works," Sakuma said. "I'm just your deputy. We're going to have to discuss this with the prosecutor at some point, so you can come with me next time I go to the Public Prosecutors Office."

"Okay."

"Is there anything else? Anything you're unsure about or want to ask the defendant?" Sakuma looked at Mirei and Ayako in turn.

Ayako tipped her head to one side and said nothing.

Once again, it was Mirei who spoke. "The thing I'm struggling to get a handle on is the culprit's humanity."

"Meaning?"

"His desire to apologize and make amends to the family of the falsely charged man who killed himself strikes me as . . . a worthy sentiment. In addition, he went to the trouble of tracking the two women down and traveled regularly from Aichi to Tokyo—there's nothing half-hearted about that. So why should someone who was capable of such compassion to other people commit a murder, particularly a premeditated one?"

"The prosecutor seems to have had his doubts from the get-go, when the accused made his confession. He suspected that while it was probably pangs of conscience that impelled the accused to track down the family, the motive behind his regular visits to Tokyo might have been different."

"Different how?"

"An ulterior motive," Sakuma said. "The Asaba family consists of a mother and daughter. Orie, the daughter, is a single woman of around forty. It's not a leap to suspect Kuraki harbored feelings for her."

A look of surprise came over Mirei's face. She looked down at the file. "There wasn't a word about that in here."

"That's true. The prosecutor in charge of the investigation thought it was a possibility, so he got the police to look into the matter very thoroughly. Ultimately, they could not turn up any evidence that the defendant was pursuing her. On the contrary, the police reported that it was the mother and daughter who were very affectionate toward the defendant. The prosecutor even summoned Yoko Asaba, told her that Kuraki was the true culprit in the thirty-three-year-old murder, and then asked her how she felt about him. Obviously, the prosecutor was expecting her to change her tune on Kuraki when she learned that he was responsible, even indirectly, for her husband's death and all her misery."

"How did that turn out?"

Sakuma slowly shook her head in response to Mirei's question. "Apparently, what she said was that the whole thing was a shock that she had to process. As far as she and her daughter were concerned, Mr. Kuraki was a customer of their restaurant and he had always been good to them. When the prosecutor heard that, he decided not to summon the Asabas to testify. The prosecution isn't interested in witnesses who don't serve their specific purpose."

There was a sardonic note in Sakuma's voice, perhaps because she had been a prosecutor herself once.

"So the narrative becomes that Kuraki was going to see the widow and the daughter in pure good faith. Do you think that will be taken into consideration for his extenuating circumstances plea?"

"It may nudge the jurors into thinking that he's not an irredeemably bad man."

"If that's true, then why would he—?" Unable to articulate the words *murder my father*, Mirei bit her lip and left the question unfinished.

"That's a very good point," Sakuma said. "And one you might want to mention in court."

23

CHECKING HIS PHONE after his movie let out, Godai saw Nakamachi had called. As he walked, he pressed the name to return the call and lifted the phone up to his ear.

The phone rang twice, then a cheery voice said, "Nakamachi here."

"It's me. You called?"

"Sorry to bother you, Godai. It's nothing big, just something that's bugging me. Have you read the latest *World News Weekly*?"

"*World News Weekly*? No, I haven't."

World News Weekly magazine covered topical everything from politics and social issues to crooked business dealings and celebrity scandals.

"They've got a feature on our case."

Godai gripped his cell phone harder. "How was it covered?"

"In considerable depth. The article even mentions the 1984 case in Aichi Prefecture."

Godai stopped in his tracks. "Okay. I'm going to pick up a copy right now."

"Have you eaten yet?"

"No, not yet."

"Are you free? I'd like to discuss this with you."

Nakamachi suggested the robata-yaki grill restaurant in Monzen-Nakacho, and they agreed to meet at eight.

After picking up a copy of *World News Weekly* at a nearby bookstore, Godai went into a café and started to read.

The article, which had the title "Should the Statute of Limitations Mean Amnesty: What Happens When Murderers Go Free," was featured very prominently in the magazine, written by a Nanbara.

"A little before eight o'clock in the morning of November 1, the body of a man was found in a car illegally parked on the street in Tokyo's Minato Ward," it began. Then there was an overview of the crime, containing previously publicly released information, such as the victim's identity and the fact that the money in his wallet had not been taken. The article went on:

> A certain Tatsuro Kuraki was arrested as a result of the investigation. According to police sources, Kuraki said that he revealed details to Shiraishi about a crime he had committed earlier in his life and on which the statute of limitations had elapsed. The lawyer then pressured him to come clean and Kuraki murdered him to cover up the crime.

The article went on to explain that the earlier crime was the 1984 murder of the financial adviser, which it described in detail, before continuing as follows.

> According to Mr. A, one of Kuraki's then coworkers, the police interviewed Kuraki because he'd found the corpse. He was neither suspected nor arrested at the time. And a man who was able to evade justice for one murder thanks to the statute of limitations later went on to take another life.

The article continued:

> The statute of limitations for murder was abolished on April 27, 2010. The revision, however, applied only to cases on which the

statute of limitations had not yet expired. As a result, people who had committed murder prior to 1995—meaning that the statute had run its course—couldn't be put on trial. Consider this extreme example: For a murder committed on April 28, 1995, the perpetrator could now be arrested and brought to justice. However, if the murder had been committed on April 27, just a single day earlier, the perpetrator could not be punished in a court of law. How can we, the Japanese public, tolerate anything so patently irrational and unfair?

Oh, I get it. When Godai reached that point, he realized what the thrust of the overall piece was. The journalist had done a little probing into the more recent murder case, but the goal of the piece was simply to highlight the unfairness of the fact that even though the statute of limitations had been abolished, the abolition did not apply to all cases.

The next section of the article detailed other murder cases where the statute of limitations had expired, as well as public opinion on the matter, and interviews with some victims' families.

On the one hand, you have murderers who have not been brought to account for their crimes because of the statute of limitations. On the other hand, you have the victims' families who continue to suffer. There is no statute of limitations on their emotional pain.

This seemed to have nothing to do with Shiraishi's murder. He was skimming through the rest when a passage near the end caught his attention.

Let us now revisit the case of Kuraki. Through my reporting, I uncovered that the crime committed many years ago has other victims in addition to the murder victim and his family. Another man was arrested in Kuraki's place. This man died by suicide in a *police cell*, proclaiming his innocence all the while.

The family of the wrongly arrested man declined to comment.

Regardless, it is easy to imagine they must have lived in shame and suffered greatly these past years.

What, I wondered, does the real perpetrator think about this?

I confronted Kuraki's son on the issue. This is his answer:

"Regardless of what the statute is now, back then, the statute of limitations was fifteen years. Personally I would like to think that my father has atoned for his past crime."

In other words, since the proverbial slate has been wiped clean for the past crime, the son wants the court to decide his father's sentence based only on his most recent crime. If you were on the jury, how would you feel? Do you think it's fair to ignore Kuraki's past crime?

THE ROBATA-YAKI PLACE was as busy as ever. However, Nakamachi had made a reservation, so they were promptly seated at a large table in the corner. After clinking their beer glasses, they immediately started discussing the *World News Weekly* feature.

"Weren't you surprised that the journalist managed to find the 1984 Higashi-Okazaki case?" Nakamachi asked, lowering his voice.

"I certainly admire his investigative skills." Godai plopped the magazine on the table.

"He spoke to some of Kuraki's old coworkers."

"I imagine the journalist just tried to speak to everyone who knew Kuraki back in the day. Apparently, he did. Once you know that the previous crime Kuraki committed was a murder, then, as the piece makes clear, it had to be from before 1995. At any rate, it can't have been a walk in the park. This journalist is quite tenacious."

"How do you think the TMPD top brass will react to the piece? I mean, after they took such care to avoid the 1984 incident and protect the Aichi police?"

"My guess is not badly. This all would have come out once the court case got underway; then there would be a real media circus over breaking details. The information coming out in small leaks like this weakens the public outrage. And since it's a weekly magazine that broke the story, the TMPD stay on good terms with the Aichi police. And for all we know, the prosecutor may be pleased about the article. Once the trial is underway, big swings in public opinion can affect the attitude of the jury. So if there's going to be any uproar, sooner is better than later."

"Fair enough," Nakamachi said as he popped edamame into his mouth.

"There's another part that surprised me more," Godai said, flipping open the magazine and jabbing a finger at the end of the article. "It's this bit where the journalist confronts Kuraki's son. That's Kazuma Kuraki, isn't it? Do you think he really went and interviewed him?"

"I guess so. He wouldn't have written any of this otherwise."

Godai snorted. "It's odd that Kazuma agreed to be interviewed. Normally, you'd expect a 'No comment.'"

"Perhaps he thought it would help his father in the trial."

"Maybe—but this is going to have the opposite effect. The conventional wisdom is that the family of the perp should not cause any trouble and appear apologetic."

Godai pictured Kazuma Kuraki's fine-featured face. He didn't look like the sort who'd get all emotional and make excuses for his father. Perhaps he'd been tricked into the interview.

A plate of freshly grilled shiitake mushrooms and shishito peppers was delivered to the table in a delicious aroma of soy sauce. Godai reached out for a skewer of mushrooms.

Nakamachi picked up the magazine. "The journalist went to see the Asabas as well."

"Seems so. Doesn't sound like he got much out of them."

"The Asabas now know that Kuraki was the real culprit. I wonder how they feel about that."

"I was wondering the same thing. I heard that Yoko was called in by the prosecutor, but who knows what they said."

Godai had never told the Asabas anything about the connection between the 1984 death and Kuraki.

"We caught the criminal, but a whole lot of baggage came with him," Nakamachi said gloomily.

"That's the way with murder cases. This case is above our pay grade now. All that remains for us is to sit on the sidelines and watch the trial play out," Godai said before refilling Nakamachi's empty beer glass.

After leaving the restaurant, they headed together for the subway station. Although neither of them said anything, they walked right past the station and only came to a stop when they stood in front of Asunaro.

"I wonder how the Asabas are doing," Nakamachi said, looking up at the building.

"Who knows? Much the same as ever, probably," Godai said.

"You don't think they read *World News Weekly*?"

"They probably did, but I don't see something like that knocking them off their stride. They're tough, those two."

He was turning away from the building when a man emerged. Plump and shortish, he looked a little under fifty. On his square face, he wore a pair of gold-framed glasses.

"Oh," said Nakamachi.

"What is it?" asked Godai, speaking quietly.

Nakamachi leaned in to Godai's ear. "That's Kuraki's lawyer."

"Seriously?" Godai's shoulders jerked, and he stared after the man who was now walking down the street away from them.

"He came by the precinct a few times before Kuraki was officially charged. Horibe is his name."

No way was this a coincidence. Horibe had clearly come to Asunaro for a reason—but what was it?

"Perhaps he was asking the Asabas to be character witnesses for Kuraki," Nakamachi said. "Remember what you told me? That if anyone was going to call the women as witnesses, it would be the defense, not the prosecution."

"I did say that. Never thought he'd actually do it, though." Godai looked up at the building, pondered a second or two, then shifted his gaze to Nakamachi. "Thanks for inviting me out tonight. It was fun. Next time you're free, let's grab another drink."

Nakamachi's eyes widened in surprise.

"Wait a moment—you're planning to go into Asunaro, aren't you? Take me with you."

Godai gave a wry smile. "It's personal curiosity, really. Look, if I take you with me, it will be obvious we're there for the investigation. Sorry—I need to go in alone."

Nakamachi frowned with disappointment. "You're right. Just promise you'll tell me what you found out."

"Will do. See you around."

"Good luck."

Godai nodded, gave a casual wave, and headed for the building. *Why's he wishing me luck?* he thought.

He checked his watch. It was 10:45 PM. The Open sign was still hanging on the door of Asunaro. Godai stepped inside.

Yoko Asaba, dressed in her smock, came scuttling up to him. "I'm sorry. We are about to—" She broke off mid-sentence. She must have recognized him.

"I know, you close at eleven. That's not a problem." Godai looked around the restaurant. There were still two groups of customers seated at tables. "I'd prefer to sit at the counter."

Yoko's chest rose and fell as she took a deep breath to steady her nerves. "This way, please," she said. Donning her best hostess smile, she led him to his seat. Orie Asaba was standing frozen behind the counter. Godai wished her a good evening and sat down.

Yoko brought him a hot towel. "What will you have?" she asked.

"Sake would be good."

Yoko raised her eyebrows questioningly. "Are you allowed to drink?"

"I'm not on duty right now." He glanced at Orie before returning his gaze to Yoko. "Anything you'd recommend?"

"How about this one?" Yoko opened the drinks menu and pointed to a brand called Banzai. "It's nice and dry."

"One of those, chilled."

Yoko went behind the counter and decanted the sake from a big bottle into a glass sake cooler.

"Here you go." Orie placed a little bowl containing shrimp and wakame seaweed with vinegar in front of Godai. Tonight's appetizer, he guessed.

Yoko brought over a cut-glass sake cup and poured his drink. Godai took a sip, then nodded approvingly. The sake had a delicious bouquet and went down smoothly.

"Do you like it?" Yoko asked.

"It's superb."

Godai picked up his chopsticks and tried the appetizer. It paired nicely with the sake.

Godai glanced over at the table seats. Both groups of customers were engaged in a lively conversation. None of them had any interest in what was going on at the counter.

"I just saw Mr. Horibe on his way out," Godai said, looking up at Orie.

Yoko, who was standing next to her daughter, was busy tidying up. Her hands froze suddenly.

"Are you surveilling us?" Orie asked.

Godai smiled wanly and shook his head.

"Of course we're not. I just happened to see the guy, and that gave me the idea of dropping in myself."

Orie glanced at Yoko. Godai could guess what the look meant: *Should I believe this guy or not?* "Right," she said flatly.

"Excuse me," called out one of the table customers.

"Coming," Yoko said and made her way over with their check.

"Horibe was delivering a letter," Orie said, leaning forward slightly and speaking in a soft voice.

"A letter?"

"A letter Kuraki had given him."

"Really?"

Godai wanted to ask what the letter had said, but he stopped himself. They had solved the case—it wasn't his business.

The other customers had finished paying and left the restaurant. Yoko came back and sat down next to Godai.

"He wanted to apologize to us," Yoko said. "Kuraki, in his letter."

"Oh yes?"

"I guess you knew all along, Inspector Godai. That Kuraki was the true culprit in the Higashi-Okazaki case. And despite being well aware of the fact, you didn't see fit to mention it to us. Am I right?"

"I was following my superior officer's orders." Godai knew that it sounded like an excuse.

"Well, either way, the prosecutor ended up telling us."

"You must have been surprised."

"If there's anyone who wouldn't be surprised at a piece of news like that, I'd like to meet them. But if you were to ask me if I hate Mr. Kuraki, I honestly don't know what to say." Yoko went on, "He was kind to us for many years, and I always felt that he was a good person. No, I still do think he's a good person. I believe that his hand was forced and that he had no choice. If he was a genuinely bad person, then he wouldn't care about a wrongfully charged man who died by suicide, much less that man's family. It wouldn't have been easy for him to locate us. I don't think that's what the prosecutor wanted to hear when he came around."

Godai extracted the folded magazine from his inside jacket pocket. "Have you read this?"

Yoko blinked and smiled wearily. "Orie came across it this morning and bought a copy. There's no point in reading trash like that."

"It's horrible. Making up stories about us like that," Orie said with a pout.

"Did the journalist who wrote this come to see you here?" Godai asked.

"No, our apartment," Yoko said. "He just forced his way in. So high and mighty. He'd dug up stuff from over thirty years ago and was peppering us with questions. We told him we weren't interested in being pawns in his game and sent him packing. The article said something about us not wanting to rake up the past; we said no such thing."

"Did the journalist know that Kuraki was a regular here at Asunaro?"

"Come to think of it, he never asked. He'd probably have been even more persistent if he knew."

Yoko poured him another cupful of sake. The sake cooler was now empty.

"Did Mr. Horibe come just to deliver the letter, or did he have anything else to say?" Godai asked, then he scowled and scratched his head. "I'm sorry. You don't need to answer that."

"We've nothing to hide, so I'm happy to tell you," Yoko said. "He came to see how we're getting on. Apparently, Mr. Kuraki was worried about us."

"I gave Attorney Horibe a message for Mr. Kuraki from us: that we're doing fine and that he should take care of himself and focus on making things right."

Looking at Yoko's face, Godai got a surprise. There was a soft smile on her wrinkled face, and the gleam in her eyes made it clear that she was sincere.

The mother and the daughter really both adore Kuraki, Godai thought.

Godai gulped down the remaining sake in his cup. "I should go. Could I get the check?"

"It's on the house," Yoko said.

"No, you can't do that."

"Don't worry about it. Next time, just bring a few of your friends with you."

Godai had not been expecting this. He was rising from his seat when the door behind him opened with a clatter. He turned and saw a man in a beige coat enter.

He thought Yoko would tell him they were closed for the night, but she said nothing. Instead, Orie spoke. "Didn't we say around twelve?"

There was surprise, criticism, and a hint of friendliness in her tone. Clearly, they knew this person.

"My thing finished earlier than planned," said the man as he began to take off his coat. A quick glance was enough for Godai to see that the suit he had on underneath was of superior quality.

He pegged his age as somewhere in the mid-forties. He had a strong nose and a pointed chin, while his closely cropped hair looked very clean.

The man said nothing and sat down at one of the tables without so much as a glance in Godai's direction. He started fiddling with his phone, ignoring everyone else there.

"Thanks for dropping by tonight, Mr. Godai," Yoko said to him. "We look forward to seeing you again."

Godai picked up on her signal: *Leave now and don't ask any questions.*

"Thank you. That was delicious," he said to Yoko, then he bowed to Orie and made for the door. He glanced at the newcomer from the corner of his eye. His posture had not changed.

24

The intercom buzzed while Kazuma was washing the dishes. As he toweled his hands dry, he checked the monitor to make sure it was Horibe, then let him in.

Kazuma hurriedly cleared the dining room table of the remains of his only meal of the day, instant noodles.

The front doorbell rang. Kazuma let the lawyer in.

They sat down on either side of the table. "Let's start with your biggest concern," Horibe said, extracting a copy of *World News Weekly* from his briefcase. "I called their editorial department this evening."

"How did it go?"

Horibe made an unhappy face. "Well, they said the complaint wasn't valid and will not be printing any corrections."

"But I didn't say half the things they have me saying in there. Just give me a minute," Kazuma said. He pulled the *World News Weekly* over to him and opened it to the relevant page. "I never said this," Kazuma said, pointing at a passage.

Horibe's troubled expression stayed in place. "They say they have a recording."

"A recording?"

"From Nanbara, the journalist. He used his phone to record his interview with you. The editors are very proud of their journalistic integrity. They claim to have carefully reviewed the original recordings."

"They say they have a recording and that this is what I actually said?"

"They're not saying it's *exactly* what you said. They edited and condensed your remarks. When the journalist asked you if you thought your father had atoned for his past crime, they were adamant that you replied that you'd 'like to think so.' Do you recall saying that?"

Now that Horibe mentioned it, Kazuma did remember that particular exchange was after the discussion of the statute of limitations. Unsure how best to reply on his father's behalf, he had been flustered and confused.

"I get the impression you do remember now."

"He misconstrued what I really think."

"And I believe you. Journalists have all sorts of tricks to get people to say what they want. As a lawyer, it's hard not to admire their skill in asking leading questions. If they have a recording, then there's absolutely nothing we can do. If it comes up again, then you'll just have to explain yourself clearly and forcefully."

"Should I put an explanation up on social media?"

Horibe's eyes widened in horror. "Absolutely not. It will only add fuel to the fire. For now, just do nothing."

"People are complaining to my employer."

"We'll let your employer handle those. You don't need to worry. Companies have professionals who deal with this stuff."

Kazuma sighed deeply and rubbed his eyes. He had a mild headache. The ramen he'd eaten earlier sat heavily in his stomach.

Yamagami, his boss, had called around lunchtime and not out of simple concern. Apparently, the article had inspired another wave of complaints.

"It's outrageous to equate the expiration of the statute of limitations with actual atonement for a crime. You shouldn't have a man like that as an employee. You need to fire him immediately"—was the gist.

Yamagami then tore into Kazuma: Why had he spoken to a magazine? And given that he had, why didn't he think before he opened his mouth?

Kazuma had no idea what Yamagami was talking about, but after the call, he went straight out to buy the *World News Weekly*.

The article left him speechless. He had no problem with the larger social argument, but the comments attributed to the "suspect's son" at the end of the article were clearly fabricated. Kazuma had no recollection of anything of that sort, and he'd said so in his call to Yamagami to explain.

Kazuma spoke to Horibe soon after ending the call.

"I understand. Look, let me review the article, and I will lodge a complaint with the publisher." Horibe's tone, though, was tired. "But you must be more careful. Don't randomly agree to interview requests in the future."

Kazuma hung his head in shame. "I will be careful."

"I just came from seeing the Asabas." Horibe sounded a bit more cheerful. "I delivered a letter from your father to them."

"A letter? What did it say?"

"It was a letter of apology. Tatsuro said that he was truly sorry; he confessed his guilt in the 1984 murder case and admitted Junji Fukuma would have been cleared had he come forward. He was deeply remorseful about both the first crime and the second. That's the gist."

"Did the Asabas accept his apology?"

"Yes," Horibe replied. "They were very gracious."

"What do you mean?"

"Yoko Asaba gave me a message for Tatsuro." Horibe took a notebook out of his briefcase and flipped it open. "'We're doing fine. You take good care of yourself and atone properly for the crime you committed.' Well—doesn't seem to be much animosity there, does there?"

"I don't know."

"I went to the restaurant during business hours, so we couldn't have a proper talk. Still, I got the impression that they were both concerned about Tatsuro's well-being and would even be willing in certain circumstances to go to bat for him."

"In what way?"

"The prosecution isn't summoning the Asabas as witnesses. That could mean that we might be able to get them to serve as character witnesses for us."

Horibe's suggestion surprised and puzzled Kazuma. "But do you think they'll be willing to do that? They lost a loved one because of my father."

Horibe leaned forward. "The false charge against Junji Fukuma has nothing to do with Tatsuro. It was the police's mistake. You could even make the case that the police are also to blame for Tatsuro getting away. Have you seen *The Shawshank Redemption*?"

"No," Kazuma replied.

"It's about a banker who's falsely convicted of murder and sentenced to life in prison. In the second half of the movie, this guy shows up who knows the identity of the real murderer. The true culprit, he says, bragged about how a banker had been wrongly arrested in his place. Now that's evil. But Tatsuro never lost his desire to apologize to the Asaba mother and daughter. They recognize that, which is why they harbor no animosity toward him. It just shows you how deep a bond Tatsuro built with them."

Kazuma recalled his recent visit to Asunaro. He hadn't told the women who he was, but there was that one brief moment where his eyes met Orie's, and he was worried she might have recognized him.

If what Horibe had said just now was true, maybe Tatsuro had shown the women family photographs. They might know his face.

"Is everything all right?" Horibe asked, perhaps because Kazuma remained so quiet.

"I'm fine. Yes, I think it would be great if the Asabas testified as character witnesses."

"The meeting I had with them tonight was a first step. Next time, I might ask. We definitely need to proceed with caution. It will backfire on us if we come across as smug and too quick to presume on their kindness." Horibe returned his notebook to his briefcase and picked up the *World News Weekly*. "Should I leave this with you?" he asked.

Kazuma shook his head. "Please don't."

Horibe put the magazine into his briefcase. "That's everything from me. Is there anything you wanted to ask?"

"Did you ask my father about that thing?"

"What thing?"

"About the Higashi-Okazaki incident. I asked you to see if my dad . . . if he intended to keep that whole thing secret from his family forever."

"Oh." Horibe reached up and adjusted his gold-framed spectacles. "I did ask Tatsuro. He said that he planned to carry the secret to his grave."

Kazuma slowly shook his head. "No big surprise."

He tried asking himself what he would have done if his father had revealed his crime to him. Would he have advised him to go public? No, definitely not. He would have gone along with his father's plan to keep it secret.

"I suppose my father is still refusing to see me?"

"I'm trying to get him to come around, but he just keeps saying the same thing: that he's too ashamed and that he doesn't mind if you break off all contact—or rather he *wants* you to break off all contact."

Kazuma looked up at the ceiling. He felt slightly dizzy.

"Is there anything else?"

"What's happening with the victim's family? You mentioned them planning to use the victim participation system."

"I gather they're pushing ahead with their preparations. The lawyer who's representing them has started having meetings with the prosecutor."

"So they—the victim's family—are familiar with the case."

"That would depend on how much information the prosecutor is sharing with them. In a case like this, I don't see him hiding anything, so they should have a pretty clear picture."

"What would you think of my going to formally apologize to them? Last time I suggested it, you warned me that they'd only bombard me with questions about the case."

Horibe frowned. "I think you're better off not doing that. The family clearly has things to say and questions they want to ask Tatsuro—not you. I suspect they would see your apology as meaningless."

"Okay, but it would make me feel better."

"That's a selfish response."

The crisply delivered response left Kazuma speechless. *I am being selfish—Horibe is right.*

"Some defendants want to literally prostrate themselves in front of the victim's family in court. But that's not usually what the families want. Antics like that are usually seen as a theatrical attempt to win sympathy. In most cases, the prosecutor will object, and the judge will step in to stop the defendant. It's the same story with character witnesses. I may get you to testify in court, but you need to remember that you're addressing the judge and jury, not the victim's family."

Horibe's words, which he enunciated so clearly and coolly, seemed to drop heavily, one by one, into the pit of Kazuma's stomach.

"I understand," Kazuma gave in.

"Right. I'll be on my way," said Horibe, rising to his feet.

"Oh . . . Attorney Horibe, is there anything I can do to help?"

Horibe pursed his lips, then stretched out his hand and patted Kazuma on the shoulder. "For now, I just need you to endure."

Once again, Kazuma found himself at a loss for words. He sat there vacantly as the lawyer wished him good night and headed for the front door.

25

THEY HAD ARRANGED to meet in the lounge of a hotel in Akasaka. Mirei checked her watch—it was still about ten minutes before the agreed time. There was no sign of the other person yet.

The waiter asked her how many people were in her party. "Two," Mirei said. "I'd appreciate if you could find us a table in a corner somewhere."

"Very good, madam," said the waiter. He led her to a table overlooking a courtyard. It was far enough from the next table, so there was no need to worry about being overheard.

Mirei sat down and checked her phone. She had a text message from a friend who was a full-time homemaker but had previously worked with her as a flight attendant. The two had stayed close, and the friend had come to Kensuke's funeral.

> Don't get upset by the nonsense spewed by that pseudo-intellectual buffoon. He's just trying to make a name for himself by saying something different from everyone else and trying to stir the pot.

Mirei felt conflicted as she read the message. On the one hand, she appreciated the encouragement of her friend, but at the same time, she felt that the situation wasn't quite that simple. Still, it would be rude to ignore her, so she replied with, "Thanks! Don't worry, I'll hold my own."

Mirei then scanned the news and was relieved not to come across anything new or disagreeable.

That morning, she'd discovered an upsetting piece of news. Someone had posted about how the online debate around the *World News Weekly* piece had really caught fire. A political commentator from one of the gossipy news shows on TV had posted a comment on the article. The comments were now flooded with arguments.

This is what the TV commentator had posted.

> The statute of limitations on murder has been abolished. But that doesn't mean that anyone will be prosecuted for murders where the statutory time limit has expired. It's not a matter of debate; it's a matter of the law. Nobody other than the individuals directly involved have the right to express an opinion on this matter. Shiraishi pressured Kuraki to come clean, but the decision about what to do was Kuraki's and Kuraki's alone. We all have skeletons in our closet. When somebody leans on you to divulge your past misdeeds, to fight back is the most natural thing in the world. Look, I'm not saying that justifies the murder, but I do think the lawyer is partly to blame. If it had been me, I would have asked Kuraki what he did and felt the day the statute expired. After all, that's an unusual circumstance and would say more about Kuraki than anything else.

Mirei read the original article and recognized the name Nanbara. That had to be who her mother had told her about, the one who had pushed his way into their house.

She felt underwhelmed by the article itself. There was nothing factually wrong with it, but the whole thing seemed to be missing the point somehow.

The article ended with a question. *"Do you think it's fair to ignore Kuraki's past crime?"* As Mirei saw it, this was the most crucial issue Nanbara raised.

One thing that had really exasperated her was what Kuraki's son had said about his father having "fully atoned" for his earlier crime. While that was a legitimate way for a family member to feel, coming out with a remark like that before a trial struck her as irresponsible.

Still, exploiting other people's misery for commercial gain was all you could expect from the tabloids.

Then, this morning, all hell had broken loose.

Mirei could see why people might react strongly to what the TV commentator had said. "Are you siding with a killer who literally got away with murder? Just think how the family must feel" was the broad interpretation of his comment. This particular TV personality, however, was known to make provocative pronouncements for attention and to promote his career. He must have known this would create a media storm.

Mirei, however, had her own reasons for being bothered by the comment.

She loathed the way he presented Kensuke's putting pressure on Kuraki to come clean about his past crime as if it were an indisputable fact. For her part, she still refused to believe her father would ever have behaved that way. She took no comfort from the volume of blowback the comment had generated or from her friend's supportive message.

She was putting her phone in her bag when a shadow appeared over her. She heard a voice say, "Hello." Looking up, she saw Azusa Sakuma sliding her backpack off.

Mirei rose to greet her, but Sakuma gestured for her to stay seated.

They ordered a couple of coffees from a nearby waiter.

"I just got off the phone with the prosecutor. He confirmed we're good to go at the agreed-on time," Sakuma said.

"Great. Thank you for setting this up," Mirei said.

"You seem a little tense." Sakuma studied Mirei's face.

"I can't help it. This is my first time going to the Public Prosecutors Office."

"You can relax. We're not the defendants in this case." When the lawyer smiled, her eyes crinkled behind her black-framed glasses. "Easier said than done, I know."

"Okay."

The coffee arrived. Mirei added some milk, then took a sip.

"Ms. Sakuma, did you see the article in the *World News Weekly*?"

Sakuma picked up her coffee cup. "Yes, I read it," she said. Her face was expressionless. "It shouldn't affect us or the case."

"But everyone who read it is having a field day speculating about what kind of man my father was. Then this political commentator guy off the TV posted a comment on social media that has triggered a whole flurry of counter-posts. I really don't like it."

Sakuma pondered for a moment or two, then nodded. "I understand. Here's what I'll do: I'll ask the publisher if they're planning to publish any sort of follow-up piece. If they are, I'll formally request they show us the article prior to publication."

THE PROSECUTOR IN charge of the trial was a Mr. Imahashi. He had a strikingly high forehead and a prominent nose. His broad shoulders filled out his suit well. Mirei guessed he was in his mid-forties.

Azusa Sakuma had advised Mirei to be as honest as possible with the prosecutor, so she was candid about the doubts she had felt when reading the transcripts, particularly her sense that the things Kensuke allegedly said seemed quite out of character.

Imahashi nodded frequently as he listened. "I understand where you're coming from. You have every right to be concerned about anything that reflects badly on your father's compassionate nature.

"However," he went on, "as Ms. Sakuma may have told you, when it comes to interactions between the defendant and the victim, the only resource available to us is the defendant's account. As far as I can judge, his account does not sound fabricated, nor does it contradict the evidence. While it is possible that the precise words he uses may differ slightly from what your father actually said, that does not change our approach to the trial. What do you think?"

"I'm not talking about the *words* my father used. I'm saying he would never think or behave like that in the first place. Why should he attack a person's past when the statute of limitations had expired? Or push them to disclose the crime? It doesn't make sense for his character."

"But your father was stabbed by the defendant. If that is not what happened, then why would he have been stabbed?"

"What if the defendant is lying?"

"Tatsuro Kuraki?" Imahashi scratched his forehead. "Why should he do that?"

"I have no idea."

Imahashi grunted again thoughtfully, then held up an index finger. "You could be right. As you have suggested, maybe your father did not speak in that manner; maybe he wasn't as aggressive as the defendant says. Surely, though, it's possible that the defendant misunderstood him? What your father said and how he said it is not relevant now. What matters is how Kuraki *took* what your father said."

"In that case, my father was murdered because of a misunderstanding." Mirei had thrust out her lower lip and was speaking more loudly.

"True—if that was indeed the case," said the prosecutor. He spoke blandly with barely a flicker of expression on his face. "But none of us can know whether a misunderstanding occurred or not. Kuraki can't help us there. In his view, he's telling us the truth."

"But his truth might not be *the* truth."

"Indeed. But that's not an essential debate to the case."

Mirei tilted her head to one side. "You don't think so?"

Imahashi intertwined his fingers on top of his desk. "Let me give you a hypothetical. As you rightly observe, there is a possibility that Kuraki is lying. Since there was a gap between the crime and his arrest, he had plenty of time to cobble together his story. Kuraki stated that he sought Shiraishi's advice because he wanted to leave his estate to the Asabas—but that too could be a lie he made up to appear sympathetic. Maybe Kuraki never mentioned the Asabas to Shiraishi; maybe all that happened was that he got drunk and in an indiscreet moment told Shiraishi that he had gotten away with murder. Maybe Shiraishi didn't react. Maybe he didn't criticize or put any pressure on Kuraki at all. Nonetheless, Kuraki went on to get paranoid, worrying that Shiraishi was going to tell someone, and he killed him. Personally, I wouldn't be surprised if the truth is something closer to that."

Mirei blinked and drew herself upright in her chair. "But if that is what really happened, doesn't it change everything?"

"It changes nothing. Think of it like this: The route may have changed, but the destination, the outcome, remains the same. Kuraki still committed murder to keep Shiraishi from talking. Either way, the motive is egotistical and selfish. Because we know *what* the motive is, the chain of events that prompted the motive is neither here nor there. The defendant is free to describe them as he sees fit. Can you accept that?" Imahashi asked her.

"No. I can't come to terms with my father being presented in court as a . . . a bully who wielded justice as a weapon."

"I can sympathize. From the legal perspective, however, delving deeper into this issue is of no strategic benefit to us. No one is contesting either the fact of the murder or the murder method. The gravity of the act itself is what has the biggest impact on sentencing. So the issue is the victim being killed and his corpse being abandoned. Since the motive itself is not actually important here, the jury will only start getting confused if we start asking questions about it. I want to avoid getting bogged down in a debate about the rights and wrongs of criticizing someone for a crime that the statue expired on—"

"But Azusa Sakuma has told me that my father's attitude to Kuraki immediately before the murder is very important. She thinks that the question of why Kuraki did not stop himself could become a point of contention."

Mirei glanced at Sakuma to gauge her opinion. Sakuma gave a discreet nod.

"If the defense is going to focus on anything, it'll likely be that," Imahashi said. "It's a clear case of premeditation, though, because the defendant came armed. He may claim he was hesitant to make himself look better, but personally, I don't expect that to have much impact. As I said just now, I think we should let Kuraki say what he wants to say."

"That's it, then, is it?"

"I think that's the best strategy for us. It will reduce the possibility for extenuating circumstances."

"What about the Asaba women? I've heard that they don't blame Kuraki."

"I have no intention of summoning either the mother or daughter as witnesses. The defense may put them on the stand, but whatever they say, I can't see it being enough to prove that Kuraki feels remorse for his earlier crime. After all, the Asabas were not the direct victims of Kuraki's past crime. The victim was—" Imahashi flicked open the file in his hand and skimmed though it. "Here we are. The victim was Shozo Haitani. If Kuraki felt any genuine remorse, surely the logical thing would be for him to go and apologize to Haitani's family? So far, the defense has presented me with no evidence of him doing so. That's a point I plan to emphasize in court."

The prosecutor had so many tricks at his disposal. Mirei knew she was being manipulated, but she could not find the words to protest.

"If you're prepared to accept my approach, then could we start the meeting and discuss the trial? I don't have a lot of time," Imahashi said, glancing at his watch.

Mirei did not agree, but she had no choice but to go along with him. Besides, she knew from her father that preparing for a trial was very time-consuming.

"Please, be frank with me," Imahashi said. "As the victim, what sort of questions do you want to put to the defendant in the trial?"

Mirei glanced over at Sakuma. The lawyer gave her a big nod of encouragement.

Mirei inhaled. "We want to ask: What sort of person do you see yourself as? Are you a remorseful person who sincerely wants to apologize to us, the victim's family, who have suffered so much because of you? Or are you a completely selfish person who killed someone to prevent your past crime being revealed? If you are in fact both of those things, then which face will you show us, and what will you do for us, the newly bereaved victim's family?"

When she got to the end of her prepared speech, Mirei looked at the prosecutor to gauge his reaction.

There was a frown on Imahashi's face. Then, still frowning, he huffed. Mirei was just starting to worry that he must have disliked her speech, when he clapped his hands. "That was wonderful," he said.

26

HE WALKED ALONG the one-way street, apartments and offices lining either side, leading to a junction with a much wider road. There was no traffic light, just a stop sign. A small truck came to a brief halt, then made a cautious left turn.

Kazuma kept on walking and turned right onto the main street. On the wide sidewalk, a jogger in a windbreaker glided past a woman pushing a stroller.

Right in front of him, there was a bridge: the Kiyosu Bridge spanning the Sumida River. The windows of the buildings on the opposite shore glowed red in the setting sun.

He paused to take a deep breath, then resumed walking. It had been his own idea to visit the place. Having come this far, he couldn't turn back now.

Kazuma trudged silently forward, his eyes fixed on the ground. It was only when he reached the far end of the bridge that he raised his head and looked to the right.

A path ran just below the river embankment. The Sumida River Terrace.

Finding the staircase, he went down. He remembered that it had been mentioned in Tatsuro's statement.

Kazuma pulled out his smartphone and found the photograph of the murder scene that Horibe had sent him along with a detailed map.

Horibe had warned Kazuma against visiting the scene of the crime when he had announced his intention over the phone. "I really don't think it's a good idea." When Kazuma asked why, he brusquely said that it was a meaningless waste of time.

"Tatsuro has to face the crime, not you. You'd be better off thinking of how you can get back to a normal life."

"But I want to see the place for myself at least once. I need to visualize the crime and the place where he committed it. *Please*."

He heard Horibe sigh. "I can't stop you if that's what you want to do. But let me just give you a quick word of advice. Walk straight through the place. Give it a casual glance, and then get out."

"You're saying I shouldn't linger?"

"A minute or two is fine, but there's nothing to be gained from agonizing over it. You're not planning to bring flowers or anything like that, are you?"

"It hadn't occurred to me, no."

"Good. Because that's absolutely something to avoid doing. You don't know who could be watching. If word leaked out that a member of the perpetrator's family was placing offerings at the murder scene, there'd be hell to pay. Public opinion is harsh and brutal. It would be mocked as theater designed to get a more lenient sentence for your father." There was an edge to Horibe's voice. Kazuma read between the lines. *Don't make waves when I'm busy prepping for the trial.*

"Okay, I get it. I'll be careful."

Kazuma made his way along the riverside terrace, his phone held out in front of him.

He came to a halt. *This is the place in the picture.* He glanced around. The way it looked now, no one would ever imagine this place had been the site of a murder. At the time, the place had been a dead end because of construction work; now, with the work finished, people strolled right by.

Tatsuro would never have chosen this place if it had been this busy. But what would he have done instead? He'd have had to find somewhere else. Given that the murder took place before seven in the evening, finding a place without any witnesses would have been a challenge. Had he failed to find anywhere suitable, Kazuma supposed, Tatsuro might have abandoned his plan, at least for one day.

Kazuma started to feel angry about the construction. Why hadn't anyone stopped to think that blocking the place off and diminishing its visibility could create a safe haven for crime? Even as he had the thought, Kazuma knew that his resentment was nothing more than deflection.

Looking around, Kazuma couldn't help thinking Tatsuro really had found the ideal location.

Tatsuro claimed to have found the place between arriving in Tokyo and meeting up with Shiraishi. That seemed a bit too convenient. Had he really come across this place completely at random?

At the same time, Kazuma didn't believe that Tatsuro had scoped out the place in advance. Had he done so, his movements that day would have been different.

Tatsuro said that after getting to Tokyo from Nagoya, he had walked from Tokyo Station to Otemachi Station, where he had caught the subway to Monzen-Nakacho. But if he was already familiar with the river terrace, then surely he would have taken the train to Suitengumae Station? The river terrace was about one and a half kilometers' walk from Monzen-Nakacho, but only half that distance from Suitengumae Station. Today, Kazuma himself had walked not from Monzen-Nakacho but from Suitengumae.

It seemed unlikely that Tatsuro was trying to conceal the fact that he'd chosen the location in advance. Why would someone who had made a full confession and was prepared to face the death penalty lie about that trivial point?

No, just as it said in the statement, Tatsuro must have traveled to Monzen-Nakacho Station and only then started looking for a suitable place for murder. It was just a twist of fate that construction work had turned this into a blind spot in the bustling metropolis.

As he gazed at the Sumida River floating placidly by, Kazuma couldn't help but wonder. Had the murder *really* happened here? No matter how hard he tried, he couldn't picture Tatsuro, his own father, stabbing someone with a large kitchen knife.

A pleasure boat slid by in front of him. Kazuma had never been on one himself. What did the terrace look like from a boat? he wondered. By seven, the sun would have already gone down, so it would probably be impossible to make out people on the shore. Surely, though, no killer would go through with the crime if a boat was passing by at that moment? That must mean there hadn't been any boats on the river at the time. Another piece of bad luck.

Just as he was about to head back to the stairs, he noticed an approaching figure. It was a young woman in a gray coat. He drew a sharp breath when he saw what she was carrying: A white lily. A powerful sense of premonition gripped him, constricting his chest.

The woman shot a brief glance in Kazuma's direction, then looked away.

Kazuma started walking. The sight of the woman preyed on his mind. Unable to prevent himself, he turned back for a second look before mounting the stairs.

She was placing the lily on the ground. Then she knelt down in front of the flower, pressed her palms together, and closed her eyes. No doubt about it, she was praying.

Kazuma stood there, rooted to the spot. He had to get out of there, but his legs simply refused to obey him.

Although she only prayed for ten seconds or so, it felt like an age to Kazuma. When she finished her prayer and looked up, he was still there, staring at her.

They were about twenty meters apart. Their eyes met briefly, then they both looked away at the same moment. Although it was only a split second, Kazuma felt violently unsettled. He walked off at a rapid pace, too frightened to look back.

Even after he got up to the main road, he kept on walking. He was kicking himself for forgetting Horibe's warning and lingering too long. But no—he hadn't forgotten; he just couldn't be oblivious to that woman.

Who was she? There weren't many people likely to leave flowers and say a prayer in such a place. The location of Kensuke Shiraishi's murder hadn't been made public.

Guessing from her age, she was probably Kensuke Shiraishi's daughter. Horibe had been notified that Shiraishi's family intended to take advantage of the victim participation system, and documents listed Shiraishi's daughter as the family representative.

What had she been praying for? Certainly not just for her dead father to rest in peace. Perhaps, with the trial about to start, she had been vowing to settle the score. The defendant had admitted his guilt, so there was no dispute about the basic facts of the case. What would constitute a win? Was she hoping to secure the death penalty?

Overwhelmed by emotion, Kazuma struggled to catch his breath. He couldn't deal with the idea that the woman hoped his father would be sentenced to death.

Had she guessed that he was the son of the man accused of the murder? If she had, what did she think about him, and how did she feel toward him? Would she loathe any relative of the man who had murdered her father as much as she must loathe the man himself?

Kazuma stopped and looked around. Where was he? In his agitated state, he had walked to some unfamiliar place. He pulled out his phone to check on his location.

He was far from the Sumida River now—near Asunaro.

Should I visit them? Kazuma thought. *I'd like to ask them what Tatsuro did in their restaurant.*

Although the thought was little more than a whim, it struck Kazuma as a brilliant idea. He started walking with a new lightness in his step. Kazuma knew exactly what was really going on. He was desperate to forget the woman praying at the crime scene—she had burned herself into his mind and refused to leave it.

Kazuma made his way along the busy sidewalk until he reached the restaurant. Being on his own today, he felt slightly diffident. He hesitated to climb up the stairs.

Screwing up his courage, he was making his way toward the stairs when a young man came down them. No, not a young man. He was a teenager—mid-teens, probably. His hair was spiky, his face boyish and his frame slim. He was wearing a parka with a gilet on top.

A woman appeared behind. Kazuma started. It was Orie Asaba.

Orie turned to the boy and said something. Without making eye contact, the boy nodded a few times sulkily, then stalked off. Orie watched him as he receded into the distance.

Eventually, she spun around and had just begun to climb the stairs, when she glanced in Kazuma's direction. She froze in her tracks. Embarrassed, she looked down at the ground.

Kazuma's breathing was rapid and shallow as he walked up to her. "You're Orie Asaba, aren't you?"

Orie lifted her head. "Yes," she said in a barely audible voice.

"My name is Kazuma Kuraki. I'm Tatsuro Kuraki's son."

"I know."

"I know you must be busy, but I wondered if I could have a quick word. Have you got a couple of minutes?"

Orie's lips moved feebly, but no sound came out. She was clearly discombobulated.

"All right," she finally said. "You'd better come up to the restaurant. . . . We're busy cleaning up for the night."

When they got to the second floor, Orie told him to wait a moment and went into the restaurant alone. He guessed she was explaining the situation to her mother.

A moment later, the sliding door was pulled open. Orie nodded at him. "Come on in."

Kazuma thanked her and stepped inside.

Everything in the restaurant was neat and tidy, ready for the next day's batch of customers. Yoko Asaba was standing behind the counter. Kazuma walked over and apologized for disturbing her at her place of work.

"You were here a few days ago with a friend, weren't you?" Yoko said. "I didn't realize, but Orie told me after you'd left."

Kazuma turned and looked at Orie.

"So you *did* recognize me. I thought so."

"I realized as soon as you came in. *He looks like Mr. Kuraki*, I thought, so I kept my eye on you. Some of your mannerisms were identical to your father's."

"I'm sorry. I was too cowardly to introduce myself. I assumed you must hate my father, now that you know what he did."

The mother and daughter exchanged a look. It was Yoko, the mother, who spoke.

"The prosecutor summoned us. He was the one who told us that Mr. Kuraki was the true culprit in the old Higashi-Okazaki murder. We were shocked. Of course. To be honest, we don't really understand why Kuraki didn't hand himself over to the police at the time. Our lives would have been a lot less difficult if he had. We wouldn't have lost a husband and a father, and we wouldn't have been scapegoated and had people talk about us behind our backs."

"I know. It's awful. I'd like to apologize on my father's behalf." Kazuma made a deep bow.

"No need for that. You're his son. You have not done anything wrong."

Noticing that Yoko was making her way out from behind the counter, Kazuma straightened up again.

"Why don't you sit down?" Orie said, indicating a chair. Kazuma thanked her and sat down opposite Yoko.

"Given all that happened, there are certainly things I can blame Mr. Kuraki for. At the same time, there are other things I have no problem with."

Kazuma blinked and looked at Yoko questioningly. "Like what?"

"Mr. Kuraki was always very kind to us. Whenever he came here, he would always discreetly inquire how the business was doing. If I said things were a little on the slow side, he would order the most expensive things on the menu. And he always used to say, 'If you've got any problems, ask for my advice. Don't be shy.' We always wondered why he chose to come all the way to our place from Nagoya. After all, he could easily get all the Nagoya and Mikawa dishes he wanted back at home!"

"But you can't *not* hate my father. You must detest him."

"That's the funny thing. Weird though it may be, I don't feel a smidgen of hate for him. How should I put it? It still hasn't registered; it doesn't feel real. The prosecutor said the same thing as you. 'You have every right to loathe Kuraki: It's because of him that your husband came under suspicion and ended up taking his own life.' The thing is, though, people's feelings don't change from one moment to the next like that. Besides—and I know this is going to sound strange—as I see it, it's thanks to Mr. Kuraki that I was finally saved."

"You were saved?"

Kazuma was taken aback. Had he misheard her?

"In my case, the people I've reserved my hatred for over the last thirty-something years are the police. I still believe that it's them who killed my husband. They arrested him and tortured him, even though he was innocent. They claim not to have forced his confession out of him, but I know that's a lie. My husband had a short fuse, but he was also as stubborn as a mule, and he hated lying. There's no way he would ever kill another human being. No, I know why he hanged himself. It was because he couldn't stand the psychological torture the police put him through and chose to die as a means of protest. The police have never once apologized to me. They painted him as a criminal and claimed he died by suicide only because he realized he could not escape justice. It was the same story with public opinion. Even though there was no actual proof of my husband's guilt, everyone chose to see us as the family of a murderer. That's why we left. But there are mean people everywhere. They spread nasty rumors and destroyed our happiness just when we had finally secured it—"

"Mother!" Orie interrupted sharply. She was shaking her head to warn her that she was being indiscreet.

Yoko sighed. "The truth is that I have lived my whole life in shame. Nobody who knows about our past is prepared to take our side. It's so ironic. Of course, the only person who knew what had really happened was Mr. Kuraki. And he could sense how much we had suffered and did his best to offer us moral support. That's true of his motivations for committing this latest crime too—he did it because he didn't want his relationship with us to be destroyed, right? I think he really did want to apologize and make amends to us."

"If he really wanted to apologize, don't you think that he ought to have told you everything a lot earlier?"

Yoko grimaced. "Of course I do. But that's unrealistic. When you get to my age, you know that human beings are weak creatures."

She expressed her opinion so firmly that Kazuma averted his eyes in embarrassment.

"Mr. Kuraki could have still kept it secret."

Kazuma was puzzled by Yoko's remark. "Sorry, kept what secret?"

"The Higashi-Okazaki murder. He could have invented a completely different motive for this more recent crime—that they'd gotten into an argument over something stupid, I don't know. The penalty for that would probably be less severe. But no, he made a full confession. Because he did that, I was finally able to clear my husband of the false charge. A newspaper just called me a few minutes ago. They asked, 'Can we interview you about your years of suffering?' I'm fielding calls like that all the time now. Some of the reporters even show up at our apartment. I turn them all away, but still there's no doubt that the stain on our name has been wiped clean. That's what I meant when I said Mr. Kuraki saved us.

"But honestly." Yoko leaned on the counter and tipped her head to one side. "Do you think it's weird for me to see things like that? The prosecutor said he couldn't understand my point of view."

"I don't know. Not sure I'm qualified to say."

As Kazuma groped for the right words, Yoko smiled and said. "No, of course not. You're right. I apologize for putting you on the spot."

Horibe was right, Kazuma thought. *The Asabas might testify on Tatsuro's side.*

"Hey." Orie shot a look at Kazuma. "You said you wanted to hear what we had to say. Is this the sort of thing you had in mind?"

"It is," Kazuma replied. "I wanted to know what my father was like when he came here. It really does seem like my father was trying to atone for his past crime."

"Do you think there was another reason?" Yoko said. "The prosecutor did ask me one odd question."

"Odd how?"

"He asked me if Mr. Kuraki was, well, courting my daughter. The detective asked me the same thing. They seem to think that Mr. Kuraki was coming here for her." Yoko jerked her chin in Orie's direction. "Naturally, I said that nothing of the kind had ever happened."

So the prosecutor suspected that Tatsuro had an ulterior motive for visiting the restaurant. It struck Kazuma as a pessimistic point of view, but being cynical was probably part of the prosecutor's job.

"I interpreted my father's conduct more as self-indulgence than atonement, but I feel a bit better based on what you've just told me. Thank you." As he said this, Kazuma rose to his feet and bowed. "I'm sorry to have imposed, especially when you're busy shutting up shop."

"Have you been to visit him yet?" Orie asked.

"No," Kazuma said. "I'm told my father doesn't want to see me. That he's too ashamed of himself."

"Really?" Orie frowned.

"It's important to take care of yourself," Yoko said.

"Of course. I'll ask his lawyer to relay your message to him."

Yoko shook her head slowly. "That's not what I meant. I meant you. Things can't be easy for you either."

"Oh . . . uh . . . well . . ."

"Listen, I have a pretty good idea what the immediate family of the perpetrator of a crime goes through. I went through it myself."

Unsure how to respond, Kazuma lowered his eyes.

"Kazuma? It is Kazuma, right?" Yoko went on. "It's okay just to disengage when it all gets to be too much. Shut your eyes. Cover your ears. We all have our limits."

"Thanks. I'll keep that in mind. I'd better be going," Kazuma said as he made for the door.

He turned back and looked at Orie before going down the stairs.

"I saw you saying goodbye to a young man just now . . ."

"That was my son," Orie said, rather warily.

"Oh, you're married?"

Kazuma was surprised. No husband had been mentioned anywhere in his father's testimony.

"Not anymore. My ex got custody of our son, but he sometimes comes around to say hi."

"Oh, right."

Kazuma felt guilty asking such an intrusive question, and he awkwardly said goodbye.

It was only when he exited the building and was walking along the sidewalk that he realized he had not merely been tactless but had touched on a very delicate subject indeed. He recalled something Yoko had said. *"But there are mean people everywhere. They spread nasty rumors and destroyed our happiness just when we had finally secured it—"*

She must have been referring to what her daughter had gone through. The happiness she "had finally secured" was to have married and had a child and a loving family. Then maybe some rumors about her father got out, resulting in her divorce. That would also explain why the father had gotten custody of their son. Kazuma turned around and looked up at the building. The lettering of the name *Asunaro* on the sign seemed a little faded in his eyes.

27

Mirei was a little lost. A taxi happened to drive by, so she hailed it. She apologized to the taxi driver for asking to be taken somewhere so close. Luckily, he did not mind.

She had not been in the cab for long when she regretted her decision. The driver was sticking to the main roads and intersections. Tatsuro Kuraki, who would have been doing his best to keep a low profile, would never have chosen this route. *Next time, I will walk the whole thing*, she thought.

The taxi took less than ten minutes to reach Monzen-Nakacho. Her father would probably have paid the seven-hundred-yen fare with a thousand-yen note and refused the change, but Mirei paid with her smart travel card.

She exited the taxi and began walking, looking around as she did so. It was her first time in this part of Tokyo. Despite its historic old-Edo vibes, she knew that the whole area had been burned to the ground during World War II air raids.

She checked her location on her phone. She quickly reached her destination, a two-story café.

She glanced at the far side of the street before going in. There it was. Asunaro.

After buying a caffè latte downstairs, she made her way up to the second floor and sat at the far end of the counter against a small window. According to the records, her father, Kensuke, had come to this café twice, staying over two hours on his second visit. No one knew exactly why, but the assumption was that he'd come to keep an eye on Asunaro across the road. Having heard about the two women from Kuraki, Kensuke might have been scoping them out.

If Kensuke had indeed heard about the women from Kuraki, his interest made sense—but why should he have come *twice*? Had he made a second foray after failing to learn anything on his first visit? Wouldn't he have been better off just going straight to Asunaro the second time around? He didn't need to reveal his identity. If he'd just acted like a regular customer, he could have seen the mother and daughter. He couldn't seriously expect to learn anything significant from this sort of distance.

Mirei was gazing at the building across the street as she pondered this question. A figure dressed in a blue down jacket came to a stop just outside it. Mirei caught her breath.

It was the same man—

Today was the third time she had gone to place a flower where her father died. Despite trying to be fast and discreet, she always worried about being noticed.

And today, when she went down to the Sumida River Terrace, there had been a man wearing a down jacket near the crime scene, lost in thought.

He had marched off as soon as Mirei started walking in his direction, which only made her more suspicious.

After she had placed her flower on the ground and said a prayer, Mirei had turned to find the man still hovering nearby, looking in her direction. Their eyes had met, just for a moment.

He had to have some connection to the crime. If nothing else, he knew the location of Kensuke Shiraishi's murder, a piece of confidential information that the prosecutor had warned Mirei and her mother not to share.

Now that same man reappeared here outside Asunaro. Why?

At this point, a woman and a teen emerged from the building. They exchanged a few words, and then the young man walked off.

The next moment, something unexpected happened. The man in the down jacket spoke to the woman and, after a brief exchange, the two of them vanished inside the building.

Mirei's mind was racing. Wasn't that the daughter of the proprietor of Asunaro? So who was this man, and why had he come to see her?

Could it be—

Could it be Tatsuro Kuraki's son? There were rumors about him floating around online, as a gossipy friend had told her. Apparently, he worked for a well-known advertising company. According to the same friend, a photo of the son's face from his high school days was also circulating. Mirei hadn't seen it, but she had seen a photo of Tatsuro Kuraki among the documents Azusa Sakuma had given her. It was a gentle and intelligent face, not at all what a killer should look like.

Although she had only caught the briefest glimpse of the man in the down jacket, she thought she had detected a resemblance to Tatsuro Kuraki.

If the man was Kuraki's son, then what was he doing at Asunaro?

Mirei recalled something that Sakuma had said. The Asabas bore Kuraki no ill will and might even appear in court as character witnesses for the defense.

Had the son come to ask them to do that? No, that had to be the lawyer's responsibility, not something the perpetrator's family would get involved in.

The perpetrator's family—Mirei ruminated on the phrase.

A perpetrator's family had done nothing wrong. They bore no guilt. Perhaps a parent ought to feel a degree of responsibility for the actions of their children. But for a child to suffer for the sins of the father was simply unfair.

Mirei imagined that Tatsuro Kuraki's son was struggling. There were thousands of people online looking for someone to blame. There were countless posts attacking Mirei's father, and he was the murder *victim*, for goodness' sake! The most popular comment was that "he got what was coming to him." Tatsuro Kuraki had confessed his past crime to Kensuke

Shiraishi, and it was the lawyer's responsibility to respect confidentiality. For Shiraishi to pressure him to come clean publicly was an act of betrayal, and he was a fool not to recognize he was driving Kuraki into a corner. There were also abusive posts directed at Mirei and her mother. She had skimmed then. "I would call this coercive justice. I bet Shiraishi's wife and daughter don't see it like that, though. I guarantee that when the trial gets underway, they'll be holding press conferences and milking the sympathy."

How stupid can you get? She did her best to stay off the internet because of all those thoughtless comments.

If people related to the victim were treated this badly, then anyone associated with the perpetrator must be going through hell. Murder was a dreadful, horrible thing that caused nothing but misery.

Mirei finished off her caffè latte, which had gone cold, and rose to her feet. Her visit hadn't yielded what she'd been hoping for. She would not return to this café, she decided.

She was about to head to Monzen-Nakacho Station, when she glanced at the building on the opposite side of the road. She started. The man in the blue jacket had reemerged. He was walking along with his eyes fixed on the ground, also heading in the direction of the subway.

As she made her way along the street, Mirei eyed the man on the opposite sidewalk. He did not seem to have noticed her. His head was still bowed and he walked with a heavy tread.

If she kept walking to the station, she might bump into him. If they ended up in proximity, he would probably recognize her. Then what should she do? How should she behave?

She still hadn't decided what to do when she reached the subway entrance. She went down the stairs. He had to be going down the stairs in the entrance on the other side of the street at the same time. They might literally run into one another!

She reached the bottom of the stairs and set off down a long underground walkway. The ticket barrier leading into the station was around the corner. Beyond that, there was another underground walkway, where he would presumably appear.

Mirei took her smart travel card out of her bag and slowly walked toward the ticket barrier. She couldn't stop herself from glancing down the passageway before she tapped her card on the sensor.

There he was. He was walking toward her, looking ahead. It was perfect timing; their eyes met. He came to a sudden stop.

Averting her eyes, Mirei pushed through the ticket barrier. She found the sign for Nakano-bound trains and went down to the platform. A train was arriving. Although she knew that she could probably catch it if she broke into a run, she deliberately opted not to. She was hoping he would catch up to her. Why, she did not know.

The doors of the train slid shut just as she stepped down onto the platform. Mirei walked the length of a single subway car, then came to a stop.

As she turned toward the train tracks, the blue down jacket was in the corner of her eye. He neared, then finally came to a stop nearby.

"Excuse me," he said timidly. "Are you related to Kensuke Shiraishi?"

Struggling to keep her breathing under control, Mirei turned slightly in his direction. "I am," she said, without making eye contact.

"I thought so. . . . I'm the son of Tatsuro Kuraki," he said softly.

Mirei glanced at him. "Oh, really?" she said, then looked away again.

"I must offer, uh . . . Honestly, I don't know how I should even begin to apologize. . . . I, uh . . ."

"Please, let's not do this here," Mirei said. She was startled at how harsh her voice sounded despite her best efforts to speak gently.

"Oh, I'm sorry."

He lapsed into silence. He stood there without moving away. The seconds ticked by in uncomfortable silence. Mirei felt planted to the ground.

"You were at that restaurant," Mirei said, gazing at the tracks. "Asunaro, I mean."

"How do you know that?"

"I was in a café on the opposite side of the street. I just happened to catch sight of you."

"That's a surprise."

"Was your visit connected to your preparations for the trial?"

"No, not at all. I went to ask the Asabas about my father. You know, this whole thing, I just can't believe it. No matter how many times people talk me through the details, I just can't believe my father would do anything like this. I can't stop thinking that perhaps he made the whole thing up. That's why I decided to try to do a little investigating of my own," he said. "Sorry. I shouldn't have said that. Just pretend I didn't."

Unsure how to react, Mirei said nothing. She did not feel uncomfortable. Somehow, she knew he was sincere. Any normal person whose father was accused of murder completely out of the blue would have their doubts. To suspect that some kind of mistake had been made was the most natural thing in the world.

An announcement that the next train was about to arrive came over the loudspeaker.

A moment later, the train pulled in and the doors slid open in front of them. After waiting for a few passengers to exit, Mirei got on, followed by Kuraki's son. They ended up standing next to each other. The train was crowded, so it would be ridiculous to make a big deal of going and standing somewhere else. Mirei stayed put.

"Where's home for you?" she asked.

"I live in Koenji. I just remembered something I've got to do, though, so I'm going to get off at Kayabacho, the next stop."

"Oh yes?"

Mirei herself would change trains at Nihonbashi, one stop after Kayabacho. She was wondering whether to share that information, but he didn't ask.

She could feel the train slowing down. They would be in Kayabacho any second now.

The train emerged into the station. "Well, I'll say goodbye," he said quietly.

"Um," Mirei said. Her eyes met his, but this time she did not look away. "I don't think your father's telling the truth either. What he said—that's just not who my father is."

Kuraki's son's eyes widened in surprise. He struggled for words. The train doors slid open before he could figure out what to say and he exited the train without a word.

The doors closed. The train left. Through the window, she could see him looking after her like a lost puppy.

Maybe I'm looking at him the same way, Mirei thought. *Everyone believes that the true perpetrator has confessed and that the truth of the crime has been laid bare. They're planning to conduct the whole trial based upon that supposed "truth." But some of us don't accept that version of the truth.* Until now, Mirei had thought that she and her mother were the only ones. Now there was someone else: someone from the perpetrator's family.

She'd probably never see Kuraki's son again. If she did, it would be just a fleeting glance across the courtroom. If they did bump into one another again, it would probably be a repeat of today.

Mirei frowned. She had caught herself planning when to next leave flowers for her father. Why did that make her feel so strangely agitated?

28

KAZUMA PICKED UP a taxi at the station. He felt a brief stab of worry when he told the driver to take him to Sasame. Would he make the connection with the murder in Tokyo?

"Sasame's not the smallest place. Where d'you want exactly?" asked the elderly looking driver, speaking with a thick local accent.

"The District 3 intersection."

"Oh yeah, I know the place," the driver said disinterestedly.

The Kuraki house was a bit far from the intersection. Kazuma, however, was afraid that specifying an address too near his father's house might clue the driver in.

Was he being paranoid? Kazuma had no way of knowing how conscious the local community was that a Sasame resident had been arrested for murder.

Luckily, the driver was not the talkative type. Kazuma briefly considered asking if anything unusual had happened in the neighborhood recently, but ultimately, he decided against it. Sometimes you had to let sleeping dogs lie.

He looked out of the taxi window. It was his first time back in two years, since attending a distant relative's memorial service. The rest of the family had given him a hard time about never coming to visit, then grilled him about what his plans were for his father's old age. Tatsuro himself had said, "It will work out fine, so just leave Kazuma alone." His other relatives looked rather annoyed, given that they had only brought it up for his sake.

Kazuma had not heard anything from his relatives. According to Horibe, Tatsuro had sent letters to them as well, though what he had said in them Kazuma could only suspect: It was likely the same thing Tatsuro had said to him. An apology for his crimes and permission to wash their hands of him.

Families in the area tended to be very close-knit. The Kurakis, no exception to this rule, were always getting together for some reason or another. Before moving up to Tokyo, Kazuma had been forced to participate in all of these family events.

Just because Tatsuro had sent those letters didn't mean that he, as Tatsuro's only son, had the right to ignore his relatives. The proper thing to do would be to visit them all and make a formal apology. Right now, though, he didn't have the strength of will.

He wasn't back to make amends but to investigate. He wanted to learn more about his father's past to understand what really happened.

Kazuma's childhood memories of his father were still fresh in his mind. Tatsuro had been conscientious, kind, and caring. He was solid as a rock, someone that the whole family could depend on. Was he really supposed to believe that was a mask hiding the face of a killer?

A mistake. It has to be. The thought ran obsessively through his mind.

The fact that Tatsuro was involved in the 1984 murder appeared to be true. According to the *World News Weekly* article, Kazuma had discovered the body. That much at least was probably correct, given that the journalist's source was a onetime work colleague of Tatsuro's.

But why, if he really was the culprit, had Tatsuro not been arrested back then? In mystery novels and detective shows, the person who found the body went under the microscope. Tatsuro claimed that the police hadn't treated him as a suspect because they had no real evidence against him. Kazuma found it hard to believe that the police would be so quick to give someone a pass. The whole country would be awash in unsolved cases if that was how the police investigated.

No, something wasn't right. The more he thought about it, the more convinced he was that Tatsuro wasn't telling the truth.

He suddenly remembered a remark someone had made, a remark that was seared into his brain.

"I don't think your father's telling the truth either. That's just not who my father is." It was the last thing Kensuke Shiraishi's daughter had said to him.

What did she mean by "not who my father is"? It sounded to Kazuma as though she disagreed with the presentation of Shiraishi in Tatsuro's statement.

Kazuma, however, couldn't recall any remarks that were actually critical of Kensuke Shiraishi. The impression he had gotten from the statement was of a good, kind man with a strong sense of justice. That had to mean that Mirei was having trouble accepting the statement's account of Kensuke Shiraishi's behavior.

Shiraishi was described as putting pressure on Tatsuro to come clean. What she'd been trying to tell him was that her father would never do a thing like that.

Kazuma belatedly realized something blindingly obvious: being related to a murder victim was excruciating. For a beloved family member to be killed was bad enough, so wanting to find a motive for the crime that made sense was only natural. Of course, the victim's family members would want to read the perpetrator's statement and question everything. Normally, that was the focus of the trial, but as things stood now, the trial was going to be based on an assumption that everything in Tatsuro's statement was true. Perhaps that was the reason Shiraishi's daughter was so angry.

An extraordinary sensation took hold of Kazuma as he pictured her face. Although their positions were so different—he, the son of the perpetrator; she, the daughter of the victim—he had the sense that they were both in pursuit of the same thing. She would probably be furious to learn he felt that way, he reflected.

His mind was still racing when he reached his destination. Before getting out of the taxi, Kazuma donned a face mask. There was a risk of bumping into someone he knew—plenty of his old elementary and junior high school classmates still lived in the area. Luckily, it was winter. Anyone in a face mask outdoors in summer would stand out like a sore thumb. Flu infection rates were high at the moment—that was good news for him, too.

Only after taking a careful look around did he head for the family house. He felt like a spy sneaking into enemy territory.

Everyone in town traveled by car, so there were fewer pedestrians compared to Tokyo. Even so, there were still some. Whenever anyone came toward him, he covered the upper part of his face by pretending to adjust his hair.

He had told Horibe over the phone about his plan to visit, justifying it by claiming to be worried about the now-empty house. However, Horibe's reaction had hardly been positive, just like when Kazuma had visited the crime scene.

"It's your family house and not my place to advise you against going back. Still, you should prepare for a possibly unpleasant experience."

Horibe explained that the police had searched the house and seized any evidence they found that would corroborate Tatsuro's statement.

"The prosecutor doesn't seem to have found anything they could use in court. The police search did, however, make everyone in the neighborhood aware of the arrest. If you go back, there's every chance that people will harass you. You know, say you've given the place a bad name, things like that."

"I know. That won't faze me."

"The best thing to do is not be noticed. I really hope you can check on the house without any trouble and make it safely back to Tokyo."

Kazuma thanked the lawyer, although inside he felt conflicted. Every time they spoke, Horibe always gave the same message: "Don't do anything uncalled for. Keep a low profile. Be discreet."

Kazuma had nearly reached the family home and was feeling more anxious than ever. He glanced around as he walked toward the house. He was almost level with it when he heard the sound of voices. He quickly walked on by.

After going around the next corner, he retraced his steps and approached the house for a second time. Seeing that there was no one else on the sidewalk, he dashed up to the front door and jammed the key into the lock. The noise of the key turning in the lock sounded horribly loud. He opened the door and slipped inside. After clicking the lock on the door behind him, he breathed heavily. This was the most nerve-racking homecoming of his life.

Once his heart had slowed a little, he slipped off his shoes and stepped into the house properly.

He had lived there until his late teens. Now, as a full-grown man, it seemed smaller. Had the corridor really been this narrow? He felt as if he were seeing it for the first time.

He looked around the living room. The incense-like smell that permeated the house brought on a surge of painful emotions. The house where he had spent such a happy childhood now felt sad and abandoned.

He went over to a cabinet against one wall of the room. The top shelf had small, wooden sliding doors, the middle shelf was visible through glass doors, and the bottom part had sliding wooden doors and some drawers. The teabowls and teapots on display had not changed since Kazuma was a boy. He recalled Tatsuro grumbling about how nowadays everyone drank ready-made tea in plastic bottles and no one bothered to brew it properly in the pot anymore.

He opened the doors of the top shelf. Inside, it was crammed with canisters of green tea, English tea bags, and pots of jam. He examined one of the jams. Unopened, it was more than ten years past its sell-by date. The same was probably true of the green tea and the English tea bags.

Finally, he slid open the bottom doors. Inside were rows of files and notebooks. He pulled out a notebook at random. It was an old household account book. He recognized his mother's handwriting. Why she always insisted on keeping several decades' worth of records was a mystery; perhaps his mother had regarded them as quasi-diaries.

Everything in the cabinet belonged to Kazuma's mother, not Tatsuro. The police must have been disappointed.

Kazuma was replacing the file on the shelf when, to his surprise, he noticed a book with a thick spine right in one of the far corners. *Perhaps not everything here is my mother's after all*, he thought.

It was a photo album. Not a simple one but one with a rather ornate cover. He remembered leafing through it as a boy, but he hadn't seen it since, because the family had long ago stopped taking commemorative pictures.

He slowly flipped open the front cover. The picture on the first page was of his parents' marriage. Tatsuro, dressed in a hakama, was standing beside Kazuma's mother, who was seated in a chair with her hair done in the traditional wedding bunkin-takashimada style.

His mother's name was Chisato. She had worked for the same company as Tatsuro, which is where the two of them had met.

How young they were! The colors in the picture had faded. On one side, someone had written their wedding date. It was two years before Kazuma had been born.

There were several pictures of Chisato and Tatsuro on vacation together on the following pages. Behind them was one of those massive ropes used to cordon off sacred precincts. "Izumo Taisha Grand Shrine" read the caption off to one side.

Kazuma remembered his father telling him that he and Chisato had gone to Izumo Taisha Grand Shrine for their honeymoon.

On the next page was a photograph of a naked baby lying on a futon. It was Kazuma himself, of course. After their honeymoon, the next big family event commemorated in the album was his birth.

There followed a run of pictures of him with his parents at the seaside, mountains, parks—

He came across a photo from Christmas. Flanked by his parents, he was grinning at the camera in a Santa Claus costume. The date printed on the margin of the picture was December 24, 1984.

1984—that was the year of the murder.

Kazuma scrutinized the picture. Tatsuro was sporting a pair of reindeer antlers on his head and looked delighted. It was hard to see a murderer in him there.

Kazuma turned over the page. His hand froze. What on earth was this group photograph? He and his parents were standing in front of the house with a cluster of ten or so men. It was dated May 22, 1988. Beside the photograph, someone had written in a firm hand: "Moving into our very own dream house."

Moving into this house was one of Kazuma's first memories. Men carrying loads of boxes in from a truck was seared into his brain. He had always thought the men were professional movers, but the people in the picture were actually Tatsuro's workmates. When Tatsuro was still working, he would sometimes have to go out on Sundays to help his junior colleagues move. That was the norm in Japanese companies back then. Maybe, thought Kazuma, it helped build team spirit.

There were a few more family photos after that, but pictures stopped featuring both his parents after Kazuma's elementary school enrollment ceremony. From then on, it was all school photos: field trips, sports, and summer camps. There was the occasional picture of him paddling in the sea or making the ritual shrine visit at New Year's with his parents, but usually it was just him and his mother. Presumably, because Tatsuro was behind the camera.

Kazuma put the album back. The photographs had provoked a bittersweet nostalgia. But he hadn't come to Nagoya to take a trip down memory lane; he was here to look into Tatsuro's past.

But what exactly should he be looking for? A diary would be the best source, but he had never heard his father mention keeping one. Besides, if there had been such a thing, wouldn't the police have confiscated it?

The smartest thing was just to look out for anything old. He needed to find some insight into what Tatsuro was thinking and doing three decades ago. The police might have passed over seemingly meaningless things only a family member could identify.

Kazuma went to the room off the living room. Originally, it had been a guest bedroom. Since Chisato's death, however, Tatsuro had spent most of his time there.

His parents' bedroom had originally been on the second floor, but Tatsuro couldn't be bothered going up and down stairs, and he almost never had people stay over. Kazuma's room was still up on the second floor. He wondered what sort of state it was in. Although his father probably aired it from time to time, it was probably just as messy as he had left it.

He opened the door of his father's room and flipped on the light. He took a good look around before stepping inside. The room looked less as if it had been searched and more as if someone had scrupulously tidied it up. A low table with a desk lamp on it stood on the tatami mats surrounded by a few flat cushions. He examined the bookshelf: It seemed to contain as many books as before. He opened the chest of drawers beside it. The clothes inside were all neatly folded and stacked.

The only thing out of place was one of the drawers, which was almost empty. Digging into his memory, Kazuma recalled that this was where his father kept his correspondence and his printed bank statements. The police must have taken them away.

There were a few more drawers below that one, both of which seemed emptier than before. Kazuma had no idea what had been in them.

At the bottom of one of the drawers, he found a thick brown envelope containing some old documents.

He sat down on one of the cushions and spread the contents of the envelope on the table. They turned out to be the official registration documents and deeds for the house.

There were also old statements from Tatsuro's company savings plan and a mortgage contract. Kazuma remembered his father telling him that he had borrowed the money he needed to buy the house from his employer because the interest rate they offered was much lower than a bank's. He'd mentioned something about not being able to quit his job until he'd repaid the loan.

Kazuma gave a start. A detail from the Higashi-Okazaki murder case had flashed in his mind. Tatsuro's supposed motive for the crime was his desire to conceal the fact that he had been in an auto accident.

If I lose my job, I will lose access to the funds I need to buy a house. Was that what Tatsuro had thought when he reached for the murder weapon?

These thoughts made him feel heavyhearted. He had just dropped one of the financial statements onto the table, when the doorbell rang. Surprised, he sprang to his feet.

Who can be ringing the bell at a time like this? He left his father's room and found the nearest intercom. "Hello, who's there?" he said.

"I have a delivery," said a man's voice.

"Huh? . . . Okay, I see."

Kazuma was puzzled as he replaced the receiver. Who would be sending anything to this address? Surely they would know that no one was living here.

He went to the front door. Before opening it, he looked through the peephole. There was a man in delivery company overalls. Kazuma unlocked and opened the door.

"Mr. Kuraki?"

"That's right."

"And your first name?"

"It's Kazuma."

The man nodded and touched his left ear. Kazuma noticed that he was wearing an earpiece.

The man extracted something from his jacket pocket.

"I'm from the police. We got a report that a suspicious person had broken into the house. I'm here to check."

The man held up a police badge. He swiftly put it away again, glanced behind him, and raised a hand in the air.

A van was parked just outside the gate. Two people appeared from behind it. One was a uniformed policeman, the other an older man in a hooded anorak. Kazuma started when he saw his face. It was someone he had known for years: Mr. Yoshiyama, their next-door neighbor.

"You are under no obligation to answer this question; however, I'd be grateful if you could tell me what you're doing here."

"What I'm doing here? 'Not much' is the answer. Since my father isn't here, I just came to check on the place."

"That makes sense." The policeman scrutinized first Kazuma and then the entrance hall behind him, then drew himself briskly upright. "I can confirm that there is nothing amiss. I will now withdraw. Goodbye, sir," the policeman said. He marched out of the gate and climbed into the van, which sped off, followed by the uniformed policeman, who was on a bicycle. Only Mr. Yoshiyama was left. There was a look of embarrassment on his face.

Kazuma jammed his feet into Tatsuro's sandals and went out onto the street.

"It's good to see you. It's been a long time," he said to Yoshiyama.

Yoshiyama rubbed his head. His hair was thinning. "I'm sorry. I thought some no-good had broken in, so I called the police. I had no idea that it was you."

"Were you watching from the van?"

"Yes. They asked me to identify the person who came to the door. When you came out, I told them it was you."

Once again, Kazuma became aware of his position. The Kuraki family had a special significance for the Aichi Prefectural Police and that was why they came running when someone called in even the smallest things. The policeman must have dressed as a deliveryman so that the suspect didn't make a run for it. For all Kazuma knew, there could have been more police inside the van.

"I'm really sorry. It got a bit out of hand."

"No, it's I who should be apologizing to you and the other neighbors for this business with my father."

"I was well and truly shocked, I can tell you."

A car drove by. Kazuma thought that the driver had turned to take a closer look at the two of them.

"We shouldn't stand out here talking. Come to mine for a cup of tea?"

"I don't know . . ."

"No need to stand on ceremony. It's just me, you know."

Giving in to the older man's coaxing, Kazuma went into the next-door house.

They sat down on either side of the low glass table in a living room decorated in a hybrid Japanese-Western style.

"Honestly, I still can't believe it. That old Kura from next door could have killed a man," said Yoshiyama after bringing in a freshly brewed pot of Japanese tea.

"Have you been seeing much of my father lately?"

"I have. I'm on my own here all day ever since my wife started a part-time job. Your father and I often went to neighborhood association meetings together."

"I didn't realize you two were so close. That only makes it worse. I apologize again."

Yoshiyama emitted a half groan. "Don't think you need to apologize, Kazuma. Come on, that's enough. Lift your head up."

The older man held out a teacup for him.

"I'm repeating myself, I know, but I just cannot believe it. My old friend Kura. How did things come to this? And this business of him being the real culprit in another murder from thirtysomething years back. That's not like the Kura I know."

Something suddenly occurred to Kazuma. "Didn't you used to work at the same factory as my father, Mr. Yoshiyama?"

"That's right, I did. We were both at the Anjo factory, though in different sections. Old Kura was in production, and I worked on the assembly line. We used to play cards during our lunch break."

"Did you notice anything odd about my father back then? I mean, it's hard to think that killing a man wouldn't have changed him."

"I don't know." Yoshiyama grimaced and cocked his head. "It's so long ago, I can't really remember."

"I'm not surprised."

"However," Yoshiyama said, "I suppose my not remembering means that nothing made an especially strong impression on me. Old Kura was probably his same old self."

"My father never mentioned the Higashi-Okazaki case to you, then? He never told you he'd been questioned by the police because he was the person who discovered the body or anything like that?"

"Now that you mention it, I do have a hazy memory of that, but I can't recall if Kura himself told me. Either way, didn't make much of an impression."

Yoshiyama's account sounded plausible enough. There probably hadn't been any noticeable change in Tatsuro right after the crime took place. Still, Kazuma was well aware that it did not mean his father was innocent.

"Drink your tea. It'll get cold."

"Thank you very much."

Kazuma picked up his teacup. The warmth in his fingertips seemed to express Yoshiyama's kindness and concern for him. Having steeled himself to be snubbed by the neighbors, he felt pleasantly relieved.

"What are you going to do with the house?" Yoshiyama asked. "I assume you won't be moving in yourself, will you?"

"No, I can't do that. I'll probably sell it. Whether I can find a buyer is another matter."

"Huh. I'm sorry to hear that. We got on so well as neighbors. I don't know if you've heard, but the land next to mine is being divided up into lots and sold for housing. I mentioned it to your dad."

"Oh, really?"

"Most of this area was originally developed by a home builder in the same business group as our former employer. We got a good deal on the land. That's why loads of people from the firm live around here."

"Yeah, I knew about that."

Tatsuro had told him that he used to bump into a number of his former coworkers whenever he went to the neighborhood association meetings.

"Sell the house, huh? That's a shame. Still, what can you do? I remember when your family moved in. I helped with the move, you know."

"You did?" Kazuma wondered if Yoshiyama was in the photograph he had been looking at earlier.

"You were just a little kid. Yeah, Kura bought us soba noodles two weeks in a row."

"Soba noodles? Two weeks in a row?"

"Yes, house-moving noodles."

"Why two weeks, though?"

"It was raining on the day he originally planned to move, so he had to cancel. Unfortunately, the next Sunday was an unlucky day in the Buddhist calendar, so just in case, old Kura brought a few boxes of stuff by car in the pouring rain on the first Sunday and ordered some take-out noodles, which the two of us ate together. Then the next Sunday, we did the whole move. That was when he presented the traditional moving gift of noodles to all his new neighbors. I got a packet of those too, so he treated me two weeks in a row!"

Kazuma pictured the photograph of the group from the day of the move. *So originally Tatsuro had been planning to move in a week earlier.*

But—!

Kazuma's heart started pumping hard. He put a hand to his chest. He had just had a shocking realization. Or was he misremembering things?

"What's wrong?" Yoshiyama was looking at him quizzically.

"Nothing. Look, I'd better be going. Thanks for the tea."

"Okay, you hang in there. Look after yourself. Don't lose hope."

"Thanks. I'll be fine."

Kazuma got to his feet, bowed crisply, and headed for the front door. He was grateful for Yoshiyama's kindness, but right now, there was something he needed to check.

He went back to the house, dashed into the living room, opened the tea cabinet, and pulled out the photo album. He turned to the page with the picture from the day of the move.

He was right!

The date on the photo was May 22, 1988. However, the original plan had been to move a week before that—May 15.

May 15, 1984, was the date of the murder of the financial adviser in Higashi-Okazaki.

Would Tatsuro really have chosen the anniversary of the murder as his moving day?

29

WHEN MIREI RETURNED home, there was no sign of Ayako in the living room or in the kitchen, so Mirei made her way upstairs. She could hear sounds coming from her father's study.

Ayako was sitting on the floor, removing books from the shelves and packing them into cardboard boxes.

"Hey, I'm back," Mirei said.

"Hi there." Ayako turned around. She must have heard the front door open, as there was no hint of surprise in her expression. "Just wait a minute and I'll start getting dinner ready. I've made us a stew."

"I couldn't care less what's for dinner. . . . Are you throwing out Dad's things?"

"I guess I am." Ayako scratched her head. "I don't mind leaving his things as they are; but I'm worried that unless I get rid of them, I won't be able to move on."

"You definitely don't want to leave his things as they are," said Mirei, walking into the room and sitting down on the bed. She tried to remember when it was that her parents had started sleeping in separate rooms. "Since you're going to have to get rid of his stuff anyway, sooner's probably better than later."

"That's what I thought. Plus, we don't know how long we'll stay living here." Ayako looked up at the ceiling as she said this.

Mirei was taken aback. "What do you mean?" she asked. "Are you thinking of moving?"

"Why not?" said Ayako as she clambered to her feet. "You'll be moving out at some point, and this place is too big for just one person. It's hard to maintain too."

"Yeah, maybe. . . . I suppose," Mirei said.

She didn't feel comfortable with the direction of the conversation. While Mirei didn't intend to stay single, she had no immediate plans to marry and move out.

"We need to think about the future," Ayako said, sounding fretful.

"The future?"

"I mean money-wise. We've lost your father's income."

"That's true," Mirei said, speaking in a quiet voice. She'd been worrying about the same thing.

Kensuke's legal practice had already been shut down, and his cases were assigned to another lawyer.

"We have some savings, but we will need to rein in our spending. Depending on how things go, we may be better off downsizing."

Mirei was taken aback: She would never have expected Ayako to say something so practical and sensible. She tended to think of her mother as a full-time housewife who knew nothing of the real world and its problems. Now here she was, doing her best to grapple with their situation and plan for the future.

"I'll give you a shout when dinner's ready," Ayako said and left the room.

Seated on her father's bed, Mirei cast another glance around. The room was dreary. The only decoration was a single family photograph on top of the bookshelf. It had been taken years ago. Mirei was wearing a long-sleeved kimono.

She rose from the bed and went and sat in the desk chair and opened the desk drawer. Pens and pencils, seals, and bottles of pills were arranged neatly inside.

There were also lots of cards: mostly membership cards, plus a few seldom-used credit cards and some insurance cards.

She came across a dentist's patient ID card. On the back of it was a grid where the receptionist would write in the dates and times of appointments. Mirei started when she noticed one of the dates: "3/31 16:00."

March 31—

It was the day when the Yomiuri Giants had played the Chunichi Dragons at the Tokyo Dome. In his statement, Tatsuro Kuraki claimed to have gone to that game and met Kensuke.

Did that mean Kensuke had gone to the dentist *before* going to the ball game? Mirei wondered.

She mentioned it to Ayako over dinner. "That's probably the day he had a tooth out," her mother promptly replied. "You know that your father had a few implants? Well, it was one of them."

"But the game started at six o'clock. Would he really have gotten a tooth taken out just two hours before?"

"Why not? Your father wasn't one to make a fuss. It may hurt a little, but it's nothing a painkiller or two can't solve."

"Still, don't you think it's odd to go and see a baseball game on the same day?"

"Maybe he thought the game would take his mind off the pain. A change of scenery."

"I wonder."

Something didn't quite add up.

She decided to visit the dentist's. She wanted to ask them some questions about Kensuke's March appointment. She was pretty sure that she wouldn't get a straight answer on the phone.

The dentist was located on the second floor of a building in Jingumae. Mirei knew that it closed at half past six. She got there ten minutes early, waited in the corridor outside, and when the half hour came around, went through the automatic glass doors.

The reception counter was right there. The young receptionist, who was busy writing something, looked up.

"I'm sorry. We're not seeing any more patients today. And we operate an appointment-only system," she said, speaking rapidly but with a hint of apology in her voice.

Mirei nodded. "I'm not here for my teeth. There's something I need to ask you about my father." As she said this, she took Kensuke's patient card out of her bag and laid it on the counter.

"Ah, that's Mr. Shiraishi's . . ." The receptionist's face stiffened.

After hesitating for a moment or two, she asked Mirei to wait and disappeared into the back.

A minute later, a man in a white coat emerged. Mirei pegged his age at a few years younger than her father.

"You have a question about Mr. Shiraishi?"

"Yes, about his treatment here. Specifically on March 31." Mirei pointed to the date on the back of the card.

"Why do you need to know?"

Mirei shot him a look. "Do I have to tell you?"

The dentist grunted and frowned pensively. "We're not allowed to reveal information about patients without their permission. And that includes members of their family."

"Yes, but my father's dead. Did you not know?"

The dentist's face didn't change. He must have heard the news.

"I understand. Please follow me," said the dentist crisply.

He led Mirei into a small room with a plate saying Consultation Room on the door. There was a large computer monitor on the desk.

The dentist introduced himself—his name was Dr. Mizuguchi—and then pulled an X-ray image of Kensuke's jaw onto the monitor.

Mizuguchi pointed to a tooth at the back bottom right.

"This is an implant. Can you see?"

"Yes. It's got a screw in it."

"That's right. To make an implant, we remove the tooth, insert a titanium screw into the bone, add a base, and then attach a crown. I recommended an implant, because in your father's case, the bone was badly damaged by periodontitis."

"I imagine you can't do the whole thing in one go?"

"No, you can't. It takes time, and you have to do it in stages. The treatment for this tooth was only finalized in August."

"So what exactly did you do on March 31?"

"All I did that day was to take out the old tooth. Normally, I'd proceed directly to the insertion of the screw, but the aperture that remained after the extraction was too big for that, so I postponed it to our next appointment."

"How long did the procedure take?"

"Extracting a tooth doesn't take long. Around twenty minutes, I'd say."

The card read "3/31 16:00." That meant the session would have been over by four thirty.

"How does it feel after having a tooth out? Is it painful?"

"It depends on the individual. It's painful for some people. Wisdom teeth aside, you're fine if you take a painkiller."

"Could you go out that same evening, say, to watch a baseball game?"

"A baseball game? Shouldn't be a problem. There might be a little swelling," Mizuguchi said. Having no idea where Mirei was going with her questions, he looked slightly puzzled.

"You don't advise your patients to take it easy after an extraction?"

"I encourage them to avoid strenuous exercise and steer clear of drinking."

"Drinking?"

"After pulling a tooth, you want the wound to heal as fast as possible. Ingesting alcohol increases blood flow, which increases the likelihood of bleeding, so I always tell my patients not to drink anything that first evening."

The dentist's remark triggered Mirei's memory.

"Beer would be off limits too, then?"

"Yes, beer's not allowed either. Ideally, you want zero alcohol intake."

"Did you tell my father that?"

"I'm pretty sure I did. More than that—" Mizuguchi opened a drawer in his desk and removed a single-page printout. "I would have given him one of these."

Mirei took the document from the dentist. It was a list of things to avoid following a tooth extraction. Alongside warnings against overenthusiastic gargling and forceful nose-blowing, it clearly said not to drink for twenty-four hours.

"Can I keep this?"

"Be my guest."

"Thank you. You've been very helpful." Mirei rose to her feet and bowed deeply.

30

TAKAHIRO HORIBE'S OFFICE was on the second floor of an old mixed-use building. The middle-aged office manager sat at a counter just inside the entrance. She greeted Kazuma with a warm smile of recognition.

"Attorney Horibe is in a meeting with another client just now. Can you wait a moment?"

"Absolutely."

Kazuma sat down on a leather couch against the wall.

A flat-screen TV hung on the opposite wall playing one of those daytime talk shows. A gaggle of writers and journalists were discussing a well-known female TV personality who had been arrested for drugs. Recently, Kazuma had been doing his best to stay away from the internet, but when he had to go online, this particular scandal was everywhere.

Kazuma had been involved in marketing for a proposed talk show of which the woman was to be one of the hosts. In meetings, she came across as a grounded person with strong opinions—nothing like the silly, featherbrained persona she presented for the public. He had been a fan of hers ever since; clearly, though, there was another side to her.

Guess I'm no judge of character. Since he had misjudged his own father so completely, how could he honestly expect to understand someone he barely knew?

A door opened, and an old man emerged from the back of the office, bowed to the woman at the counter, and went out.

The phone on the reception counter started ringing. The office manager picked it up, said a few words, then looked over at Kazuma. "Please go on in, Mr. Kuraki."

Kazuma made his way along a narrow hall to a small meeting room at the back of the office.

He went in. Horibe was on his feet, shuffling documents. "Please," he said, gesturing for Kazuma to sit. "I went to see your father," he continued, intertwining his fingers on the table. "I asked him about that matter you brought up."

"What did my father say?"

Horibe glanced away before returning his gaze to Kazuma. "He said that it hadn't really occurred to him."

"Hadn't occurred to him? Hang on a second. How did you phrase the question?"

"Exactly as you said to me. I voiced your doubts directly. He committed the first murder on May 15, 1984. Why, then, did he choose to move into his new house exactly four years later to the day, on the same May 15? Didn't he feel odd about that particular date?"

"And he just said that 'it hadn't really occurred to him'?"

"He said that while he'd not forgotten the crime he had committed, he didn't think about the date as an anniversary. Work was busy at the time of the move, so he chose the most convenient day that wouldn't interfere with his job."

Kazuma shook his head vigorously.

"That's nonsense! How could he forget something like that? You see how crazy it is, don't you, Mr. Horibe? I'm right, aren't I?"

Horibe nodded reluctantly. "It's certainly atypical behavior. That's why I felt it worthwhile to ask. I thought he might have attached some special significance to the move."

"What do you mean?"

"I mean commemorative significance. It would give Tatsuro a reason to make the day special."

Kazuma looked slightly baffled. "I still don't get it."

"Assuming that he moved on May 15, that day would go on to assume special significance as an important family anniversary. So if Tatsuro subsequently started going to pray at a shrine or a temple that day, the natural assumption would be that he was celebrating the anniversary of the move. Nobody would suspect he was commemorating a crime. I'm saying it could have been a decoy maneuver. Now, if that was the real reason why he arranged to move on that day, it would prove that he felt remorse for his crime. It may even be something I could use in court."

Kazuma looked long and hard at the square-faced lawyer in his gold-rimmed glasses. "You really think so?"

"What?"

"That you can use it in court."

"Absolutely." Horibe straightened himself and looked intently at Kazuma. "I'm a defense lawyer. Finding things that will be advantageous in court is my job. Unfortunately, though, this one's a dead end. Since Tatsuro claims that the link between the two days hadn't even crossed his mind, it could backfire on us and be used to prove that he felt no remorse whatsoever."

"But that's not why I brought it to your attention."

Horibe frowned. "So why did you?"

"My point was that if Tatsuro really had murdered another human being on May 15, then there's no way he would have moved into his new house on the same day of the year. As a young man, my father always dreamed of buying his own home. The fact that he hung on to his mortgage payment records and receipts from the repair reserve fund proves how much it meant to him. He would never have chosen that day of all days to move into the home he had dreamed of for so long. . . . It's totally impossible."

"Like I told you, he says he didn't think about the date."

"That's just crazy. The reason he didn't turn himself in to the police before was because he was waiting for the statute of limitations to run out. He'd never 'forget' the date of the murder. My father's lying. He has to be—"

"Stop," said Horibe, raising his right hand. He sighed. "I see where you're coming from, but to start arguing about the basic facts at this stage is simply not good strategy. Tatsuro himself admits to having committed the Haitani murder. Nothing anyone else says has any weight in comparison."

"But—"

"No," Horibe cut him off. "That's enough. Stop obsessing."

Kazuma felt the energy draining out of him. He'd gone back to the family home in Nagoya, spoken to Yoshiyama, the neighbor, and finally unearthed this little glimmer of light amid all the darkness. Was it all for nothing, after all?

"Listen," said Horibe. "If you can't accept my advice and are so sure that your father is lying, then I suggest you find out why. If you can find a plausible reason for his behavior, I'd be prepared to reassess."

"You want me to find out why he's lying to us?"

For some reason, an image of *her* face—the face of Kensuke Shiraishi's daughter—swam into his mind.

31

"You're quite sure about that? That it was Mrs. Ryoko Ishii who suggested the trip to Atami?"

As Godai asked the question, he leaned forward.

The woman opposite him looked slightly alarmed as she nodded. "I'm one hundred percent sure it was her. I told Ryoko what days worked for me. She then picked a date and booked the accommodation for us."

"Did you discuss things in person or by email?"

"We texted."

"Have you still got the texts?"

"Yes, I have." After some tapping and swiping, she showed them to Godai. "Here they are."

Godai looked at the screen. The text exchange confirmed her account.

"Under no circumstances should you delete those messages," he said. "They're very important pieces of evidence."

"Okay." The woman looked worried. "You've already arrested the man who killed my mother, so why are you continuing with the investigation?" she asked as she put her phone away.

"There are just a few matters of fact we need to confirm. Thank you for meeting with me today. I appreciate your help." Godai picked up the check and got to his feet.

After exiting the coffee shop and saying goodbye, Godai called Assistant Inspector Tsutsui at the station incident room.

"That sounds like a step in the right direction," Tsutsui said. "The prosecutor was here a moment ago. The unit chief will be pleased with this information. Now get back here."

"Will do," Godai said and ended the call. It felt good to have finally found something.

A dismembered body had been found deep in the mountains of Okutama to the west of Tokyo the previous month. It had taken about a week to identify the remains. The body belonged to Ryoko Ishii, a wealthy widow of sixty-two who lived in Chofu in the west of Tokyo with her twenty-six-year-old daughter.

The police promptly set up an investigation. Godai was part of the team sent in.

However, the investigation seemed to have hit a dead end, because it was unclear exactly when Ryoko Ishii had first gone missing. Her daughter, who'd been studying in England, only realized that her mother had disappeared when she got back to Japan. While overseas, the two women had used text and email to stay in touch, and the daughter hadn't noticed anything unusual in the messages.

When the police checked the house, they found clear evidence of robbery. Ryoko Ishii's cash cards and credit cards were missing. An examination of her transaction history revealed withdrawals from her savings accounts and uncharacteristic patterns of credit card use starting at the end of August.

One man in the security camera footage they reviewed caught their attention: a twenty-eight-year-old self-styled musician by the name of Numata, who was the daughter's ex.

The evidence against him was irrefutable. Numata's prints were found on a leather case at the murder scene. The case contained bank statements and other documents.

When questioned, Numata admitted to having disposed of Ryoko Ishii's body. He was immediately arrested. For a brief moment, Godai and his teammates thought their job was done and they could relax.

Numata, however, denied committing murder.

He confessed to having used the cash and credit cards, but insisted that Mrs. Ishii had given him permission to use them after he told her that he was having trouble making ends meet. She had given him all the relevant PINs at the same time.

Numata's explanation of the situation was: He went to thank Ishii for the money, only to find that she had hanged herself. Worried that the discovery of the corpse would cause a furor that would distract the daughter from her studies, he decided to conceal the dead woman's body. He claimed to have taken over Ishii's phone, assumed her identity, and kept up the exchange of messages with the daughter.

Godai wondered whether Numata seriously believed that anyone would swallow a story so ludicrous. Since then, things had taken a turn for the worse. According to the prosecutor, there currently wasn't enough for him to put together a viable criminal case.

The problem was the cause of death. The body was in such a degraded state that it was impossible to pinpoint the cause of death. No murder weapon had been found. In other words, there was no physical proof Numata had killed the woman.

The prosecutor had decided that his best strategy would be to refute Numata's claim about Ryoko Ishii having died by suicide. If he could prove that statement false, then he could disappear all other claims.

Still, it wasn't going to be easy. Proving that Ryoko Ishii had no reason to take her own life was difficult. Ultimately, no one can ever really know what secret torments other people have in their hearts.

The prosecutor decided to initiate a thorough investigation into Ryoko Ishii. The aim was to prove that she wouldn't have taken her own life.

The police had made a number of discoveries. Among them was the fact that Ryoko Ishii had taken out a life insurance policy just over a year earlier. Her daughter was listed as the beneficiary. The policy, however, contained a clause that no money would be paid out if the policyholder died by suicide within the first two years. That suggested that even if Ishii was resolved to end her life, she would have waited until she had passed the two-year mark.

They also discovered that Ryoko Ishii had discussed her plans to renovate her house with a large number of people. Renovating seemed unlikely to be a concern for anyone who was seriously contemplating suicide.

Recently, Godai learned that Ryoko Ishii had been planning a trip with a friend to a hot-spring resort. The idea that the person who had proposed such a trip should kill themselves just before the vacation seemed far-fetched.

Looking forward to making a triumphant return to the incident room, Godai was on his way to the police station when his phone rang. His eyes widened in surprise when he saw the name of the caller on the screen. It was Mirei Shiraishi.

"Godai here."

"Uh . . . this is Mirei Shiraishi, the daughter of Kensuke Shiraishi, who was murdered last year. . . ."

"Yes, I remember you. What can I do for you?"

"There's something I need to talk to you about. It's to do with my father's death."

"What exactly might that be? If it's something administrative, the local precinct will—"

"No, it's directly connected with the investigation," Mirei said emphatically. "I believe the investigation was mishandled."

Godai's grip on his phone tightened automatically. "That sounds serious."

"Which is why I need you to listen to what I've got to say. Have you got the time to meet? I'll go wherever's convenient for you."

Godai glanced at his watch and sighed. Even if the police's battle was over, the family's battle was only just beginning. He could not ignore her in good conscience.

"You choose the place. I'm happy to go wherever's easiest for you."

Around a half hour later, Godai sat across from Mirei Shiraishi in a café. Seeing her again reminded him just how good-looking she was.

"Thanks for making time for me," Mirei said with a bow.

"Not at all. Now, what did you want to tell me?"

"It's this," she said as she laid an appointment card from a dental clinic on the table. What she went on to explain, pointing out the date and time jotted on the back of the card, gave Godai a jolt.

Mirei explained that Shiraishi had had a tooth extracted that afternoon and was under strict instructions not to consume any alcohol for twenty-four hours.

"My father's not the kind of person to ignore medical advice like that. If he was told not to drink that night, then he wouldn't do so," she said firmly, showing Godai the printout she had gotten from the dentist.

Godai was at a loss for words. Mirei's case was compelling.

"You're telling me that you think Kuraki's lying?"

"Don't you agree that that's the only possible explanation?"

"Okay, but what can I do when things are so far along . . . ?"

"What are you saying—that things have gone too far for a change of course and you're just going to sweep it under the rug?" Mirei was glaring at him.

Godai sighed. "Have you mentioned this to anyone else?"

"I told our lawyer. The woman who's helping us with the victim participation system."

"What did she say?"

"That she'd try bringing it to the prosecutor's attention but that she didn't expect much from him."

The lawyer's probably right, Godai thought. There wasn't going to be any arguing about the basic facts in the trial, so presenting any extraneous information at this stage was futile. "The culprit has been arrested and provided a full account of his motive. Isn't that enough for you?"

"But what about the truth? I want to know the truth. Don't you, Detective Godai? You've put so much work into the investigation. Are you really happy with a solution that's founded on a lie?"

"It's not necessarily a lie—"

"It's a lie," Mirei said, her voice growing louder, and she jabbed a finger at the printout on the table. "If you think he's telling the truth, then explain this."

Godai said nothing. He could not.

"Look, I'm sorry," Mirei said. Her voice was quieter and less insistent now. "I know what I'm saying is only going to cause trouble. That's doubly true for you, Detective Godai, but I've no one else I can turn to."

"It's no trouble. If justice hasn't been done, then it's my job to do something about it." Godai looked intently at Mirei. "Will you let me handle this? I'll do some digging of my own."

"You will?"

"I can't guarantee I'll get you the outcome you want."

"Thank you. I appreciate it." Mirei looked reassured as she bowed her head in gratitude.

Even as Godai nodded back at her, he could feel himself starting to sweat. He was not sure that this was a problem he could solve.

Nakamachi was already at a table at the back of the restaurant when Godai got there at 8:00 PM.

It was the same place they always went. Godai ordered beers for them both.

"Wasn't expecting to drink with you here again so soon," Nakamachi said, loosening his tie.

"It's my fault. You'll just have to humor me."

"I can manage that. Honestly, though, I was surprised when you got in touch."

Immediately after parting from Mirei Shiraishi, Godai had phoned Nakamachi and explained the situation to him.

The waitress brought them a couple of draft beers, and they clinked glasses.

"So what did you find?" Godai asked.

"You mean about Kensuke Shiraishi's movements on March 31, right? It was all there in the investigation records." Nakamachi pulled out his notebook. "Ms. Nagai, Shiraishi's assistant at the firm, was interviewed about this. Shiraishi's desk planner showed him leaving the office at half past three that day and not coming back. The appointment was listed as a 'personal matter.' There was nothing in the planner about a client meeting."

"Okay, so let's assume he left the office at three thirty to get to the dentist at four. I don't suppose there was anything in the planner about him going to the Tokyo Dome after that?"

"I wouldn't really expect him to put that in his work schedule. His assistant didn't know about the game."

"But she's worked for him for years, hasn't she? Strikes me that his first outing to a ball game in a long time is exactly the sort of thing he'd bring up at the watercooler."

"Do you think it was by chance or on purpose that he didn't mention it?"

"Or did he never even go to the game *at all*?"

Godai's interjection prompted a sharp intake of breath on Nakamachi's part. "That's heavy-duty. It completely undoes the whole case."

"You haven't mentioned it to anyone else, have you?"

"Of course not."

"Good. Let's keep this between ourselves for now."

"Got it. But"—Nakamachi lowered his voice—"what are you planning to do?"

"I don't know yet. That's what I'm going to start thinking about now."

The waitress happened to walk by, so Godai ordered a few dishes.

"Are you busy right now, Godai? What are you working on?" asked Nakamachi, changing the subject.

"Something very challenging. We've arrested the culprit, though." Godai gave a brief outline of the case.

"Oh, right. The murder of the wealthy widow out in Chofu. I've heard about it. The suspect came up with some wacky pretext."

"You've got to admire the guy's capabilities as a storyteller. Of course, it's nothing that out of the ordinary."

"What do you mean?"

"All criminals want to evade punishment. That's why they fabricate stories. So what about Kuraki? If we assume that the statement he gave us is false, then why would he lie? It won't get him a lighter sentence, so why bother lying at all?"

"I dunno," Nakamachi grunted, cocking his head.

Godai tipped the remainder of his beer down his throat and looked around the restaurant.

This was the place the two of them had come after arresting Kuraki. He could remember feeling a sense of foreboding even then—a sense that rather than emerging from one labyrinth, they had just been drawn into a new one.

Those misgivings hadn't disappeared over time, Godai realized. If anything, they'd grown stronger.

32

THE YOUNG COUPLE emerged from the famous jewelry store smiling. The woman was looking particularly pleased. Had they found that perfect wedding ring?

Kazuma wondered if he would ever have a life like theirs. It wasn't wedding rings or marriage that he really cared about; it was the carefree smiles and laughter that he envied.

Kazuma arrived for their reservation five minutes early. They seated him at a quiet table in a corner.

At 3:00 PM, Kazuma glanced toward the staircase and saw the man he was meeting come into view. He strode confidently. The note of cunning in the suntanned and unshaven face was even more pronounced than the last time they had met—or was that just prejudice speaking?

"It's been awhile." Nanbara smiled wanly and sat down opposite him.

"Thanks for meeting me at such short notice," said Kazuma with a little bow.

"No trouble. Was a bit surprised, I admit."

"Thought you might be."

Kazuma was the one who had reached out to Nanbara to ask him questions. He'd expected the journalist to turn him down flat. Instead, Nanbara had accepted and proposed both a time and place.

The waitress came to get their order. Nanbara ordered a coffee and Kazuma did the same.

"I'd like to start with a disclaimer." Nanbara pulled a ballpoint pen out of his shirt-front pocket. "This pen's a voice recorder, and I intend to record our conversation with it. Are you okay with that?"

"Be my guest."

"Great." Nanbara pressed a couple of buttons on the pen and laid it on the table.

"You recorded our last conversation too, didn't you?" Kazuma said, looking at the pen. "When you came to my apartment and asked me all those questions."

"Recording every conversation is the first rule of journalism," Nanbara said without a trace of embarrassment. "I heard from the editors at *World News Weekly*. You made a complaint through a lawyer."

"I didn't like what the article implied."

"Different people see different things in the same piece. All the comments I attributed to you were condensed versions of things you actually said. Do you disagree?"

"I think you played me very cleverly."

"So? Did you bring me here just so you could vent?"

"No, that particular ship sailed long ago."

The waitress came over and placed a coffee in front of each of them. Nanbara used the interval to scrutinize Kazuma.

"That article wasn't quite up to snuff," Nanbara said after the waitress had moved away. "I was aiming for hard-hitting, but it didn't quite get there. Since a lot of the cases are decades old, it's hard to produce content that feels urgent, even when you write about the feelings of the victims' families. Guess we all strike out from time to time." Nanbara smiled ironically as he poured milk into his coffee and stirred it in with a spoon. "Okay, so if you're not here to grouse about that article, what are we doing here? On the phone, you said there was something you wanted to ask me."

After taking a sip of his black coffee, Kazuma took a deep breath and started to speak. "I want to ask you about one of the crimes my father committed. Not the recent one; the one he committed in 1984."

"You mean the murder of the financial adviser in Higashi-Okazaki, right?" Nanbara said, eager to be as precise as possible. "Well, what about it?"

"Given that the police have yet to make a public statement about the case, how did you go about your research?"

"That's what you want to talk about?" Nanbara looked rather disappointed. "What you said to me when I doorstepped you was enough for me to deduce that the crime had to be murder, so I tried to talk to anybody who knew him back then. In those days, the employees of big companies hardly socialized outside their own firms, so I knew that the best bet was to get my hands on the firm's employee register. Loads of the employees still lived in that area."

"In your article, you mentioned a former coworker of my father's who remembered him being interviewed by the police, didn't you?"

"They interviewed your father as the person who first discovered the body. Pretty clear evidence he's guilty, but in the end, I wasn't able to definitively confirm that Tatsuro Kuraki was the culprit. What do you expect? I mean, it's such an old case. Even so, in the article, I insisted on Tatsuro's guilt. That was a deliberate choice. I promised my editors that I was ready to take full responsibility if I was wrong and the police or Tatsuro himself started complaining. For myself, I was one hundred percent sure that wouldn't happen." Nanbara's tone was polite enough, but his face glowed with smugness.

"Did you talk to anyone else?"

"Several people, but I didn't get anything interesting out of them. That was when I had the idea of talking to the victim's family. Haitani, the murdered man, had once been married, but he was single and childless at the time he was killed. You know, that was my biggest miscalculation and the main reason I couldn't produce a well-rounded article. My original plan was to focus on exploring how the family members of murder victims in cases where the statute of limitations has expired feel when they find out that the same perpetrator has gone on to kill somebody else." Nanbara shrugged as he sat there with a coffee cup in one hand.

"You couldn't find any surviving family members?"

"Like I said, Haitani didn't have a wife or children. Regardless, I did a little digging and managed to unearth someone—just one person—of interest. Haitani had a younger sister whose son worked for Haitani."

"Haitani's nephew, in other words?"

"Right. The sister's dead, but the nephew is still alive. He lives alone in Toyohashi. He's in his mid-fifties now, so he was in his early twenties when the murder happened. His name's Sakano."

"Did you manage to see him?"

"I did. Wanted to get the juiciest story possible, didn't I? Once again, though, things went awry. It was a complete waste of time." Nanbara deposited his cup on the table and held out his hands, palms upward, in a gesture of mock despair.

"How come?"

"To start with, Sakano hadn't even heard about this latest murder. When I told him about it, he was like, 'Why should I care?' He was more interested after I explained the link between this case and the old one from 1984. He remembered his uncle's murder, and he remembered Tatsuro Kuraki, although he'd forgotten his name. He told me that he and Kuraki were the ones who found the body and reported it to the police."

"He was there, then. What was the 'miscalculation' you mentioned just now?"

"The fact that Sakano didn't get the least emotional." Nanbara scowled. "Like I said, I wanted the guy to go batshit crazy when he learned that the man responsible for his uncle's murder had not only gotten away with it due to the statute of limitations but had even killed again. The article would have been so much better if he'd produced a few juicy quotes dripping with rage and hatred. Instead, he was more like, 'Oh, is that what happened?' His response had zero emotional weight. What do you think he said when I asked him if he was angry? *That he simply didn't care.* That the identity of the perpetrator made no difference to him."

"So he wasn't overly fond of the victim?"

"Far from it—he absolutely despised his uncle. He only took the job answering the phone because he couldn't find any other work. 'I couldn't stand working for that creep. The man was a scumbag who cheated old people out of their money,' he said. He could think of any number of people with a reason to kill Haitani, he said, and wasn't surprised that he ended up dead. The nephew actually said he knew how Tatsuro Kuraki must have felt when he killed Haitani. As he saw it, Kuraki had every reason to lose it, with Haitani not only forcing him to work as his driver but also extorting money, even though the original accident wasn't remotely serious. Sakano was very candid with me, but nothing he said was right for the article I had in mind."

"I see."

Maybe Nanbara was just trying to manipulate him; but knowing that the victim's closest relative felt no pain or sense of loss gave Kazuma some consolation. The shorter the chain of misery, the better.

"Is there anything else you want to ask?" Nanbara said.

"Yes. This is the thing I'm most curious about: Why did the police fail to suspect my father? Wouldn't the person who discovers the body automatically become a prime suspect?"

"That's a good question. It bothered me too. I tried looking it into via a friend in the force, but we couldn't get a clear answer. Chiefly because, more than thirty years later, there's no one left with a grasp of the actual events. Plus the records of the case have been all shredded."

"They have?"

"However." Nanbara cocked his head to one side. "That Sakano fellow I was talking about said something odd. He said that while he wouldn't be at all surprised if Kuraki *had* done it, he remembered Kuraki having an alibi."

"An alibi?" Kazuma straightened up in surprise, and he leaned in toward the other man. "Is that true?"

"I can't say. The way Sakano tells it, the detective who was first on the scene carefully questioned both himself and Kuraki. He remembers thinking vaguely at the time, *Oh, this guy's got an alibi.* He doesn't actually know if Kuraki's alibi was corroborated, though."

"Surely if the alibi was phony, it wouldn't have taken the police long to find out? Doesn't that suggest that they *did* manage to corroborate his alibi? That would also explain why my father wasn't investigated. Don't you think that's what really happened?"

"Please, Mr. Kuraki, there's no need to shout."

Kazuma looked around the café. Luckily, there was no one sitting close by.

He gulped down a mouthful of water from his glass and, making a conscious effort to keep his voice down, continued. "Look, the police would only have been suspicious if they'd discovered that his alibi was fake."

"Now just hang on a minute." Nanbara held up a hand. "I see where you're going with this, but don't shoot the messenger. All I've done is to tell you what Sakano told me. Obviously, you don't want your father to be the murderer—*but he confessed to the crime.* Like it or not, those are the facts. There's no room for doubt."

Kazuma said nothing. Nanbara made a valid point.

"Have you got any other questions? If not, I should be going." Nanbara picked the pen recorder up off the table.

"Can you give me Sakano's contact details?"

Nanbara gave him a quizzical look. "Why? You planning to meet up with him and check up on things for yourself?"

"I don't know. Maybe."

"You'd be wasting your time."

"If you don't mind . . . I'd really appreciate it."

Nanbara sighed. Then he pulled out his phone, tapped the screen, grabbed a paper napkin from the end of the table, and jotted something on it with his ballpoint pen.

"Here's Sakano's address and phone number," he said, sliding the napkin across the table.

"Thank you." Kazuma carefully folded up the napkin and put it in his pocket.

"Sakano's not much of a drinker," Nanbara said, apropos of nothing.

"Though if you plan to take him a gift, he has a real sweet tooth. When I met with him, he was munching his way through a fruit sundae."

A little taken aback at this unsolicited advice, Kazuma nodded. "I'll bear it in mind."

"I still think you'll be wasting your time," Nanbara said again, his voice low.

Kazuma ignored him. "Oh, before I forget, are you planning to publish a follow-up to the original article?" he asked.

Nanbara shook his head. He looked distinctly unamused. "No plans right now. Not unless there's some major development."

"Uh-huh." Nanbara put his pen recorder back into his shirt pocket, glanced at the bill, and pulled out his wallet.

"No, no. This one's on—"

Nanbara raised his other hand, cutting him off. "There's no reason you should pay for me. Besides, you need to save whatever money you can. Things are only going to get more difficult for you from here on in."

Kazuma had nothing to say. He hung his head in silence.

Nanbara deposited his share of the bill on the table, stood up, and wished him goodbye. Not wanting to watch as Nanbara made his way out, Kazuma turned and gazed out the window.

A fine rain had started falling, and umbrellas were springing open here and there in the street. Kazuma shook his head. He hadn't brought an umbrella with him.

33

GODAI WAS FINISHING a report at his desk when the name *Mirei Shiraishi* flashed up on his caller ID. The case of the wealthy widow who'd been murdered, dismembered, and dumped in the mountains of Okutama was finally winding to a close.

"Hello. Godai here," he said, lowering his voice and looking around. There was no one else nearby.

"It's Mirei Shiraishi here. Sorry to bother you. Have you got a moment?"

"Sure, go ahead."

With his phone to his ear, Godai walked briskly out into the corridor. He didn't want anyone hearing that he was speaking to the family of a closed case.

"I know why you're calling," Godai said, keeping his voice low. "It's about that Tokyo Dome business, right? I'm sorry. I've had my hands full with another case and haven't gotten around to it yet. I've nothing new to report," he said honestly.

"I expected as much. I'm not calling to chase you up. I want some information from you."

"Oh yes? What?"

"You know *that man*'s son . . . the son of the defendant, I mean?"

Godai inhaled with a sucking sound. This was the last thing he had expected her to say. "Just to confirm, by 'the defendant,' you mean Tatsuro Kuraki, right?"

"Correct."

"Of course. I know Kuraki's son. What about him?"

"I was hoping you could give me his contact information."

Godai could not stop himself from gasping. Her request was so unexpected.

"I need that information. Badly." Mirei's tone was grave—urgent, even.

"What for?"

"To find the answer to something that's bothering me. I'm simply unable to believe that Kuraki's statement is truthful. I want to run that idea by his son."

"Now listen here, Ms. Shiraishi, I don't think you want to do that. It might be different if you were hoping to get an apology from him. As a general rule, though, it's not a good idea for the victim's family to approach the family of the perpetrator. It might be seen as intimidation."

"I've no intention of intimidating anybody."

"You may not, but we don't know how he will feel."

"I disagree. I don't think he's prone to assuming the worst like that."

"Why? Have you met the guy?"

"Just once. By chance."

"When? Where?"

Mirei Shiraishi was silent for a moment, then said, "Am I obliged to answer that?"

"No, you're not. There's no need to say if you don't want to."

"It's not that. It's just a little complicated. The short version is, I bumped into him where my . . . at the crime scene near the Kiyosu Bridge. I had gone to leave flowers, and he happened to be there."

"Okay." Godai could see how that could happen.

"We said hello and exchanged a few words. At the time, I didn't think

I should ask him for his details, and we went our separate ways. I didn't think I'd see him again; now with everything that's happened since, I want to ask him some questions."

Godai peered around to check that no one was listening, wondering how best to deal with her request. "Look, I understand how you must feel, but it wouldn't be appropriate for me to give you that information. It's personal information, plus it's covered by police confidentiality rules."

"I won't tell anyone that you told me."

"I'm sure you're sincere, but we don't know how this might play out. If it leads to trouble, then I'll be in hot water."

"I'll be careful. And I promise not to cause any trouble whatsoever."

He released a weary sigh into the phone.

"So you won't help me?"

"I'm sorry. I hope you can understand. At some point, I do mean to look into that business of whether Kuraki and Shiraishi really did meet at the Tokyo Dome."

"Well, okay. Thank you. Sorry for disturbing you." The disappointment in her voice was palpable.

"Don't mention it. If there's anything else you need, feel free to call me."

"Thank you. Goodbye," said Mirei and ended the call.

Godai, his phone still in his hand, crossed his arms on his chest and leaned back against the wall.

Since Mirei Shiraishi was using the victim participation system, she had to be getting detailed information from the prosecutor's office. Presumably, she was struggling to accept the very facts of the case. Otherwise, she wouldn't be trying to contact the defendant's son. She was a strong-minded woman, the kind who would have no inhibitions about acting recklessly.

He uncrossed his arms and made a call. It was quickly picked up.

"Nakamachi here," said a quiet voice.

"This is Godai. Can you talk?"

"Give me a moment."

A few seconds of silence. He guessed that Nakamachi was looking for somewhere private to speak.

"It's fine now," Nakamachi said, speaking at a normal volume.

"Sorry to bother you."

"No problem. I was in one of the unit chief's stupid briefings, so thanks for giving me a reason to slip out. Are you calling about that Tokyo Dome thing?"

"That's the one. Learned anything?" He heard a groan.

"I did some digging, but I couldn't turn up anything new on Shiraishi's movements on March 31. Frankly, I don't think there's anything new out there to be found."

"You think so too, huh? Maybe it's just too late in the game."

"It's not exactly the same, Godai"—Nakamachi lowered his voice—"but I did come across something else in the file that bothered me."

"Oh yeah? What?"

"I'd prefer to tell you in person. Might you be free anytime soon?"

"What's with the sudden formality? I'm just putting the finishing touches on a troublesome case. This evening is fine for me."

"Then this evening it is. Same place okay?"

"Okay by me."

They agreed to meet at seven o'clock and ended the call.

THE YOUNG WAITRESS at the restaurant must have recognized Godai, because she escorted him straight to the table at the back as soon as he arrived. Nakamachi was already seated and working on a tablet. Noticing Godai approaching, he wished him a good evening. There was an uncharacteristic hint of tension in his voice.

"Seems we've been recognized as official regulars here," Godai said after ordering two draft beers and a selection of small dishes.

"Funny thing about this place, I don't bring other people here. I only come when I'm meeting you, Godai."

"Same with me. Anyway, you were busy working. Don't stop on my account."

"You mean this?" Nakamachi pointed at the tablet. "Just something bugging me that I wanted to check out. This is what I'm looking into."

Nakamachi turned the tablet around so Godai could see the screen. It showed the TV broadcast schedule from a newspaper.

Their beers arrived, and they clinked glasses.

"What's so interesting about TV listings?" Godai asked.

"Take a look at the date."

"The date?" Godai shifted his gaze to the top of the screen.

"Respect for the Aged Day," Nakamachi said. "It's something that came up in Kuraki's statement. He claimed to have been watching TV on Respect for the Aged Day when a program came on about wills and bequests. He said that's what gave him the idea of leaving his estate to the two Asaba women to make amends."

"So he did. It had slipped my mind."

"The police interviewer asked him what program it was. Kuraki said that he'd forgotten the name but that it was one of those soft news talk shows. No one did any follow-up after that. I asked a journalist friend to send me the relevant back catalog. Different regions have different programming, and this is a local Aichi newspaper."

"Clever."

This young detective is sharp as a tack. Godai had sensed that right from the beginning.

"I've read all the program descriptions," Nakamachi continued, "and as far as I can see, no such show was broadcast on that day. Several channels ran special Respect for the Aged Day features; they were mainly about the challenges older people face or ways to improve their quality of life. I couldn't find anything about wills or bequests. My impression is that the broadcasters probably felt that a subject associated with death was not in tune with the whole theme, and they would have given it a wide berth."

"Let me have a look." Godai pulled the tablet toward him.

As he scanned the page, phrases like *How to stay healthy* and *Better ways to enjoy your second life* caught his eye. He reckoned Nakamachi was probably right: The program coordinators probably saw wills and bequests as too morbid for Respect for the Aged Day.

A couple of dishes arrived at their table. As he pecked at the food and drank his beer, Godai tried to put his thoughts in order.

The fact that a topic wasn't mentioned in the program listings didn't necessarily mean that it hadn't actually been discussed on the air. A show could well have featured some discussion about estate planning.

"Is this what you wanted to discuss with me?"

"No, think of it as a bonus. I know you're busy, and I don't want to waste your time on something as trivial as this. It was just a warm-up. Let's move on to the main act. I told you over the phone that I'd found something concerning in the investigation. It was a business card. It was discovered in Kuraki's desk in Nagoya."

Nakamachi tapped at his phone, then turned the screen toward Godai. "Here it is," he said, showing him a photograph of a business card, labeled as evidence.

Godai leaned in for a closer look. The card belonged to a man by the name of Ryozo Amano. But it was the man's job title, not his name, that brought Godai up short. *Ryozo Amano, Attorney-at-Law, Amano Law Office*, the card said.

"Another lawyer . . . ?"

"Now look at the address."

Godai did as Nakamachi said and directed his gaze to the address at the bottom of the card. *It was in Nagoya.*

"So what? Kuraki knew a Nagoya-based lawyer."

"But don't you think it's strange?"

Godai took a swig of beer, wiped his mouth, and looked over at Nakamachi. He knew what the younger detective was going to say. "Kuraki told us that he contacted Shiraishi because he had no idea how to bequeath everything to the Asabas. But if Kuraki already had a relationship with a local lawyer in Nagoya, surely it would have made more sense for him to discuss the matter with him? Why would he seek advice from Shiraishi, someone he'd only just met?"

"And why would he come all the way to Tokyo to do so?" Nakamachi's eyes were shining.

"I can see why this is sticking in your craw. Can you forward the photo of the card to me?"

"Yes, sir." Nakamachi tapped at his phone.

Godai picked up a skewer of grilled onion.

"The thing is, we don't actually know how well this Amano lawyer and Kuraki knew one another. It's quite possible that they just met and exchanged cards and had no relationship beyond that. If that were the case, then there's nothing strange about Kuraki choosing to contact a lawyer he befriended at a ball game instead." As Godai said this, he bit into a piece of onion. The pungent aroma tickled his nostrils.

"I think you're right," Nakamachi said as he put his phone away. "At the same time, why would he bother to hang on to Amano's card if they didn't have some sort of relationship? Maybe if Kuraki were a politician, someone focused on building a network of contacts, but he was a completely ordinary fellow—and retired to boot."

"All good points." Godai checked his phone to see if the photograph of the business card had come through. "I guess the quickest thing to do would be to go and see this Amano and ask him about his interactions with Kuraki."

"Shall I handle that? I can go to Nagoya on my next day off."

"That'd be great, but . . ." Godai's voice trailed off.

"What's the problem?"

"He's a lawyer. It's hard to imagine him casually sharing any information with you unless you have a warrant. There's attorney-client privilege, you know. He may tell you if Kuraki came to see him; he definitely won't tell you what the meeting was."

"Yeah . . . you're probably right." Nakamachi sounded slightly discouraged. "What do you propose instead?"

"Give me a moment to think."

An idea percolated in Godai's head, but he wasn't ready to share it or its possible repercussions.

They drank their beer and ate their food in silence for a while. It was Nakamachi who spoke first.

"Oh, by the way, the prosecutor in the Kuraki case is busy causing trouble now, when the trial's about to get underway."

"How come?"

"Apparently, he ordered the precinct cops to gather more corroborating evidence of Kuraki's statement. It seems the prosecution don't have all the physical evidence they need."

"It's a bit late for that. Anyway, what better evidence is there than a confession? Is the prosecutor worried Kuraki might retract his statement in court? There's no way that's going to happen."

"I agree. Still, I guess the prosecution has to consider all possibilities. The evidence is all circumstantial; the only solid piece they've got is the fact that Kuraki knew the location of the crime scene when it hadn't yet been disclosed to the media."

"Undisclosed information. That should do the trick."

"Apparently, they recently found something online that could be a problem."

"What?"

"Some social media post. Someone who saw the forensics team at work on-site posted that the murder scene was probably very close to the Kiyosu Bridge. The post predates Kuraki's arrest. Although a social media post isn't the same as an official news report, its existence is enough to cast doubt on whether the crime scene location really was undisclosed information."

Godai took another swig of beer, then he shook his head. "Social fucking media. The greatest pain in the ass of the modern world."

"Kuraki has an old-school flip phone rather than a smartphone. The thing doesn't record mobile location data. The guys who were told to dig up more supporting evidence are pissed. They're like, orders or no orders, looking for something that's simply not there is a total waste of time. They may put me back on the case before long."

"So no fingerprints or DNA were ever found?"

"Nothing. Nor was there any evidence Kuraki actually came to Tokyo on the day of the murder. And that's after trawling through all the footage

He started walking north along Ohashi Boulevard, the main road running through the town. Sakano had suggested meeting at a café that specialized in Japanese sweets. As Nanbara had said, Sakano had a sweet tooth.

He had been walking for a few minutes when the buildings on either side abruptly became significantly shorter and the sky seemed to expand above his head. It was gray and growing darker. Kazuma hoped it wouldn't rain, although he'd brought an umbrella this time.

He turned off the main street. Kazuma checked his location against the map on his phone as he walked. In no time, he had reached his destination. The building was retro-looking, from some time in the mid-twentieth century, with a large battered sign.

A showcase displaying a variety of Japanese sweets stood by the front entrance. Kazuma barely glanced at them as he went inside.

There were only two groups of customers in the place: a couple of women and a lone middle-aged man in a tracksuit. The man glanced up from a weekly magazine, caught sight of what Kazuma had in one hand, and scratched the bottom of his nose. Kazuma was carrying a paper bag, their prearranged signal.

Kazuma walked over to him. "Are you Mr. Sakano?" he asked.

The man nodded. He was plump with a round, unshaven face.

"I'm Kazuma Kuraki. Thanks for agreeing to meet at such short notice. I really appreciate it." Kazuma handed the other man his card.

Sakano glanced at it carelessly. "Well, sit down, then."

Kazuma thanked him and sat down opposite him. Sakano must have already eaten—there was an empty bowl and a spoon on the table in front of him.

A middle-aged woman dressed in a smock came over to take Kazuma's coffee order.

"Make mine a red bean soup with rice balls—oh, and another cup of green tea," Sakano said.

Kazuma suspected that Sakano had gotten there early on purpose. It was an opportunity to indulge his sweet tooth at someone else's expense. Maybe that was why he'd agreed to meet.

"This is something I picked up at Tokyo Station. It's for you." Kazuma placed the paper bag on the table. Inside it was a sponge cake filled with banana cream.

Sakano grinned as he peered into the bag. "You shouldn't have. But thanks."

Kazuma drew himself upright and looked straight at the other man. "Could I ask you a couple of questions?"

"Fine by me. What do you wanna know?"

"I understand that in 1984, the year the murder took place, you worked for the victim. Is that correct?"

Sakano slipped the cake box back into the bag and nodded. "I'd no choice in the matter. The firm I'd been working at went under, so I didn't have a job. My mom told me to take the job answering phones for my uncle. I didn't know him well, but once I started spending time with him, I was shocked. I'd no idea what a total shit the guy was."

"Yes, Mr. Nanbara told me. He said when you learned that my father was the actual perpetrator, you said you couldn't care less."

"And I don't. The whole thing happened over thirty years ago, and that creep, he was just begging to be killed. When he was murdered, I thought, *Well. It's finally happened.*"

The woman in the smock brought over the red bean soup, the green tea, and the coffee.

Sakano picked up his spoon and dragged the bowl of red bean soup toward him. Before tucking in, he said, "But I'd be lying if I said I wasn't surprised by what Nanbara had to say to me. Finding out that your father, Mr. Kuraki, was the killer didn't bother me. Nah, what surprised me was finding out that the electrician fellow, the guy who killed himself, was not guilty after all. I was so sure he'd done it."

"Why?"

Sakano crammed a spoonful of soup into his mouth, then cocked his head. "I'm no people person, still, no matter how you slice it, he was the shadiest of us all. That's why the cops arrested him right away."

"Does that mean you know the circumstances of his arrest?"

Still clutching his spoon, Sakano waved his hand from side to side. "I don't know about evidence or any shit like that. All I know is that if I'd been a detective, I'd have arrested the electrician too."

"Can you tell me why?"

"Sure. Back then, the electrician guy came into the office to complain all the time; you know, saying that Haitani had swindled him. That's why he was there at the office that day too. When he rolled up, Haitani was out, and I was the only person in the office. Anyway, the electrician, he decided to wait till Haitani came back. It was a pain in the ass, but I couldn't very well tell him no. With just the two of us there, it was awkward, so I went out looking for my uncle. I spent nearly an hour checking his local haunts. I didn't find him, so in the end, I decided to go back to the office. That's when I ran into Mr. Kuraki—your dad—just outside the place. Come to think of it, actually, that was Kuraki's second time there that day."

"His second time?"

"Mr. Kuraki had also shown up when I was stuck in the office with the electrician fellow, but when I told him that Haitani wasn't there, he went away. So, yeah, that was his second time. Anyway, the two of us go up into the office and we find the body. Cherry on the cake, our electrician pal is nowhere to be seen. So, stands to reason he did it. Signed, sealed, and delivered."

Kazuma pictured the scene as Sakano described it. It was only natural for suspicion to fall on Junji Fukuma, the electrician.

"My father now claims that he was the one who stabbed Haitani to death and that he'd just climbed into his car to make his getaway when he spotted you and got back out of the car, pretending that he had just gotten there."

"Oh yeah? Well, if that's what he's saying, I guess it's probably true. Never occurred to me at the time, though."

"I understand that you told Nanbara that you thought Mr. Kuraki, my father, had an alibi?"

Sakano put his spoon down on the table and raised his teacup. "I vaguely remember something like that, yeah. The police turn up and ask us a load of questions—stuff like, 'Where were you before you came back to the office and found the body?' I told them that I'd been doing the rounds of all the local coffee shops and bars looking for Uncle Haitani. Then Kuraki, he gave his own explanation to the cops. I remember thinking at the time, *Oh, this guy's got an alibi too. That means the electrician must've done it.*"

"What did my father say to the police? He must've told them where he had been. Can you remember?"

Sakano took a sip of his tea and gave him a dirty look. "It's more than thirty years ago."

"I'm sorry."

Sakano reached for his spoon and started eating whatever was left of his red bean soup. "It's like I said, if Kuraki says he did it, then that's got to be the truth. Like I told you on the phone, I got nothing big to share."

"Okay. Thanks."

Kazuma picked up his cup. The coffee in it was almost cold.

ON THE BULLET train back to Tokyo, Kazuma felt even gloomier than he had on the way out. Although he hadn't been expecting much, he thought he might uncover at least a glimmer of hope.

He still couldn't figure out why the police hadn't investigated Tatsuro for the murder. He could see why Junji Fukuma was treated as the prime suspect. Even so, there wouldn't have been anything strange about the police investigating Tatsuro's alibi. No, *strange* was far too weak a word. *There was simply no way the police would not follow through.*

But if the police had managed to find evidence to corroborate Kuraki's alibi, they would have eliminated him as a suspect.

It was dark by the time he reached Tokyo Station. Glancing at his watch, Kazuma saw that it was a little before 7:00 PM.

Suddenly, the idea of going to the Kiyosu Bridge popped into his head. It was around this time of the evening that the murder had taken place.

Taking the subway and walking would take too long, so he hailed a taxi. Luckily, the streets were quiet, and he was there in less than ten minutes.

He had just started walking down the same stairs to the Sumida River Terrace, when he looked up at the bridge and came to a stop.

The Kiyosu Bridge was brightly floodlit, but the surrounding area was in semidarkness. Underneath the bridge, it was pitch-black.

He resumed walking slowly down the stairs. The terrace at the bottom was rather dark, but not so dark that he couldn't make out the shapes of things. It was dark enough that people on the far bank or riding on pleasure boats on the river wouldn't be able to see anything. The place had also been blocked off for construction at the time of the murder. An ideal spot for murder.

Despite the lateness of the hour, there were still a few loiterers. The occasional jogger went by.

A woman was standing looking out at the river, the hem of her coat flapping. Kazuma started when he caught sight of her profile. It was Kensuke Shiraishi's daughter, the same woman he had run into here the other day. Kazuma gasped audibly and stopped in his tracks.

Although he hadn't been that loud, she must have heard him. She turned in his direction. Her eyes widened.

It wouldn't be right to pretend not to have seen her and to walk away. Kazuma bowed to her. "We met the other day."

"So we did," she said with a thoughtful frown.

"Do you come here every day?" Kazuma asked.

"Often, but not every single day, no." She spoke stiffly.

"To leave flowers?"

"Sometimes. Like on the day we met."

"Right."

"Do you come here often?"

"This is only my second time. There was that time and today."

"Right."

Kazuma took a deep breath, then said, "If it's uncomfortable for you and you'd rather I didn't show up here, I'm happy to stop coming."

She briefly lowered her gaze, looked up at Kazuma, and curtly shook her head. "I've no right to ask that of you." As she said this, she turned and looked out at the river. "I come here because I want to try to understand my father's state of mind. I want to understand what was going through my father's head when he pressured another man to come clean—when he didn't need to."

"What are you saying? That the father you knew would never do that?"

"Never," she said crisply and turned to face Kazuma. "He'd never do that. Tatsuro Kuraki's testimony is false. It's a heap of lies."

"I . . ." Kazuma's voice was hoarse. "I'm hoping that it's lies too. From the bottom of my heart, I'm hoping that everything Tatsuro confessed to—your father's murder included—is a fabrication."

She looked into Kazuma's eyes. "I've found one piece of evidence. Evidence that proves Tatsuro Kuraki is lying."

"What is it?"

"About how the two of them first met. Kuraki's claim that he ran into my father at the Tokyo Dome—*it's simply not true.*"

She went on to tell Kazuma how Kensuke Shiraishi would not have been drinking beer that day because he'd had a tooth out a few hours earlier.

"Well, I know for a fact that my father went to the Tokyo Dome on that day," Kazuma said. "I'm the one who got him his ticket."

"Yes, but my father wasn't there. Which means he never met Tatsuro Kuraki."

"So where did they meet, then?"

"I have no idea. And I don't know why Tatsuro Kuraki should choose to lie about it. But if that part of his story is false, don't you think he could be lying about his motives too?"

Her tone may have been emotional, but the point she was making was logical. *She's smart*, Kazuma thought. "Have you discussed this with anyone else?"

"I got my lawyer to relay my concerns to the prosecutor. He showed zero interest. I also mentioned it to a detective. Godai. Do you know him?"

"Oh, him. . . . Yes, Godai visited me immediately after the crime. What advice did he give you?"

"He said he'd try to look into it but that I shouldn't get my hopes up. No doubt he's got other fish to fry.... I asked Godai for your contact details so I could get in touch with you. He turned me down flat."

Kazuma was puzzled. "You wanted to get in touch ... with me?"

"The last time we met, you told me that you thought your father might not be telling the truth and were doing some investigating of your own. Do you remember? I wondered if, like me, you'd managed to find out something."

"I've found out several things. None of them are conclusive, though."

"Can you share them with me? Or are they all things you plan to use in court?"

"They're not. I shared them with our lawyer. He wasn't interested. It's probably fine to tell you."

"Before you do," she said, holding out her open right hand. "Could I ask you your name?"

"Oh, sorry. My name is Kazuma Kuraki." He clumsily produced a card from his jacket pocket.

She took it and squinted at the letters in the dark. "I'm Mirei."

"So you're Ms. Mirei Shiraishi."

"I see your cell phone number is printed on your card. I'd rather not give you my phone number just yet. If you think I'm not being fair, I'm happy to give you your card back."

"That's okay. If you have no use for my card, feel free to toss it."

"Okay." Mirei Shiraishi tucked Kazuma's card into her coat pocket.

"The first questionable thing I dug up was connected to the 1984 crime. The murder took place on May 15 ..."

Kazuma then explained how Tatsuro had planned to move into his newly built house on the same day, May 15, exactly four years later.

"Tatsuro ended up postponing the move to the weekend after due to bad weather. Since that second Sunday was an unlucky day in the Buddhist calendar, he moved a few of his things on the fifteenth as a token gesture. Don't you think that's odd? My father told our lawyer that the anniversary 'never crossed his mind.' Look, I know I'm his son and I'm biased, but there's just no way he's that unfeeling a person."

Mirei Shiraishi looked at him solemnly. "That would be abnormal."

"And then there's one more thing. It's something the journalist who wrote the *World News Weekly* article told me."

According to Nanbara, Kazuma explained, the second man who had found the body with Tatsuro was convinced that Tatsuro had given an alibi. He related his whole trip to Toyohashi to hear what the man had to say for himself.

"I'm starting to believe that my father really did have an alibi. It would explain why the police crossed him off the suspect list so quickly."

"So you think that your father's claim to have murdered Haitani in 1984 could be a lie?"

"I do. But I'm biased. He's my father."

"If you're right about that, then his confession to my father must automatically be false too."

"Exactly. And the stuff about your father pressuring my father to come clean."

Kazuma looked at Mirei. She looked back at him. As the seconds passed in silence, Kazuma felt a bond of sympathy tying them together—or was that just his imagination?

"Let's say that all your hypotheses are correct," she said. "What possible reason could your father have to assume responsibility for a thirty-year-old murder?"

It was an obvious question to ask.

"I don't know. Perhaps . . ." One possible explanation had popped into Kazuma's head.

"Perhaps what?"

"Perhaps he's protecting someone."

"But the statute of limitations has expired on that murder. What's the point of him coming forward as the perpetrator at this stage?"

It was a valid question.

"I see what you mean. . . . Oh!"

A word had come back to him: *redemption*.

"What is it? Have you thought of something?" Mirei Shiraishi asked, an intense expression on her face.

"Yes, I have. It's pretty speculative, though."

"Let me be the judge of that."

"My father confessing to being the true perpetrator in the 1984 case was the salvation of a couple of people. I'm talking about the Asabas, the mother and daughter who run the Asunaro restaurant. The last time I saw them, they were so happy that the false charge against Junji Fukuma had finally been expunged. They'd suffered so much, being shunned and scapegoated for three-plus decades."

"So what you're telling me is that you think the original charge wasn't wrong and that Junji Fukuma was the real culprit. Because your father felt sorry for the two women, he confessed to being guilty, hoping to exonerate the man."

"I think that *could* be what happened. . . . Pretty speculative, huh?"

"I don't think so," Mirei Shiraishi said, vigorously shaking her head. "Since the statute of limitations has expired, your father can't be called to account for that crime. Given that he was going to be arrested anyway, the idea that he assumed responsibility to help save some people he cared for seems quite plausible to me."

"If that is what happened, then my father's motive for murdering Mr. Shiraishi must also have been different."

"I guess so."

Kazuma saw Mirei Shiraishi's face stiffen. Although they were chatting and even agreeing about things, ultimately, he was the son of the man who had killed her father.

"Unless we act, then the trial will proceed based on a false statement," Kazuma said, avoiding her eye. "Given that my father killed your father, whatever his motive may have been, perhaps that doesn't matter."

"No, it does matter." Again, she spoke with great force. "I want to know the truth. I won't be satisfied until I know what Tatsuro Kuraki's real motive was."

"I'm with you. What should we do, though?"

"Let me think. Really think about it. I'll give you a call if I come up with anything worth running by you."

Kazuma was in awe of her determination. *This woman isn't just clever, she's tough as nails.*

"Okay. I'll try to do some thinking too."

A look flashed across Mirei Shiraishi's face, then she pulled both her smartphone and Kazuma's card from her coat pocket. She punched his number into her phone with her right.

Kazuma's phone started to vibrate, and her number appeared on its screen.

"I feel I can trust you."

"Thank you. Is it . . . uh . . . okay for me to call you if I discover anything?"

"Of course." Mirei Shiraishi smiled faintly. "I should go. It was good to talk to you."

"Likewise."

Mirei Shiraishi turned smartly on her heel and walked away. Kazuma could not take his eyes off her as she disappeared into the distance.

35

GAZING UP AT the elegant apartment building glowing in the sunshine, Godai gave a contemptuous jerk of the head. *It really is exactly the sort of place you'd expect some fancy-pants ad agency executive to live.* Even a simple one-bedroom apartment would probably set you back 150,000 yen a month.

He pressed the intercom in the outer lobby. "Hello," came a flat voice. Godai spoke his name into the microphone. The doors slid open.

Godai rode the elevator to the sixth floor and rang the bell of apartment 605.

The door opened, and Kazuma Kuraki appeared. He was wearing a sweatshirt with a fleece on top. A glance was enough for Godai to see that both items were expensive. Kazuma definitely looked thinner and exhausted—or was that just Godai's self-projection?

"Sorry to drop by out of the blue like this." Godai ducked his head apologetically.

"It's okay. Like I said on the phone, I've got something I want to tell you too."

Kazuma led Godai inside. Sure enough, it was a one-bedroom apartment, if generously sized. There were a couple of armchairs in the living room, but Kazuma offered him a dining chair instead—better for serious talking.

"Why don't you go first?" Godai said once he was seated. "What is it you want to tell me?"

Kazuma Kuraki nodded. He spoke rather slowly. "I understand that Mirei Shiraishi asked you for my contact details?"

Godai stared back at the other man in shock. "How do you know?"

"She told me."

"*She* told you? You mean Mirei Shiraishi?"

"Right."

"Did she reach out to you?"

"We ran into one another by chance, near the Kiyosu Bridge."

"Ms. Shiraishi mentioned that to me. I thought you hadn't exchanged contact details on that occasion."

"We ran into one another a second time."

"Again? What, at the same place?"

"Yes," Kuraki said.

Two *chance* encounters in succession? Not likely, Godai thought. "Do you go to the bridge regularly?"

"No, that was only my second visit. Ms. Shiraishi told me she goes quite frequently."

Perhaps Mirei had been going there whenever she was free in the hope of bumping into Kazuma Kuraki. She seemed headstrong enough to do something like that.

"What did you two discuss?"

"Plenty. Mainly things we had doubts about. She told me that her father had a tooth pulled the day my father claims to have first met him at Tokyo Dome. Oh, and she mentioned she'd raised the matter with you."

"She did, yes. Said he's not the kind of person to drink beer at the ballpark the same day he'd had a tooth out."

"A smart catch. Compelling too."

"I agree."

"For my part, I told her that I'd looked into the 1984 incident and found an inconsistency of my own."

Godai's eyes widened. The self-assurance in Kazuma Kuraki's tone surprised him. "You looked into it? Really?"

"I'm stuck at home on furlough. I've got nothing but time on my hands." Kazuma gave a self-mocking smile, then went on to explain how Tatsuro Kuraki had moved into his new house exactly four years to the day after the Higashi-Okazaki murder. Godai was alarmed.

"If that is true, it's certainly a cause for concern."

"*It is true.* And there's something else." The light in Kazuma's eyes shone even more fiercely. "I'm starting to think that my father had an alibi for the time of the 1984 murder."

"An *alibi*!" Godai flinched. It was the last word he'd expected to hear. "What do you mean?"

"I went and spoke to someone who was directly involved in the case." Kazuma went on to explain who that "someone" was.

"Just hang on a second. What you're trying to tell me here is that Tatsuro has confessed to a murder he didn't actually commit?"

"I suspect so, yes."

"But why on earth should he do that?"

"For redemption."

"*Redemption?*"

"You'll probably accuse me of jumping to conclusions with what I'm going to say now."

Godai was dumbfounded at Kazuma Kuraki's theory that Tatsuro Kuraki had devised a scenario to exonerate Junji Fukuma in order to help his widow and daughter.

Godai looked intently at Kazuma. "That's some pretty creative thinking."

"I know that my hypothesis sounds crazy. But I've not been able to get it out of my head since it first occurred to me."

Godai groaned quietly, rubbed at his forehead, and tried to sift through everything he had just been told. His mind was in chaos.

"Have I unsettled you?" Kazuma looked at him shyly.

Godai pulled his hand away from his forehead, resettled himself in his chair, and looked straight at the other man. "You know that most people would automatically dismiss your theory as absurd."

"I know."

"The thing is," Godai continued, "rather to my surprise, it all adds up. I tried to pick holes in it just now, but I can't. Okay, so if we run with this theory of yours, we find ourselves confronting a couple of questions: Why did Tatsuro murder Shiraishi, and why is Tatsuro concealing his real motive?"

"Exactly. That's where I got stuck."

"Hence your wanting to speak to the detective in charge of the case and see how he would react?"

"Yes, I wanted to get your opinion."

"I just gave you my opinion. You've been extraordinarily perceptive. And I assure you, I'm not being sarcastic when I say that."

"Thank God. Making you waste your time on some self-indulgent fantasy is the last thing I want to do. Anyway, I've said everything I wanted to say to you. Now, what I'd really like you to do is to redo the entire investigation with this theory of mine in mind."

"Let me be straight with you, Mr. Kuraki. That'll be difficult. At this point, your theory is entirely speculation. I can certainly propose reopening the investigation to the higher-ups, but unless we can provide hard evidence for doing so, I guarantee they'll turn me down flat."

"I thought as much." Kuraki's shoulders seemed to sag.

"New facts could still come to light, so I'll be sure to keep your theory in mind."

Godai's words were cold comfort to Kuraki. "Please do that."

"That reminds me, I've a question of my own for you. Do you know if Tatsuro owned a prepaid phone?"

"A prepaid phone?" Kazuma was puzzled. "Sorry, I don't know."

"How about the electronics shops in Osu? Was he a regular visitor there?"

"Osu? Back when he was buying gadgets and stuff for the house, he went there often. Recently, though, I don't know."

"Apparently, it's just like Akihabara in Tokyo. You can pick up a lot of illegal stuff like unregistered phones and modified communications equipment. Was Tatsuro interested in stuff like that?"

"My dad? No, definitely not. Why do you ask?"

"In his statement, he claims to have bought a prepaid phone from some random guy in the Osu electronics district."

"My father?" Kazuma cocked his head to one side. "First I've heard about it. He's the last person in the world to do anything dodgy." His display of incredulity appeared genuine.

"Okay, let's move on to something else. I gather you recently went to Toyohashi. Are you thinking of going home again soon?"

"I've no immediate plans, no."

"There's something I want you to take a look at." Godai tapped his phone a few times and placed it in front of Kazuma. On the screen was the photograph of the other lawyer's business card.

"What's this?"

"Something we came across in Tatsuro's business card holder. Does it mean anything to you?"

"Nope." Kazuma shook his head, then looked up as if something had occurred to him. "The fact that my father had this card in his possession—does that suggest that he had dealings with this law firm?"

"We can't say for sure; it seems a reasonable assumption to make."

"But isn't it a bit odd? The reason he got in touch with Mr. Shiraishi was because he didn't have anyone else to advise him on his estate—at least, that's what he claimed. But this card suggests he had some sort of link to this law firm in Nagoya. Surely, the normal thing would be to consult with them first?"

He's sharp, Godai thought. Kazuma had anticipated everything that Godai was about to say.

"My thoughts exactly. Which is why I'm asking you."

"It's certainly worth looking into. I hope you'll investigate the matter further." Kazuma looked imploringly at Godai.

The detective had to disappoint him. "I'm sorry. I've not received an order to that effect from my superiors. They don't think this business card is of any special interest. As far as they're concerned, it's just something that one of the local policemen came across in the house search."

"That's insane." Kazuma shifted his gaze from the screen of his phone up to Godai's face and back. "Why won't *you* investigate it?"

"Because my superiors regard the case as closed. The suspect's statement is solid and contains no major inconsistencies. Even if I take this card to my superior officers, I can't see them changing their position. They'll just tell me not to rock the boat."

"I can't believe it." Kazuma scowled. "There's got to be something you can do. It's ridiculous, not being able to act without the explicit permission of your superiors."

"That's not normally how things work; in this particular instance, I'm not at liberty to act independently—a detective from Tokyo without a warrant who suddenly shows up at a Nagoya law firm to ask if they know a certain Tatsuro Kuraki. There's no way they're going to give me an answer. They have a duty of confidentiality. However"—Godai looked steadily at Kazuma as he continued—"if it was Kuraki's son who went, the firm might well respond differently."

"What do you mean? That if I ask, they'll tell me why my father had one of their cards?"

"Just asking them outright won't work. Son or not, they still have a duty to protect his privacy. But with the right approach, I think you could get them to spill the beans."

"The right approach?"

"I want you to pretend that I'm just thinking aloud here. Whether you act based on what I'm going to say, that's up to you." Godai moistened his lips as he said this.

AFTER LEAVING KAZUMA Kuraki's apartment, Godai was still not sure about the ethics of his actions. He knew he'd probably broken police regulations, but he tried to persuade himself that he had only done so to get to the truth. Nonetheless, he couldn't shake off the sense that he had toyed with the emotions of a young man desperate to believe in his father's innocence. Kazuma Kuraki probably wouldn't be getting much sleep tonight.

Still, that theory of his had been a real bombshell—falsely confessing to spare the Asabas.

But why would the two women mean so much to him? One could understand that Tatsuro Kuraki wanting to atone for Fukuma having been wrongly charged if he was the real perpetrator of the 1984 murder, but if he wasn't actually responsible, that changed everything.

Godai consulted his watch. It was a little after five. He hailed a taxi that was passing and instructed the driver to take him to Asunaro.

Godai reached Asunaro at exactly half past five. Since it was opening time, there were probably no customers yet. Godai wanted to ask again about the relationship between the two women and Tatsuro Kuraki. Particularly Orie, the daughter. Was there really no romantic involvement there?

He had just begun climbing the stairs when a man in a beige coat started making his way down from the second floor. He passed Godai and went out of the building onto the sidewalk. Godai knew that he had seen that face somewhere before. It didn't take him long to place the man. He was the man who had turned up at the restaurant just before closing time the last time Godai visited.

Godai dashed back down the stairs and looked frantically up and down the street. Spotting the man in the beige coat, he sprinted after him. "Sir, excuse me, sir!" he shouted.

The man stopped and turned around, a questioning look on his face.

"I'm sorry to stop you out of the blue," Godai said and tried to look friendly. "I'm from the Tokyo Metropolitan Police."

The man blinked in surprise. "What do you want?"

"I saw you leaving Asunaro just now."

"Yes. What about it?"

"I apologize if I'm wrong about this, but aren't you Ms. Orie Asaba's ex-husband?"

The man seemed a little taken aback. "I am, yes."

"Could I have a word with you? It should only take a minute or two," Godai said in the humblest tone he could.

"Is it about that murder?"

"That's right, sir."

"Then you're wasting your time. I know nothing about it."

"I'm fully aware of that. We're currently trying to speak to the friends and associates of anyone connected to the case. I'd really appreciate your cooperation. It won't take long."

The man looked grumpily at his watch. "Oh, all right then."

"Thank you, sir." Godai nodded in gratitude.

A few minutes later, Godai and the man were seated across from one another in the café on the other side of the street.

Godai produced his police badge, taking care that it would not be seen by the other customers. The man gave Godai one of his cards. His name was Hiroki Anzai. *Assistant Director, Secretariat, Ministry of Finance.*

"I've seen you at Asunaro before, Mr. Anzai. You came in just before closing time."

"Oh, so were you that late-night customer?" Anzai nodded as he held his paper coffee cup in one hand. He remembered the night in question.

"I was aware that Ms. Orie had been previously married. I thought you might be her ex."

"Right—look, why do you want to speak to me?" Anzai took a sip of his coffee.

"You obviously know about the murder. Was it Orie who told you?"

"No, it was a relative of mine."

"A relative? How come?"

"The *World News Weekly*. A relative of mine who reads the magazine called me. 'The man in the article, the one who killed himself in police custody, isn't that the Asabas he's talking about?' So I read the article, thought he might be onto something, and called Orie to check."

"And you found out that your relative was right?"

"Something like that, yes," Anzai concurred, a strangely morose look on his face.

"I gather that you are occasionally in contact with your ex-wife."

"Well . . . not that often, but she has visitation rights."

"Visitation rights?"

"With our son."

"Ah, I saw a photo of him at the Asaba apartment. He looked to be grade four or five."

"Well, he's in grade eight now. The number and the timing of the visits isn't fixed, so we coordinate them in advance."

"Is that why you were at the restaurant today?"

"No, it wasn't." Anzai pondered for a moment or two, glanced around the café, then brought his face closer to Godai's. "I'm going to tell you this because it's better than you listening to any random gossip. Orie and I didn't divorce because we fought or anything. We divorced because of the whole business with Orie's father. Orie had told me when I proposed to her. I chose to believe her when she said that her father had been wrongfully accused. Since that was almost twenty years later, I assumed that everything would be fine, provided we were discreet. My parents were very fussy about my elder brother's choice of a wife, but they couldn't have cared less about mine. I'm only the second son. I told them that Orie's father had died in an accident when she was young; they didn't suspect anything. In fact, we had no problems for quite a while after getting married. We had a kid, and we thought we would be together forever.

"Until something happened."

Godai nodded. The pain was visible on Anzai's face.

"My father is a municipal assemblyman. My brother was supposed to take over from him, but he got seriously sick, and I ended up being his designated successor candidate for a while. That upended our lives. Without my say-so, the local supporters' association and various members of my extended family started trawling through my personal history for anything problematic. This vetting, it's a gauntlet that all politicians have to go through. Anyway, that was when they discovered Orie's father's case. As you'd expect, it blew up into a major problem. I told them that I'd never had any great desire to follow in my father's footsteps. They were adamant that my discreetly stepping down wasn't enough, because if word got out, it would impact negatively on my father's reputation. My father excoriated me for not having been more open with him when I got married. Said that had he known, he would have virulently opposed my marriage."

Godai believed him. Politicians lived in a Darwinian world of kill or be killed. The old case was excellent ammunition for a political enemy to exploit.

"So you decided to get divorced?"

"Orie was the one who made the decision. She asked me to divorce her."

"Orie asked you?"

Anzai propped his elbows on the table. There was a distant look in his eyes. "Orie said that she knew what she was getting into when she married me. She knew that we might have to split up if anyone found out about her father; she'd been through similar things before. I told her that we should ride it out together, but she wouldn't change her mind. She didn't want us to stay married in the face of my family's disapproval, and she couldn't bear to see all the pain she was causing me and our son. The people in the support association were busy doing their best to keep the story out of the papers, so separating right away was the best thing to do. She was cool and not in the least distressed when she suggested this. Listening to her, I ended up feeling that my notions of staring down prejudice were rather sophomoric, and I couldn't come up with any counterarguments."

"You were in a difficult position too."

"A difficult position?" Anzai gave a snort of laughter and shrugged. "It was nothing compared to what Orie has gone through. Anyway, giving her complete access to our son was the absolute least I could do. Now that he's old enough, he goes and visits her by himself. Anyway, then the *World News Weekly* comes out with this article about how Orie's father had been wrongly accused. That moved the goalposts again."

"Because your divorce had been for nothing?"

"I wouldn't go that far. Had we not gotten divorced, we would have been bullied and persecuted plenty. Now things are going to change. My family didn't like me letting my son see his mother. The tide will turn on that one. The reason I've been dropping in to Asunaro recently is because Orie and I have been discussing what to do about our son's education.

That's why I was there today." Anzai picked up his paper cup, drank some coffee, put the cup back down on the table, then looked hard at Godai. "There you have it. Was that clear enough for you?"

Anzai was very much a politician's son. He had the gift of gab. His account was lucid, logical, and left no room for doubt.

"Very clear indeed." Godai looked at Anzai's fine-featured face. "Are you thinking of getting back together with Orie?"

Anzai waved a deprecating hand. "Not going to happen. I actually remarried seven years ago. I have two children with my current wife, a boy and a girl."

"I didn't know."

Anzai appeared to be in his mid-forties, so seven years ago he would have been in his late thirties. Getting remarried at that age was understandable enough.

"My present wife isn't involved in the education of my son from my first marriage. That's why I needed input from Orie."

"But you have no special feelings for her anymore?"

"Feelings of a sexual or romantic nature, no. I think she's a wonderful woman. I sincerely hope that she will find someone who can make her happy."

"You never got the impression that there was such a person? One of the restaurant customers, for instance?"

Anzai tipped his head to one side and looked slightly bemused. "I don't know. . . . I make it a point to never go during business hours, so I can't really say."

"I see."

"I should tell you," Anzai said, "there was this time when I was on my own with Mom. She said something that stayed with me."

"By 'Mom,' you mean Orie's mother, Yoko Asaba?"

"That's right."

"What did she say?"

"'Anzai, you don't need to worry about Orie anymore. She's found someone she feels she can rely on.'"

"When was this?"

"About this time last year, I suppose. I didn't think it would be polite to pry, so I simply said that it sounded like very good news. I don't know how the relationship developed after that." At that point, Anzai directed a doubtful look at the detective. "Is this really going to be of any use to you?"

"Yes, very much so," Godai said.

36

MIREI WAS AT Azusa Sakuma's office. The social niceties out of the way, the lawyer's eyes widened in surprise behind her black-rimmed spectacles at the first thing out of Mirei's mouth.

"What did you just say?" Sakuma asked.

"What I said was, I want to meet, face-to-face, with the defendant, Tatsuro Kuraki. I want to visit him in the detention center, and I'd like you to come with me."

Holding Mirei's gaze, Sakuma took a deep breath to calm herself down. "Why do you want to do that?"

"Why? Because I want to see what kind of person he is. I want to see him, talk to him, size up his character. Then I'll ask him one simple question: *Why are you lying?*"

Sakuma interlaced her fingers on the top of her desk. "Is it Kuraki's claim to have met your father for the first time at the Tokyo Dome that you're having trouble with?"

"That's *one* of the things that's bothering me. I have nothing but questions. I can't bring myself to accept Kuraki's supposed motive: My father would never be so dictatorial."

"It does seem likely that the defendant embellished parts of his statement, as Prosecutor Imahashi made clear to us. However, since these embellishments have no impact on the gravity of the final outcome—namely, Kuraki killing a man in his own self-interest—there's nothing to be gained from discussing—"

"But the prosecutor's wrong!" Mirei exclaimed, cutting Sakuma off. "We're not talking about someone using a little creative license here and there. Let me ask you point-blank: Can you confirm that Kuraki did not fabricate his statement entirely? Have you any evidence to show that the whole thing's not just one big web of lies?"

"You need to calm down. What's gotten into you? Has something happened? You're not yourself. Has someone been putting these ideas into your head?"

Mirei started back and looked askance at the lawyer. "No, that's not it."

"Yes, it is. Someone's been putting ideas into your head."

"It's nothing like that."

"Then what's going on? Mirei, be honest with me. I am representing you. Everything I say and do should align with your wishes, and I can't do my job unless you're open with me. Frank and honest sharing of information is the cornerstone of the victim participation system."

Sakuma spoke with urgency. Mirei knew that there was nothing to be gained by withholding the whole story.

"Well, the truth is . . . I met with his son," she confided, feeling a little unsure of herself.

"*His* son? *Whose* son?"

"The son of Kuraki, the defendant."

"You're kidding me! When?"

"It was an accident. When I went to leave flowers at the crime scene."

"Then what?"

"The son . . . he is also struggling to believe his father's statement and has been doing some investigating of his own. He thinks that his father's lying about being the real perpetrator in the 1984 case. If he's correct about that, then the motive Kuraki gave for murdering my father must also be false."

Sakuma shook her head, a cynical look in her eye.

"The son is on the other side of the case. Of course he's going to look for evidence that's advantageous to the defendant."

"That's not what he's doing. He said, 'Whatever the real motive, if my father really did kill your father, then I suppose I'll just have to live with that.' In other words, he may not *want* to believe that his father is a murderer; he is willing to accept it, but only if it's actually true. Since he can't accept his father's statement, he is taking matters into his own hands. That's why I want to meet Tatsuro Kuraki, the defendant. I want to see for myself what kind of man he is."

Sakuma adjusted her glasses, blinked a couple of times, then looked intently at Mirei.

"What? Why are you looking at me like that?"

"You seem to have a lot of sympathy for the son of the defendant."

Mirei felt her heart racing. "All I'm saying is that we feel the same way: Both of us want the truth. And he's not the one who murdered my father. He's suffering because of this crime. He's a victim too. Or do you disagree?"

"No, you're right. I'm sorry. I was out of line." Sakuma gave a crisp nod of apology. "I see how you must be feeling, Mirei. At the same time, I really can't approve of you going to see the defendant at this stage. That's my professional opinion, and I'm sure that Prosecutor Imahashi would say the same thing."

"Why? Why shouldn't a member of the victim's family get to see Kuraki?"

"It's not officially prohibited; it's more about you participating in the case. At the trial, you're going to be working with the prosecutor to uncover the full truth about the crime. That process depends upon a multiplicity of objective facts. If you meet the defendant one-on-one, you'll have to put any prejudices or preconceptions to one side. To be frank, I don't think there's much to be gained from a single meeting. I'm not saying that because I don't think you're a good judge of character. I am just stating it as a simple matter of fact. For instance, if Tatsuro Kuraki did and said all the right things when he was with you, surely you wouldn't automatically assume that he was being sincere?"

"Probably not. I still want to meet him, though."

"Don't do this. I'm asking as a favor." Although the lawyer spoke softly, her voice had an uncompromising edge.

Mirei looked down at the floor and sighed. "All right then."

Sakuma squatted down a little and looked up into her eyes. "Are you sure you're not planning to sneak in secretly to see him?"

That was precisely what Mirei had been thinking. "You really don't want me to go, do you?"

"Absolutely not." Sakuma crossed her arms. "Let it go. If you won't agree, I'll have no choice but to step down."

"Okay, okay," Mirei said, agreeing reluctantly.

"You still seem to be caught up with the motive."

"Kuraki's story about the two of them meeting for the first time at the Tokyo Dome is false; that means his account of his relationship with my father is false too. Why should the motive be any different?"

"I see what you mean. It's a separate issue, but what are your thoughts about sentencing?"

"Sorry . . . sentencing?" stammered Mirei. It was not something she had given much thought to.

"Most of the families of murder victims seek the severest punishment possible. Basically, that means aiming for the death penalty and then settling for life imprisonment if you fail to get it. Most of the families look to the prosecutor to take a very strong line. I was wondering where you stand. Your mother seems to favor the death penalty."

"What I want . . . is to discover the truth and then to make up my mind after that. How is anyone supposed to judge the gravity of the defendant's crime if no one even knows the facts of the case?"

"Ah, *the truth*." Sakuma glanced away for a moment before returning her gaze to Mirei's face. "All right. Just for the sake of argument, let's say that the motive Kuraki gave in his statement is false. Do you think that his real motive may be even more malicious and cold-blooded than the false one?"

"I've no idea. How am I supposed to know?"

"Kuraki committed the murder to silence your father and to conceal a murder he'd committed many years ago. That's how I'd sum up his motive. The jury will see his selfish motivation because Kensuke Shiraishi did absolutely nothing wrong. Prosecutor Imahashi thinks he can secure the death penalty if he proves the whole premeditation angle, so he has asked the police to do some additional investigative work for him."

"Additional investigative work? Such as what?"

"Kuraki claims to have used a prepaid phone to call Shiraishi on the day of the murder. He's also claiming to have purchased the thing two years ago, meaning that—just like the knife he used as the murder weapon—he did not buy the phone specifically to commit the crime. Prosecutor Imahashi doesn't believe this. He sees the prepaid phone not as something Kuraki just *happened* to have in his possession but as something he acquired only *after* deciding to commit the murder. The prosecutor can build a stronger case for premeditation if the police can find where Kuraki bought the phone and show that he procured it immediately before committing the crime."

Mirei pictured Prosecutor Imahashi with his sphinxlike face. He seemed the kind of man who would see a trial as a game and feel real joy in victory.

"We've gotten a little off track," Sakuma went on. "What I was trying to say is that we stand a good chance of getting the death penalty if we just leave everything to Prosecutor Imahashi. Let us say, however, that Kuraki is hiding something and that his motive was actually different. That won't be a problem for us if his real motive turns out to be even crueler and more heinous than the one in his statement. But if it turns out that extenuating circumstances forced his hand, he could well end up with life imprisonment rather than the death penalty. Would you be okay with that, Mirei?"

"That's not my call. I want to learn the truth; getting the death penalty for Kuraki is not a priority. I just want to know what really happened."

Sakuma thought for a moment, then she nodded. "Okay, let's communicate our position to Prosecutor Imahashi. We don't find the defendant's statement about the circumstances leading up to the murder credible, and so we want the prosecutor to consider the possibility of a different motive. I'm assuming that works for you?"

"Sounds good. Thank you."

"I do need you to understand something. There's a limit to what Prosecutor Imahashi can do at this point in time. We've built the case on the back of a scrupulous police investigation. Of course, everything could still change if new facts came to light."

"Sorry to be a broken record, but that's exactly why I want to confront Tatsuro Kuraki about his claim to have met my father at the Tokyo Dome."

Sakuma shook her head to make clear that it wasn't going to happen.

"If you tell Tatsuro Kuraki that Shiraishi would never have drunk beer at the ballpark the night after having a tooth out and his response is simply to say that that's all very well, but Shiraishi really *was* drinking beer, which is why he included that detail in his statement, then we're at a dead end."

"What if we say it in the courtroom instead? It would certainly make the jury suspicious about the veracity of the defendant's testimony."

"That's not a good strategy. Coming out with a question like that in open court will only confuse the jury. If we're going to accuse the defendant of lying, we need proof. And before we do anything like that, we'd need to explain the approach we're taking to Prosecutor Imahashi. Decide on a game plan to expose the defendant's falsehoods. If we don't do that, the prosecution's whole case will fall apart."

Mirei sighed. "Trials aren't easy."

"It depends what you want from them. They're certainly not easy if the pure, unadulterated truth is your goal. With regard to the motive, I think we're pretty close to the truth as these things go."

"How come?"

"Because the defendant has gone out of his way to confess to a crime on which the statute of limitations has already expired. There's nothing to be gained from lying about something like that, is there? The other way around would make more sense: His real motive was to conceal his past crime, and he cooked up a false motive to stop that being found out."

Mirei pointed at Sakuma. "That's it."

"What?"

"Kuraki *does* have something to gain."

Mirei outlined the theory Kazuma Kuraki had expounded to her: the theory that Tatsuro had confessed to the 1984 murder to help the Asaba family.

"Kuraki can't be punished for the crime, because the statute of limitations has expired. He thought he might as well claim to be responsible to get people to remove the stigma the Asabas have faced."

Sakuma gasped. "That's a pretty bold theory."

"And a plausible one?"

"Not wholly implausible. But in the absence of any proof, it's nothing more than a little fantasy. A story cooked up by a son who cannot accept that his father is a killer."

Mirei scowled. "That's a nasty way of putting it."

"Sorry if I upset you. The problem is, unless the defendant changes his current statement, we have no choice but to accept it as it stands. There's simply no way we can prove Tatsuro Kuraki is *not* guilty of a thirty-plus-year-old murder."

Mirei felt a chill around her heart. "What you're telling me is that trials don't always succeed in uncovering the truth. I feel like I've lost confidence in the whole charade."

"Defendants always have the right to remain silent. There are plenty of cases where they exercise that right and truth is the first casualty. Don't lose faith in the system. The trial's not even started yet."

"Thanks, Attorney Sakuma. I'm not a child. I know the world's not always a fair place." Mirei got to her feet. "I'll be getting going."

"There's still some time before the trial. I'll try to come up with an approach that will be acceptable to you."

"I appreciate that." Mirei was about to leave the room when she stopped abruptly and swiveled around. "Why hasn't he apologized?"

"Apologized?"

"Kuraki has admitted his responsibility and appears to be remorseful. But despite that, there hasn't been even the hint of anything like an apology addressed to us, the victim's family. Nor has Kuraki's lawyer come to see us with any letter of apology entrusted to him by the defendant. Why do you think that is?"

"I'm not in any position to—"

"Don't you think it's because the defendant doesn't *want* to apologize to us? Because he thinks what he did was justified?"

"I doubt it. Quite a few defendants don't apologize."

"I wonder."

Sakuma looked at Mirei reprovingly. "Please don't tell me you're thinking of discussing this with the defendant's son."

"Would that be wrong?" Mirei said, finally picking up on the lawyer's negative reaction.

Sakuma raised her hands in agitation. "You mustn't. People could get the wrong idea if you two are seen together."

"I'll do whatever it takes to find out the truth."

"Please don't do anything rash. It won't do you or anyone else any good."

"I'll bear that in mind."

"Mirei . . ." There was a look of resignation on Sakuma's face.

"Goodbye then," Mirei said and left the lawyer's office. She felt bad, but making a promise she was only going to break was the last thing she wanted to do.

Emerging out onto the street, she felt the cold wind on her cheeks. In her wound-up state, it felt good. She had been pretty bold, if she did say so herself.

An image of Kazuma Kuraki's face swam unexpectedly into her mind.

His beautiful, sincere eyes had made a strong impression on her. She could see in them the tenacity with which he was confronting the harsh realities of life. That tenacity would make him very good at his job. Now his life had suddenly taken a dark turn. He must be desperate.

Mirei was surprised to find how sympathetic she felt toward him. Was it because she was able to contemplate the crime dispassionately despite being the daughter of the victim? Was it something to do with Kazuma's character and its impact on her? Or was it for some other reason? She didn't know. All she knew for sure was that she harbored no ill will toward him.

When she got home, Ayako was waiting for her with dinner ready. The main course was fish meunière. It was one of Ayako's best dishes.

"Azusa Sakuma called me a moment ago. Said you went round to her office to see her," Ayako said, pausing from eating.

"That's right. Is there a problem?" Sensing a rebuke coming, Mirei willed herself to stay calm.

Ayako laid her knife and fork on the table. "I recognize that you have some doubts and are doing your best to address them. I'm the same: If there are any facts that remain hidden, then I'd like to discover what they are. But what do you think you are doing, engaging directly with the other side?"

"'The other side'?"

"The perpetrator's family. The son. Attorney Sakuma told me you'd met with him. She asked if you'd gotten my consent for the meeting. I was dumbfounded. Why didn't you say anything to me?"

"I didn't think it worth mentioning. Is that a problem?" Mirei calmly ate her fish meunière while avoiding eye contact.

"Of course it's a problem. He's our enemy. Can't you see that?"

Mirei slowly chewed her fish, swallowed it, and only then looked up.

"Enemy? That's nonsense. Tatsuro Kuraki may be a killer, but the other people in his family aren't responsible for his actions, are they?"

"Maybe not, but once the trial gets underway, anyone in his family becomes our enemies. They'll do whatever they can to get him a lighter sentence."

"That's not how he thinks."

"Who's this 'he'?"

"The defendant's son, duh." Mirei jammed a forkful of salad into her mouth.

"Don't take that tone with me, young lady. That's the son of the man who murdered your father."

Mirei put down her fork and looked her mother straight in the eye.

"I need to know the truth, and I'll see whoever I want and join forces with whoever I want to get it. You'll never get to the truth with the attitude you're taking. Never."

Ayako glared back at her. "'Truth isn't an easy thing to find, and sometimes in the end it's barely worth finding.' That's what your father liked to say. Many defendants aren't capable of explaining their motivation. They're all like, 'Oh, you know, I just sort of stole it'; 'Before I knew what I was doing, I'd killed the guy. I don't really know why.' I bet you Kuraki's the same. The man had issues of his own, but in the end, he acted thoughtlessly and impulsively. There's no doubt about that. You gain nothing from obsessing about his motive. We should be focusing on making sure that he gets a punishment that fits his crime. *End of story.* I want the death penalty for him. If we can get that, then there's no need to sweat the small stuff. I'm asking you as a favor to me: Don't rock the boat. Meeting with the son of the killer is an outrageous thing to do."

"Oh, outrageous, is it?"

"Are you even listening to me? Can't you understand?"

"Sure, I'm listening. Now I know exactly what you think. You're not wrong, but I have my own life. And right now, that life is on hold. I can't move forward with things the way they are. For me, getting the death penalty doesn't change that."

"Mirei!"

"Thanks, Mom. That was a lovely dinner, as usual. You're always so sweet." Mirei stood up as she said this.

37

That's the current team lineup, is it? Kazuma thought as he inspected the Chunichi Dragons calendar tacked to the wall. He had seen the players' names in articles, but this was his first time matching faces to the names. He had little idea what positions they all played or who had what player number.

Tatsuro often took Kazuma with him to ball games when he was a boy. Seeing the pros in action had made a big impression, but eventually, his interest in baseball had waned. Although Kazuma did keep tabs on the scores, that hardly qualified him as a baseball fan. Nor did he have a favorite team.

By contrast, as an avid Dragons fan, Tatsuro went to games several times a year. Knowing that had prompted Kazuma to get a ticket for the opening Dragons versus Giants game. Kazuma vividly recalled his father's reaction when he told him over the phone. It was the first time he'd heard his old man say, "No fucking way!"

Tatsuro must have been thrilled to get to go to the Tokyo Dome. And he was undoubtably surprised to get such a good seat in the infield too.

And Kensuke Shiraishi was in the seat next to his—

Kazuma only got that far when he started having doubts. How had Shiraishi managed to get his hands on a ticket? Tickets for the season opener at the Tokyo Dome weren't easy to come by. Perhaps he had used his professional connections, or maybe he had bought it through online resale.

But if he had gotten his ticket by either of those routes, surely there would be some evidence of him having done so? Had the police managed to track that evidence down?

No, they haven't, Kazuma thought. When Mirei Shiraishi argued that her father was unlikely to have gone to the Tokyo Dome after a same-day tooth removal, Godai had failed to come up with proof. The police would have told Mirei if they knew for sure how Kensuke Shiraishi had procured a ticket.

Kazuma had a thought. He pulled out his smartphone and typed in a memo. He would raise the matter with Mirei Shiraishi the next time they met.

Would he get the chance to see her again? She'd told Kazuma that she would contact him if she had any ideas about uncovering the truth. At the end of the day, that meant she'd only reach out if she absolutely had to. Getting together with the son of her father's killer was probably the last thing she wanted to do. The other day, to his own surprise, he had felt that the two of them had some kind of affinity; later, he realized that he had been letting his imagination run away with him, and he despised himself for it.

He was lost in thought when a voice called, "Mr. Kuraki?" He looked up. The woman at the reception counter nodded in his direction.

"Please go to meeting room number three." The woman pointed to the doorway of a corridor.

He went down the hall. The door was open, and Kazuma went on in. A gray-haired man with a good-natured smile on his face was sitting behind a small desk.

"Mr. Kuraki, isn't it? Close the door behind you and take a seat."

Kazuma did as he was told.

"My name is Amano," said the old man, handing him his business card that read *Ryozo Amano, Principal, Amano Law Office*. The design was slightly different from the card the police had found in Tatsuro's home.

"I gather that you're here today to talk to me about your father's estate. What precisely is it that you want to discuss?" Amano asked as he ran his eyes over the form he was holding.

"Here's the situation. My father is currently drawing up his will, and it seems that he's planning to leave his estate not to his only son—that's me—but to some other people who are not family. Is that feasible under Japanese law?"

"I see," Amano said with a nod. "Now if you were to ask me, 'Does my father have the right to draw up such a will?' then I would have to tell you that yes, it's not a problem, legally speaking. What your father says in his will is entirely up to him. If, however, you were to ask me, 'Does him writing such a will guarantee that the estate will be settled the way he wants?' then I would have to say that outcomes tend to vary on a case-by-case basis and that sometimes the testator doesn't get what he wants. If you don't mind my asking, is your mother still alive?"

"No, she's dead."

"You said that you were the only child?"

"Yes, that's correct."

"Well, that greatly simplifies things. Provided that you give your consent, your father is free to leave his entire estate to someone else."

"What if I don't consent?"

"Then he can't leave his whole estate to them. In that case, your father is free to dispose of up to half his estate as he wishes, and you automatically have the right to inherit the rest of it. We call that your *legal entitlement* as the heir, which would form the basis of any discussions. If you want to, you can let the other party or parties have a greater share of the estate. If you don't want to do that, then, as I said, you automatically inherit half."

Kazuma nodded. "As I thought."

"As you thought?"

"I did a little research for myself before coming. My father seems to believe he can make over his entire estate to strangers, regardless of my view on the matter. I overheard him saying as much on the phone. He even said that he'd gotten confirmation from a law firm."

Amano looked baffled. "That makes no sense. I can't see any lawyer giving him such an opinion. If you don't mind me saying so, I'm inclined to think that your father hasn't really consulted a law firm. It sounds more like his personal assumption."

"No, he really does seem to have consulted a law firm. You see, I found this business card." Kazuma pulled out his smartphone, gave the screen a few swift taps, and pulled up the photo of Attorney Amano's own business card, sent by Godai via email. "Here," he said, and showed the phone to Amano.

The expression on the gray-haired lawyer's face underwent an abrupt change. He had not been expecting to be shown his own card.

"The quickest thing would be for me to ask my father directly what he's planning to do, but since I'm not even supposed to know that he's drawn up his will to begin with. . . ."

"Could you jot down your father's name for me?" Amano gave him a pen and a piece of paper.

Kazuma wrote out Tatsuro's name in full. "Please give me a moment," Amano said, then he left the room.

Kazuma exhaled loudly through his nose as he stared at the door that Amano had shut behind him. Despite his nerves, so far things seemed to be going well.

Godai had suggested the approach to take—making the lawyer nervous so they would check their records and tell him if his father had been there and what he'd discussed.

Kazuma knew that there were limits on what Godai could himself do and that the detective was pushing him, but he also knew that no malice was involved. Godai too had started to think that there was a whole other reality concealed beneath this murder case.

"I've managed to confirm some details. Your father did indeed come to see me. It was in June the year before last. I remembered him as I was going through the records."

"What sort of advice was he after?" Kazuma asked, his heart racing.

Amano sat down and gave a little nod.

"The same issue: the procedure for leaving an estate to people outside the family. It's odd, though. I'm sure I gave him an explanation of your legal entitlement as his child. I'm guessing that your father either misunderstood or forgot what I said. I can talk him through it all again if that's the case."

"I see." As Kazuma said this, his voice trembled with excitement. He had to fight to keep the emotion out of his face. "I'll run it by my father and contact you again if necessary. Many thanks for your time today." He got to his feet.

"Have you got all the information you need?"

"Yes, thank you."

"I hope I was of some use."

"Very much so." Kazuma's voice was almost shrill.

As he emerged from the building where the law firm's offices were, he clenched his right hand into a fist. He would have whooped in triumph if there hadn't been other people in the street. He had been right. A year and a half ago, Tatsuro had gotten a briefing from Amano. That meant he had no reason to go and seek the same advice from Kensuke Shiraishi. And that story about him coming up with the idea of leaving his estate to the Asabas after watching a TV program on Respect for the Aged Day was also untrue.

What's my next step? After such an important discovery, doing nothing was simply not an option.

He tried to set things straight in his head as he walked through the towering skyscrapers to Nagoya Station.

Should he speak to Attorney Horibe about confronting Tatsuro? There wasn't much chance of Tatsuro admitting to lying. Kazuma suspected it would just be a rerun of what happened when Horibe asked Tatsuro why he had moved on the anniversary of the 1984 murder. He would admit to having visited the law firm, but wiggle out of it with some excuse about having struggled to make heads or tails of Amano's advice or having forgotten it altogether.

When push came to shove, Kazuma didn't completely trust Horibe.

The lawyer wasn't a bad man and he was trying to do his best, but it never occurred to him to doubt anything Tatsuro said. As Kazuma saw it, in his eagerness to find things that could help reduce his father's sentence, Horibe had very early abandoned any idea of contesting the facts of the case.

Should he tell Godai what he had found out? The detective—who must have known that Kazuma would go and see Amano—was sure to be interested in the outcome. Kazuma imagined his eyes lighting up at the news.

Truth be told, there was another face that swam into Kazuma's mind before either Horibe's or Godai's. Mirei Shiraishi's. She was skeptical of Tatsuro's account of how he and Kensuke Shiraishi had met. Her skepticism would only be reinforced by this latest development.

But was it okay for him to contact her?

Mirei had said yes when he had asked her if he could ever reach out. He didn't think she was just being polite. But did this latest information merit him reaching out to her? Was it weighty enough to justify the son of the killer contacting a family member of the victim? For his part, he saw it as a significant breakthrough, but perhaps he should hold off until something more important turned up.

On his last visit to his father's place, he'd sorted several weeks' worth of accumulated mail. It had completely slipped his mind to provide the post office with a forwarding address. He had finally set one up online, but he still needed to go and collect the letters that arrived in the interim. The mailbox was just to the side of the gate at the front of the house. His plan was to collect the mail and head directly back to the station without going inside the house.

He checked his watch once he was on the platform. The train wasn't due for another five minutes. Kazuma pulled out his smartphone and rather timidly selected Mirei Shiraishi's number. He exhaled heavily before pressing the green Call button. He put the phone to his ear and closed his eyes. He felt flushed and out of breath.

The phone rang. Twice. Three times. No answer. Kazuma hung up after the fourth ring. It was the middle of the day. She was bound to be at work. He was a fool for even trying to call her on a weekday!

A minute or two later, the Kodama train pulled slowly into the station and came to a stop.

The train had not been moving long when he got a call. The caller ID indicated that it was Mirei Shiraishi. Kazuma scrambled out of his seat, answering the call as he made his way to the vestibule between the cars.

"Hello?"

"It's Mirei Shiraishi. You called a moment ago?"

"I've got some news. Is now a good time?"

"Yes, fine. What is it?"

"I just went to see a law firm in Nagoya. The police found one of the firm's business cards among my father's personal effects. I had this idea that if my dad already knew a local law firm, he didn't need to go and get advice about his estate from Mr. Shiraishi."

"How did it go?" There was audible tension in Mirei Shiraishi's voice.

"My father *did* go to see the Nagoya firm in June the year before last."

Kazuma then told Mirei everything that Amano had told him. She said nothing. The silence became so drawn out that Kazuma began to worry that the connection had been lost.

"Kazuma." Her voice was grave. "What do you plan to do now?"

"That's something I haven't decided. I thought I'd fill you in first."

"I appreciate that. This is a crucial piece of information."

"I'm glad you think so."

The announcement that the train was about to arrive in Mikawa-Anjo came over the speaker.

"You're on the bullet train?"

"Yes. On my way to the family house to pick up the mail."

"Have you got anything planned for later today?"

"Not really. Just heading back to Tokyo."

"I see . . ." Mirei's voice trailed off.

The train slowed abruptly. Kazuma braced himself, his phone still clamped to his ear.

"What time do you think you'll be back in Tokyo?" Mirei asked.

Kazuma did some rapid mental calculations. If he hurried, he could be back at Mikawa-Anjo Station by four. He'd been planning to return to Tokyo on the slower Kodama, but he could always double back to Nagoya and switch to the faster Nozomi there.

The train came to a stop, and the doors opened. Kazuma climbed out onto the platform.

"I can be back in Tokyo by six thirty."

"Six thirty? And you have nothing on after that?"

"No."

"Well, how about meeting at seven o'clock? I'd like to hear more about this law firm business and talk about next steps."

It was exactly what Kazuma had been hoping to hear. "That works for me. Where should we go?"

"Somewhere where we can talk. Do you know a good place near Tokyo Station?"

The place he had met with Nanbara fit the bill. Kazuma told Mirei Shiraishi the name and address of the café, and they agreed to meet there.

After the call, Kazuma felt buoyant, and then guilty for being excited. Words like *outrageous* and *insensitive* seemed inadequate to describe his feelings: actively looking forward to meeting the victim's daughter just before his father was about to go on trial for his murder!

He reminded himself that Mirei Shiraishi was only meeting him as part of her fight for the truth. The fact was that she had no desire to see the face of her father's killer's son.

Just like on his last visit home, he took a taxi from the station to Sasame. In the taxi, Kazuma put on the face mask he had brought with him as a precaution against being recognized. Even though Yoshiyama from next door had been friendly last time, Kazuma suspected he might be the exception rather than the rule.

Kazuma got the taxi to stop just ahead of a small crossroads around the corner from the house. As he paid, he asked the driver to wait. "I'll be back in a couple of minutes," he said.

"You will? You'd have been much better off letting the meter run," laughed the old taxi driver, who obviously wasn't expecting an influx of hails. It was a quiet neighborhood, Kazuma realized. Not the sort of place where murderers lived.

He got out of the taxi and walked quickly away. After turning the corner, he looked around to make sure that no one was watching, walked toward the house, took yet another look around, and then went through the gate.

There were all sorts of letters in the mailbox. He grabbed them all with one hand, stuffed them into his bag, and hurried back onto the street.

He returned to the waiting taxi and asked to be taken back to the train station.

"You see, I was right about it being cheaper to keep the meter running, wasn't I?" said the driver as he switched the engine back on.

Kazuma took all the mail out of the bag and examined it. A single slightly oversize envelope stood out among the junk mail and the utility bills. The logo read *Toyoda Central University Hospital*, above which the words *Dr. Tominaga, Chemotherapy Dept.* had been added by hand.

The addressee was Mr. Tatsuro Kuraki. Without a moment's hesitation, Kazuma tore the envelope open.

38

Standing in the street outside the café where she and Kazuma had agreed to meet, Mirei was of two minds. There were still ten minutes to go until seven o'clock. Mightn't she look a little desperate if she went in and sat down before Kazuma had even arrived? Although she desperately wanted to hear what he had to say, she didn't want to come across as needy. Still, it would be just as weird to go off for a walk to kill time.

She shook her head and went through the automatic doors. Why was she overthinking? His opinion of her didn't matter. She had just arrived early. That's all there was to it.

The first floor was a bakery, and the café was on the second floor. She went up the stairs and surveyed the large room, deciding where to sit, when she noticed a man rising to his feet near the window. Kazuma Kuraki, who was dressed in a suit, raised a hand to say hello. *What have I been so worried about? He's been here all along.*

"I hope I didn't keep you waiting long," Mirei said as she sat down.

"You didn't, but I'm glad I got here early. I wouldn't want to keep you waiting." He seemed to be just as anxious to be tactful as she was.

The waitress brought them water. Mirei ordered a latte and Kazuma a regular coffee.

"Sorry to contact you out of the blue like that," Kazuma said.

"It was a bit of a surprise, but I'm interested to hear the details."

"Yes, of course."

Kazuma tapped his smartphone a few times, then placed it flat on the table in front of Mirei. The screen displayed a photograph of a business card for the Amano Law Office.

"Apparently, the police came across this in my father's collection of business cards. Godai asked me if it meant anything to me. I had to say no."

"Are the police looking into it?"

Kazuma shook his head. "No, and they don't intend to either."

"How come?"

"The investigation is over and done with as far as they're concerned. The only reason Detective Godai showed me the card was because he was curious about it personally. He had his own doubts."

"Is that why you went to Nagoya?"

Kazuma nodded. "I went to see the attorney on this card. Like I said on the phone, he told me my father went to get his advice on whether it was legally okay for him to leave his property to people outside the family. Amano seems to have been very clear with him that, as his son and heir, I had a legal entitlement to a share."

"That also means that your father had no reason to seek my father's advice. Tatsuro Kuraki—your father—is lying about running into my dad at the Tokyo Dome and asking his advice. And he's extremely likely to be lying about his motive for the murder."

"There's something else in the Tokyo Dome episode I have my doubts about."

Kazuma suspected that the police had not tracked down the source of Kensuke's ticket. If they knew where he had gotten it from, then surely they would have given Mirei a straight answer?

The waitress served their drinks. As she did so, Mirei looked hard at Kazuma. Kazuma did not look away, returning her gaze with equal intensity.

"The big question for us is what to do next," Kazuma said as he picked up his coffee. "I'd like to confront my father through his lawyer, but past experience suggests he'll just give me some excuse. I also intend to discuss it with Detective Godai, but I've no idea what, if anything, he can do about it."

"Same here. I need to think carefully before deciding whether to mention this to our lawyer. Even if I told her, I doubt she could do much with it. The prosecutor seems to be confident that he'll win the case easily enough if the trial goes ahead without Kuraki modifying his statement. I've realized that the prosecutor and our lawyer care much more about that than getting to the actual truth."

"I feel the same way. My father's lawyer is obsessed with pleading extenuating circumstances to get a more lenient sentence for my father, and he seems pissed at me for refusing to accept that my father actually did it! If I bring this Amano to his attention, he'll probably tell me to stop interfering and quiet down."

"'Quiet down'? That's exactly what—" Mirei was going to say "our lawyer's always telling me" but she broke off mid-sentence.

"Sorry?"

"Nothing. It's not really relevant."

In fact, it was highly relevant to Kazuma. Mirei didn't want to mention Amano to Azusa Sakuma, because then she would be admitting that she had met Kazuma again. Sakuma was sure to be upset and snitch on her to her mother.

Mirei reached for her latte. It tasted as good as it smelled. She couldn't remember the last time she had drunk coffee from a porcelain cup. Her regular place used paper ones.

Looking out the window, she could see down into Ginza. Another similar experience she had had recently flashed into her mind. She had gone to the café that Kensuke had supposedly visited. That café wasn't as nice as this one; the latte she'd had there had come in a paper cup. She'd been watching Asunaro when Kazuma Kuraki had shown up—

Something was puzzling her. She turned to Kazuma.

"What is it?"

"Why do you think he went to that place?"

"Sorry? What place?"

"The café across the street from Asunaro. My father visited it twice before his murder. The second time, he stayed there for quite a while, apparently. The police think that he went to see the Asaba women. But what possible reason could my father have had to go to the café, if Tatsuro Kuraki never consulted him about settling his estate on the Asabas in the first place?"

Kazuma nodded slowly. "That's something else to think about."

"If he really wanted to see how the Asabas were doing, then going to the restaurant would make a lot more sense than surveilling the place from across the street."

"I agree. I think I need to take a second look at the old murder. I don't know how much an amateur like me can accomplish, but I think that that's where we'll find the truth behind everything that's happened."

"What year did the first murder take place—1984, was it?"

"That's right."

Mirei took a sip of her caffè latte and tilted her head quizzically.

"Is something bugging you?" Kazuma asked.

"Just a thought. Maybe I should look into it too."

"Look into what?"

"The past, of course. If Kuraki's statement is false, then maybe my father had some sort of connection to the Asaba family. It might even explain why he was keeping an eye on Asunaro from that café."

"Hmm, what sort of connection are you thinking of?"

"I really don't know. Still, I'd like to look into it for myself nonetheless."

1984—it was years before Mirei had even been born. Her parents had been university students. They'd started living together a few years after graduating and then gotten married after Ayako became pregnant.

She glanced at Kazuma, who was staring off into the middle distance. "What are you thinking about?" Mirei asked.

"I'm wondering why my father is lying . . . what on earth he's trying to hide."

"You think your father's hiding something?"

"Maybe not hiding *something* so much as protecting *someone*."

"Someone being the Asabas?"

"Probably, yes," Kazuma continued. "Protecting them at the cost of his own life."

"His life . . ."

Kazuma must have only just realized what he had said. A look of horror spread over his face, and he shook his head. "I'm so sorry. I didn't mean that my father's life is more important than your father's. Just ignore what I said."

There was something odd about his eagerness to brush the whole thing under the carpet. Mirei could sense that he was hiding something, but she bit her tongue because of the pain visible on his face.

YOU'RE BACK LATE," Ayako said when Mirei got home.

"One of my old flight attendant colleagues got in touch. We went out for coffee in Ginza."

"That's not like you."

"Yes, it is. I do it all the time."

"Normally, you go for a drink with your old airline friends. Can't recall you going to a café before."

Mirei realized that her mother was right and wanted to kick herself. She should have come up with a better excuse.

"Oh, my friend was trying to be nice. She didn't think that a drink was the mood just before the trial. I didn't mind. Anyway, today we had a coffee and left it at that."

"Going out for a drink from time to time's a good idea. A nice change of pace for you."

"It's not some kind of girls-go-wild scenario. I'm done with all that." As Mirei said this, she turned away from her mother and headed for her bedroom. The longer she talked to her, the greater the chance she'd dig herself into a hole. Ayako was sharp.

She was used to having dinner alone with her mother. Perhaps because of their earlier exchange, Mirei poured them both a glass of white wine.

"Did you find any old albums when you went through Dad's things the other day?"

"Albums?"

"Yes, albums of photos from when he was a kid or a student?"

Ayako nodded. "I just found one. Since he was an only child, his parents took tons of pictures of him. I don't know what to do with them. While we can't hang on to them forever, tossing them out doesn't feel quite right either."

"Is it in his room?"

"I think I put it in the bottom shelf of the bookcase." Ayako looked dubiously at Mirei. "Anyway, what do you want to do with your dad's old photo album?"

"Just to have a look. I realized that I know nothing about Dad's childhood. He never talked about it."

Ayako broke into a grin. "Don't you mean that when he did, you simply weren't interested?"

"Maybe." Mirei looked at her mother. "You met Dad when you were at university, didn't you? How old were you?"

"I was twenty-one and had just started my senior year. Your father was prepping for the law exam. He'd just turned twenty-three that April."

"So you were already in your senior year."

"We were studying different subjects, so we ran in different circles. There was this cherry blossom–viewing party, and that's where I met him. Most of the cherry blossoms were already off the trees because it was mid-April. Nobody really cared. That's not really what the party was all about," Ayako said wistfully.

"What was Dad like in his student days?"

"That's a difficult question." Ayako cocked her head to one side. "My first impression was of someone serious and reliable, not a whole lot more than that. I only realized there was more to him once we started dating."

"What do you mean?"

"He was a serious student, and on top of that, he worked really hard. Plenty of people study like crazy to pass the national bar exam, but your father was also working multiple jobs. I couldn't believe that he could drive himself so hard without destroying his health. I only found out why he was like that when I asked him about his family. He was raised by a single mother. He told you that, right?"

"I know that his father died when he was young."

"In a car accident when your father was in junior high school. The person responsible was in a stolen truck and had no driver's license. He ended up in jail, but he wasn't in a position to pay compensation. Zilch. They'd lost the family breadwinner, but they just had to suck it up and get on with their lives."

"I didn't know."

"'Don't like complaining about the hard life I've had,' your dad always said. Though he did tell me." Ayako wanted Mirei to know that she'd been someone special in Kensuke's eyes. "Luckily for them, they had a place to live. You probably remember it? That little house in Nerima?"

"I remember it. With the rice paddies right out front."

Mirei had often visited as a child. Her grandmother, who was hale and hearty, always spoiled her with lots of delicious food.

"Your dad lived with Grandma in that house for the first two years after graduating university. He only moved into his own place when he got his first job with a law firm. He must have been twenty-five or twenty-six by then."

"And you weaseled your way in."

Ayako frowned. "That's not a very nice way to put it. I had my own apartment, but we decided that sharing made better economic sense. It was Dad who suggested it."

Mirei had her doubts, but she kept them to herself.

Nothing her mother told her struck her as strange. The elephant in the room was the year 1984 or anything prior. Kensuke would have been twenty-two in 1984. He only met Ayako a year later.

"Did you know any of Dad's friends from his student days?"

"I've met a few of them. That's about it."

"Can you contact any of them?"

Ayako cocked her head to one side. "Their details may be in the address book on his phone. I don't know if Dad is still in touch with them. Haven't heard him mention them recently."

"Okay, let's go through his address book later. You can tell me if there are any names there you recognize."

Kensuke's smartphone was in an evidence bag somewhere. They had, however, been given a copy of the contact data.

"Okay. What are you thinking of doing?"

"I'm not sure. I just know I want to find out more about Dad's life. Here we are using the victim participation system, but with us knowing next to nothing about Dad, the actual victim, I'm worried we won't be able to make a good case."

"I see," Ayako said, looking far from convinced.

After dinner, Mirei went into her father's room. The old photo album was there in the bottom of the bookshelf. It was thinner than she had expected.

She opened it. The first thing to catch her eye was the picture of a naked baby lying on a futon.

She turned over the page and came across a cluster of pictures showing the baby Kensuke with a couple—his parents, obviously. Mirei could recognize her grandmother's face. *She was a pretty young woman*, she thought.

Her grandfather was a well-built, earnest-looking man. She remembered Kensuke telling her that he used to work for a trading company and did a great deal of business travel.

There were a few snapshots featuring an elderly couple. They had to be Mirei's great-grandparents. Her great-grandfather was a Kyushu man, born and bred, Kensuke had told her. He had moved up to Tokyo and married there. Both of them had died while Kensuke was still young, so he knew little about them. Looking at the album, Mirei realized that both her father and grandfather took after her great-grandfather.

Once Kensuke got to kindergarten, he was by himself in most of the pictures, though the photograph of his primary school enrollment ceremony featured him and his parents together.

Mirei stopped turning the pages when she came across one particular picture.

Kensuke was with an old woman whose face Mirei didn't recognize. She looked around seventy. She was wearing a thick coat and a muffler, so it must have been winter. Kensuke, who looked like a first or second grader, was wearing a tracksuit and a baseball cap.

But it was what was behind the two figures that really caught Mirei's attention: row upon row of ceramic tanuki, Japanese racoon dogs. They were standing on two legs, like the ones outside shops and restaurants.

Where is this place? Who is this old lady?

Mirei looked for any similar pictures, but the old woman did not reappear. There were pictures of Kensuke as a junior high schooler, just a few snapshots and group photos of him at high school and university, then him at his first law firm.

Busy working part-time jobs between intervals of studying, he probably wasn't having enough fun to want to capture the moment.

She turned back a few pages. She couldn't get that picture of her father and the old lady out of her mind.

Mirei went down to the first floor carrying the album. Ayako was in the kitchen washing the dishes.

"Mom, have you any idea who this is?" Mirei opened the album and showed her the photograph.

"Oh, that one. Noticed it myself a few weeks ago. No idea. Going by her age, perhaps a friend of your father's grandma or grandpa."

"Where is this place?"

"Shiga Prefecture," Ayako said offhandedly.

Mirei scrutinized her mother's face. "Shiga Prefecture? How do you know?"

"Those ceramic racoon dogs, they're Shigaraki ware. And Shigaraki is in Shiga." Her tone implied Mirei should use her brain more.

"So there's this old lady who lives in Shiga, and Kensuke's grandma or grandpa take him to visit her?"

"Maybe. Though your father never said anything about it to me."

Mirei picked up the album and went back upstairs. She googled Shigaraki ware on her phone just to be sure. Her mom was right.

This can't be important, she thought. *The Kensuke in the photo looks less than ten years old. The picture was taken almost fifty years ago. There's no way I need to go that far back into Dad's past. It's pointless.*

Nonetheless, Mirei couldn't let it go. For some reason, the photo bothered her.

As she stared at it, she realized why. It was the cap Kensuke was wearing. The mark with the interlocking *C* and *D*—wasn't that the logo of the Chunichi Dragons?

She checked on her phone. It was. So Kensuke had been a Dragons fan at that age.

Although Mirei herself was not interested in baseball, she'd read Kuraki's statement. The statement had Kensuke telling Kuraki that he first became a Chunichi Dragons fan because he hated the Giants and the Chunichi Dragons were the team who had stopped the Giants from winning the Central League Championship ten years in a row.

She did some digging online. The Dragons thwarting the Giants' bid for the V10 crown—according to the internet, that had happened in 1974. Kensuke would have been twelve at the time.

Mirei was convinced that she had caught Kuraki in yet another lie. *Even the man's account of why Kensuke had become a Dragons fan was an invention!*

She wanted to share the news with Kazuma. They had exchanged email addresses at the café. Mirei took a photo of the picture in the album on her phone and sent it to Kazuma along with a message explaining that she had found proof that Kensuke had been a fan of the Chunichi Dragons *before* the V10 upset in 1974.

Her phone rang a moment later, and her heart jumped.

He must have been so surprised that emailing felt too slow!

"Hello."

"It's Kazuma Kuraki here. I got your message."

"What do you make of my idea? I think I'm onto something."

"I agree. There's no way the kid in the photo's twelve years old."

"Definitely. Tatsuro Kuraki has got to be lying."

"Yes. I'm actually calling about something else, though."

"What?"

"You know all those ceramic racoon dogs in the background?"

"Yes. Apparently, the photo was taken on a trip to Shiga Prefecture. The racoon dogs are Shigaraki ware."

"I don't think so. That place isn't Shiga. I know where it is."

"Really? Where is it, then?"

"I'm pretty sure it's Tokoname."

"Tokoname?" Mirei had heard the name, but she had no clear image of the place.

"It's a town famous for its pottery. And it's in Aichi Prefecture," Kazuma said. There was an edge to his voice.

Aichi Prefecture. The words echoed in Mirei's head.

39

IT WAS ALREADY dark by the time Godai and Nakamachi emerged from Kazuma Kuraki's condominium. Godai checked his watch. They'd been with him for about an hour, and what he'd told them had surprised and unsettled them. He'd brought up not one but multiple issues.

Kazuma had called around midday to say that he wanted to give them an update. When Godai asked about what, Kazuma explained that he had been to Nagoya to visit the law firm on the card and wanted to share his findings.

Godai knew he needed to hear this and promised to drop by that afternoon. He invited Nakamachi to accompany him as soon as he got off the phone, and Nakamachi had immediately said yes.

"Where do you fancy eating, Godai?" Nakamachi asked as they walked along the street. "Our usual place?"

"No, no." Godai waved his hand in front of his face. "Let's go somewhere nearby. We need to start strategizing. That's not something we can do in a taxi with the driver listening in, is it?"

There was an abundance of pubs and restaurants to choose from. They found a place in an old wooden house on a narrow street and went inside. There was a vacant table in the corner.

They consulted the menu and ordered from a set list of draft beers with a few appetizers.

"Right, then," Godai said. "What shall we tackle first?"

"Do you think we're up to the job?" Nakamachi smiled sardonically. "Every issue Kazuma brought up spells trouble for us."

"We can't send this up the chain yet. Our superiors will just yell at us to stay in our lane. Anyway, I propose we start with the Amano Law Office."

"Kazuma Kuraki went to see them. I know you encouraged him to go, Godai, but I'm impressed with his can-do attitude."

"It really matters to him. He's committed, so he uncovers details."

According to Kazuma, Tatsuro had visited the Amano Law Office in June two years previous to inquire about the feasibility of leaving his estate to someone outside the family.

Nakamachi nodded. "That's a major new piece of information. There's no way Tatsuro would seek out a lawyer in Tokyo to ask for exactly the same advice."

"Then why would Tatsuro arrange to meet someone he'd only bumped into once at the Tokyo Dome?"

The waitress brought their beer and food: edamame, deep-fried squid tentacles, and cold cubes of tofu.

After toasting Nakamachi, Godai helped himself to edamame as Nakamachi spoke.

"Kazuma seems pretty skeptical about the whole 'we first met at Tokyo Dome' scenario too."

"The way he deduced that we don't know where Kensuke Shiraishi got his ticket from. He's pretty sharp."

"It certainly made my ears burn. Because we don't know! Ultimately, we just hypothesized a few scenarios not based on any solid evidence: Maybe Shiraishi bought a resale ticket on the day of the game; maybe he was given a ticket by a friend. Either way, we never reached a convincing solution and just sort of left the question hanging."

Godai groaned. "We've got no answer to the question Mirei Shiraishi raised about her father being unlikely to drink beer at Tokyo Dome on the same day he had a tooth out either. Perhaps we need to reconsider that whole Tokyo Dome episode."

"That photograph was the coup de grâce. The one of Kensuke Shiraishi as a little boy."

Godai nodded emphatically. "Quite a discovery."

"There's no two ways about it—the kid in the photo's only six, possibly seven, years old. Shiraishi would have been twelve in 1974 when the Dragons stopped the Giants winning their championship. It doesn't match what Kuraki said in his statement. Impressive, finding that inconsistency."

"As Kazuma said, he wasn't the one who caught it. It was Mirei Shiraishi."

"That was another surprise. You don't normally find a bereaved member of the victim's family teaming up with someone from the perpetrator's family and sharing their information." Nakamachi shook his head in amazement.

"That's true, but with those two, it's different. They share a common cause."

"Oh? What's that?"

"Neither of them believes the official version of events. As far as our superiors at the police are concerned, the case is signed, sealed, and delivered; meanwhile, all the prosecutor and the lawyers care about is the upcoming trial. Technically, the families on either side of the case may be in opposition, but their goal is the same, so there's nothing weird about them joining forces."

"I suppose not. At the same time, I can't quite get my head around it. I can't get a handle on their feelings." Nakamachi popped a piece of chilled tofu into his mouth and tilted his head quizzically to one side. "Light and dark. Night and day. The whole thing, it's perverse."

"You're waxing poetic today! You're right, though. I don't think the two of them are completely comfortable with being thrown together. Look at Kazuma Kuraki. He wasn't exactly bursting to tell us about his interactions with Shiraishi. He knows that it comes across as odd."

"Be that as it may," Godai said, continuing the discussion, "you know something else that bothered me? The location of that photo of the young Kensuke and the old lady. Kazuma's convinced that it's Tokoname, a town in Aichi. The location of the 1984 murder committed by Tatsuro Kuraki was Okazaki, also in Aichi. Should we see it as nothing more than a coincidence that both places are in Aichi? I got the impression that Kazuma is starting to think that Kensuke Shiraishi might have some connection to the earlier crime. Mirei seems to think so too. She's told Kazuma she's going to sift through her father's past."

"As a theory, it's pretty wild. All the more so when it comes from a couple of amateurs. Aichi is the country's fourth-most populous prefecture. There's every chance that some distant relative of Kensuke Shiraishi might still be living there."

"You could be right. Those two have a problem with Kuraki lying about Shiraishi's reasons for becoming a Chunichi Dragons fan. Why did Kuraki even need to tell that particular lie? It's got nothing to do with the case." Godai laid down his chopsticks and leaned his elbows on the table. "How about this: Let's say that Kuraki is lying about *everything* to do with how he met Shiraishi. Let's say that they actually met in some completely different way—and that he wants to conceal the fact. He comes up with a fanciful place for them to meet, and the Tokyo Dome pops into his head. Why? Because he really did go to the opening game of the season there. He also knew that Shiraishi was a Chunichi Dragons fan. As he was thinking what to say, he realized that there was something improbable about Shiraishi, who was born and raised in Tokyo, being such a passionate Dragons fan that he would watch a game by himself from the infield stand. His solution was to come up with the story of him having become a full-on Chunichi Dragons fan when they thwarted the Giants' ten-championship run. Plausible?"

"Just a minute. If Shiraishi really was a Dragons fan, then he'd have his own reasons for being one. All Kuraki had to do was be honest about it. If he didn't know why Shiraishi was a fan, he needn't have brought it up in his statement."

"My point exactly." Godai pointed a finger at Nakamachi. "Kuraki knew the real reason why Shiraishi was a Dragons fan, but he thought he'd be better off concealing it. Why? Because the real reason is that the Chunichi Dragons and Aichi Prefecture itself were a big part of Shiraishi's life. Kuraki cooked up the lie because he didn't want the police connecting the dots. How's that for a theory?"

"Aichi was a big part of his life—in what way?"

"It was a place he frequently went to as a child, meaning it had a formative influence on his life. It's also the place where Kuraki and Shiraishi first met."

Nakamachi choked on his beer and spluttered. He patted himself on the chest and got his composure back, then directed an inquiring look at Godai. "You think they met that long ago?"

"I'm just asking the question: What if they did? It would change every single aspect of our case."

"'Change' sounds like the understatement of the year to me. Don't you think we should inform our superiors?"

"I'd like to, but we can't propose reopening the case until we have some absolutely conclusive piece of evidence. At the very least, we need something that will subvert Kuraki's statement." Godai drizzled soy sauce onto the chilled tofu. "How's the search for supporting evidence progressing?"

Nakamachi grimaced and cocked his head to one side. "*Swimmingly* is not the word that comes to mind. It's the same old story: We can't find any physical evidence. We've got a written confession, but the prosecutor's going to need more than that to eliminate the jury's doubts if he wants to get the death penalty. He's terrified that the defense counsel might rein in the jurors by claiming that his client is concealing the truth."

"What's going on with the prepaid phone?"

Nakamachi spread his palms wide. "We came up empty, sadly, even with the help of the Aichi Prefectural Police. Despite canvassing all the vendors at all the electronics stores in Osu, they didn't find anyone who seemed likely to have sold one to Kuraki."

"That episode is another one that sticks in my craw. When I asked Kazuma Kuraki about it, he said, yes, his father often went to Osu, and no, he simply wasn't the sort of person who'd buy anything suspicious like a prepaid phone. I think the prepaid phone story's another fabrication, though why Kuraki should lie about it, I can't imagine."

"Try this on. Kuraki actually used a *borrowed* cell phone to contact Shiraishi. In his statement, however, he claims to have used a prepaid phone because he doesn't want to reveal the identity of the person who lent him their cell phone and get them into trouble."

"Sounds plausible enough. You're saying that Kuraki might have had an unwitting accomplice. It strikes me as a little risky, though. If for some reason Kuraki hadn't managed to get rid of Shiraishi's phone, the incoming call log would have given it away."

"No, that's true. Hey, I've just had an idea." Nakamachi's hand stopped in midair where he reached for the deep-fried squid with his chopsticks.

"What is it?"

"If Kuraki's aim was to avoid any record of the call being left on his own cell phone, then all he needed to do was to use a pay phone. If he used a pay phone, he wouldn't even need to get rid of Shiraishi's phone."

Godai put his beer tankard down on the table and looked intently at Nakamachi.

"Why are you staring at me like that? Did I say something dumb?"

"It wasn't dumb at all. It's a very good point. All Kuraki needed to do was to use a pay phone. So why didn't he?"

"Maybe he thought using a pay phone would arouse Shiraishi's suspicions. When you call from a pay phone, it shows up on the display, you know."

"Yes, but the first time he called Shiraishi using that prepaid phone was on the day of the murder. You don't think it occurred to him that Shiraishi might be suspicious when an unknown number came up on the screen?"

"A pay phone and an unknown number . . . They're both suspicious in their own ways."

"So why did Kuraki use a prepaid phone, then? Though, of course, we have no way of knowing if that's something else he's lying about."

"Yeah, with him having smashed the thing and chucked it into Mikawa

Bay, we're totally screwed. With pay phones, at least, you can't smash them to bits or cart them off somewhere else! Plus, since there aren't many left and not many people use the things these days, there's a high chance of fingerprints surviving on them. Putting on my policeman's hat, I'm rooting for the pay phone option."

Offhand though Nakamachi's comment was, it triggered something in Godai. He leaned his forehead on his left fist and thought long and hard.

It came to him like a ray of light piercing the darkness, only gradually assuming a clear and intelligible shape. It was an idea that hadn't occurred to him before, a theory in which, for all its outlandishness, he felt almost complete confidence, and it came together in the blink of an eye.

He smacked his fist into the table with an almighty thump. "I messed up."

Nakamachi jumped. "What's gotten into you?"

"I screwed up big-time."

"Screwed up? How?"

"I need you to look into something pronto. It's too much for one person to handle alone, so I'll have a word with your superior officers. I'll also speak to my unit chief. He'll probably give me a hard time for breaking protocol, but now's not the time to worry about that. If this hunch of mine is right—" Godai took a deep breath before he went on. "Then we've got a shocking new fact on our hands that is going to turn the whole case on its head."

40

THE BUILDING HAD a retro modern design that looked like something from the Showa era, although, according to the official website, it was much more recent.

Mirei drew herself up to her full height and went in through the main doors. There was a bank of elevators at the back of the spacious lobby. They all went to different floors. Mirei got into the one for the fifteenth floor alone. After pressing the button, she placed her right hand on her chest. She was feeling nervous.

The elevator arrived. There was a glass door immediately in front of her, and Mirei went in. A woman in uniform was sitting at a reception counter just off to the right. "Good afternoon," she said, smiling.

"My name is Mirei Shiraishi. I have an appointment with Mr. Hamaguchi, the managing director."

"Could you wait a moment, please?" The woman picked up the receiver, said a few words, and put it back down again. "I'll take you in. This way, please."

She escorted Mirei to a large, immaculate, and luxuriously fitted-out room. There was a marble coffee table surrounded by easy chairs and probably space for ten or so people. Not quite sure where to put herself, Mirei sat in the chair nearest to the door.

When she'd showed the contact list in Kensuke's smartphone to Ayako, her mother had picked out five names that she recognized from Kensuke's college days. She had singled out one of them, a certain Toru Hamaguchi, as someone who was particularly close to Kensuke.

"I've only met him a couple of times. He's the person whose name always comes up when your father reminisces about his university days. I think they used to go skiing together."

Mirei asked what Hamaguchi did for a living. Ayako wasn't sure.

"All I know is that he's not in the legal profession. I think Dad said that he got a job with a regular company after graduating from law school. He hadn't mentioned him much recently, so I thought they fell out of touch."

Mirei decided to contact Hamaguchi anyway. He was the only one of the five for whom there was also an email address. Perhaps Hamaguchi and her father had kept in touch by email, even if they never saw each other face-to-face.

She emailed him and after introducing herself and apologizing for contacting him out of the blue, she explained how Kensuke had lost his life and that she was looking into various aspects of Kensuke's past in preparation for the trial. She wanted to speak to someone who had known him as a young man, and she would be grateful for even a few minutes of his time.

She was surprised when his reply came back in less than an hour. Hamaguchi already knew that Kensuke was dead. "I heard about his death from a friend of mine. Since the funeral was private, and the trial is pending, I felt it was not appropriate to get in touch," he wrote.

While he had not seen Kensuke in person for nearly ten years, they'd indeed kept in touch by email. If Mirei wanted to see him and talk about his memories of their student days, he'd be more than happy to oblige. He appended his company details to the end of the email. It was a well-known insurance company, and his job title was managing director and chief executive officer.

She heard a metallic click behind her. As Mirei swiveled around in her chair, the door slowly opened, and a man with thinning hair and a kindly smile on his face came in. Mirei hastily rose.

"You're fine as you are; no need to get up. Please, sit and make yourself comfortable." As he said this, the man proffered his business card.

Mirei received it respectfully with both hands before presenting him with her card in return. "Thank you for making the time to see me."

"Not at all, not at all. Oh, I see you work for Medinix Japan?" Hamaguchi said as he scrutinized her card. "Quite a few of my friends are members. Currently, I get my checkups with one of our associated companies, but I might well sign up with you after I retire."

"I hope you will. I promise we'll take good care of you."

Hamaguchi nodded, smiled, and made his way to an easy chair across from Mirei. Though he wasn't tall, he held himself well and exuded calm authority.

"I have seen a photograph of you," Hamaguchi said. "It was from just after you were born. It was on a New Year's card from your father. I always thought he'd got married in a big hurry, and then I understood why. Even though I was at the wedding, I had no idea they were expecting! I didn't notice a thing. Those two really pulled the wool over my eyes." He smiled wistfully at the memory.

"But you haven't seen much of my father recently?"

"Every so often, we'd exchange emails saying that we ought to get together soon, but the timing never seemed to work out. If we'd managed to meet up, I'm sure it would have been just like old times, a complete gabfest." Despite Hamaguchi's smile, there was a tinge of sadness in his eyes.

There was a knock on the door. A woman slipped into the room and served them green tea, then withdrew.

"Please, have it while it's nice and hot."

At Hamaguchi's prompting, Mirei reached out and picked up the cup. "Thank you."

Hamaguchi took a sip of tea. "I was horrified when I heard what happened." His face was grave. "I don't know how far to trust the news reports. Was his killing really motivated by a personal grudge?"

"That's what the perpetrator said in his statement. He said that he'd inadvertently revealed something from his past to my father that he was desperate to keep secret."

Hamaguchi frowned and shook his head. "So terrible."

"Anyway, as I wrote in my email, I was hoping you could tell me about my father when he was young."

"I'm very happy to. Where should I start?"

"It doesn't matter. Anything that made a strong impression."

"Something that made an impression?" Hamaguchi put down his teacup and crossed his legs. "If someone asked me to sum up your dad in a single phrase, I'd describe him as one great big bundle of energy. When he studied, he studied like crazy; he could pull an all-nighter and then go straight into class without nodding off. And when he wasn't studying, he'd be working nonstop, either at his part-time jobs or preparing for the national bar. Your dad was a big reason that I decided not to pursue a career in law. I just thought, if that was what one was expected to do, then it was beyond me!"

Mirei remembered that: Her father always had boundless energy.

"Did my dad have any hobbies or interests?"

Hamaguchi grunted and cocked his head thoughtfully.

"What did he do for fun? He liked reading books and watching movies as much as the next guy. I can't think of anything he was especially passionate about. He always liked to say that wasting time was the thing he hated most. Although gaming consoles were all the rage back then, he never so much as touched one."

"So he was mostly studying or working during the university vacations. Did he never take any time off?"

"He did go on the occasional short trip. One winter, we went skiing together. A bargain-basement bus tour sort of thing. We spent ten hours being bounced around on the bus, got there in the morning, changed, and then went straight out onto the slopes. It's the sort of thing you can only do when you're young." Hamaguchi was starting to look a little misty-eyed.

"Did he ever say anything about going to Aichi Prefecture?"

"Aichi . . . ?" Hamaguchi's eyes widened.

Mirei worried that she had been a bit too abrupt. "A place called Tokoname. It's a town famous for its pottery."

"Tokoname," Hamaguchi repeated. "You're asking me if he ever went there?"

"I found a photograph that suggests my father had some sort of connection to Tokoname. Since he never mentioned the place to us when he was alive, we have no idea what sort of connection it might be."

"I see." Hamaguchi nodded. "I do remember Shiraishi going to Nagoya on the express bus from time to time. I don't know whether he was going to Tokoname."

Mirei blinked in surprise. "Are you sure?"

"Absolutely. I was renting my own apartment back then. Whenever Shiraishi went to Nagoya, he'd ask me to tell people that he was staying at my place. He always made overnight trips, and it seems like he wanted to keep them secret from his mom. After coming back from Tokyo, he'd always bring me a present. I got a lot of eel pies!"

"My father went to Nagoya without telling his mother what he was doing?"

"Yes, I think so. I asked him if he had a girlfriend there. No, he said, there was someone he needed to look in on from time to time on behalf of his late father. I always imagined it was someone who had been close to his father in some way, though I never came out and asked."

It's got to be the old woman in the picture, Mirei thought.

"Is there anything else you remember about his visits there? It doesn't matter how trivial."

"Anything else? Let me think." Hamaguchi crossed his arms and leaned back in his chair.

"Did my father make these trips to Nagoya throughout his time at university?"

"No. I seem to remember that at some point he stopped going. Oh yes, that's it. I remember now." Hamaguchi smacked his knee and gave a vigorous nod. "It must have been the autumn of our junior year. I was teasing him and he completely lost it."

"Teasing how?"

"He'd been going to Nagoya every month or two, then there was this period when he didn't go at all. I asked him why, and he said it was because he didn't need to go anymore. He mumbled and was rather evasive, so I said, 'Oh, I know what's going on. You *did* have a girlfriend there and she's kicked you to the curb.' He got this really fierce look on his face, and he yelled at me, 'That's not what happened! You think you're being funny?' He was so aggressive, I was completely blindsided."

"Wow . . ."

"Neither of us ever mentioned the subject again. Honestly, I'd forgotten all about it until just now."

Mirei remembered what Ayako had said. She had met Kensuke in April, when he was just starting his senior year. If Hamaguchi was right, at that point, Kensuke was no longer making his visits to Nagoya. It made sense that Ayako knew nothing about them.

"Well? Was any of that of any use?" Hamaguchi asked.

"It was very useful indeed. I really appreciate you making the time to see me."

"Feel free to get in touch if there's anything else you want to know. I'm happy to share stories anytime."

"I appreciate it."

"I know it's not polite to ask, but how old are you?"

"Me? I'm twenty-seven."

"Is that right? That means there's still plenty you don't know."

Not understanding what Hamaguchi meant, Mirei gave him a quizzical look.

"Know about your father, I mean. When we're young, none of us could care less about our parents' youth. It's only after your father dies and you go through his things that you start making all sorts of surprising discoveries. It's an experience I've had myself. When my father died three years ago, I found a copy of my grandfather's family register and learned that my father had once had a baby sister. I had absolutely no idea. My father never mentioned her. Under normal circumstances, I'd never have bothered looking at the family register, so I could have gone through my whole life without knowing."

"The family register..."

"Are you all right?"

"Yes, yes, I'm fine. Thank you. It was nice to talk and learn something new."

"I gather that the perpetrator's been arrested. Still, with the trial coming up, things won't be easy. Take good care of yourself. If there's anything I can do, don't hesitate to get in touch."

Mirei thanked him and made a deep bow.

41

WHEN KAZUMA TOLD Attorney Horibe what he had found out at the Amano Law Office, his father's lawyer's reaction was just as uninterested as he'd expected. The sour expression on his face seemed to say "So you've been playing at detective again, eh?"

Horibe said, "I understand the point you're making. It certainly is peculiar. Still, I don't think it merits any follow-up."

"What do you mean by 'it'?"

"I mean how your father met Shiraishi, the history of their interactions. Your father made the mistake of confiding his past crime to Shiraishi; then, terrified that Shiraishi might reveal it to someone else, he killed him in a frenzy. As long as those basic facts stand, nothing else matters much. Poking around at things of no relevance to the trial is of no use. We don't assume that because the defendant has made a confession he has told us the whole truth and nothing but the truth. That's not what happens most of the time. Even when defendants admit to having committed a crime, they try to make themselves look better, and they stay vague about crucial details. It's standard behavior, nothing special," Horibe said in the tone of a teacher speaking to a slow-witted student.

It was exactly the response Kazuma had expected.

He decided not to tell Horibe about the rest, the Dragons part of the story. It would be nothing more than a waste of time.

However, Kazuma did have one piece of news for the lawyer—and no one else.

"There's something I need to show you." Kazuma picked up his bag off the floor and balanced it on his knees.

"Oh, what is it?"

"This," Kazuma said, holding an envelope out toward him.

Horibe took the envelope and frowned distrustfully. "Toyoda Central University Hospital... from the chemotherapy department."

"Open it and read it."

"Surely this is Tatsuro's private correspondence? I cannot read it without his permission."

"I'm his son, and I say it's okay."

"Strictly speaking, opening another person's mail is against the law even for the addressee's children. Or are you not aware that it's a crime? People who open sealed correspondence without reason can be punished with up to twelve months in jail or a fine of up to two hundred thousand yen—"

Kazuma shook his head, no longer trying to conceal his annoyance. "I couldn't give a flying fuck about etiquette. There's got to be a serious reason for a busy hospital doctor to go to the trouble of sending someone a letter. Surely in an emergency, the issue is moot?"

"It depends on the circumstances; however, if you feel that strongly..." With a sigh, Horibe finally raised the flap and extracted some folded documents from the envelope.

Kazuma watched Horibe's face as he read them. The disinterested expression on his face gradually took on a certain rigidity. Horibe looked up. "Tatsuro has colorectal cancer?"

"He had an operation for it eight years ago. It was stage three."

"And the cancer's recurred?"

"Apparently so. I didn't know."

In the letter, the doctor was asking Tatsuro which hospital he was planning to go to for chemo treatment. Having no idea what Dr. Tominaga was talking about, Kazuma had called the hospital. What he had learned from the doctor had surprised him.

Tatsuro had been going to the hospital for regular screenings. Recurrence of the cancer had been confirmed about a year ago, and it had since spread into several of his lymph nodes. After radiotherapy, Tatsuro had a course of chemo. Tominaga was the doctor in charge of his treatment.

Although the drugs had a positive impact, they also had considerable side effects. Tatsuro suffered from fatigue and chronic nausea. Tominaga had experimented with different combinations, but at a certain point, Tatsuro announced that he wanted to pause the treatment. He justified this by claiming that he was moving, and he promised to look into resuming his treatment later at another hospital.

Tominaga asked him to give him the name of his new hospital once he had moved. After that, Tatsuro disappeared. When none of his phone calls were ever answered, Tominaga sent the letter by mail.

Tominaga clearly knew nothing about the incident in Tokyo. After some debate, Kazuma explained to him that Tatsuro was in custody for a criminal offense.

"Are you telling me that he's not receiving any treatment right now?" Tominaga asked in a startled voice.

"I don't think so. I mean, he didn't mention the cancer to me, and I'm his son."

"I need you to speak to him right now and get him to get the necessary treatment. Maybe there won't be any dramatic developments today or tomorrow, but this is not a problem he can afford to do nothing about." There was real urgency in Tominaga's voice.

Kazuma had not shared this piece of information with Mirei or Godai. He didn't want it to look like he was angling for sympathy. But he had to tell Horibe.

After recounting his phone conversation with Tominaga, Kazuma looked Horibe in the eye.

"Can you find out what my father is thinking about his cancer? What is he planning to do? Ask him why he didn't tell me about the recurrence or his decision to discontinue his chemotherapy, and what he wants to do next."

"I'll do that," Horibe said with a nod. "This is urgent. First thing tomorrow, I'll go to the detention center."

"I appreciate it."

"It's always possible that—" Horibe resettled his gold-rimmed glasses on his nose. "That Tatsuro thinks he's past any hope of recovery."

"That's certainly what I think. Why do you see it like that, Mr. Horibe?"

"Because everything makes a lot more sense that way."

"Everything?"

"When your father found out that the cancer had come back and spread, he must have realized that he didn't have long to live. That made him want to come clean to Shiraishi about the crime from his past. Who knows, perhaps anybody would have wanted to do the same. I suspect he chose Shiraishi because he was a lawyer and someone he could trust— *that's it!*" Horibe raised his index finger as if a brilliant idea had struck him. "For Tatsuro, the question of what to do with his estate was no longer a nebulous problem. It was urgent and pressing. Having consulted the law firm in Nagoya, he understood the technicalities of leaving his estate to someone outside his family. The problem then became whether he could actually do it. He picked Shiraishi and asked him to make sure that his estate went to the Asabas after his death. Shiraishi then came back at him with a completely unexpected counterproposal. If Tatsuro genuinely wanted to show he was sorry, then how about telling the truth while he was still alive? This threw Tatsuro into a panic. There he was, hoping to enjoy what little time he had left with the Asabas, and now it looked like he was going to be robbed of this last pleasurable part of his life. In his agitated state, he went and did something completely beyond the pale: He murdered Shiraishi."

Having rattled off his theory, Horibe took a deep breath and said, "So, what do you think?"

"I'm impressed," Kazuma said, "at your ability to come up with a narrative like that on the spot." There was no hint of sarcasm or irony in his voice. His admiration was genuine.

"It's my job, you see. With this scenario, I can see the jurors feeling sympathy for your father. What do you think?"

"I think you're right. It's good—at least in terms of helping my father get a reduced sentence."

Horibe looked at Kazuma dubiously. Hadn't the young man liked what he said? "What are you trying to tell me?"

"I agree with your idea that my father has accepted death as inevitable. Everything other than that, I disagree with totally. Let me tell you how *I* see things. My father wanted to use what little life he had left to him to protect something or someone, and he was ready to do whatever it took to do so. His whole statement is a lie. He's hiding something big. I suspect that my father could be lying about having murdered Shiraishi—No, I am quite sure that he is lying about it."

Weariness spread over Horibe's face. "Are you going to start trying to overturn the facts of the case at this stage? Kazuma, that just won't—"

"I know you'll never approve of what I'm trying to do. I know you won't support me unless Tatsuro himself withdraws his statement. Anyway, I'd like you at least to ask my father about his illness. That's at the root of everything."

"Fine, I'll do that," Horibe said. *Spare me from clients' families!* His annoyance was written all over his face.

Kazuma left Horibe's office and was about to head for the train station when he got a call. It was Mirei Shiraishi. Kazuma walked over to the curb and picked up.

"Hi, Kazuma Kuraki here."

"It's Mirei Shiraishi. Can you talk?"

"Yes. What's up?"

"I need to see you right now. There's something I've got to tell you. Are you free?"

Kazuma's grip tightened on the phone at her words. "Anytime. Now's fine for me."

"I see. Where are you now?"

"Shinjuku."

"I'm near Ueno. Shall I come to you?"

"How about we meet in the same café as last time? It's a quiet place to talk." Kazuma looked at his watch. It was almost half past four. "I can probably get there by five."

"Great. I'll see you there."

"See you soon," Kazuma said and ended the call. He realized that his pulse was racing. Was he excited to find out more about the case, or was he just happy to hear her voice? He did not know. All he knew for sure was that the prospect of meeting the daughter of the man his father was accused of killing didn't depress him at all.

He arrived at the café at exactly five o'clock. When he went up to the second floor, Mirei Shiraishi was already there, sitting by the window.

"Sorry to have kept you waiting."

"Not at all. Sorry to have asked you to meet at short notice."

The waitress brought them a couple of glasses of cold water. Mirei Shiraishi ordered a caffè latte, just like the time before. Kazuma felt like having the same thing, so he ordered one for himself.

"What was it you wanted to tell me?"

"I actually want to ask you a favor." Mirei Shiraishi looked at him earnestly.

"What is it? Anything I can do, I'm happy to help."

"That's kind of you to say. It's a big favor. I want you to go somewhere with me."

"Somewhere? Meaning where, exactly?"

"It's . . ." Mirei rubbed a nervous hand on her chest. "Tokoname. I want you to come with me to Tokoname in Aichi, to the place in that photograph."

42

GODAI FELT ENCOURAGED when he saw the person who followed the director and the commissioner into the meeting. He had not been expecting the head of TMPD Homicide. The atmosphere in the room turned tense. Everyone got to their feet and bowed at the senior officers.

The head of Homicide was a short, broad-chested man. Only after he settled into his chair did anyone venture to sit down themselves. Unit Chief Sakuragawa was the only man who remained standing. He turned and looked at the three men of higher rank.

"May I begin?"

The director, with his sharply chiseled features and gold-rimmed glasses, glanced over to the commissioner and head of Homicide for confirmation. The head of Homicide gave a curt nod.

"Please proceed," said Unit Chief Sakuragawa.

"Thank you, sir. It's necessary to go into considerable detail, so I'd like to ask the detective in charge of the case to do the presentation. Do you have any objection to that?"

The head of Homicide and the commissioner said nothing.

"No, that's fine," the director said.

"Thank you, sir."

Sakuragawa caught Godai's eye.

Godai got to his feet, introduced himself to the three senior officers, then went and stood beside the flat-screen monitor at the far end of the big table. From Tsutsui on up, everyone else in the meeting was of assistant inspector rank or higher. They already knew a certain amount about the case. The tension was visible on every face.

"I am going to tell you some important new facts that have come to light. Kuraki's confession contained a number of inconsistencies. He says that after committing the crime, he smashed the phone and threw it into the sea. The prosecutor requested we confirm the existence of this prepaid phone as corroborating evidence of the premeditated nature of the crime. Regrettably, we have not been able to do so. However, since we felt that there was something questionable in his whole story of the prepaid phone, starting with where he had acquired it, we suspected that Kuraki could have contacted and lured the victim using other means—namely, a pay phone. We therefore teamed up with the local precinct to review the footage from all the security cameras in the vicinity of pay phones near the Kiyosu Bridge."

"I've got a question," said the commissioner, raising his hand. "Why should the defendant go to the trouble of lying about something like that when he's already admitted to murder?"

Godai looked at Sakuragawa. He wasn't sure if now was the right time to answer that particular question.

"We'll address that issue a little later, if you don't mind, sir."

The commissioner acknowledged Sakuragawa's response with a nod.

Godai tapped a few keys on the computer keyboard. A map of the Kiyosu Bridge area appeared on the monitor.

"There are four pay phones within a four-hundred-meter radius of the Kiyosu Bridge. There are security cameras installed near each, and it's possible to make out, at least to a certain degree, the faces of anyone who uses the phones. We went through all the footage from the relevant time period on the day of the crime. We found only one person who used any of the four phones. It was a phone located here in Kiyosumi Ward District 2."

After pointing with his finger at one spot on the map, Godai again tapped his keyboard. The screen was now showing security camera footage of a liquor store with a pay phone just to one side of the door.

The date and time stamp at the bottom left of the image was from 6:40 PM on October 31.

A figure appeared on the left of the screen. After glancing around to check that no one was watching, the figure approached the pay phone and removed a wallet from a pocket, presumably to extract a telephone card.

The figure then picked up the receiver and jabbed at the buttons. The call was quickly answered. Glancing around anxiously from time to time, the figure talked for a while before eventually replacing the receiver, retrieving the phone card, and once again vanishing out of the left-hand side of the image. From appearance to disappearance, around two minutes had elapsed in total.

Godai pressed a key and froze the image. "This is all the footage I have to show you."

"Have you identified the individual?" asked the commissioner.

"We have," replied Godai. "The individual is related to a person of interest in the case. However, none of the investigative team interviewed this person directly."

"What is this individual's relationship to the defendant, Kuraki?"

"There's no direct relationship. Nonetheless, this individual is profoundly implicated in the murder the defendant discussed in his statement."

The head of Homicide whispered something into the commissioner's ear. The commissioner nodded, turned, and said something to the director on his other side. Unable to hear what they were saying, Godai felt uneasy.

The director turned to look at Godai. "When were you planning to answer the question the commissioner put to you a few minutes back?"

Godai glanced over at Sakuragawa. The unit chief gave an emphatic jerk of the chin.

"I'll do it right now, sir. We believe that Kuraki lied about having used a prepaid phone in his statement in order to conceal the existence of the individual that used the pay phone."

"You're saying that the person who lured the victim to the riverside was not the defendant but the individual in this footage?" the commissioner asked.

"Correct, sir," said Godai.

"Are you telling us that the person in this video footage is an accomplice working in cahoots with the defendant?"

Godai hesitated a second. He shot a glance at Sakuragawa. The unit chief looked uncomfortable and was chewing his lip.

This is not the right time for tiptoeing. Facts are facts.

"We don't think so," Godai said, addressing his superior officers. "There was no pressing reason to use a pay phone near the Kiyosu Bridge if the sole purpose of the call was simply to lure the victim there. The individual in the footage lives a long way away from the bridge. We believe that this individual is the principal offender and not an accomplice, that they are the true perpetrator of Kensuke Shiraishi's murder; that Kuraki was cognizant of that fact; and that he deliberately falsely confessed to protect the individual."

There was no sign of surprise in the faces of the three superior officers. Word must have leaked around the station that the wrong man had been indicted. That would explain the head of Homicide's presence.

Foreknowledge did not make Godai's report any easier to digest. The three senior officers, looking rather sour-faced, talked among themselves. The head of Homicide spoke less than the other two men, restricting himself to the occasional brusque nod.

"Unit Chief Sakuragawa," said the director. "Is this person a flight risk?"

"For now, we don't think so. Our assumption is that the individual in question has no inkling that they are under suspicion."

"How do you plan to prove they're the perpetrator? Using a pay phone near the crime scene doesn't even clear the bar for circumstantial evidence." The director had been given a detailed briefing in advance by Sakuragawa, but asked for the benefit of the head of Homicide and the commissioner.

"The first step will be to ask this individual who they called on the phone that day, after promising to respect their privacy, of course," Sakuragawa said. "If they are not the perpetrator, they should be happy to answer that question. We will also ask them to take a DNA test. We will check their DNA against foreign DNA found on the victim's clothing. After that, we will check relevant location data. It is highly likely that despite using a pay phone, the individual has a cell phone they were carrying on the day of the incident."

Having heard what the unit chief had to say, the director turned and looked at his two colleagues.

"Fine. You get on and do that," the director ordered. "We'll work out how to deal with the prosecutor."

"Yes, sir," said Sakuragawa.

The head of Homicide pulled himself to his feet, and the commissioner and director followed suit. Godai watched them leave the room and sat down heavily on one of the chairs. His armpits were drenched in sweat.

"Nice job, Godai," Sakuragawa said. "We're off to the races. I want you to interview the person of interest. If you plan to bring them in for voluntary questioning, do it here rather than the local precinct. Have you met this individual before?"

"No, sir. I've just seen a photograph. And an old one at that."

"Got an address?"

"Yes, sir. Shoto in Shibuya Ward."

"That's a posh neighborhood. Best to keep a low profile. We don't want to attract attention."

"Yes, sir."

Sakuragawa sighed heavily and then left the room.

Someone gave Godai a hearty slap on the back. He swung around on his heel.

"Quite the shit show we've got on our hands," Assistant Inspector Tsutsui said with a jovial shrug.

"I screwed up."

"Really?"

"When I was interrogating Kuraki, I told him how there were thousands of security cameras dotted around Tokyo and that the one surefire location was in the vicinity of pay phones. I told him that we'd go through all the security camera footage with a fine-tooth comb. That must have made Kuraki realize that he needed to act or else. He was aware that the real perpetrator had called from a pay phone. Since there were no other options, Kuraki chose to frame himself instead. I can still see him confessing to the crime. Out of the blue, he suddenly began to deliver a full and detailed account, as relaxed and fluent as you could wish. He reckoned that that was the only way he could stop the police investigation in its tracks. I really screwed up," reiterated Godai.

"Don't beat yourself up about it. This is not your garden-variety crime; it's murder. The trial could end in a death sentence. For an innocent man to be willing to step in and take responsibility for such a heinous crime—it's the last thing anyone would imagine."

"That's true, I guess. The real issue is *why* Kuraki was prepared to step in like that." Godai turned to look at the PC monitor, tapped the keyboard, and rewound the footage. A profile was visible on the screen.

Godai had seen a photograph of the individual when he went to the Asabas' apartment. It was a picture of a primary schooler. At the time, he had not asked the child's name. Now he knew what it was.

His name was Tomoki Anzai. According to his father, Hiroki Anzai, he was now in eighth grade.

43

KAZUMA SAVORED THE sensation of the cold air on his skin as he stepped down onto the platform at Nagoya Station. His cheeks were flushed and hot. He'd been tense throughout the train journey. The mingled anxiety of not knowing what lay ahead and a sense of heightened expectation that they were getting closer to the truth was coursing through his veins; the fact that Mirei Shiraishi was sitting right next to him was also a factor. Until a day or two ago, he would never have dared to imagine her traveling with him.

"We switch to another line here, don't we?" Mirei Shiraishi asked.

"Yes. We need to walk to Meitetsu Nagoya Station. It's very close."

The Meitetsu Nagoya Station building was vast. Kazuma made his way through the milling hordes of people, looking back occasionally to make sure that Mirei Shiraishi still followed.

They got to the ticket barrier in no time. Kazuma announced that he would go buy the tickets, but Mirei Shiraishi followed him to the ticket machines. He couldn't very well object if she offered to pay her share and had no choice but to take the coins she offered him.

It was two days since their rendezvous in the Ginza café when Mirei Shiraishi had asked him to travel with her to "the place in that photograph."

Kazuma had been surprised at her reason for wanting to go. She had a hunch about the identity of the old woman in the photo, she said. She was Kensuke Shiraishi's grandmother—Mirei's great-grandmother.

"I checked my father's and grandfather's family registers. The procedure's tiresome, but at least you can do the whole thing by mail. I discovered that my grandfather was actually the stepson of my great-grandmother."

"Just a minute. By your grandfather, you mean Kensuke's father, right? That's who the stepson was."

Kazuma needed to repeat what Mirei said to get the details clear in his head. She was talking about so many generations ago that he found it difficult to follow.

"My great-grandfather got divorced. The woman I thought of as my great-grandmother was actually his second wife, and my grandfather was the child he had with his first wife."

"And his first wife . . . ?"

"She's the woman in the photograph. The family register lists Tokoname in Aichi Prefecture as her birthplace. I'm guessing that she probably went back to Tokoname after the divorce."

The woman's name was Hide Niimi, Mirei said.

"I don't know whether or not Hide remarried, but since my grandfather was her child, then his son Kensuke—my father—is her grandson. It's only natural for my grandfather to have wanted to show off his grandson to his mother—without telling my great-grandfather and his second wife anything about it. I'm guessing that the photo was taken on a secret trip my grandfather took to Tokoname, bringing my father with him."

As he listened to Mirei, Kazuma could imagine the situation vividly, even though it was so long ago.

"One of my father's university friends told me that he used to make frequent visits to Nagoya by express bus back then. I'm guessing that he was visiting Hide Niimi."

Mirei's conjecture sounded convincing to Kazuma. He could not think of any other plausible explanation, and he told her as much.

"It's what we do with this information that's important. In the fall of his junior year, my father stopped visiting Aichi Prefecture. He told his friend that he no longer needed to go."

"*He no longer needed to go* . . . probably because his grandmother had died?"

"Very probably. I meant to check Hide Niimi's family register but didn't have the time. Still, there's something else that's bothering me."

"Oh yes? What?"

"My father's junior year was 1984. May of that year is when the incident you mentioned took place."

Kazuma felt a chill run up his spine. "What? You think Kensuke Shiraishi was involved in that case?"

"I don't know. I could be barking up the wrong tree. Either way, I need to know in order to be sure. That's why I'm asking." Mirei Shiraishi looked at him, her eyes glowing with determination. "I'm asking you to come with me to the site of this photograph."

Kazuma found everything she said quite startling, but he had no reason to turn down her request. After a little back-and-forth to find a mutually convenient time, they had decided to go to Tokoname that day.

Kazuma also had Tatsuro to worry about. Horibe had gone to see him at the detention center the day before. "Did the doctor from the hospital really send a letter to my house? The stupid old busybody," Tatsuro had said sourly when the lawyer asked about his cancer.

When Horibe asked what he planned to do about the disease, Tatsuro had simply announced that he no longer cared.

The chemo was unpleasant, and although he had stuck out the full course, complete recovery was out of the question, and there was no guarantee of him surviving very long. That was why he had decided he would be better off enjoying whatever time he had left, only everything had turned to shit.

"I don't care if I get the death penalty. If it puts me out of my misery, then bring it on, I say. Please, just bring this whole thing to an end as fast as you can, Attorney Horibe. I'm sure it's a pain in the ass for you too, right?" Kuraki was smiling as he said this.

When Horibe later relayed this exchange, Kazuma was more convinced than ever that his father was lying. Tatsuro wasn't the sort of person to give in to despair.

But why was Tatsuro lying? Kazuma hoped that this trip to Tokoname might furnish a clue and help solve that mystery.

The train pulled into the station, and Kazuma and Mirei Shiraishi climbed aboard. It wasn't very crowded.

Kazuma tried to remember when he'd last visited Tokoname. He hadn't been there since moving to Tokyo. The last time must have been when he went with a girl he was dating in high school. He wondered if the little lanes lined with ceramic sculptures would still be there.

"Could you just show me that address again?" he asked.

Mirei Shiraishi took her phone out of her handbag. "Here you go." The screen showed an old family registration certificate. Her grandfather Shintaro Shiraishi's.

Kazuma could make out the legal domicile of Hide Niimi. It was given as Onizaki in Chita in Aichi Prefecture, an address that no longer existed. Mirei Shiraishi explained that Onizaki had merged with Tokoname, losing its name in the merger.

"As far as I could tell from my internet research, the place is now part of the Kabaike District of Tokoname. I couldn't narrow it down any more than that."

"That should be enough for us to figure it out. We can ask the locals for help when we get there."

They didn't know whether Hide Niimi's house was still standing or not. *Tokoname's an old place without a great deal of population turnover,* Kazuma thought. *We've got a good chance of running into someone who used to know Hide Niimi.*

The train pulled into Tokoname. They emerged from the station to a line of waiting taxis.

A white van was parked slightly apart from the taxis with a man in a suit standing next to it. Kazuma recognized the logo of the car rental company on the side of the van. He went over and introduced himself.

"Good afternoon, sir," the man said. He opened the van's sliding door.

Once they were both settled in their seats, the van started to make its way along the main road. There were no tall buildings. A vista of old houses with tiled roofs stretched into the distance.

They stopped at the rental car company's office, which was just around the corner and turned out to be surprisingly small.

Not sure what the streets of Tokoname were like for cars, Kazuma had arranged to rent a smallish SUV. Once the paperwork was complete, he asked the man at the desk how to get to Kabaike.

"Go east along this street here, then turn left onto Route 252 and straight from there."

It was so simple he would not need the GPS, the clerk added with a laugh.

It was a long time since Kazuma had driven a car, so he set off cautiously.

"Tokoname seems like a very historic place. I honestly had no idea," Mirei Shiraishi said as she looked out at the town.

"Well, it's got a long history of pottery-making. It goes way back to the Heian period, maybe even earlier. Pottery from this place has been found all over Japan."

"How interesting."

After delivering this rote response, Mirei Shiraishi muttered the words *that photo* under her breath.

"You know that photo of my father as a little boy standing in front of all those ceramic racoon dogs? Maybe it wasn't just a family photo, and there was an element of regional pride in there. Perhaps his grandma wanted him to know that there was something special about the place she lived."

"That's a good point. Perhaps you're right. . . . No, I'm sure you are."

Kazuma had a sudden idea. He pulled onto the side of the road and checked their location using his smartphone instead of the GPS.

"You know I told you that I had an idea where that picture was taken? The truth is, it's very close to where we are now. Shall we swing by for a quick look before heading to Kabaike?"

Mirei's eyes were shining. "That would be great."

"Excellent. I've not been there for ages, so I'm eager to go."

They drove back to the vicinity of Tokoname Station and parked in a paid lot. If the map was right, their destination was only a few minutes' walk away.

They turned off the main road, walked a little way up a side street, and came to a signpost that read *Tokoname Pottery Path: Pedestrian Entrance. No through traffic.*

"Is this the place?" Mirei asked.

"I think so."

The street was a gentle upward slope. The street gradually narrowed as they made their way along it. You definitely wouldn't want to try it in a car.

Old houses that looked like traditional farms started to appear. A little farther on, and there were small items of pottery placed on either side of the footpath.

They were at the foot of Denden-zaka, one of the most famous stretches of the footpath.

"Ooh, what are those?" Mirei exclaimed. The wall running along one side of the hilly path was made of round-mouthed pottery jars laid on their sides, one on top of the other.

"Those are Tokoname ware shochu jars."

They advanced a little farther up and emerged onto a stretch known as Dokan-zaka, where the wall was made of earthenware pipes. The pipes too were Tokoname ware.

There was the occasional small pottery shop. All of them had plenty of pottery animals on display; items with a racoon dog motif were particularly prominent.

"My guess is that the photo was taken somewhere on this footpath," Kazuma said. "Since it was almost fifty years ago, things were probably very different from today, but the rows and rows of ceramic tanuki lined up along the sides of the path—this is the only place that fits the bill."

Mirei Shiraishi seemed to be getting a little emotional as she surveyed the scene. Noticing that her eyes were moistening, Kazuma looked away. *She must be thinking about her father*, he thought.

They continued walking and finally arrived at a large multichambered ascending kiln. Kazuma knew that it was one of the biggest kilns of its kind in Japan. The ten chimneys of different heights, one beside the other, made for a truly impressive sight.

"I wonder why my father never mentioned this place. It's beautiful. I wish he'd brought me here."

Kazuma wanted to be careful and not say the wrong thing. They were going to have to confront the answer to that question soon enough.

They went back to their car and set out again for Kabaike. Kazuma estimated they would be there in ten minutes.

They drove in a straight line along a single-lane road with private houses and small shops on either side. Most of the shops had their metal shutters down and appeared to be permanently closed. It was a common enough sight in provincial towns in Japan. Presumably, someone had built a shopping mall a short drive away.

They were at Kabaike Station in no time, and Kazuma slowed down. He had spotted a small post office on the right-hand side of the road.

"What's up?" Mirei asked.

"Let's try asking them."

"You mean the post office?"

"Yes. I have an idea."

He stopped in front of a store that looked as if it had shut down years ago.

The two of them went into the post office, where a middle-aged woman at the counter greeted them with a friendly hello. One other person, a man, was standing at the counter; a few other clerks were at work at desks behind him.

"Excuse me. I was wondering if you could help me," Kazuma said. He then told the woman that they were looking for the house of someone who had lived in the area around fifty years ago but were having trouble because they only knew the old address.

An older man at one of the desks behind the counter must have overheard, as he walked over to them. "What is the address?"

Mirei tapped her phone and showed them the photograph of Hide Niimi's family register.

The old man slipped on a pair of reading glasses and squinted at the screen. "I see what you mean about it being old. It's from before the towns were merged."

He beckoned them into the office area behind the counter, then told them to wait before he disappeared. Although the two of them had no business being there, the other staffers didn't give them so much as a second glance.

The man reappeared a few minutes later. He had a thick file under his arm. Kazuma spotted a date on it: 1965.

The man opened up the file on his desk. It contained photocopies of old maps.

"Right, so Onizaki would be . . . around here. Now what was the name of the person you're looking for?"

"Hide Niimi," said Mirei Shiraishi.

"Oh yes. Here it is. The Niimi house. It's near the fishing harbor."

He was pointing at a particular square on the map. Kazuma could just make out the name *Niimi* in small characters. Kazuma pulled up a contemporary map on his phone and started looking for the same place. Beside him, Mirei Shiraishi did the exact same thing.

"What's there now?" Kazuma asked.

The man smiled wryly. "Any of our mail carriers could tell you soon enough, but I'm guessing you're heading there right now. You'd be better off asking for yourselves. We can't just come out and tell you who's living there now."

The man was right. That would be a serious infringement of privacy.

"Of course not. We appreciate your help."

They thanked him and left the post office.

"That was very worthwhile," Kazuma said as they strolled back to the car.

"Thanks to your quick thinking. I'm so glad you came with me today."

"My pleasure. Anyway, we'd better carry on. The house will be harder to find once it gets dark."

They reached their destination in a matter of minutes. It was a residential district with a lot of tired-looking houses. There was no shortage of monthly parking lots for residents, but no public parking. With no choice in the matter, Kazuma parked on the roadside, and they set off on foot, while checking the maps on their phones.

"This has got to be the place," said Mirei after they'd done a couple of circuits of the immediate neighborhood. She sounded disappointed.

"Let's try talking to the people who live nearby. There are plenty of old houses, so we may well come across someone who knew Hide Niimi."

The two of them went from house to house, asking the residents if they remembered the old Niimi house. People were a little suspicious at first, but relaxed as soon as Mirei pulled out the photograph and explained they were looking for the house because Hide Niimi was her great-grandmother.

Several of the locals remembered that there had been a Niimi house. However, nobody remembered anything about the woman who had lived there.

At the seventh house they visited, the Tomioka house, they struck gold. "If it's Mrs. Niimi you're interested in, Grandpa's certainly mentioned her to me," said the woman who answered the door, a housewife in her forties. It turned out that by "Grandpa," she meant her father-in-law.

"Could we have a quick word with him?" Mirei asked.

"Sure you can. He's at a fisheries cooperative event right now. He should be back any minute. Do you want to wait?"

"Absolutely. We'll wait outside in the car. Could you call us when he gets back?"

"I can do that, but you're very welcome to wait here. He's due back any minute now."

Mirei looked inquiringly at Kazuma.

"Then we'll take advantage of your kind offer. A proper sit-down talk will certainly be better."

"Sounds good to me. Please, come on in." The woman beckoned them inside.

She escorted them into a Japanese-style room with a family altar. A boy of junior high school age peeked in at them from the passage before vanishing.

Kazuma got a little uncomfortable when the woman produced tea for them.

"Oh, you really shouldn't," protested Mirei, looking rather red.

"You've come all the way from Tokyo. It's the least I can do," the woman said. The expression on her face quickly changed to thoughtful. "I moved here about twenty years ago when I got married. The house was still there back then. No one was living in it, though. One time when the subject happened to come up, I remember Grandpa saying that an old woman called Niimi used to live there. Pretty sure he said she lived alone."

Kazuma and Mirei exchanged a look.

There was the rattle of a sliding door being pushed open and the sound of a man's deep voice.

"Ah, he's back." The woman stood up and left the room.

They could hear hushed voices from the passage. Eventually, the woman returned with an old, sturdily built, and deeply suntanned man. He looked every inch the retired fisherman.

"Sorry to intrude on you like this," Mirei said, sitting primly with her legs folded under her on the floor. Kazuma also bowed.

"What's this all about? You want to know about Mrs. Niimi?" the old man said as he sat down on the floor. His voice was disconcertingly loud.

"My father used to come and visit her when he was a little boy." Mirei pulled the photograph up onto the screen of her phone and showed it to the old man.

"What's that? Uh . . ." The man opened a cabinet and took out a pair of glasses. After putting them on, he took the phone from her and squinted at the screen, then nodded as he said, "Aha. That's right, that's right. That's her. That's Mrs. Niimi. Hide, I think her name was. But this is a very old picture."

"Did you know her personally?" Mirei asked as the man handed the phone back to her.

"Me, no. My mother was friends with her. My ma was unusual for this neck of the woods; she'd gone to a posh all-girls' school and fancied herself as a bit of an intellectual. What with Mrs. Niimi being a primary school teacher, I s'pose they were birds of a feather. Used to talk about books and things together."

"What was Hide Niimi like?"

The man tipped his head slightly to one side, then began to speak. "Hard for me to say, really. I didn't have much to do with her myself. Cheerful and good-natured, I think. Like I said, my mom was a bit of a snob and always quick to judge other people. Never heard her say a bad word about Mrs. Niimi, though."

"Really?"

There was a look of relief on Mirei's face as she said that. Since this was her great-grandmother they were talking about, praise didn't hurt.

"Did Hide Niimi have a family?"

"Probably did, but as far as I can remember, she always lived alone. Let me think . . ." The old man frowned and scratched one of his temples as he dredged his memory. "I heard she'd been married. That's why her son would come by to see her from time to time, right? I remember my mom saying something about him 'coming from different stock' after he managed to win a place at a top university in Tokyo. Or am I getting mixed up? No, the ages are all wrong. Mrs. Niimi was already an old woman by then. There's no way she could've had a son at university."

Pressing a hand to his forehead, the old man tried to get his thoughts straight.

"How about this?" Mirei said. "Maybe that young man was her grandson."

"You're right. That's right. My memories got all tangled up. It's the grandson. My mother told me. Mrs. Niimi's son died. She complained to my mother that she couldn't attend the funeral out of consideration for the new wife and her family. Still, the grandson came by himself to visit her after that. Yeah, my mother told me she'd met the grandson quite a few times."

"Do you remember anything about him?"

"The grandson, you mean? I don't know anything firsthand. All I know is what I heard from other people. Anyway, at some point, Mrs. Niimi just wasn't there anymore."

"You mean she moved?"

"I suppose. Because something awful happened to her." The old man furrowed his silver eyebrows.

"Something awful?"

"Mrs. Niimi's parents had a lot of money, and she was pretty well off herself too. Still, as a woman who had to take care of herself, she must have been worried about the financial side of things. She got into investing—more like speculating, really. The problem was, her financial adviser was a complete crook, and she ended up losing a boatload of money. She was trying to get the money back from the adviser, when he was murdered. Then she was truly up the creek without a paddle."

Kazuma started. "That murder happened in Okazaki, didn't it?"

The old man's wrinkled eyes widened in surprise. "That's the one, that's the one. Impressed that a youngster like you knows that. Back when it happened, my mom couldn't stop going on about how the murdered man was Mrs. Niimi's financial adviser. She got a second shock later when it turned out that the guy had been ripping Mrs. Niimi off big-time."

Kazuma was flabbergasted. *Kensuke Shiraishi's grandmother was defrauded by the man at the center of the Higashi-Okazaki financial adviser murder case.*

Mirei just sat there, frozen stiff. A glance was enough for Kazuma to see how unnaturally rigid her face had become.

"Uh, what's wrong? Have I put my foot in it?" The old man looked between them.

"It's nothing," Kazuma said, intuiting that Mirei was in no fit state to answer his question. "Is there anything else you can tell us, like what happened to Mrs. Niimi after that or where she moved to?"

The old man shook his head. "No idea. I haven't thought about her or spoken of her with anyone for years now. Doubt anyone else round here even remembers her."

"No? Well, thank you so much for everything."

"Was I any use?"

"You were extremely useful."

Kazuma thanked the old man once more, then glanced across at Mirei. Despite her stupefaction, she came to herself with a start and bowed briskly.

Neither of them said a word as they left the Tomioka house and went back to their car. It was only after he had switched on the ignition that Kazuma spoke.

"Is there anything else you want to look into while we're here?"

Mirei shook her head. "I don't know," she said in a barely audible voice. "Mr. Kuraki . . . How about you?"

"Can't think of anything off the top of my head. I feel we should share this information with Detective Godai. What do you think?"

Mirei sighed. "Yes, I think this has become too big for us. For you and me."

"I agree. So, should we head back to Tokyo?"

"Let's do that," said Mirei. Her voice was muffled.

They barely spoke in the car or the train back to Nagoya. It was the same after they boarded the Nozomi bullet train and sat down in their reserved seats.

Kazuma had no way of knowing what was going on inside Mirei's head. Kazuma himself was bewildered. He had no idea how to interpret or even process what they had learned.

The murder of the finance executive in Higashi-Okazaki was a more than thirty-year-old case. Tatsuro had confessed to being the killer—and now it turned out that Kensuke Shiraishi had a connection to the case.

How could Kazuma possibly make sense of it?

A nebulous thought started to coalesce in some deep corner of his mind. It was too momentous and horrible for him to articulate. There was no way he could share it with Mirei.

Or maybe she was thinking the same thing.

Maybe the beautiful woman sitting beside him was imagining the same scenario herself.

A grim, ominous story untouched by redemption.

Kazuma turned and tried to sneak a look at Mirei's profile. As he did so, the fingertips of his left hand brushed her arm. He hastily pulled back. His heart was pounding in his chest.

Then he felt something against his fingers. Mirei was pressing her arm closer to him.

He cautiously intertwined his fingers with hers. She did not resist.

Still looking straight ahead, he gave her hand a squeeze. She squeezed his hand back.

God, how I wish the two of us could just escape this! he thought.

44

Just as Sakuragawa had said, Shoto in Shibuya Ward was jam-packed with posh houses. Each of them had its own unique design, as if the residents were all competing with their neighbors in the good-taste stakes.

Hiroki Anzai's house was Western in style. It had no front gate, and there were a couple of parking spaces on either side of the path leading to the front door. One fancy foreign car was parked in the left-hand space, but the right-hand one was empty. Perhaps it was for visitors.

He checked his watch: 1:00 PM. Today was a Saturday, and the detective responsible for surveilling the house had confirmed that none of the Anzai family had left it.

Godai made a call on his cell as he looked up at the house. The name was already saved to his contacts. Someone quickly picked up.

"Yes?" said a man's voice. He sounded quite composed.

"Is that Mr. Anzai?"

"It is."

"I'm sorry to disturb you over the weekend. My name's Detective Godai, and I'm with Tokyo Metropolitan Police Homicide. We met the other day."

Anzai gave a grunt of recognition. "What can I do for you?"

"I'm actually standing right outside your front door. I have some questions for Tomoki."

"*You want to speak to Tomoki?*" Anzai sounded astonished.

"That's right. May I come in?"

"What do you want to ask him about?"

"I'd prefer to tell him directly."

He heard a sharp inhalation of breath at the other end of the line. "Could you give me a minute?"

"Very good, sir. I'll be waiting out here."

Anzai ended the call without saying another word, obviously rattled.

Godai looked up at the second-floor windows. He thought he could make out people moving behind the curtains.

"You're not worried he'll let the boy sneak out, sir?" asked a junior detective.

"It's not going to happen," Godai said tersely. "Anzai's just reacting like a father. He's got no idea what's going on, so of course he's shaken up. The idea of helping the boy get away won't even cross his mind."

The junior detective nodded. Godai only brought three officers with him, including the driver. He'd planned to have one keep an eye on the back door of the house, but there turned out not to be one.

Neither Nakamachi nor any of the other precinct detectives were there. Sakuragawa's orders were for Godai to hand over the new suspect to the precinct only after building a rock-solid case against him.

Hiroki Anzai called him back.

"Godai here."

"Anzai. Sorry for being slow to get back to you. My son's here in the house, but he's in no fit state to see you. Can we reschedule this, perhaps tomorrow or the day after?" Anzai was doing his best to sound calm, but Godai could hear a slight quiver in his voice. He wondered if Tomoki had gone to pieces at the news that the police were outside.

"I regret to say that this is an urgent matter. We have to speak to him today. How about if I interview him, one-on-one?"

"No, I . . . uh . . . Can't you hold off till this evening?"

"I'm afraid that's impossible. Otherwise, we'll have to take him back to headquarters. Since your son is a minor, I think it's best for all concerned if we can do this at a civilized hour."

"Headquarters? You mean the Tokyo Metropolitan Police Department Building in Kasumigaseki?"

"I'm only saying that we *might* have to take him there. It's not definite." Godai was being deliberately disingenuous, lying as earnestly as possible.

"All right . . . look, can you give the boy an hour? . . . No, no. Make that thirty minutes. I have some questions of my own for him."

"What are they?"

Anzai stammered something, then lapsed into silence.

"Well, be as quick as you can about it. We'll take proper care of him. I hope you understand that."

Anzai said nothing. Godai could picture the anguish on his face.

"Do you think my son is involved in that murder case?"

"We don't know. It's a possibility. Which is why we want to talk to him."

Anzai sighed heavily. "Can I be present at the interview?"

Godai had been expecting this request. Sakuragawa had told him how to reply.

"You're welcome to do so," Godai said.

Again, Anzai hung up without saying a word.

As Godai was watching the house's front door, it swung open, and Hiroki Anzai emerged in a navy-blue sweater.

Godai ordered the junior detectives to stay back and walked up to the doorstep. He greeted Anzai with a nod of the head. "Sorry about this."

"What's Tomoki done?" Anzai looked desperate as he asked this.

"That's what we're here to find out. What did you tell him?"

"Nothing. I just said the police were here."

"How did he react?"

Anzai shook his head wearily. "He didn't say anything. Just kind of snorted . . . *But I know.*"

"Know what?"

"I know the signs. That boy—the more upset he is, the less emotion he shows."

Listening to Anzai, two thoughts occurred to Godai. That the man was smart and coolheaded. And that he was a good father.

"Please." Anzai beckoned him into the house.

Immediately inside the door, there was a spacious entrance hall. Godai slipped off his shoes. "Where are your wife and the other children?"

The detective watching the house had told him that the whole family was at home.

"They're upstairs. I'm afraid we won't be able to offer you any tea."

"Don't worry about that. Is Tomoki up there with them?"

"No, he's in his bedroom."

Godai looked up at the stairs. "So he's by himself?"

"Yes."

"In that case, could you bring him down right away? I'm a little worried about him."

Teenagers' emotions were complicated. The last thing Godai wanted was the boy slitting his wrists.

Anzai's face stiffened. He went up the stairs.

Godai's fears proved groundless. A minute or two later, Anzai came back down with the boy in tow.

"Shall we go in here?" Godai asked.

Anzai led the young man into the back of the house. Godai followed.

The sun poured in through the large plate glass window in the living room. Godai sat down facing Tomoki Anzai across a marble coffee table. Hiroki Anzai sat off to one side.

Tomoki was a thin youth whose slim jaw and neck were those of a child. He kept his eyes fixed on the ground and well away from Godai.

"Tell me, Tomoki, do you have a smartphone?"

His face blank, Tomoki gave a small nod in response to Godai's question.

"I'd be grateful if you could answer verbally."

"Give the man a proper answer," Anzai growled.

Godai raised a restraining hand before repeating the question: "Do you own a smartphone?"

"Yes," Tomoki answered.

His voice was weak and reedy and slightly hoarse.

Godai opened the briefcase he'd brought with him. He extracted a printout of an image from the security camera and placed the paper in front of Tomoki. "This is you, isn't it?"

The father craned forward for a better look. The son just darted a quick glance at it. Godai noticed that he caught his breath.

"Well? It is you, isn't it?"

"Yes . . . I think."

"You *think* it is. That's an odd thing to say. That is you, so you should be able to give me a clearer answer than that."

The father was itching to interrupt. This time, however, he managed to keep himself under control.

"Okay, yes, it's me," Tomoki mumbled.

"Sorry? You're going to have to say that a bit louder."

Tomoki took a deep breath and said, "It's me."

"Thank you," Godai said.

"Just a moment ago, you admitted to owning a smartphone, so what are you doing here using a pay phone? Did you just happen to forget your phone that day? I see you've got a phone card there. Do you always keep one in your wallet?"

Tomoki said nothing and hung his head.

"My next question: Who were you calling? A friend? An acquaintance? You'd better tell the truth, because it's something we can easily check up on."

Once again, the kid said nothing. It was exactly the reaction Godai had been expecting.

"All you need to do is to tell me who you were calling, then I'll leave. It doesn't matter who it is. I'll get up and go without asking you any more questions. That's a promise. Come on, you can tell me."

Godai now noticed that Tomoki was shaking. He couldn't tell whether it was from confusion or fear.

"Answer the man, Tomoki," Anzai said in a low voice.

"Why?" Tomoki said. "Why are you asking me this?"

"Sorry? *You're* asking *me* why?" Godai responded.

"You already know, don't you? You know who I called," Tomoki said without lifting his head.

Godai straightened his spine and resettled himself on the chair. He was nearly there. "I need to hear you say it."

Tomoki raised his head and looked at Godai for the first time. Godai was startled at the expression on his face. A faint smile played on the young man's lips.

"The person I called was Mr. Shiraishi. Is that good enough for you?"

Godai exhaled heavily just as Anzai burst out, "You can't be serious!"

"If you know his first name, could you give me that too?" Godai said.

"I know it. It's Mr. Kensuke Shiraishi," Tomoki answered defiantly.

Godai took a notebook and a ballpoint pen out of his briefcase and placed them in front of Tomoki.

"Do me a favor and write the name here. Along with your name and today's date."

Tomoki picked up the pen and began to write. After completing the name *Kensuke Shiraishi*, he paused to think for a moment, then wrote something else. Godai's eyebrows jumped when he peered over at the page.

I killed Mr. Kensuke Shiraishi was what the youth had written.

45

THE INSTANT SHE heard the ring of the doorbell, Mirei's chest tightened with dread. Could it be a bearer of bad news?

Ayako would answer the intercom. Mirei hoped it was just a delivery.

There was the sound of footsteps coming up the stairs, coming closer. Mirei's hunch was right—she just knew it.

A knock on the door. "Come in," Mirei said.

The door opened. Ayako stood there silhouetted with the corridor behind her. The lights were off in Mirei's room.

"Are you awake, Mirei?"

"Uh-huh," she said from beneath her quilt. "Who was that at the door?"

"It's the police: Godai, the first detective who came round here."

Mirei let her breath out. She was right. Still, there was some comfort in the knowledge that it was Godai.

"He says he's got some important news for us. And he wants you there."

"Okay." She sat upright. "What time is it?"

"It's after six."

"Oh, okay."

Outside, it was dark. Although Mirei barely managed to sleep, the day had gone by quickly.

"I need a minute. I've got to make myself presentable."

Mirei hadn't eaten anything that morning and had spent the entire day in her room. She knew she must look awful.

Ayako switched on the light. "Mirei, are you all right?"

"What do you mean?"

"I mean that... yesterday, you said you weren't feeling well. What's going on? Did something happen at work on Friday?"

Friday was the day before yesterday, before her trip to Tokoname with Kazuma. She had not told her mother about it.

"Detective Godai is waiting," Mirei said. "Why don't you fix him some tea?"

There was a look of exasperation on Ayako's face as she turned to go.

"Mom?" Mirei said.

Ayako swung back toward her.

"We should be ready for some bad news."

Ayako frowned suspiciously. "Why?"

"Detective Godai definitely won't be bringing us good news."

"I don't need you to tell me that. Your father was murdered. There's nothing good about that."

"It's worse. Worse than you can imagine. Devastating. Horrible."

Ayako's face stiffened. Mirei felt guilty. She shouldn't have gone that far. Still, her poor mother would have to learn the truth somewhere down the line.

"What do you know, Mirei? Tell me."

"I don't need to tell you. That's what Detective Godai's here for." Mirei rolled out of bed and went and stood in front of the window. When she pulled back the lace curtain, her gloomy face was reflected back at her in the glass.

Ayako left the room without another word. There was something final about the sound of her footsteps descending the stairs.

Mirei sat down at the small table and pulled her makeup bag toward her.

Suddenly, she found herself thinking about Kazuma Kuraki. What was he doing right now? What was he thinking about? What was he planning to do tomorrow?

She recalled everything that had happened in Tokoname. Had it been a mistake to go there? She'd ended up learning something she would have been better off not knowing.

She didn't want to think about it, but she couldn't stop herself. Although she tried her best to suppress the sinister narrative taking shape in her head, the effort backfired.

She prayed that Godai was there for a different reason entirely.

There was little chance of that, though. As she applied her lipstick, she told herself that she should prepare for the worst.

Godai stood up and wished Mirei good evening when she came into the living room. He was wearing a suit and tie. It was the same outfit he'd been wearing the last time they met, but he came across as more formal because of the rigidity of his facial expression. Mirei sat down, and Godai followed suit.

"I've made tea," Ayako said.

"Don't want any," Mirei said brusquely. She looked at Godai. "What's this about?"

Godai rubbed his hands on his knees.

"The first thing I need to say is: What I'm going to tell you today is not officially allowed. Some of my colleagues thought it would be better to conceal it from you, the bereaved family, for now. Looking ahead, however, I think that the sooner I share what we know, the better. It was my decision to come here today. That means that everything I'm about to tell you is unofficial and off the record. Can you promise me that you will not share it with anybody else?"

Mirei looked at Ayako. They exchanged a nod, then told Godai they agreed.

"Thank you." Godai ducked his head in gratitude.

"Let me get right down to it, then. We have a new suspect in the Kensuke Shiraishi murder. The likelihood that Tatsuro Kuraki, the suspect who is currently in detention, is responsible has declined very significantly.

In fact, the charges against Kuraki will soon be dropped, and he will be released from detention."

"What do you mean?" Ayako burst out. "How could this happen?"

"It's just as I said. The person we believe to be the true perpetrator of your husband's murder has given us a highly credible statement, and we already have amassed a considerable amount of supporting evidence for it. His statement is far more compelling than Tatsuro Kuraki's, and we believe that he is telling the truth."

"Who is it, for God's sake?" Ayako asked, her voice ragged.

"I'm sorry, but I'm not yet at liberty to say."

"Please tell me. I won't tell anyone."

"I'm sorry, I can't do that. When the time is right, I promise I will tell you."

"That's simply . . . simply not good enough."

"Mom," Mirei said. "Just give it a rest."

Ayako's eyes widened in shock.

Mirei turned toward Godai. "Is that everything you came here to say? I'm betting there's something else that you need to share with us."

Godai looked back at her solemnly. "You're right. There is something else."

"I knew it. And this thing is more than the real identity of the murderer." For all her agitation, she spoke with complete fluency.

"What are you talking about, Mirei?" her mother said.

"What was the motive?" Mirei asked Godai, ignoring her mother's question. "The perpetrator's reason for killing my father—how did they explain that?"

Godai looked searchingly at Mirei. "Do you know something about it?"

"I do. It's related to my dad's past. Dad was involved in a crime that took place in Aichi Prefecture more than thirty years ago. I'm right, aren't I?"

She could feel Ayako tensing beside her.

"Why do you say that?" Godai asked.

"It's a long story. Suffice it to say that I went to Tokoname the other day."

"Tokoname." Godai frowned in puzzlement. He didn't seem to be familiar with the place.

"It's where my dad's grandma used to live. I did some investigating of my own there. All I really learned was that Kensuke does have some connection to an old murder case, though I don't yet know exactly what his role in it was. I have my own ideas—ideas that I sincerely hope are wrong. So what really happened? I'm guessing you know. Or am I wrong?"

Godai looked intently into Mirei's face, then nodded. "Yes, I know."

"Then tell me. I can handle it."

Godai nodded and took a deep breath to settle his nerves. "Let me answer your earlier question, the one about motive, first. We have learned the motive was revenge. The actions of Kensuke Shiraishi plunged the perpetrator's whole family, up to and including the perpetrator, into misery. Killing Shiraishi was payback."

"What did my father do to ruin their lives?" Mirei was determined to ask the question despite already knowing the answer.

"More than thirty years ago, a man was arrested in connection with the case you mentioned just now, the murder of the financial adviser in Higashi-Okazaki. The police believed this man to be guilty, but he insisted on his innocence right up until he took his own life in a police cell. As you well know, in his statement, Tatsuro Kuraki admitted to being the actual perpetrator in that murder case. According, however, to the individual we now believe to be responsible for your father's murder, Kuraki was lying about that too. The individual claims that Attorney Shiraishi was the true culprit in the 1984 case, and that is what inspired him to take his revenge."

Every word that Godai uttered sank into the very depths of Mirei's heart like large rocks hurtling down into soft marshland. At each impact, she felt an indescribable sense of loss, though, very much to her own surprise, there was no pain.

She had arrived at the truth. From now on, there was no more getting lost. There was nowhere she needed to go and nothing she needed to look for. The thought gave her a strange feeling, almost like a sense of achievement. Resignation and acceptance turned into a sensation of peace and comfort.

46

GODAI WAS THERE waiting when Tatsuro Kuraki walked out of the detention center. The detective asked Kuraki to accompany him to TMPD headquarters on a voluntary basis. Kuraki raised no objections and climbed into the police car with a benign expression on his face. All he had by way of luggage was a single travel bag.

Kuraki was no longer suspected of or charged with a crime. Although guilty of interfering with a police investigation, it was not clear yet whether he would be charged for the offense.

Rather than having Kuraki sit wedged between a pair of uniformed policemen, Godai sat next to him in the back seat of the police car.

"I've caused you all a great deal of trouble," Kuraki said by way of apology once the car had moved off.

"Any chance of you telling us the truth now?" Godai said.

Kuraki sighed and turned to look out the window. "I suppose I'm going to have to."

His complexion was a good color even if he did appear to have lost a lot of weight over the last three months. His profile, as he gazed into the distance, radiated peace. He had the aura of someone who has seen and understood everything.

The car arrived at the Tokyo Metropolitan Police Headquarters, where Kuraki's interview was to be conducted. Unit Chief Sakuragawa wanted to handle the questioning himself. For his part, Godai had demanded to sit in.

"So where do you want to start?" asked Sakuragawa once they were seated across from one another in the interview room.

Kuraki smiled wryly and tilted his head to one side. "Where indeed!"

Sakuragawa turned and looked at Godai. "Where would you like him to start, Detective Godai?"

"Let's go the traditional route and start with the old case from 1984," Godai shot back.

Sakuragawa turned back to Kuraki. "Are you okay with that?"

Kuraki briefly closed and reopened his eyes. "I suppose so. That's the only sensible place to begin. I warn you, this is going to be a very long story."

"Not a problem. We've all been looking forward to hearing it, so we're here for the long haul. Right, Godai?"

"Sounds good to me, sir." Godai bowed his head.

"All right, then," Kuraki said, and he launched into his account.

MAY 1984

KURAKI HAD JUST turned thirty, and life was good. Three months before, his son, Kazuma, had been born. He had married his wife, Chisato, two years earlier, and the two of them had been dreaming of having a child. One year older than her husband, Chisato had gotten pregnant just as she began to worry about her age.

The factory where Kuraki worked was a subsidiary of one of Japan's large automakers. Around one thousand people were employed there. Roughly half of them were machinists.

The auto industry was booming, and they were worked to the bone. They were all supposed to get two days off a week; in reality, they only got one or two Saturdays off a month. There was plenty of overtime, something that Kuraki, who had a new family to take care of, welcomed, as it increased his paycheck.

Kuraki commuted to the factory by car. His white sedan was made by the parent company. It was comfortable enough, despite being secondhand. Since Kuraki didn't wash it very often, it was always streaked with grime.

On the morning of *that* day, just as they always did, Chisato and little Kazuma waved goodbye as he set off to work. They rented a cheap apartment, but Kuraki had plans to buy a house in the near future. He'd been paying into a housing fund since joining the firm and had a tidy sum saved.

The two-lane road was on the busy side. There was a hill approaching, and Kuraki knew that once he got over the summit, he would be confronted by a long line of backed-up cars because of the slow traffic signal ahead.

A man was cycling along the edge of the road in the same direction as Kuraki, his dark suit flapping in the breeze. *Hard work pedaling up a hill like this*, he thought as he overtook him. Glancing at him as he went by, he was struck by the ill-tempered scowl on the cyclist's face.

Once Kuraki got to the top of the hill, there, sure enough, was the line of cars. He vacillated a second or two before deciding to turn off onto a side road. He could turn left at the bottom of the hill. It was a bit of a detour, but he would still get to the factory faster that way.

He was nearly at the foot of the hill and was drifting to the left when it happened. A glimpse of something in his peripheral vision, and a moment later, something crashed to the ground right alongside his car. It had to be a person. *Oh god, I hit them*, he thought.

He hastily stopped the car on the side of the road and jumped out.

Squatting on the ground was the cyclist he had passed a minute or two earlier. His face was distorted, and he had his hands pressed to his back.

"Are you okay?" Kuraki asked. "Are you hurt?"

The man did not move. He said something through tight lips. Unable to make out the words, Kuraki bent down. "What did you say?"

"I'm in agony," the man mumbled.

"Oh... I'm so sorry."

The man responded to Kuraki's apology by extending his right hand at high speed, palm upward. "Your card."

"Sorry?"

"Give me your business card. You've got a job, so you must have a card. And your driving license." The hand waved impatiently. "Get a move on."

Kuraki took his card and driving license out of his wallet and handed them to the man, who compared them to each other. He then produced a ballpoint pen from the inside pocket of his jacket.

"Your home address and phone number. On the back of the card."

"What, my card?"

"Of course I mean yours. For fuck's sake," the man replied rudely.

Kuraki dutifully jotted down his home address and phone number on the back of his card. When he held it out, the man snatched it back from him and examined it greedily. "So what is this? A new-build condominium? An apartment?"

The man must have noticed that the address had a number in it. When Kuraki told him that it was an apartment, a look of disdain came over his face. Was he disappointed to be dealing with someone comparatively poor?

"I'll go and call the police. And an ambulance."

The man looked at him sourly but gave a small nod.

There was a pay phone about thirty or forty feet away. Kuraki dialed both emergency numbers. Due to his agitated state, it took him a while to explain the situation. He then called his company and told a clerk that he was feeling sick and was going to take the day off. She seemed to take him at his word.

His calls taken care of, Kuraki returned to the site of the accident. The man was now sitting cross-legged on the ground, smoking a cigarette. A briefcase, which must have been strapped to the rack on the back of his bicycle, was now on the ground beside him.

"I am so sorry," said Kuraki, renewing his apologies.

The man said nothing. He thrust a hand into his briefcase and pulled something out. It was his card.

Kuraki took it and read it. It read *Shozo Haitani, CEO, Green Enterprises.*

"I'm screwed," Haitani muttered, half talking to himself. "I had a ton of meetings scheduled for today. Why the hell did this have to happen?"

"I really can't apologize enough," Kuraki said, bowing humbly.

"Call the number on that card. A young guy should answer. Tell him that I've been in an accident and that he'll need to cancel all my morning meetings."

"Okay." Kuraki turned back around, card in hand, and ran to the phone booth, where he called the number.

"Green Enterprises," said a male voice. He certainly sounded young.

Kuraki duly relayed Haitani's message. Naturally enough, the young man at the other end was startled. "You said Haitani's been in an accident? How serious is it? Is he badly hurt?" he asked.

"No, no. He's sitting talking normally and smoking a cigarette. I don't think it's anything serious."

"Oh, it isn't?"

Kuraki thought he detected a note of something akin to disappointment in his voice. Unsure what to make of the young man's reaction, Kuraki hung up.

He heard the ambulance siren just as he emerged from the phone booth.

When the paramedics saw how light Haitani's injuries were, they reacted not with relief but annoyance at being called for such a trivial incident. They nonetheless bundled Haitani into the ambulance and drove off, siren wailing. Haitani had given Kuraki the key for his bicycle, which Kuraki had promised to drop off at Haitani's office.

A police car drove up a minute or two later, and the site inspection got underway.

Kuraki gave as thorough an account as he could to the traffic policeman who was asking the questions. It was, of course, as thorough as possible from Kuraki's own perspective. The truth was that he had very little idea how the accident had transpired.

In total, there were three policemen conducting the inspection. They carefully examined the road surface, Kuraki's vehicle, and Haitani's bicycle, but their faces were confused. There was much puzzled tilting of heads.

"We'll be in touch in the next day or two," they eventually told him. Kuraki was now free to go. He had been expecting them to take him with them to the police station. Apparently, that was not necessary.

He drove back to his apartment, where he told Chisato about the accident. She was horrified. As he told his story, the color drained from her face, which went taut with anxiety. "And . . . what's going to happen now?"

"I don't know. It'll depend how bad the man's injuries are. Frankly, I don't think they're serious."

"Did you tell your firm?"

"No. I want to keep this whole thing under wraps."

"Good idea."

Kuraki's employer was extremely sensitive about traffic violations and traffic accidents. If you reported yourself as having being involved in any incident, the personnel department would be notified automatically, and it would have a negative impact on your next performance assessment. Sometimes the personnel people even posted the details of the accident on the company bulletin board. Although they only ever used people's initials, you didn't have to be a genius to work out who it was.

Kuraki called a taxi to take him to the site of the accident so that he could collect Haitani's bicycle.

Having arrived, he climbed onto the bicycle and set off for the address on the card Haitani had given him. His office was in a building overlooking the plaza in front of the railway station. He popped into a Japanese sweets shop he passed on his route and bought a mixed box of azuki bean paste wafers.

When he reached his destination, the building turned out to be more run-down than he had been expecting, with paint peeling off the façade in places. Green Enterprises was on the second floor. He left the bicycle on the sidewalk and climbed the stairs.

On a door spotted with patches of rust was a nameplate with the words *Green Enterprises.*

He pressed the doorbell. He heard it ringing inside.

The door opened, and a young man popped out. He was casually dressed in a shirt and jeans.

"Oh, hi . . . Mr. Haitani called a moment ago. He should be here any minute."

"Is it all right if I wait inside?"

"Don't see why not," the young man said after a little hesitation. Perhaps he wanted to show he didn't have the authority to make such decisions himself.

Kuraki walked into the office. He estimated it was about twenty-five square meters. There was a large table in the middle piled high with a heap of boxes, documents, bottles, and some pieces of equipment. The shelves around the walls were overflowing with files.

The young man went and sat down at a desk by the window and started reading a comic. There was a phone and a fax on the desk.

Kuraki sat down on a chair.

"How did Mr. Haitani sound on the phone? Any news on his injuries?" he asked.

The young man didn't bother looking up from his comic. "Dunno," he said indifferently.

Kuraki took another look around the office. There was nothing there to suggest what the company actually *did*. Was this young man the sole employee? If he was, he wasn't exactly dressed for the part.

The phone on the desk rang, and the young man picked it up.

"Green Enterprises here. . . . I'm sorry, but Mr. Haitani is currently away from his desk. . . . Ah, it's you, Mr. Tanaka. It's always a pleasure to speak with you. . . . If that's what you're calling about, I'll be sure to get Mr. Haitani to call you back later today. . . . Absolutely. I promise I'll give him the message. Thank you. Goodbye." The young man had conducted the whole conversation lolling back in his chair and not bothering to put down the comic he was reading. While his language had been polite enough, the tone had been wooden, as if he were reading from a script.

The young man replaced the receiver and turned his attention back to his comic.

There was a clang as the door swung open. Seeing Haitani, Kuraki got to his feet.

"Oh, you here?" Haitani scowled as he walked in. He had a slight limp in his right leg. "God, it hurts. It really hurts. What a total disaster."

"I can't apologize enough," Kuraki said. "How are the injuries?"

"Why d'you even need to ask? I can't even walk right. Three months for a full recovery. Three goddamn months. Doctor told me I've got to take it easy. What are you going to do for me?"

"But the bones are okay?"

"Just 'cause they ain't broke don't mean everything's fine. Look at the state of me."

"Oh . . . I'm sorry."

Haitani limped his way toward the desk where the young man was sitting. "Any calls?" he asked.

"Yeah, some fellow called Tanaka. Old geezer, sounded like."

"That stupid relic? Okay, you can go home for the day."

"Great." The young man sprang to his feet, slipped past Kuraki, and left the office, still clutching his comic book.

Haitani plunked himself down in the chair the young man had just vacated and pulled the phone over to him. He took a notebook out of his briefcase, flipped it open on the desk, picked up the receiver, and dialed a number.

"Oh, hello. Is that Mr. Tanaka there? It's Shozo Haitani here. I understand that you called. I'm so sorry, I'd just stepped out." When he spoke in a civil manner, Haitani sounded like a completely different person. "Ah yes. I thought that's what the call was about. I just came back from a meeting with the broker. . . . That's right, just as we hoped, the price is climbing nice and steadily. . . . Yes, of course. . . . As I explained the other day, with this particular financial product, we're not able to cancel the contract until the maturity date. . . . Yes, that's correct. So they're saying you'll just have to be patient for a little while longer. The returns you get will be better that way. . . . Exactly, exactly. Yes, I'll take care of everything. Great talking to you. Goodbye."

Haitani put down the receiver. Scowling, he jotted something down in his book and then sighed. After briefly massaging the back of his neck, he turned to Kuraki.

"Right, so what're we going to do about this?" His previous brusque manner was back.

"Did you . . . uh . . . get issued with a medical certificate at the hospital?"

"Did I get a medical certificate? I couldn't make heads or tails of it. Let me see. Where'd I put the thing?" Haitani rifled through his jacket pockets and his briefcase, then clucked his tongue loudly. "Shit. Can't find the darn thing. Not to worry. For the time being, all I want is for you to pay for my treatment today."

"Oh yes. Of course." Kuraki pulled out his wallet, wondering how Haitani could possibly have mislaid such an important document. "Have you got your receipt?"

"No. Must have lost it along with the certificate. I'll find the thing, but just pay me anyway. It was thirty thousand yen, give or take."

"Did you say . . . *thirty thousand yen?*"

Kuraki wanted to ask why the treatment had cost so much.

"You've got car insurance, haven't you? You'll get your money back, so what's the big deal, eh?"

"I don't think I can use my insurance."

"You can't? Well, that's your problem, pal, not mine. Never heard of anyone causing an accident and refusing to cover the injured party's cost of care."

"That's not what I'm saying. I just don't have that much cash on me."

Haitani glowered at him. "Well, how much have you got?"

Kuraki flipped open his wallet. He had a little over twenty thousand yen. He wasn't in the habit of walking around with large sums of cash. Besides, it was Chisato, his wife, who kept the family ATM card.

"Fine," said Haitani when Kuraki explained the situation. "I'll take twenty thousand." He looked disgusted.

Kuraki held out the two ten-thousand-yen notes. Haitani grabbed them and crammed them directly into his inside jacket pocket.

"Um . . ."

"What now?"

"I'd like a receipt for the twenty thousand. I'll pay you the rest later."

Haitani glared at him. "You calling me a cheat?"

"Absolutely not. I just think it's better to do things by the book."

"Don't you worry. I won't forget. Now we need to talk about the next few weeks. Dropping in on my most important customers is a big part of my job. In this state, I just can't do it. How are you going to help me with that?"

"I'm sorry." All Kuraki could do was bow and apologize again.

"The first thing is getting from my home to the office. I won't be able to ride my bike for a while, so we need to come up with a solution."

Haitani explained that his house was three miles away.

"The best thing would be to take a taxi, but they take ages to come, even if you make a phone reservation, and the ones you see driving around are usually taken. Um, what can I do?" Haitani pulled a card out of his wallet as he said this. It was Kuraki's business card. Haitani looked hard at Kuraki's home address, which Kuraki had jotted down on the back of the card. "What time does your job start every morning?" he asked.

"Nine. Why?"

"Okay. That's perfect. You can come and collect me at my place at seven thirty and drive me to the office. You'll still be able to get to work on time." He tossed Kuraki's card onto the desk. "Yeah, that'll work. Let's do that." It was a unilateral decision.

"What? . . . Do you mean *every day*?"

"Course I do. If you can't do it yourself, then find me someone who can."

Kuraki quickly thought it through. He couldn't ask anyone else to do it, but he could make it work if he left home at seven.

"Fine, I'll do it. Starting tomorrow, right?"

"Here's my address." Haitani jotted something down on a piece of scrap paper and handed it to Kuraki. "Driving me home from the office starts today, so be here at six."

"Hey, hang on a minute. I can do six today because I've taken the day off. Normally, I have overtime. Can't you make it eight?"

"Eight? What am I supposed to do, stuck here till eight?"

"Okay, then at least make it seven. Please."

Haitani sighed theatrically. "Oh, all right, then. Seven it is. Don't you be late, though."

"I won't. Trust me."

Haitani sank back into his chair, crossed his arms, and looked up at Kuraki. "That's that out the way. Now I need to start thinking about damages. I'll also be making a few more visits to the hospital, so I'll be billing you for those too. Make sure you've always got cash on you."

"Uh . . . okay."

A black mist of rage was spreading inside Kuraki's chest. If he gave in to all Haitani's demands, he would end up without a penny. As things were now, though, he had no means of fighting back.

Kuraki remembered the paper bag he had brought with him. Inside it was the mixed box of azuki bean paste wafers.

"I . . . uh . . . brought you this . . . uh . . ." Kuraki timidly held out the box.

"Sweets? Never eat that crap. Whatever. Just stick it down there. Next time, make it booze. Whiskey, preferably."

Kuraki was wondering if Haitani was expecting him to bring him whiskey that evening, when the doorbell rang.

"Who could that be at this time of day? Go get it, would you?"

Kuraki dutifully went and opened the door. It was a young man dressed in a tracksuit. *Probably still a student*, Kuraki thought. The young man nodded at Kuraki politely and asked, "Is Mr. Haitani in?"

"That's me. And who are you?" boomed Haitani from the far end of the room.

"Oh . . . uh, my name is Shiraishi. I'm the grandson of Mrs. Hide Niimi."

"Mrs. Niimi? Oh, the old lady. Is she well? We've not been in touch recently." Haitani was being quite polite seemingly in light of the young man's age.

"She's okay. There's something I'm worried about and need to discuss with you, though. My grandma has problems getting around because of her legs, and she says the whole business is too complicated for her to understand in the first place."

"I wonder what she could mean. I don't recall saying anything terribly complicated to her." Haitani's ingratiating tone was a sharp contrast to the way he treated Kuraki.

"My grandma told me. How you talked her into investing her money."

"I don't know about me talking her into anything. She came to me looking for advice, and I told her what the options were. Where's the problem in that?"

"My grandma says it wasn't just a consultation. You emphatically told her that keeping her savings in the bank was the wrong thing to do."

"That's her interpretation. We were just chatting. I got the sense that she was worried about her advancing age, so I explained that there was a range of options available if she was interested in increasing her capital."

Haitani's explanation did not seem to satisfy the young man.

"All my grandma said to you was that she would think about it. Then you started bringing round a bunch of people she'd didn't know from Adam and forced her to sign up for a load of investment products."

"As I said a moment ago, I think what we're dealing with here is a simple difference of perspective. Claiming that I forced her to sign up for anything—that's a very strong way of putting it. I was acting out of the goodness of my heart."

The young man shook his head, a fierce expression on his face. He was starting to lose his temper. "That's very considerate if that is the truth. Regardless, my grandmother wants to cancel all the contracts she signed with you."

"Cancel them?" Haitani frowned. "What are you talking about?"

"I'm saying that she wants her money back. I have brought along all the securities my grandmother purchased from you." The young man opened the bag he was holding and took out a large envelope. "This is the deposit certificate for a golf club membership, and these are the certificates for the leisure club and resort hotel memberships. The total face value comes to twenty-eight million yen."

Kuraki was astonished at the sums involved.

"If your grandmother wants to cancel the contracts, she'll need to address herself to the individual companies. I believe she has the business cards of all the relevant people."

"We've already called them. They all said the same thing: You can't cancel without notice."

"Then there's nothing you can do, is there? To cancel, you'll just have to wait for the maturity date."

"According to my grandmother, she was told that she could cancel anytime. Told by *you*."

"I never said anything of the sort. All I did was introduce her to the different firms' representatives."

"But you told her that she should come to you if she had any problems."

"Now that I did say. So does she have a problem?"

"Yes, she wants to cancel all the contracts. *Give her her money back.*"

"Are you just plain fucking stupid, kid?" Haitani slammed his fist down onto his desk. "That's an issue for your grandmother and the companies to sort out. It's fuck all to do with me. If she's not happy with the terms of the contracts, she'll be better off talking directly to the representatives. Look, kid, I'm busy. Time for you to get going. Go on, get lost." He waved his right hand dismissively.

"No, but—"

"I said get lost." Haitani made as if to stand up, then winced in pain. "Fuck, that hurts." He turned and looked at Kuraki. "What are you gaping at? Get that stupid kid out of here."

Kuraki couldn't quite understand why he had to get involved, but in his situation, he could hardly say no. He had no choice. He went up to the young man and politely asked him to leave.

The young man bit his lip in exasperation, glared at Kuraki, spun on his heel, and stalked out.

Kuraki watched the door close behind him before turning back around. His eyes met those of Haitani.

"Why are you looking at me like that?" Haitani glowered at him. "Got something you want to say to me?"

"No, it's just that . . ." Kuraki could not hold the other man's gaze. He had to look away.

"I'm not feeling too good. I'll be leaving early today. Come back at five."

"Okay. Goodbye."

Without making eye contact, Kuraki opened the door and left the office.

He discussed the situation with Chisato when he got back home. She frowned.

"Who is this guy? There's something off about him."

"His business looks shady, and he's slippery. Refusing to show me his medical certificate isn't normal behavior. I've fallen into the hands of a thug." Kuraki was stroking baby Kazuma's face, who was sleeping tranquilly. Out of nowhere, a black storm cloud had gathered over his calm, contented existence.

"Shouldn't you contact the insurance company?"

"Yeah, well . . . ," he grunted.

Kuraki was not eager to use his car insurance. He was insured through his company. That came with lower premiums. However, he had been warned that if he made a claim, all the facts of the accident would be passed on to both his employer and the parent company. Because of that, no one in Kuraki's firm made claims for minor accidents.

"If he's demanding large sums of money from you, surely you have no choice."

"You're probably right. As far as I can see, though, his injuries aren't serious. The costs shouldn't be too high."

They agreed that for now the best thing was to wait for the police to get in touch.

Although five o'clock was still a long way off, Kuraki didn't feel like doing anything. He spent the time lounging around watching TV. Nothing he watched really registered. The only thing that cheered him up was the sight of baby Kazuma wiggling his little arms and legs around when he woke up.

Kuraki got to Haitani's office at five on the dot. "Here, take this," Haitani said brusquely, holding out his briefcase. He clearly expected Kuraki to carry it for him. Swallowing his anger, Kuraki took it silently.

Although Haitani still had a limp, walking did not appear to be that much of a struggle for him. Kuraki couldn't help feeling curious about the results of his hospital examination.

"This car is filthy. You should wash it more often," Haitani said, opening the door and climbing into the back seat.

"Sorry about that," Kuraki said, then wondered why on earth he needed to apologize.

Haitani gave him directions as he was driving. It took less than fifteen minutes to get to Haitani's house. It was a small, old, detached house with a token garden, but no space for a car.

"Tomorrow. Seven thirty sharp. Don't be late." Haitani climbed out of the car.

Kuraki put the car in gear. He took a second look at Haitani's house before driving off. The windows were all dark. Perhaps Haitani lived alone.

The thought that he would be coming here on a daily basis depressed him. *How long am I going to have to do this?*

He gave a small shake of the head and accelerated away.

Starting the next day, Kuraki became Haitani's unpaid driver. As per Haitani's request, he picked him up and drove him to the office at seven thirty. Every evening, he went back to the office and gave him a ride home. He managed to get his overtime cut back by telling his boss that his wife was sick.

If that had been the extent of it, he could have managed. But Haitani demanded money from him on an almost daily basis: taxi fares, money for medicines, money for bicycle repairs, and on and on and on. He always produced receipts, but they were always questionable-looking handwritten things. Kuraki found one where the number *3* had clearly been altered to an *8*. In the absence of concrete proof, he just had to grin and bear it.

Worse still, Haitani occasionally called Kuraki's workplace to make his demands. "If you've got a problem with me, then put your superior on the line instead," was his favorite line. He knew that Kuraki had not told his employer about the accident and he was making a veiled threat: *Do as I say, or I'll report you to your boss.*

Several weeks went by in this way. Then one day, as per usual, Kuraki had driven to Haitani's office after leaving the factory. He saw someone standing outside the door. It was the same young man who had been there a few days earlier. He appeared to recognize Kuraki. "Where's the boss?" he asked.

"Isn't he in?" Kuraki pointed at the door.

"Door's locked. He must be out."

"You think?" Kuraki looked at his watch. It was a few minutes before seven.

"Don't you have a key?" the young man asked.

"No, I don't work here."

"Oh." The young man appeared surprised. It was a logical assumption to make. He had seen Haitani treating him like a lackey the last time he was there.

The young man glanced at his watch. "Dammit," he muttered.

"Seems like you've got issues with him," Kuraki said offhandedly.

The young man eyed him suspiciously. "Have you done any business with that guy?"

"God help me, no." Kuraki shook his head. "I hit him with my car. Frankly, it wasn't a serious accident. Still, I'm the one at fault."

"Ah." The mistrust in the young man's eyes had vanished.

"From what I heard the other day, your grandmother signed up to something with him."

The young man nodded and sighed. "My grandmother lives by herself in Tokoname. When I went to see her after being away at school, I came across this golf club membership deposit certificate, so I asked her what on earth she was doing with something like that. She said it was an investment, that she had bought a membership and then gotten this company to manage it for her. It was obvious that an old lady of eighty-two would never come up with an idea like that on her own, so I started asking questions.

Sure enough, it turned out that she only did it because someone had recommended it to her. When I pushed her a little, she admitted that she'd also been talked into buying memberships for a leisure center and a hotel resort. The intermediary in all three cases was the same man, and he had brought reps from the different companies around to her house."

"The intermediary being Mr. Haitani?"

"That's right." The young man nodded. "He came to see her with some story about how he used to work in an insurance company and that he had handled the life insurance of a deceased friend of hers. Haitani talks a good game, and my grandmother was completely taken in. She's always going on about what a 'nice young man' he is. It's incredible. But I know he's not on the up-and-up; he can't be."

Kuraki recalled how Haitani had conducted himself on the telephone. He had been polite and ingratiating. The complete opposite of how he was with Kuraki.

"He's not a man you should trust," Kuraki said. "He's greedy and dishonest. Like you say, those investments sound dodgy to me. You're right to terminate them."

"That's what I'm *trying* to do, but I'm getting nowhere. I've contacted the individual firms, but they all say either that we can't cancel at short notice or that we'll have to pay a massive cancellation fee."

The more Kuraki heard, the shadier the whole thing seemed. It sounded like a scam. It reminded Kuraki of that recent case involving gold bars and false ownership certificates. This company had sold its customers gold without actually transferring the physical gold to them. Instead, they had issued them with deposit receipts while embezzling all the money they had taken in as payment. People all over Japan had fallen victim to the scam, and the cumulative losses were estimated to be in excess of two hundred billion yen.

"So you're hoping to get Haitani to admit responsibility? That sounds like a good idea. If it is a fraud, he's definitely taking a cut."

"That's what I think. And why I'm here . . . Dammit, I don't know what to do. I need to get going or I'll miss the bus."

"Where've you come from?"

"Tokyo."

"You came all that way for this?"

"I'm all the family my grandma's got. My father's dead. My mom's got her hands full looking after the house and me, so I'm the one who goes and visits her from time to time."

The young man explained that he was in his junior year studying law and that he lived with his mother in Tokyo.

"Grandma's been kind to me since I was a little boy. It'll be a catastrophe for her if I can't get her money back. I'm not going to back down. Ever."

"Good for you, kid. If there's anything I can do, I'm happy to help," Kuraki said. He meant every word.

They exchanged contact details before the young man left. His name was Kensuke Shiraishi.

Haitani mysteriously appeared a few short minutes after Kuraki had said goodbye to Shiraishi. "What were you talking about with that kid?" he asked.

A light bulb went off in Kuraki's head. Haitani must have known Shiraishi was outside his office door and had been lying low until he left.

"Nothing much."

"You sure?"

"Why? Is there anything you'd prefer us not to discuss?"

Haitani glared at him. "What's that supposed to mean?"

"Nothing."

Haitani snorted. "Fuck it. Let's go." He marched off.

"Ah, I see your leg's better," said Kuraki, seeing that Haitani was no longer limping.

"It's painful, but I can bear it. It'll definitely be a while before I can get back on a bicycle."

You'll be driving me for the foreseeable future was the subtext.

Unusually, that day, Haitani did not pester Kuraki for money. He sat in the back in silence. He must have had something on his mind.

It was a few more weeks after the accident when Chisato telephoned Kuraki at work in the early afternoon. The police had called her to say that they wanted Kuraki to come in when it was convenient. Kuraki immediately requested permission to leave work early and headed straight for the police station.

Kuraki sat across from a policeman at a small table in one corner of the Traffic Department's office as the officer scrutinized the document in front of him. It was a diagram of the accident scene with a photograph of Kuraki's car attached to one corner with a paper clip.

"Frankly, we're a little puzzled," said the officer.

"Why?"

The officer picked up the photograph. "We inspected your car immediately after the accident. We were unable to find any evidence of a collision. I hope you won't mind if I point out that it's clearly been a while since you washed your car. Any contact or collision would have resulted in the dirt being scraped off that part of the body. Although we examined the vehicle extremely carefully, we could not find any such place."

"So you think that there was no contact?"

"That's the reasonable conclusion to draw. What probably happened is that Mr. Haitani mis-steered his bicycle when he saw your car approaching. While Mr. Haitani is quite insistent that you hit him, we're inclined to see that as misremembering. We can't write a report based on nothing more than one man's imagination."

The officer was basically saying that there was no proof that an accident had taken place.

"What do you want me to do?"

"That's the rub." The officer crossed his arms. "Have you contacted your insurer yet?"

"Not yet, no. I was planning to do that when the facts of the accident were clearer."

"The other party—Mr. Haitani, I mean. Have you discussed a settlement with him?"

"Nothing specific, no. On his side, he's certainly not holding back."

Kuraki listed all the demands Haitani was making of him.

"I can't believe it." The officer frowned. "Could you wait there a second?" He stood up and went and conferred with what Kuraki assumed to be one of his superior officers.

A minute or two later, he came back.

"I've just discussed the matter with my boss. You appear to regret your actions, and you have treated the other party with all due consideration and respect. As we don't believe in dishing out penalties indiscriminately, we're prepared to overlook this incident. Please try to drive a little more carefully in the future."

"So . . . you're not going to treat this as an official accident?"

"There's no evidence that an accident occurred."

"Do you think Mr. Haitani will accept that?"

"He probably won't be happy. At the same time, I don't think it will come as much of a surprise. From the start, we told him that this didn't meet the accident threshold."

"You did?"

"At one point, I even laid into him: Did he really have any contact with your vehicle? Was he sure he didn't imagine it?—I told him that we'd not been able to find any physical evidence and would need to do a thorough investigation before deciding whether or not to treat it as an accident."

"Really?"

It was a revelation to Kuraki. Haitani had passed on none of this to him. Everything was now starting to make sense. While Haitani had demanded multiple small sums, he hadn't mentioned damages since the day of the accident. He must have known all along that he wasn't entitled to anything.

"Now about this Haitani character . . ." The officer dropped his voice. "You need to watch out with him. Since this episode is not going to be officially classified as an accident, the less you have to do with him, the better. As for that business of you serving as his driver, you need to just say no. There was no accident, so you have no obligations to him whatsoever."

"I see. Good. That's what I'll do."

It was encouraging to get such frank advice from the police.

"I interviewed Haitani in the hospital, and the man's a snake," said the officer. "He was making out that he was in agony when all he had was a little bit of bruising."

"You're kidding!"

Kuraki explained that he had paid twenty thousand yen for Haitani's medical expenses.

The officer frowned, shook his head, and repeated, "You need to watch out with him."

Kuraki felt an enormous sense of relief as he left the police station. There was no need to worry about his company finding out about the incident. Eager to let Chisato know, he went into a phone booth and called home. She was delighted at the good news. He could hear the heartfelt joy and relief in her tone.

"We'll celebrate tonight. I'll rustle up something special."

"Nice idea. Looking forward to it," said Kuraki before hanging up. He started to hum with glee.

Nonetheless, thinking of Haitani made him angry. The man had taken a hundred thousand yen off him. Kuraki had kept all the receipts. *We've got to get at least half of the amount back*, he thought.

He looked at his watch. It was half past five. He decided to go to Haitani's office, knowing full well he would be early. He wasn't in the mood to give Haitani a ride home that night. And it wasn't just then; he was never going to chauffeur him around again.

When he pushed open the door of the office, a man he had never seen before turned and looked at him. Thickset. Probably mid-forties. With a grim expression on his face and desperation in his eyes.

The young man who answered the phone was at the far end of the room. He lifted his head from his comic book and looked over at Kuraki.

"Mr. Haitani here?" Kuraki asked.

"Not back yet. Meaning I've got to stick around and wait. Pain in the ass." The young man made a face.

Kuraki was not sure what to do. Should he wait for Haitani to come back? The trouble was that someone was ahead of him.

In the end, he decided against waiting there. He stepped back and let the door swing shut. *I'll go somewhere to kill time*, he thought.

He bought a weekly magazine from a bookshop nearby and went into a diner that had recently opened. He sat at the counter, reading the magazine as he drank his coffee. He looked at his watch after having read several articles. It was just after seven.

I'm late! There'll be hell to pay with Haitani, he thought, before quickly remembering that he no longer needed to play the lackey. All he needed to do now was to be firm and make clear that he wouldn't allow himself to be pushed around anymore.

Kuraki got into his car and headed back to Haitani's office. He parked on the street just out front. He had just gotten out of his car when he ran into someone familiar: the young man who answered the phone.

"Is Mr. Haitani back now?"

The young man cocked his head. "I don't know. He wasn't showing up, so I went out to look for him. Thought he might be in one of the cafés around here. Didn't find him, though."

"Wasn't there a customer in the office?"

The young man shrugged. "Customer? I'm guessing he only came to make a complaint."

"Is he still there?"

"Honestly don't know. Probably. The atmosphere was uncomfortable with just the two of us in there, so I slipped out."

The young man had left a customer alone and unattended in the office. Still, given the boss's character, you couldn't blame the kid.

They went up the stairs together. The young man pushed open the door of the office and went in. Kuraki followed.

The young man stopped abruptly. Kuraki walked straight into his back.

He was about to ask him what was wrong when he looked over his shoulder. His breath caught in his throat.

Haitani was lying on his back on the floor. In a gray suit; his loosened tie flipped back onto his face.

A blackish stain was spreading over his chest.

A second later, Kuraki realized the stain was red, not black.

The young man backed away, moaning. His whole body was shaking.

"We've got to call the police," Kuraki said. His voice was hoarse. "Now."

The young man glanced toward the back of the office, hesitated, and retreated a step. He would have to walk past Haitani's body to reach the telephone. Plus the receiver was off the hook.

"Better to use a pay phone. We shouldn't touch anything we don't have to," Kuraki said.

He had no idea whether the young man even processed what he said. Either way, he walked out of the room, his face ghostly pale.

Kuraki took another look at Haitani. His eyes were half-open; yet they saw nothing.

There was a knife on the floor beside the body, the blade covered in blood. Kuraki looked around the office. It was obvious that a fight had taken place.

As he started walking past the body toward the back of the office, he heard a metallic clang from the balcony. His eyes wide with fright, Kuraki instinctively glanced at the source of the noise. He noticed that one of the sliding glass doors was open.

There was someone out on the balcony. A figure climbing over the railing.

The figure looked in Kuraki's direction. Their eyes met.

It was Kensuke Shiraishi. His face, which had been so warm and friendly when they had met the other day, was now drawn and savage.

Kuraki had no idea how long the two of them stared at each other. Probably just a fraction of a second. What Kuraki did next surprised even him.

Pulling his shirtsleeve over his hand, he slowly pulled the glass door shut. He also nodded discreetly at Shiraishi as if to say, "It's okay. I'll handle things on this end."

The message seemed to get through. Shiraishi nodded back and swung his other leg over the railing. The office was on the second floor, so he should be able to climb down. In the worst case, he could always jump.

Kuraki locked the latch on the sliding glass door. Here too he was careful to leave no prints. He didn't want the police finding evidence of what he had done.

And there were other fingerprints he needed to get rid of. Kuraki picked the knife up off the floor and wiped the handle down with tissue paper. He recognized the knife. It was the one kept in the office. That suggested that the killing had been a crime of passion. The kid was unlikely to have been coolheaded enough to wipe his prints off himself.

He had just fitted the knife back into the bloodstain on the floor when he heard the siren of the police car.

The first person on the scene was a detective by the name of Muramatsu. Muramatsu asked Kuraki and the office assistant a boatload of questions. They were taken to the police station and asked the same questions all over again, this time by a different detective.

With one exception, Kuraki was candid about everything he knew. That exception, of course, was Kensuke Shiraishi. Kuraki also didn't mention that he'd shut and locked the sliding glass door and wiped the knife clean of prints.

He was kept around for several hours after his interview, but the police finally sent him home. They thanked him for his cooperation and apologized for keeping him so late. The detective didn't come out and say it in so many words, but his manner suggested that they had managed to confirm Kuraki's alibi at the diner.

Chisato was waiting for him when he got home, worry written all over her face. He could understand why. He'd extracted himself from a traffic accident only to get involved in a murder case.

As she listened to Kuraki's account, she realized that there were unlikely to be any negative consequences and gradually calmed down.

"Still, how terrifying! I wonder who did it?" Curiosity started to take over now that she was no longer worried.

"Who knows? The guy was into all sorts of shady stuff. There must have been plenty of people who hated his guts," Kuraki said in reply. He didn't mention Shiraishi, even to his wife.

That night in bed, he thought about what he'd done. He'd tampered with the crime scene and lied to the police. His actions were wrong. At the same time, he didn't want Shiraishi, who seemed like such a well-intentioned and good-natured young man, to throw his whole life away. Haitani was the one at fault; he had brought the stabbing on himself. Kuraki recalled his meeting with the traffic police. What was it the officer had said? Something about there being no point in handing out penalties indiscriminately.

Of course, the police weren't incompetent. There was every chance they would work their way back to Shiraishi and start gathering evidence against him. Perhaps Shiraishi would even turn himself in.

If that happens, thought Kuraki, *I'll come out and tell the truth*. Perhaps the police wouldn't charge him if he explained that he had felt sorry for the kid.

News reports that a suspect had been arrested started coming out three days after the murder. According to the newspaper, the suspect was a certain Junji Fukuma, a forty-four-year-old manager of an electronics store who had been involved in a money dispute with Haitani. Haitani's part-time employee had testified that Fukuma had been at the office on the day of the incident. Fukuma himself admitted to being there, but denied committing the murder, the article concluded.

It must be that guy, Kuraki thought. *The stocky one who had been waiting in the office.*

The article didn't go into any detail about what evidence there was to convince the police that Fukuma was the perpetrator. Awful though it had to be for Fukuma to be arrested, Kuraki was confident that the police would have to let him go.

The bigger issue was how Shiraishi would react to the news.

He might come forward voluntarily. He can't just look on and do nothing when an innocent man's been arrested. Kuraki steeled himself for the inevitable: Shiraishi would hand himself into the police—and then the detectives would come around to see *him*.

However—

On the evening of the fourth day after the arrest, Kuraki was watching the TV news when he dropped his chopsticks from surprise.

Junji Fukuma had died by suicide in police custody. He had twisted his clothes into a makeshift rope, then hanged himself from the bars of his cell. The guard had been distracted and not watching him.

Fukuma had not confessed to the crime despite being interrogated two days in a row. The TV played footage from a press conference where the officer in charge insisted that the interviews had been conducted in a proper and responsible manner.

"What's wrong?" Chisato asked him. "You look like you've seen a ghost."

"It's nothing. Just . . ." Kuraki had to clear his throat before going on. "I'm just shocked. At him taking his own life like that."

"I know. You don't expect the culprit to commit suicide."

But Fukuma isn't the culprit—Kuraki pushed his plate away, knowing he could never tell his wife that. He'd completely lost his appetite.

He waited eagerly for follow-up stories, but no further details were forthcoming. The police were probably restricting the reporting, as they had clearly made a mistake.

Around lunchtime on the following Saturday, Shiraishi called him. It was five days after Fukuma's suicide. Since Chisato was at lunch with a friend, Kuraki answered. As soon as he heard a tense voice ask "Hello, is that the Kuraki residence?" the young man's bloodless face swam into his mind's eye.

"I was wondering whether to call you. Can we meet face-to-face and talk?"

Shiraishi said yes. That was why he'd called.

They arranged to meet at six at the diner that had furnished Kuraki with his alibi.

Kuraki drove to the diner at the agreed-on time and spotted Shiraishi at a table in the back. He looked quite haggard.

The first thing Shiraishi did was apologize. His voice shook.

"It's not me you should be apologizing to," Kuraki said.

"Yes, I know," said the young man, his head sagging on his shoulders.

"Why don't you start by telling me what happened."

"Okay," Shiraishi said, picking up his coffee. The cup rattled on the saucer.

After taking an unsteady sip of coffee, Shiraishi began. He spoke softly, with the occasional long silence, either because he was trying to recall things accurately or because he was choosing his words with care. All in all, his account was coherent and consistent. *This kid's smart*, thought Kuraki.

Shiraishi had gone to the consumer consultation bureau of the Ministry of Economy, Trade, and Industry to inquire about the different financial products that his grandmother had been manipulated into buying. He discovered that they were suspected of being unethical and the object of many complaints and inquiries.

Shiraishi was sure that Haitani had tricked his grandmother and introduced her to his crooked cronies, knowing full well that she would never see her money again. Haitani had offered up Shiraishi's grandmother like a sacrificial lamb. Getting some nice kickbacks for himself, of course.

Shiraishi had gone to the Green Enterprises office to confront Haitani a second time. He was determined to get him to take responsibility.

Haitani was alone in the office. Something had clearly happened there. The office was a complete mess. It looked as though there had been a brawl.

Haitani's lip curled at the sight of Shiraishi. "What, now you?"

Shiraishi realized that someone had been there before he had, and there had indeed been a fight, but that had nothing to do with him. He launched into an account of what he had learned at METI's consumer consultation bureau and tried to pressure Haitani.

Haitani didn't take him seriously. He reiterated his spiel. All he had done was to introduce the company reps to his grandmother. Ultimately, she was the one who decided to sign the contracts with them. He had zero responsibility in the matter.

Shiraishi was getting increasingly enraged. He glared at Haitani, and Haitani glared right back at him, callous and contemptuous.

"You want to rough me up too, huh? If you're so desperate, then go ahead and hit me. Be my guest." As he said this, he presented his face to Shiraishi.

Shiraishi froze. Haitani snorted contemptuously.

"What's your problem? Too chickenshit, eh? I'm surprised you had the balls to show up here in the first place. Look, why not be a good little boy and piss off home?"

It was this speech that sent Shiraishi over the edge. Just at the moment, he happened to catch sight of a kitchen knife on the draining board. Before he knew it, the thing was in his hand.

The conceited grin had vanished from Haitani's face. Even so, a veteran fraudster like him was not going to buckle under that intimidation.

"Oh, so now you're gonna stab me instead, are you? You know what'll happen if you do that? *Your life will be over.*"

For all his frustration, Shiraishi knew he was not capable of stabbing the man. Struggling to suppress his feelings of humiliation, he put the knife down on the nearby desk.

Haitani impulsively picked up the receiver.

"Just because you've put the knife down doesn't mean this is over. I'm gonna call the cops on you. This is attempted murder, pure and simple. Your prints are all over that thing. Can't talk your way out of this one, son."

At Haitani's words, Shiraishi panicked. Haitani broke into a smirk, as if he could read Shiraishi's mind.

"How about this, then? I don't call the police—and in return, you never show your face here again and you stop kicking up a fuss about your poor old grandma. Well?"

He couldn't accept that.

"No."

"Then I'm going to call this in. You really think you can treat me like this? I'm serious."

When he saw Haitani thrust a finger into the phone's rotary dial, Shiraishi again reached for the knife.

At this point, his memory became rather hazy.

He thought Haitani said, "If you've got the balls, then do it, stab me," but he wasn't quite sure. Before he knew it, he had flung himself at Haitani and stabbed him.

Haitani crumpled and fell, face upward, onto the floor. The knife was still in Shiraishi's hand. He did not know if he had pulled it out or if it had slid out of the wound when Haitani fell.

He was standing there for who knew how long when he heard the sound of footsteps coming up the stairs. Shiraishi flung down the knife, slid open the sliding glass door, and stepped out onto the balcony. He didn't have enough time to slide the door shut behind him.

Someone had come into the office. He had to get away before they saw him. He peered over the edge of the balcony. The drop was manageable. Making up his mind, he swung one of his legs over the railing. At that moment, his foot caught on the edge.

Whoever was in the room was coming toward him. His eyes widened. *I'm done for.*

Shiraishi knew that face. It belonged to the man who was in trouble with Haitani because of a traffic accident.

The other man nodded a moment later. Just a crisp little nod. Shiraishi interpreted it to mean, *Go on. Get out of here fast.*

Thank you, he was thinking as he bowed back.

"I wasn't going to let that con artist wreck a young man's life before it had even begun," Kuraki commented after hearing Shiraishi's account.

"I know I did something really dumb. I wasn't thinking straight." Shiraishi couldn't meet his eye.

"You're right there. Still, I can see why you lost it. Listening to you speaking, the anger I felt toward Haitani came rushing back to me. Such a sordid, vile little man."

"That's good to hear. You let me off the hook because you understood the situation I'm in. But I took advantage of your good nature, and I didn't turn myself in."

Kuraki grunted. "You haven't spoken to anyone about this, have you?" he asked.

"No. It's not exactly the sort of thing you can bring up casually. My mother's always telling me that watching me grow up is the only thing that gives real meaning to her life. When I heard that someone had been arrested and that he'd killed himself, I just didn't know what to do." Shiraishi let out a single whimper. Kuraki was worried that Shiraishi was going to break down and cry. A tearful scene in a place like this was the last thing he needed.

"To be frank, I've been feeling guilty too. It was only because I failed to tell the police about you that suspicion fell upon a completely innocent man. Never in my wildest dreams did I imagine things would end this way!"

"What do you think I should do? Turn myself in?"

Shiraishi's question demanded thought. Kuraki was all too aware that part of the responsibility for the situation now lay with him.

"Have the police come to see you?" Kuraki asked.

"Me, no. My grandma told me they visited her and asked her a couple of simple questions."

"The young man at Haitani's firm—did you ever cross paths with him?"

"No. The only people I met there were you and Haitani."

"I see."

In that case, thought Kuraki, the chances of the police training their sights on Shiraishi had to be low. Shiraishi's grandmother must have been on Haitani's customer list, but the police investigation was unlikely to stretch all the way to her grandson in Tokyo.

"Listen, Shiraishi," Kuraki said, speaking very deliberately. "The man's name was Fukuma, wasn't it? I feel sorry for him, but going and arresting the wrong person, that's entirely on the police. He's dead now and he's not coming back, so I think it makes more sense to focus on the good of the living." Kuraki looked into the young man's eyes aglow with sincerity. "By which I mean you and your mother."

"Is that . . . Is that really okay?" Shiraishi asked. His eyes were starting to tear up.

"I think it is. If the pangs of conscience end up becoming more than you can bear, you'll just have to do what you have to do at that point."

Shiraishi blinked incredulously. He took several deep breaths and then nodded once, vigorously and emphatically.

"Thank you. I owe you."

Kuraki waved his hand in front of his face. "There's no need for that. You take care of yourself now."

"Yes, sir. And thank you very much," the young man repeated.

After saying goodbye to Shiraishi, who set off for the station, Kuraki went out into the diner parking lot and climbed into his car. As he drove off, he felt that he was leaving something behind and moving on. He hoped that the young man would feel remorse for his actions and go on to live a good and honest life in consequence.

It makes more sense to focus on the good of the living—he ruminated on his own remark. *It has a nice ring to it, if I say so myself*, he thought.

It was only many years later that he realized just how wrong he was.

47

HE HAD JUST finished the last of his tea when he sensed that someone was outside. The sliding door was pushed open a little way, and a middle-aged woman in the traditional samue outfit of cotton jacket and long trousers peered in. "Your friend is here."

She pushed the door open wider, and Nakamachi walked in.

"Sorry. I seem to have kept you waiting. My apologies."

"Trouble finding the place?" Godai said. "Don't worry. I've actually been here before."

As Nakamachi sat down on the floor and swung his legs under the table, he looked around the room. It was modeled after a traditional Japanese farmhouse.

The woman in the samue brought a cup of tea for Nakamachi and refilled Godai's cup.

"We have something we need to discuss before we start eating. Could you hold off on serving us for a few minutes?" Godai said to her.

"Very good, sir. Please use the intercom to let us know when you're ready."

"Will do."

After the woman left, Nakamachi took stock of his surroundings a second time.

"I'm impressed you know a fancy place like this! That's Homicide for you, I guess."

"I've only been here once or twice before with my superiors. This evening, there are things I need to discuss with you that I don't want anybody else overhearing."

They were in an upscale Japanese restaurant. Godai felt that a private room was the best place for a discreet conversation.

"I'm looking forward to hearing what you've got to say more than I am to the dinner," said Nakamachi. "I've only heard rumors so far."

"I owe you an apology. While I did ask you to check all the security cameras near the pay phones, I took care of everything else myself. The whole case is extremely sensitive."

"The son of a Ministry of Finance official. Just fourteen years old. It's certainly not straightforward."

"There's that, but there was also the question of whether it was right to release the previous defendant on the eve of his trial. I had to sort things out with the prosecutor, and the TMPD top brass had their own opinions on the matter too."

"I can imagine." Nakamachi nodded with conviction.

"Tomoki Anzai is currently under house arrest. We're planning to send him to your precinct tomorrow."

"So I heard. And then what? He'll be referred to the prosecutor, I suppose."

"First, the head of Homicide will hold a press conference. He's expecting all hell to break loose."

"Yes, I heard that. Anything could happen."

Godai took a sip of his tea, sighed, and looked at Nakamachi. "Did you hear what the motive for Shiraishi's murder was?"

"I did. To say it blew my mind hardly does it justice. I simply can't believe ... Shiraishi being the actual murderer in that case from years ago. And that the defendant Kuraki—sorry, I should call him *Mr.* Kuraki now—covered up for him. Frankly, though, I don't really know the exact details."

"I'll talk you through the old case once our dinner's arrived. It's a long story. Let me start by outlining what I learned about the more recent murder. Your bosses will have received my report, but I'm guessing that none of this information has yet trickled down to you."

"No chance of that. I'm just a humble foot soldier."

"Tell me about it. But this time, I just happened to have access to the information. I expect you'll have to reconfirm things at the precinct level; still, I doubt you'll be able to get a three-hundred-sixty-degree view that way."

"Thanks. Appreciate it."

"With regard to how Kuraki got to know Yoko and Orie Asaba, his new testimony is almost identical to his previous. The only difference is the fact that Kuraki did not perpetrate the 1984 murder himself but instead shielded the actual perpetrator, Shiraishi. The desire to atone for the pain he caused after his actions led to the wrong man being charged prompted him to approach the Asabas. As you'd expect, Kuraki never told the two women about his involvement in the 1984 case. At least, not until very recently."

"Until very recently? So you're saying that—"

"Yes, he came clean to Orie, the daughter, a year or so ago. All Kuraki said about it is that his guilt had become unbearable. In fact, more complex psychology seems to have been at work there."

Nakamachi tilted his head quizzically to one side. "What do you mean?"

"On that particular issue, it was actually Orie's testimony that was the most illuminating."

"Why? What did she say?"

"She told me a love story."

Godai thought back to when he had interviewed Orie Asaba on suspicion of hindering a police investigation. He had been assigned the job because he had dealt with her in the past.

"I fell in love with Kuraki"—Godai would never forget the sad smile on her lips as she uttered those words. "It wasn't just that he was a kind and good-natured soul; the thing that really attracted me to him was his solidity. When I was with him, I felt emotionally whole. I wanted to give myself to him, body and soul. Eventually, I came right out and told him how I felt about him. I was pretty confident that he liked me, I won't deny it. And I wasn't wrong. Kuraki told me that he loved me too, that given his age, he didn't want a physical relationship. I wasn't prepared to settle for that. I got a bit aggressive with him, and I even said, 'If you don't really love me, then just come out and say so.' This terrible pain came over Mr. Kuraki's face, and right then and there, he got down and prostrated himself in front of me. I couldn't believe my eyes. At first, I was thinking, *Wow, this is how far he'll go to* not *have a deeper, physical relationship.* When he started talking, the things he said were so shocking I almost passed out."

Kuraki had confessed to Orie that he had allowed the true culprit in the case that drove Orie's father to kill himself to make his getaway. Although Orie found it hard to believe, it was an unlikely story to invent.

"My mind just went blank," said Orie, recounting her emotions at the time.

Godai continued, "At the same time as this profound sense of shock, Orie could not bring herself to hate Kuraki. I'm guessing that's because while she knew that her father wouldn't have been arrested if Kuraki hadn't let the real culprit get away, her father's wrongful arrest and suicide both stemmed from police failure. You ask me, I think the real reason is simply that her love for Kuraki just won out over any other emotion."

"I second that. Did their relationship continue after this episode?" Nakamachi's eyes were shining with curiosity.

"No, in the end, the relationship stayed as it was. I think the emotional bond between them grew stronger, nonetheless. Orie didn't pass on what Kuraki had told her to her mother. It remained their private secret. Oh yes, and Orie gave Kuraki a birthday present. Got any idea what it was?"

"A present?" Nakamachi blinked, nonplussed. "Absolutely no idea. What was it?"

"A phone. A smartphone. The contract was in Orie's name. She gave it to him and told him to use it to stay in touch with her. Kuraki just had one of those flip phones, and she wanted to contact him the normal way. Kuraki accepted the phone on the condition that he got to pay the bill. Basically, they had set up a private hotline just for the two of them, which was all very sweet—except that it triggered Shiraishi's murder."

"Really? How?" Nakamachi's face had stiffened.

Godai pulled a notebook out of his jacket pocket. It seemed he was going to have to consult his notes to tell the rest of the story.

"Sometime in mid-September, Kuraki was looking for some information online when he happened to come across an organization whose name ignited his curiosity: Shiraishi Law Office. The name *Shiraishi* is hardly an unusual one in Japan, but Kuraki remembered that the young man who killed Haitani had also been a law student. That piqued his interest, so he went to have a look at the company's home page. There he found out that the head of the firm was called Kensuke Shiraishi, and there was a photo of him. Kuraki knew for sure that it was the same guy from 1984. Delighted to see that the young man had made such a success of his life, Kuraki was curious to discover how he felt about the crime he had committed all those years ago, so he just went ahead and called him. That was October 2."

"Oh, the call that was noted in the law firm's official call log, which first prompted you to go to Sasame in Aichi to interview Kuraki."

"Yes. Anyway, Shiraishi took the call and remembered Kuraki. The two men arranged to meet. The reunion took place in that café near Tokyo Station on October 6. They were caught on the café's security camera, and the camera footage was what led to Kuraki's arrest. Of course, you know all that."

"Hard to forget," Nakamachi said, nodding with his teacup in his hand.

"Shiraishi told Kuraki that the murder had stayed with him ever since, that he had been tormented by guilt the entire time. He felt awful not just about the murder itself but also for the family of Junji Fukuma. Kuraki told Shiraishi about Yoko and Orie Asaba and Asunaro. We discovered how Shiraishi acted in response to this new information by analyzing his smartphone." Godai briefly consulted his notes before continuing. "According to the location data from his smartphone, Shiraishi went for a rambling walk around Monzen-Nakacho the next day, the seventh of October. We assume that he was looking for Asunaro. Once he found the place, he settled into a café across the street. He spent almost two hours in the same café on the twelfth, as we know."

"Sounds like he wanted to get a look at the Asabas but didn't have the guts to go into the restaurant."

"Do you remember what happened when we went to Shiraishi's house right after his murder? Here's what his wife said about Shiraishi. He's not been quite himself lately. I think he had something on his mind."

"He must have been anxious. Uncertain how to act."

"For myself, I suspect that he'd made up his mind to get out of the legal profession. You remember we went and spoke to that Yamada fellow, the young man who worked in that little factory in Adachi Ward? He told us that Shiraishi had swung by to see him for no particular reason and asked him if he was comfortable in his new job. My take is that Shiraishi wanted to see how his old clients were getting on before he quit the profession entirely."

"I see what you mean. Yamada also mentioned something about Shiraishi not being quite his normal self." Nakamachi frowned and scratched his forehead. "It's all too sad," he muttered.

"For his part, Kuraki was also trying to work out what his next step should be. After a certain amount of agonizing, he decided to tell Orie about Shiraishi. He didn't think a phone call was the right way to do it, so he sent her an email instead. He used their private hotline. That message led to Shiraishi's murder." Godai looked up from his notes. "Because someone read it who had no business reading it."

"Tomoki Anzai?"

Godai nodded. "Tomoki Anzai knew the code to unlock his mother's phone because he had been playing games on it since he was a little boy. It turns out that he had a habit of secretly reading her email and texts every time they met. That was how he found out about Shiraishi. On October 27, Tomoki Anzai went to have a look at Shiraishi's office. He was working up the courage to go in when Shiraishi happened to come out. Shiraishi must have noticed Tomoki Anzai staring at him, because he went up to the boy and asked what he wanted. Tomoki Anzai introduced himself as Junji

Fukuma's grandson. Shiraishi was stunned, but had some urgent business he needed to deal with, so he gave Tomoki Anzai a card and told him to contact him later. The card had his work phone number on it."

Nakamachi shook his head and grimaced. "I can't imagine how Shiraishi must have felt."

"Tell me about it. You reap what you sow. Still, you can't help feeling some sympathy."

"So did Tomoki Anzai contact Shiraishi?"

Godai looked down at his notebook. "Yes, he called him three days later. The thirtieth. They arranged to meet at Monzen-Nakacho in the early evening the next day. Crucially, Tomoki Anzai was already using pay phones at this point. Apparently, he lied to Shiraishi; told him he didn't have a phone of his own."

Nakamachi's eyes were grave. "Meaning that he'd already considered . . ."

"That he'd already started planning. He admitted as much to me. On October 31, Tomoki Anzai left his house carrying a concealed knife. He made his way to Kiyosumi in Edo Ward, called Shiraishi using that pay phone, and asked him to come to the terrace beneath Kiyosu Bridge. He selected that particular bridge because it was isolated due to ongoing construction work. When Shiraishi rolled up at a little before seven, Tomoki Anzai took a look around to check that no one was watching and then—just like that—stabbed him with the knife. He told me that he visualized the act in his head repeatedly before actually doing it. He ran away after Shiraishi went down. He was wearing gloves, so he wasn't worried about leaving any prints." Godai put his notebook down. "That's everything he gave us in his confession."

"That's everything? I don't get it. Shiraishi's body was found in a car abandoned on the side of the road. Does that mean that someone else drove the car there?"

"That's the obvious conclusion. Your average junior high schooler doesn't know how to drive. Tomoki Anzai may well not have been physically capable of dragging the body to the car. But before we get into that, let me tell you what Tomoki Anzai did after the murder. He went directly home, without telling anyone what he had done. The body was discovered the next morning and a major investigation launched, as you well know. The murder also made it onto the news. It gave Kuraki quite a shock. He only sent Orie that mail about Shiraishi a couple of days earlier. He knew it was unlikely, but he was worried that Orie might have had something to do with the murder, so he called her. Orie knew nothing about the murder. She told Kuraki that she hadn't made any overtures to Shiraishi or spoken about him to anybody else. It was only later as she was thinking things over that she realized that there was one person who could have been reading her messages without her knowing."

"Her son."

"Precisely. The scenario she now imagined was so ghastly she had trouble accepting it as a possibility. Even so, she called Tomoki and asked him to come and see her. 'You read my messages,' she said. She wasn't so much asking a question as stating a matter of fact. Tomoki Anzai admitted it right off. Then he confessed."

Nakamachi lurched forward in his chair. "He told her that he had stabbed Shiraishi and killed him?"

"Yes. Orie said it felt as if the world had just crumbled around her."

Godai cast his mind back to his interview with Orie. When she was talking about Tomoki coming and telling her that he had killed Shiraishi, her face was a lifeless mask.

"Tomoki Anzai desperately wanted revenge. All his life, people had bullied him for being the grandson of a murderer, and that was also the thing that separated him from his mother. Although Tomoki's father had remarried, Tomoki didn't see his father's second wife as his family, nor the children she had with his father as his real brother and sister. The way he saw it, he was the grandson of a killer, and that was something he just had to live with—when suddenly along comes this message from a Mr. Kuraki and Tomoki realizes that it's not, in fact, true. It was this lawyer Shiraishi who was responsible for screwing up his family. He had a wild urge to do something about it."

Orie felt an overwhelming sense of gloom and despair after listening to Tomoki's confession. Why was a three-decade-old tragedy now wrecking Tomoki's life? Was their family cursed? She even started blaming herself. She shouldn't have married Hiroki Anzai and had a child when she was under a curse.

Naturally, Orie's first impulse was to contact the police. Feeling that she ought to give Kuraki a heads-up, she called him first. In the interview, she'd said, "Mr. Kuraki was literally dumbstruck for a while but eventually asked me to tell him more. He was so cool and collected that I worried he hadn't grasped the gravity of the situation. I couldn't have been more wrong. He asked me if Tomoki was with me. I said he was, and he asked me to put him on the line. Mr. Kuraki then asked Tomoki a large number of highly detailed questions. Tomoki then gave the phone back to me. Kuraki told me not to mention this call to the police and said I shouldn't do anything silly, because he would take care of everything."

Orie didn't hear from Kuraki for a while after that. She spent the whole day on tenterhooks, expecting the police to show up any minute.

"It's probably better if I explain things using Kuraki's testimony from now on." Godai flipped his notebook back open. "After hearing Tomoki Anzai's detailed account of the crime, Kuraki resolved to do whatever he possibly could to protect the boy because he believed that the whole situation had its roots in his actions thirty-plus years ago. That was certainly a factor. That's not all there was to it, though. Listening to Tomoki Anzai's account, Kuraki had realized that someone else had an agenda of their own."

"Someone else? Who do you mean?"

"We need to revisit a question you raised earlier. Tomoki Anzai told his mother that he had stabbed Shiraishi near Kiyosu Bridge. However, the media was reporting that his body had been found in a completely different part of Tokyo. Rather astonished by this discrepancy, Kuraki decided there was only one possible explanation: *It was Shiraishi himself who had driven the car.*"

Nakamachi gasped and his jaw dropped. "So Shiraishi was not dead after all," he said.

"He was on the verge of death, but he could still move, and he had his wits about him. Picture it: There's Shiraishi, he's losing consciousness, he's on the brink of death, yet he has the wherewithal to realize that he's got to move his car. He could have also gotten rid of his cell phone, the flip phone. My guess is that he chucked it into the Sumida River on his way to his car. Once he had driven the car to another location, Shiraishi wiped the steering wheel and climbed around into the back seat. Why did he do all that? I doubt you need me to explain it to you."

"To throw the investigation off track. No one would suspect that a minor was involved in a crime that involved the driving of a car. Shiraishi used his last moments to shield Tomoki Anzai."

"Kuraki assumed that. Shiraishi was trying to atone for his past crime by protecting Tomoki Anzai. Kuraki decided to honor Shiraishi's intention. Realizing that it was just a matter of time before the police found the link between him and Asunaro, he had already resolved to confess to the murder in Tomoki's place. He knew his story needed to be free from discrepancies or inconsistencies, and so he came up with a story that was robust enough to withstand scrutiny. In addition to shielding Tomoki Anzai, he wanted to put an end to the stigma that had dogged the Asabas for decades. The only narrative that could accomplish both those goals was that he was responsible for the 1984 murder. As you would expect, he got rid of the smartphone that served as his hotline to Orie. So the phone he smashed and threw into Mikawa Bay wasn't a prepaid mobile; it was that smartphone."

Nakamachi sighed heavily, pressing his fingers to his temples as if he were massaging away a headache. "I don't know how to feel about this. I'm amazed he was prepared to go so far."

"You've probably heard that Kuraki's got cancer. He made up his mind with full knowledge that he didn't have long left. As a show of determination and forethought, that's borderline scary. It must have been hard for Orie, though."

"Yeah . . . I suppose so."

"She told me as much. When Kuraki said he would take the fall for her son, if he had to, she was vehemently against the idea. But he was dead set on it, and there was nothing she could do to change his mind. She was utterly wretched when she saw the reports about Kuraki's arrest."

The anguish on Orie's face as she revisited that moment was seared onto Godai's retinas. "I seriously thought about ending my life," she had said. "Death seemed like the best thing for me and Tomoki. I wanted the police to know the truth of the case, so I started writing a letter. Then I realized that doing so would only make things worse for Kuraki. I really didn't know what to do."

When Godai and Nakamachi came to interview Orie after Kuraki's arrest, she was secretly hoping that they would figure out what had really happened.

"She thought that she would find peace and acceptance that way. That she would be able to look Kuraki in the eye. I think she's quite pleased at how things have turned out now. She's grateful to the police, and she even thanked me for uncovering the truth. She wasn't being sarcastic. She really meant it—she wept when she did."

Orie hadn't liked keeping her mother in the dark. And while Yoko seemed to know that something strange was going on, she never brought up the case, even when it was just the two of them.

"So that's the full picture. Took a while to plow through it all, eh?" Godai looked at his watch. He had been talking for more than half an hour.

Nakamachi groaned. "I don't know why, I feel full after hearing your story."

"Shall we skip dinner?"

"No. Let's eat. Karma really is a bitch. One murder always leads to another. More than thirty years go by, and up pops the grandson to take his revenge."

"Yeah, that's a hard one to digest. The boy and his family suffered for decades because of that false charge. When he found the person who was actually responsible for the murder, he killed him—it seems too simple when you put it like that, but the motivations of a fourteen-year-old kid are complex and difficult for adults like us to get our heads around. Even so . . ." Godai tipped his head quizzically to one side. "I do wonder what that smile of his meant."

"What smile?"

"Tomoki Anzai's. There was this faint ghost of a smile on his lips. Just before he gave me the name of the person he called from the pay phone. I still can't figure out what it meant."

"Hmm . . ." Nakamachi looked puzzled.

Godai picked up the intercom receiver. He asked for dinner to be served, put the receiver back in its cradle, and drank down the remaining green tea in his cup.

"While we tuck into our dinner, shall I tell you about what happened thirty-plus-years ago that led to Kuraki covering for Shiraishi?"

"Please do. By the way, what's going to happen to those two?"

"'Those two' being . . . ?"

"Mirei Shiraishi and Kazuma Kuraki, I mean."

"Of course," Godai said with a nod. "Light and dark, day and night—their positions have been completely reversed. Which is precisely what enables them to understand each other in a way other people cannot. I think an attachment may be developing there."

Nakamachi's eyes widened. "You're kidding me! It's almost a miracle."

"More like a dream. As detectives, we're always having to confront the nastiest aspects of human nature. From time to time, please, show me something better!"

"Excuse me, gentlemen," said a voice as Godai finished speaking.

The sliding door opened.

48

SHE WENT OUT into the hall when she heard the ring of the doorbell.

The sight of Azusa Sakuma standing on the doorstep reminded Mirei of the first day they had met. Sakuma, smaller and younger than she had expected, and her striking suit, backpack, and black-framed glasses. Mirei hadn't thought much about her appearance since. When they were busy discussing or arguing about the case, she had too much on her mind to care.

"Please." She smiled and beckoned her in. Was she alone in regarding this woman as one of the few people in the world who had her back?

"My mother's out. She's at the movies," Mirei said after escorting Sakuma into the living room.

"Really?" Sakuma's eyes widened in surprise. "What's she gone to see?"

"I don't know," Mirei said as she put the teacups on the table. "I don't think she knew herself. She'll just watch whatever happens to be on; all she wanted was *not* to hear what you've come to tell us. She left because she knew that if she stayed, she'd get curious and eavesdrop. I've got no idea what she's gone to see, but I'm confident she won't remember anything about it afterward."

Sakuma looked a little uncomfortable. "Does she see me as the bearer of bad news?"

"Oh, she was just frightened. She didn't know why you were coming, but she was pretty sure it wouldn't be for anything good. She can't handle any new revelations. Hence the vanishing act."

Sakuma lowered her eyes and gazed intently at the tabletop. "Well, she's right. What I'm here to tell you will hardly be welcome news."

Mirei clasped her hands on her knees and took a deep breath. "I'm fine. Go ahead and tell me."

"Are you up to speed with what's happening with the young perpetrator?" the lawyer asked.

Mirei shook her head.

"Since the boy is over fourteen years old, he is old enough to be tried as an adult. The case is a serious one, so it was referred to the prosecutor. After that, however, the case was sent on to the family court. The family court reinvestigated the case so they could decide what to do with him—put him in a juvenile detention facility, send him to reform school, release him on probation, not penalize him at all, or refer him back to the prosecutor. It's highly unusual for a case involving a fourteen-year-old boy to be sent back to the prosecutor, but since this was a murder, that's what happened. In other words, the case will be tried and adjudicated as if he were an adult."

Mirei felt no particular emotion as she listened to Sakuma's matter-of-fact explanation. For all the occasional interjections she made, she knew she must come across as thoroughly disengaged.

"That was when the prosecutor in charge of the case contacted me. He wanted to know if you were planning to use the victim participation system. He directed the inquiry to me because I was your victim-participation lawyer when Tatsuro Kuraki was the defendant. I told him that I didn't know you and your mother's plan and that even if you did decide to use the system, I didn't know whether you would opt for me again. I told the prosecutor that I was happy to talk to you myself, at which point he shared rather more information with me than I was expecting. That's what I wanted to discuss with you. Oh, and as this is something I am doing of my own volition, you don't need to worry about a bill."

"I appreciate you coming," Mirei said. "The police have already provided us with plenty of information about the case, though. I don't really feel the urge to know more."

"I can understand that. It's just that new facts have come to light as a result of the prosecutor's investigation."

God, was there even more for her to process? Mirei felt a sense of foreboding.

"It concerns the new defendant and will likely become a point of dispute in court. I'd like to talk you through it briefly, if I may."

Mirei really didn't want to hear it, but she could not very well leave the room. "Please, go ahead," she said, resettling herself in her chair.

Sakuma pushed her teacup to one side and briskly pulled out a file, which she opened on the table.

"Just like when Tatsuro Kuraki was the defendant, the facts of the case aren't up for dispute this time either. It's the motive that's the contested issue. The young defendant, his mother, and his grandmother all had to go through many years of hardship as a result of a false accusation. Further hardship was imposed on the defendant in the form of his parents' divorce and bullying by his peers at school. In his statement, the defendant said that he was prompted to commit murder by a desire for revenge when he found out who the real culprit was. The twist in the tale is that fact-finding interviews the prosecutor conducted with the defendant's teachers and fellow students cast doubt on that claim."

"What!" Mirei could not suppress her amazement. "You're saying he had some other motive?"

Sakuma adjusted her black-framed glasses with a fingertip, leaned forward, and consulted the file again.

"It seems that he was briefly ostracized while he was at primary school when a rumor his grandfather was a killer started to circulate, but no bullying was reported. The same is true for the junior high school he's currently attending. The prosecutor's official opinion was that the boy was not in a uniquely discriminatory environment. He therefore asked him to provide specifics: What kind of negative experiences had he gone through? What had he heard from his mother and grandmother about the hardships they went through? The young man's answers were extremely vague, and it became clear that the tales of hardship he claimed to have heard from his mother and grandmother were nothing more than figments of his own imagination."

"Why should he want revenge, then?"

Sakuma briefly looked up and nodded before resuming her reading of the file. "The prosecutor had the very same question. He cross-examined the boy very rigorously about his state of mind in the lead-up to his decision to commit murder. At that point, the young defendant provided an account of his motive that was quite different from what he had said before."

"Different how?"

"The boy," began Sakuma, directing a searching glance at Mirei. "The boy said he was *interested* in murder."

It took Mirei a moment to take in the lawyer's words. After a pause, she said, "Sorry? 'Interested'?"

Sakuma nodded slowly and consulted the file again.

"At primary school, he wasn't bullied by his peers after they discovered that his grandfather was an accused murderer. Far from it. They were afraid of him. When he realized that, he developed a fascination with the outsize psychological impact of the act of murder. Over time, he started wondering how it would feel to murder someone and fantasizing about doing so. Obviously, he was aware that murder was a serious crime and that killing another human being would mean throwing the rest of his life away, so he confined his dark desires to some corner of his imagination. That delicate balance was upset when he went into his mother's phone and read the message Kuraki sent his mother. He now felt that he had a legitimate motive to kill someone. He believed that the public reaction would be forgiving and the penalty lighter because he was avenging an old wrong. That rapidly metastasized into the impulse to act. That's roughly what he said in his statement."

Mirei felt suddenly dizzy. She put her hands on the table to steady herself. "I can't believe that's what . . ."

"He wasn't particularly concerned with concealing his involvement in the crime once he'd committed it. Apparently, he was planning to make a full and candid confession if anyone confronted him with proof."

Mirei put a hand to her chest. Her heart was racing. "What did he have to say about the police arresting Kuraki instead of him?"

"He couldn't figure out what was going on. According to the prosecutor, Tomoki knew that the grown-ups in his life were working to protect him, but he knew none of the particulars."

Mirei's hand was still pressed to her chest. She didn't say anything until she felt a little more in control. "That certainly is a big difference. The boy may well go on to give a different account of the murder too."

"I agree. As the prosecutor sees it, the boy is not only showing zero remorse but is actively justifying his actions. He regards the boy as psychologically abnormal and his declared motive of avenging the pain and suffering of his family as a rationalization of his murderous impulses after the fact. Knowing that the Japanese public is broadly sympathetic to the boy and ready to excuse—or even praise—his actions, the prosecutor wants to go to trial with a very aggressive posture. That's why he wanted me to ask whether you and your mother, the bereaved Shiraishi family, would be using the victim participation system again." Sakuma looked up from the file. "So what do you say?"

Mirei leaned back in her chair, intertwined her fingers behind her head. She thought for a while, then resumed her previous posture. "I'll talk to my mother. My sense is that we probably won't participate."

"I see." A look of mild disappointment flashed across Sakuma's face. "Do you mind if I ask you why?"

"It's difficult to put into words. Perhaps it's because I *understand*."

"You . . . *understand*?" The lawyer was plainly mystified.

"Yep," Mirei replied tersely. "I'm grateful that you came to explain the situation to me today like this. Now I have no more questions. Now I see why my father lost his life. I understand it all. The final verdict that the boy gets may matter to the prosecutor and the lawyers, but as far as I'm concerned, I could not care less. Even if his motive was more about the workings of a twisted mind than about revenge, my father was still the person responsible for twisting and perverting his mind in the first place. I know that my father drove his car to a different location after being stabbed. I believe that through his death, my father atoned for his original crime. On that morning—" Mirei exhaled heavily to settle her nerves, then went on. "On the morning of the incident, my dad was talking about snow. He asked, 'Do you think we're going to get good snowfalls this year?' We often used to go on family ski trips; recently, we did so much less. I can see now that Dad was thinking back to a happier time in his life. He knew that he was going to have to let go of all those happy memories. I think that my dad had no regrets when he breathed his last."

Sakuma nodded. "I see," she said with a sigh. "I will let the prosecutor know."

"Thank you very much."

Sakuma began putting the files back into her backpack. "Are you managing to go into work?"

"I'm on leave for now. I'll probably just quit. The statute of limitations may have expired, but I don't think there are too many firms out there that want a murderer's daughter on their reception desk."

Sakuma looked troubled. "Were the people at work treating you differently?"

"Oh, it's not just them. We're villains for the whole of Japan. I canceled the landline here because of all the harassment. And we're receiving all sorts of crap sent to us through the mail: not just abusive letters but razor blades and mysterious white powders. I was passing the really nasty, vicious stuff on to the police, but there's so much, I just gave up."

Sakuma frowned sympathetically. "That will change over time. You know what the Japanese public's like: quick to get excited and equally quick to lose interest."

"Let's hope you're right. I'm talking it over with my mom. She's all in favor of us moving abroad. The problem is, we've no idea how to go about making a new life for ourselves overseas; plus, we don't have the financial resources for it in the first place." Mirei shrugged and exhaled through pursed lips. "It's a bizarre turn of events. Until a few days ago, we were the victim's family. Now all of a sudden, we're the perpetrator's family."

"That's wrong. You're still the bereaved family of a murder victim. That's not changed. That's why I think it makes sense for you to participate in the trial."

"Please, let's not go there. I appreciate everything you have done for us, Ms. Sakuma. I was demanding and self-centered, and I caused you plenty of trouble. I should say sorry."

Sakuma hefted her backpack onto her knees and cocked her head to one side. "There's this one thing I keep thinking about. Although Mr. Kuraki had made a voluntary confession, you refused to take it at face value, and you tried to find out the real truth yourself. I wonder if I should I have tried harder to stop you. Because if I had . . . Oh, what is his name, that very capable detective?"

"You mean Detective Godai?"

"That's it. Because if I'd tried harder to keep you in check, then maybe Detective Godai wouldn't have started having doubts of his own and things wouldn't have turned out the way they did."

"So, what then? Kuraki would have been found guilty and we'd all have lived happily ever after? You can't seriously see that as a good outcome." Mirei stared intently into the lawyer's face.

Sakuma frowned and shook her head. "No, I can't."

"The whole time, I was asking myself, 'What on earth are you doing, sticking your oar in like this?' Still, there is one person who was saved by the uncovering of the truth."

Sakuma seemed to know exactly who she meant. "You're talking about Tatsuro Kuraki's son, right?"

"His life was hell when he was seen as the son of the perpetrator. I imagine he must have gotten his old life back now. Because of that, I can't see what I did as a mistake; I did what was right. And if he's happier, that's consolation for me too."

As Mirei said this, she was thinking about the picturesque pottery path they had explored together.

49

A YEAR AND A half after the Kiyosu Bridge murder, Kazuma Kuraki decided to pay a visit to Asunaro. As he strolled along the main street, he wondered what to do if the place had shut down. For all he knew, the Asabas might well have shuttered the business or relocated somewhere else. He could probably get their contact details if he pulled a few strings. But should he really go to such lengths? He wasn't sure. He still was of two minds about visiting today.

He arrived at the building. Looking up, he saw that the sign for Asunaro was still there. It didn't necessarily mean that the restaurant was still open.

He remembered his last visit. He had walked there after catching sight of Mirei Shiraishi placing flowers at the Sumida River Terrace. Orie Asaba had just been coming out of the restaurant accompanied by a boy. He now knew that the boy was Tomoki Anzai—the true killer of Kensuke Shiraishi. There had still been something childish about his features, and he didn't look remotely capable of such an act of cruelty. *Appearances can be deceptive*, Kazuma thought.

He climbed the narrow stairs. Asunaro was still in business! There was an Opening Soon sign hanging on the door, and he could see a strip of light in the crack under the door.

Kazuma took a deep breath and reached for the door handle.

The interior had not changed from his last visit. The same elegant, well-polished tables arranged in a neat row. A woman with rolled-up sleeves was busy scrubbing one of them. It was Orie Asaba. She turned to look and froze at the sight of Kazuma, like a mechanical doll whose battery has suddenly given out.

"Sorry to show up unannounced like this," Kazuma said. "I thought about calling, but it seemed better to come and give you the news face-to-face."

"The news?" Orie repeated under her breath. She pushed her cleaning things to one side, clasped her hands in front of her. "It's been a long time."

"Have you got a moment? This won't take long."

"It's fine. Sit down. I'll make a pot of tea."

"There's no need."

Orie bustled off behind the counter. Perhaps she hadn't heard him.

Kazuma pulled out a chair and sat down while Orie prepared the tea. Had she lost weight? Kazuma took another look at the restaurant. He was right. Nothing much had changed.

"Is your mother taking the day off?" Kazuma asked.

"Yoko doesn't come in much lately. She's aged a lot." Orie came back carrying a tray with the teacups on it. "Here you are." She placed a cup in front of Kazuma, then sat down opposite him.

"Thank you," said Kazuma. After a single sip, he put the cup back down on the table.

"How have you been?" she asked.

"Oh, you know. Getting by."

"How's work?"

"I'm back at my old firm. Doing a completely different job from before."

Kazuma had been transferred to a section where he had no direct interactions with clients. That was a detail he didn't feel he needed to share with Orie.

"You're in advertising, aren't you? That's nice. I'm sure your father is very proud of you."

"It's my dad I'm here to talk about." Kazuma drew himself upright and forced himself to smile. "He passed away last week."

Orie's face froze in shock.

"About six months ago, the cancer was found to have spread to his lungs. He was being treated in a hospital in Aichi. In the end, he didn't make it."

Orie started to tear up. She pressed the heels of her palms into her eyes, then took a long, slow breath. "I see. That's very sad news. Please accept my condolences."

"When did you last see my father?"

"Let me see." Orie's brow furrowed as she scoured her memory. "It was about a month after Tomoki's arrest. He came here. Didn't he tell you?"

"No. He was already back home in Anjo by then. He must have come up to Tokyo without telling me. What did you and he talk about?"

Orie sighed. "He apologized. Said he was sorry that he hadn't managed to protect Tomoki properly. 'What you did was wrong,' I told him. 'You made the same mistake you'd made before.'"

"'The same mistake'?"

"In that first incident, he let the real culprit escape despite knowing his identity. That was when everything went haywire. Right?"

Kazuma frowned and scratched one of his eyebrows. "What did my father have to say to that?"

"That he had nothing to say in his own defense." Orie smiled. "What about you? Did you get the chance to sit down and have a good talk with him ever?"

"My father discussed the two incidents—the murder from the 1980s and the more recent case—with me the day after he was released from detention. As you pointed out, he made a big mistake. If you ask me, though, his mistake was very typical of him. He's always had a strong sense of responsibility, and he wasn't afraid to put himself on the line."

"Maybe you're right. Still, I really don't think that gives him the right to make the people closest to him miserable. Least of all his own son." Orie frowned.

"He'd tell you that he only did what was necessary."

"'Necessary'? What does that even mean?"

"He told me that being arrested in place of Tomoki wasn't actually an unpleasant experience. Knowing that he was sick and didn't have long to live meant he wasn't afraid of the death penalty. But he was tormented by the idea of people shunning me and me losing my job. That cost him plenty of sleepless nights. In the end, he said, he came to see his confrontation of that pain as his true punishment."

Kazuma's memory of his father, with his face contorted as he laid bare his anguish, was as fresh as if the conversation had happened yesterday. Listening to his father, he had understood: The fear for your family is more excruciating than being hurt yourself.

"Mr. Kuraki said that?" Orie looked away, struggling to control her roiling emotions.

Kazuma glanced around the restaurant before resettling his gaze on her. "How's Asunaro doing? It certainly looks the same."

"If it's the business side you're asking about, well, it's not great, but it's not terrible either. People may write malicious crap on the internet, but this place has always been sustained by a faithful core of regulars."

"Very glad to hear it."

The whole complicated sequence of events had spread online under the moniker of the "Kiyosu Bridge Case." Even though no proper names were used, plenty of people in chat groups knew that the "restaurant run by the juvenile killer's mother" meant Asunaro.

Kazuma did his best to stay away from any such posts or articles. According to his friend Amemiya, the internet was overflowing with positive comments about "the male resident of Aichi Prefecture who got himself arrested in place of the actual perpetrator," while considerably less sympathetic to the juvenile perpetrator. There was, however, fierce criticism of "the victim who worked as a lawyer, despite having murdered someone in the past."

Still, public opinion was a fickle thing. Recently, the case barely came up, and Kazuma could surf the internet without fear of what he might encounter there.

"My father said something to me before he died. He asked me to help you and your mother and to leave a share of his estate over to you, if it was economically feasible for me."

Orie raised her right hand, with the palm facing out. "Your father and I discussed this. I turned him down flat."

"Yes, Dad told me. Still, I felt I ought to run it by you nonetheless."

"That's very kind of you. It's the thought that counts, and it's the thought that I'll treasure."

Although her tone was mild, he could feel the steely resolve behind her words. Orie wanted to live her own life without being reliant on anyone else. "Okay," Kazuma said. Why should he try to undermine her?

Despite his curiosity, Kazuma had decided not to ask Orie about Tomoki Anzai's sentence. Kazuma's sense was that Tomoki would be in detention for a certain length of time, juvenile or not. Kazuma suspected that when he got out, it would be Orie, rather than his father, who took him in.

Kazuma checked his watch. It was almost five thirty and time for the restaurant to open. He got to his feet.

"There's somewhere I've got to be. I'd better get going. Next time, I'll bring some friends along."

"Please do. I'll look forward to that." Orie smiled kindly.

Once he was back out on the street, Kazuma took a postcard out of the inside pocket of his jacket. Printed on it were the words *Official Notice of Office Relocation*.

What Kazuma had just said about needing to be somewhere was not strictly true. He hadn't yet decided whether or not to share the news of Tatsuro's death with the person who had sent him the postcard.

A vacant taxi approached as he was standing on the curb. Still of two minds, Kazuma hailed it. Climbing in, he showed the driver the map on the postcard and asked him to take him to Itabashi.

It was still before six o'clock when the taxi reached its destination.

After gazing up at the building, Kazuma took several deep breaths and stepped inside.

He rode the elevator to the fourth floor. As soon as he got out, he was confronted by a glass door with the words *Sakuma Law Office* on it. There was a reception counter immediately behind the door, but it was empty.

The doors slid open automatically as he approached. "Good evening," someone said, and a woman in a blouse and a blue cardigan appeared from the curtain behind the counter. When she saw Kazuma, she looked stunned.

It was Mirei Shiraishi. Although she was as beautiful as ever, she looked different somehow. Was it because she had cut her hair? Her face was a much healthier color than when they parted last at Tokyo Station after their visit to Tokoname.

"It's been a long time," he said.

Mirei let out a long, slow breath. "What are you doing here?"

"Well, I got this notice . . ."

"Notice?"

"This thing." Kazuma showed her the postcard. "Didn't you send it?"

Mirei took the card, looked at his name and address, and shook her head. "I didn't."

"Then who was it?"

The name *Azusa Sakuma, Chief Lawyer* was printed in the Sender box. Beside that, someone had written in *Mirei Shiraishi, Administration Dept.* by hand.

"What's going on, Mirei?" came a voice from behind the curtain. A small woman in black-framed glasses then emerged.

"Do you know anything about this?" Mirei showed her the card.

The woman with the glasses took the card, inspected it, and nodded. "Yes, I do. I sent it."

"Why?" Mirei asked.

"Because I thought it would be good for you."

"Good for me?"

The woman with the glasses smiled, handed the postcard back to Kazuma, and vanished once more behind the curtain. She soon came back, this time holding a coat and a backpack.

"I'm going to go home now. Mirei, will you lock up?"

"Uh . . . well, good night."

The woman—Kazuma assumed she had to be Azusa Sakuma—gave Kazuma a knowing grin and left the office.

Kazuma turned to Mirei. "How long have you been working here?"

"Since the summer of last year. When Attorney Sakuma moved offices, she decided to hire an administrative assistant and asked me if I wanted to join the firm."

"Does she have some connection to your father?"

"That's sort of how we met, yes. When my mother and I were planning to use the victim participation system, she was kind enough to be our lawyer."

"Oh . . . really."

The victim participation system—the phrase felt to him like some relic of a dim and distant past.

Mirei was looking awkwardly down at the floor. He could see she was struggling to keep the conversation going.

"There's something I need to tell you," Kazuma said. "My father died last week."

"Oh!" Mirei exclaimed and raised her head.

"He'd had cancer for a long time."

"I didn't know. I'm . . . I'm very sorry for your loss. May he rest in peace."

"Thank you."

"Was that what you came here to tell me?"

"Sort of . . ." Kazuma paused, pulled himself together, then continued. "At least, that's my official reason."

"Your *official* reason?"

"What I mean is that I also have another, quite different reason. A real reason. To be honest, I wanted to come as soon as I got the postcard, but I didn't have the guts. When my father died, I thought it would be a pretty good pretext, so here I am. Ever since—" Kazuma looked deep into Mirei's eyes. "I can't stop thinking about that day we went to Tokoname together. I don't think I'll ever forget it."

Mirei lowered her eyes. "I feel the same."

"It was a very painful and difficult day. But there's also something from it that I kept holding on to. When I held your hand on the train home. I don't know quite how to say this. . . . I had the sense there was an understanding, an affinity between us. That's the reason . . . That's why I'm here today." Kazuma looked down at the floor and extended his right hand. "I wanted to ask if I could hold your hand for a second time."

He hoped that she would understand how he felt. He hoped that she would do as he asked.

However, his hand remained unheld. Kazuma timidly raised his eyes. Mirei had both hands pressed to her chest and was looking studiedly off to one side.

"Sometimes I wonder if I even have any right to exist," she said in a slow, muffled voice. "My father led a normal life and built a family after killing another man and escaping punishment. Does the child of a man like that really have any right to life? My mother is a separate person from my father, unrelated to him by blood. But I have the blood of a killer in my veins. If I have any children, they will inherit that bloodline. Can I allow that to happen?"

Kazuma drew back his outstretched hand. "I bet that if I did some research on my ancestors, I'd find a killer or two in there. I mean, back in the old days, there were all those wars. . . ."

"Maybe you're right." Mirei forced her lips into a weak smile. "Azusa Sakuma said to me when she asked me to take the job, 'Crime and punishment are complex issues. There aren't ever any easy answers. I'm going to be grappling with those issues, and I'd appreciate your help with my work. Let's try to work together to find those answers.'"

Weighty words. Kazuma felt them sinking into his soul.

"You're grappling with . . . the issue of crime and punishment?" he said. "Those are certainly things I have thought about too, but I've acted thoughtlessly in coming here. I owe you an apology."

"There's no need for that." Mirei shook her head. "I'm very happy to learn how you feel about me. And I promise to tell you as soon as I do manage to find some sort of answer. If you still feel like extending a hand to me then, I hope I can respond in kind."

Her eyes were fixed on Kazuma. From the look in them, he could tell that she was not stringing him along or telling him comforting white lies. *She needs time. And she needs a man who can give her the time—a man who is prepared to wait for her.*

"I understand," Kazuma said. "I'll be on my way now. Please, though, never forget: No matter how far in the future it may be, when the day comes, my hand is open to you. That's a promise."

"Thank you," Mirei said. She broke into a smile.

A single teardrop ran down her cheek.

ABOUT THE AUTHOR

Keigo Higashino is one of Japan's bestselling novelists, and his work has been translated into more than twenty languages. He's best known for his Detective Galileo mystery series (*The Devotion of Suspect X*) and his Kyoichiro Kaga series (*Malice* and *A Death in Tokyo*). His work has been a finalist for the Edgar Award and the CWA Dagger, as well as many awards in his home country. He lives in Tokyo, Japan.